The Forbidden Man

The Legends of Ḷainjin

Book Two

(The Prequel)

The Forbidden Man

The Legends of Ḷainjin

Book Two

(The Prequel)

A novel of historic literary fiction by Gerald R. Knight

IGUANA

Published by Iguana Books
720 Bathurst Street, Suite 303
Toronto, ON M5S 2R4

Publisher: Meghan Behse
Editor: Shelley Egan
Cover design: Meghan Behse
Cover image: "We Are in Another Sea" by Herbert K. Kane. Copyright Herbert K. Kane, LLC.
Map: Hobe / Holger Behr, Public domain, via Wikimedia Commons

ISBN 978-1-77180-508-7 (paperback)
ISBN 978-1-77180-509-4 (epub)

This is an original print edition of *The Forbidden Man: The Legends of Ḷainjin.*

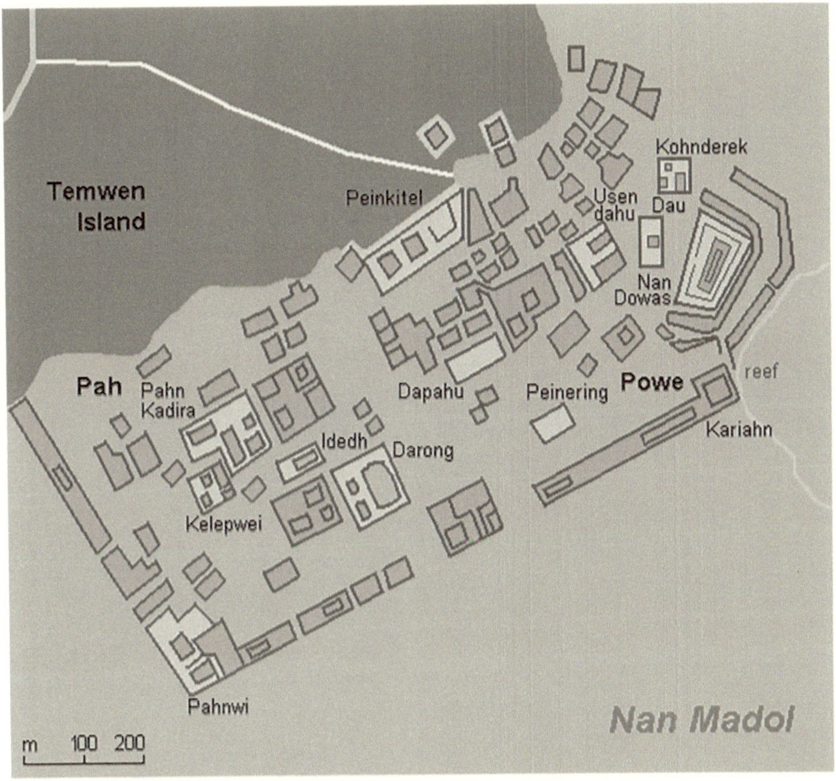

Digital rendering of the first detailed map of Nan Madol drawn by John Stanislaw Kubary in 1874

The dialogue

That fateful morning, many seasons before his destiny would lead him to Liṃanṃan[1] and the shelter of Lae Atoll, Ļainjin[2] turned yet again from the sound of the breadfruit-leaf stubs slapping the smoking pile of coral stones and smoldering, dried coconut husks before the cookhouse's welcoming hearth. Turned from the comforting sight of the fire's flare as it ate the billowing, eye-stinging smoke and filled the thatched house with warm light. He turned from the laughter of the young women chiding one another as they captured the fallen refuse from the forest canopy shading the village's neat stone-covered courtyards, as the young men returned from their early morning fishing, carrying long lines of fish freshly caught. He left behind the comradery of his fellow anglers, *jebwa*[3] dancers, and *anidep*[4] players to face the ineluctable sun storm that raged upon the surrounding sea.

He hung his netted coconut shells beneath the eave at the open cookhouse entrance, each shell filled to its mouth with clear morning *jekaro*.[5] Untied the

[1] Irooj's daughter; Ļainjin's chosen one. A name: "woman beautiful." "Li": the female prefix; "ṃanṃan": "very beautiful." The north star, Polaris.
[2] Tarmālu's son.
[3] A battle dance; a fierce reenactment of a classic fighting style passed along from previous generations.
[4] A game in which a foot-sized cube of woven pandanus leaves is kicked back and forth within a circle by clapping participants.
[5] Also called "tuba," "toddy," and various other names; the sap of the coconut palm tapped from the flower bud as it grows and continues to protrude between its mature frond leaf and the less-mature inner fronds of the palm's inner crown. The skill of making jekaro is practiced worldwide wherever palms grow.

Chief's[6] leg from the pandanus tree branch where he had been but temporarily tied and watched his long wings, iridescent black, flap but twice or thrice before the wind streaming about them lifted his glide. He abandoned his dry boathouse and bid farewell to friends, young and old alike. He bent low to accept the flowers, provisions, and farewell gifts bestowed upon him. Placed the parting gifts on his canoe deck, paddled out on the bright, calm lagoon water, and hoisted his sail amid what breeze he found. Once again, he followed it out of the comforting shelter of the surrounding colorful coral reefs through the passageway onto the treacherous, sky blue depths of the open ocean. There, yet again, he stowed the fragile mementos of the island past, unfurled his trolling line, and set his course.

Such was the pattern of his restless journey as he faithfully continued the search for the end of the story of his mother, Tarmālu. His search had started much earlier in life, as a child sitting among the elders, listening here and there for her stories. He soon learned she had left him in the care of others as she led her fleet of proas[7] out onto the open ocean, never to be heard from again. Why? To protect the precious craft from the certain damage of an oncoming storm. Why? *Emejjia wa iļometo*[8] was the reason he had always received.

It was a comment he had retained from an evening's ramblings a few nights before: the stone village attracted traders from islands south and west. Surely, any survivor of Tarmālu's fleet would tarry there, where a man could earn a fortune, before returning to Rālik.[9] Especially since she and her crew had been there many times and knew well its whereabouts.

In the past, his habitual wayfaring seemed a calling from his mother. He thought of her story as trapped in history without a proper end. He searched for someone to tell him what had happened to her. Then, as memories he had collected built up — some carelessly discarded, others more often remembered, all at risk of deteriorating like so many breadfruit leaves cast into the banana patch — they left him disoriented and without specific

[6] Ļainjin's pet frigate bird.
[7] Proa: An outrigger canoe rigged with a sail.
[8] "A boat dies slow in the open ocean."
[9] The western chain of atolls of what is now known as the Republic of the Marshall Islands.

heading. Like a proverbial banana stump repeatedly replanted, these departures had become harder to propagate and less productive as he had begun to question the likely outcome of his self-appointed search. That is, until this comment appeared out of nowhere, like a guiding star poking its light into the evening sky. This spark had flared in his imagination, cleared the smoky hesitation that lingered, and encouraged him to set sail again on one fateful — and, as it turned out, final — journey of discovery.

Yes, he was a younger man that day, with less confidence and more fear in his manner as he first set course for Pohnpei.[10] His previous voyages had been down and up the two strings of atolls that make the neck-strings of Rālik and Ratak.[11] He now headed on what he knew would be a much longer voyage into far-flung, unstrung islands amid unfamiliar seas. Could he prevail there on a much, much longer voyage? Well taught, he knew the slant his hull must cut into the broad *kāleptak*[12] swells rolling toward him, beneath him, as he angled his craft correspondingly over the sharp crests of the massive *buñtokrear*[13] swells from the opposite direction that inexorably carried him westward. Yes, he feared the voyage, but his biggest fear was, what else to expect?

He had faced the inescapable force of Tūṃur's[14] sun storm in the past with nary a mishap, but such voyages had lasted but a day or so. He knew well he could bear the constant shiver as the sea splash of the steep whitecaps lashed his skin and conjoined with the merciless wind at his back. He knew he could withstand the ups and downs of the *añōneañ*[15] waves, because to do so was the very mark of a man.

---

[10] Currently one of the principal island groups that make up the Federated States of Micronesia, located in the Eastern Caroline Islands.

[11] The eastern chain of atolls of what is now known as the Republic of the Marshall Islands.

[12] Swell that "slaps from the west"; the countercurrent of the Intertropical Convergence Zone, which periodically streams through the islands just north and south of the equator.

[13] Swell that "falls from the east."

[14] Aka Antares, the brightest star in the constellation Scorpius, including Tau, Alpha, and Sigma.

[15] "Call of the north"; the southern solstice, which annually coincides with winter in the northern hemisphere.

"*Ekūtañtañin eṃṃaan!*"[16]

Ļainjin could hear his twin grandfathers chant as the cold spew from the wave crests slapped his face and ran down his chest. This became a battle cry enunciated in the very core of his being. Chanting this as he stood at his helm, oar leveraged at his side, an insignificant speck challenging the wind and its waves raging about him, he would glance backward from time to time. Yes, with nostalgia for the comfort of the life he had left, but more to check his wake against the position of the ever-receding island. He would imagine one grandfather saying, "Expect an unpredictable ocean current to divert you from your target, so be ready to set your path to north or to south to counter your drift." This from one of the pair who had taught his famous mother to navigate. So, he studied his drift per his heading as he challenged the horizon by periodically glancing backward before his point of departure sank reluctantly into the sea.

Even as he would later lower, brace, and lash his sail to its spars. Turn his craft around into the wind, heave to, and put his craft to drift. Even as he would curl below in an exhausted attempt to rest and recuperate. Even as the continuously churning sea rocked and relentlessly tossed him about, his fear would not be that he would fail at what he knew he could do. Because his grandfathers had taught him to fear the unknown, he feared that he would fail at what he did not know to expect.

Educated, hardened, and habituated to the ways of the sea, he would remain confident until his last gasp.

He expected a reduction in spirit from his growing physical insignificance amid the vast, rainless tempest that had gradually roiled the immense ocean of mountainous swells about him.

"Expect thirst!" he heard one grandfather advise. "Be prepared to turn nocturnal, sail by night and sleep by day, ration your water, cut your course true to minimize your time at sea."

Then the other broke in. "Expect to weaken if your lures don't haul fish."

So, Ļainjin gorged like his bird when lucky, eating incessantly when he could, and never missed an opportunity to haul in nourishment.

Nor did his bird, for this was the Chief's season to soar high to spy the telltale signs of flopping terns, then to glide low above the sea among them,

[16] "A man is an inchworm at sea."

gliding effortlessly on the updrafts from its waves, and clenching his hooked beak onto anything that rose but a hand's length from their bounty. He would disappear for days at a time, usually departing and returning from the general direction of land, seemingly sleeping in the sky, seldom frequenting the perch his worker provided. Seldom requiring his worker's food, seemingly as disengaged as a young man avoiding his chores in pursuit of amorous treasures. He, too, was a younger, less confident bird. Lacking red, only brown-and-white feathers marked his still immature gular sac. He bothered not the terns he searched for. He was yet to develop a taste for the contents of their craws. He practiced rather on timing the midglide swoop that plucked a hapless flying fish successfully escaping the jaws of one seaborne predator only to enter the throat of a truly airborne one. He ate in big, satisfying gulps, as did his worker below.

"Expect cold!"

So, Ḷainjin ate more fish to heat his body. He was careful to bail any saltwater that found its way through his fore and stern mid-deck hatches into the bilge of his hull beneath the ballast decking upon which he rested when heaved to, and he kept the sleeping mat, into which he periodically crawled, as dry as possible.

"Expect to lose faith in your heading," advised one grandfather.

"Don't dismiss the first signs of your destination once they appear," yammered the other.

"Expect to tire of the incessant movement about you."

"Expect pain induced by the struggle to brace yourself at each abrupt slap of wave or gust of wind."

Yes, he expected his lips to crack and dry in the salt like the fish he would slice and lay flat on his deck to dry in the sun. He expected his skin to burn, blacken, and turn feverish in the face of the ever-splashing turmoil in which they warned he would feel "increasingly lost, isolated, and diminished."

Yet his youth, with its stubborn determination, physical strength, naiveté, vulnerability, and glorious optimism, enabled him to endure that which an older, wiser man might simply avoid. The unusual thing about him, which he himself barely recognized at the time even when questioned by others, was his ability to endure this solo. Alone, his vessel would appear on the lagoon horizon. Alone, he would disembark with his friendly manner, his fish, and other gifts and quickly engage in fellowship, partnership, and fraternity. He would dance, play games, make *jekaro*, and be gone. This was not cultural. It was not the gregarious way of the young. Solo was not common among his friends and relatives on Namorik.[17] What had turned him into a loner if not this very lonely quest to learn what had happened to her? This, no other man was likely to share. Only he could remember her smell. His solo quest would haunt him, but it would help him too. He had no companion to offer false counsel to alter course or turn back, no one else to feed or provide drink, no one he had to help, no one to place his life at risk — only himself and, of course, the Chief. Might this penchant to act alone be the very trait he would need to succeed? Only time and many more days of heroic determination would tell.

Day by day, he watched the low-blowing, somewhat circular puffs of white or light gray wind clouds ever reshape as they passed overhead from behind. They carried nary a drop of water. They varied neither by day nor by night. They streamed westward as though floating, like his bird, upon the surface of the wind or like the foam residue left on the surface of the sea in the wake of the passing whitecaps about him. Then, as though by his grandfathers' guidance, during the afternoon of his third day, he noticed a clumping of clouds to the southwest. They emerged at first with a slightly deeper shade of gray, slightly south of the course he had set. As the afternoon passed, they appeared to pile higher on a horizon that elsewhere presented a flat frontier of lighter gray. As his grandfathers had warned, he would dismiss this vision.

Despite such dismissal, chided repeatedly by his grandfathers and in the absence of conscious decision on his part, instinct bent his wrist unwittingly to point his craft toward the clouds that his eyes could not resist periodically glancing toward, thus gradually altering his course toward them. Then, as the sun set, leaving its red residual glow to illuminate and highlight them, he realized that these clouds were indeed different from the others. They appeared to be much farther away, as though unmoving and indigenous to

---

[17] Literally, "small lagoon"; an atoll in the southern Rālik Chain of what is now the Republic of the Marshall Islands. Where Ḷainjin is from.

some spot below the horizon. He memorized the angle of his course over the swells rolling westward beneath him and held fast to that heading long after it turned dark and until it was time to lash down, face the wind, heave to, and allow these same swells to rock him to an exhausted, constantly interrupted sleep. One more expectant than in nights past.

He awoke the next morning, his bow pointing to the southeast as he drifted and braced himself against the same torrent of wind and surface waves, amid these same monotonously rising and falling buñtokrear swells. Sitting in his hull and shivering in the cool morning air, he immediately peered over his bulwarks to the west, but alas, there was nothing of significance there as the sun, now rising in the east, was illuminating the details of only that half of the sky. He sat with his back secured against one side of his hull, legs bent and feet pressed for support against the other, and ate his morning meal of *jāānkun*,[18] dried fish, and water from one of many netted shell containers hanging in bunches from wooden hooks below. Then, refreshed and excited to begin the day, he removed the pole that braced the hanging lashed spars of his lateen sail, allowing them to hang free in the flurry. He hoisted the *rojak ṃaan*[19] vertical, secured its halyard, and sheeted in. Using his oar as a tiller, he turned his craft around until the wind billowed in his sail, lifting his bow off toward the west, setting his course at the same angle to the following sea that he recalled from the night before.

As the dawn lightened and the sun climbed above these same singular, rushing clouds that crowded the eastern horizon, it again began to illuminate the same clump of darker clouds he had observed the evening past. Only then did he allow himself the luxury of admitting to his smug, imaginary crew that they had been right all along. As the day progressed, the clouds grew taller, whiter, and more distinct. As expected, the buñtokrear swell from behind grew larger and more distinct yet smoother and less sharp, as if a large island with surrounding reefs beneath the clouds had begun to cut off the roll of the counterswell kāleptak and — as one or the

[18] Sun-dried sheets of pandanus pulp rolled into a log and wrapped in a sheath of pandanus leaves.
[19] Literally, "spar man" or "spar in front"; the vertical boom or yard of the triangular lateen sail.

other of his grandfathers rarely missed his opportunity to point out — its corresponding countercurrent beneath him.

He expected to see the island by nightfall, and not disappointed, he saw what he had expected from the innumerable tales listened to since boyhood. Magnificent mountains peaking up from the sea and rising into the clouds, shining green as a breadfruit leaf illuminated by the setting sun. With no more reason to conserve his energy, unable to restrain his expectations, he sailed on through the moonless night. The starlight, though blurred by the wind and the streaming clouds between, was sufficiently bright to silhouette the dark mountains of the island emerging ahead.

Did those mountains above the stone village contain somehow, some way, the story of his mother's end? Not that he expected to find her trapped there, unable to escape. Just finding an answer to what happened once she had left him would be enough to set his search to rest. There remained that conundrum: *emejjia wa ilọmeto*! If it was true that a proa was nearly indestructible in the open ocean, and she was famous for her sailing and navigation skills, what could have gone wrong? Surely, the answer was not only important to the posterity of her story but to the confidence in his ancestors' teachings too.

He sailed on until Tūṃur himself had sailed through the sky to overtake him, until the mountains had risen from the sea and loomed impressively afore. Only then did his mind turn to thoughts of his eventual landing. Did he really want to arrive exhausted, disheveled, and fawning with dehydration? No, he must drink his fill, eat, sleep, wash the stink from his body, and prepare to face his debarkation with an aura of confidence. Hence, he lifted his oar, allowed his craft to turn again to wind, and again secured its drift. However, as he curled in his mat, he was unable to allow his mind to discard its oar. He sailed on in his dreams. Even as he drifted and slept, he continued his nightmarish struggle with the sea toward the mysterious, dark mountains and the stone village that he dreamed would dominate his future.

Next morning, he awoke from his dreams to the sound of *wūnaak*[20] about him. The island, its green mountains, and the white clouds that

[20] Flock of seabirds diving for baitfish driven to the surface by tuna.

perched among them filled the horizon to the southwest. The intense light of a bright yellow sun was already streaming here and there through the wind clouds rushing upon the still ferocious windstorm. The sea churned as it whitecapped about him. His craft bobbed in the waves as it tittered and fell into the trough of one columnar swell after another, and white-and-gray terns periodically dove in a deliberate, matter-of-course manner into the convulsive whitecaps, squawking to one another amid their frantic, swirling chase. Even as the potential safety of the island loomed before him, he sensed an opportunity to receive a fisherman's welcome and pursued it.

He loosened his sheet as the outrigger float of his craft first rose and then dipped into a trough. He grabbed onto the pole that had propped and secured his rig and tugged the sheet that brought his sail with its twin spars back to him as he rose, unsecuring them from each other, then grabbing the halyard and hoisting. By that time, his craft had reached the crest of the following swell, his upraised sail proudly fluttering and wildly palpitating in the gust. Ready to lunge forth, he placed one of his lighter trolling lines with its shiny shell lure upon the outrigger deck. Once he had secured it, he tilled his craft downwind, filled his sail with wind, and set his course midway between the rapidly whirling flocks. He dropped the lure into the water and allowed the line to play through his left hand as he leveraged his oar tiller under his shoulder with his right. As the line played out, the water splashing into his face and running down his chest into his kilt, his eyes fixated on the shoreline of the island ahead and to his right. He was searching for the mouth of the fish. Even as he glanced here and there — at his sail, at the approaching waves and swells on his flank, and at the coils of line he was playing out — his eyes continually returned to the shoreline ahead of him. His grandfathers had taught him that the shape of the main island was that of a butterfly fish lying flat on the sea and facing east with small islands and fringing reefs like fins all around. And that the stone village lay just south of the fish's proverbial puckered mouth, which jutted east into the sea.

Ḷainjin did see what looked like the two lips of its pointy mouth there, jutting out to his right. Where were his grandfathers now that he needed them? From his position at sea, he had nearly passed the vantage of seeing through the narrow opening between the lips into what he thought was a deep, narrow bay leading into the island's interior. He could not spot the village yet. "Those islets just to the north and in between must be blocking my view," he thought. His grandfathers had told him the village stood out cleanly from a background of green mangrove swamps, on one of the many noncontiguous reefs that fringed the island's periphery. They had told him the reefs surrounding Pohnpei were "like a series of fan corals laid on their side." The fringing reefs he had known were flat, solid, and stark at low tide and extended outward from an islet's sandy or rocky shore, different from these. He had never seen shoreline like this — void of sand and covered by mangrove that crowded out upon the reef. He had never seen mountains, streams, or waterfalls either, but of course, his grandfathers had told him about these. He had only known the flat, squat lines of brush, coconut, and breadfruit forests, and white, sun-bleached sand amid light blue water. Among the islands he knew, the mangrove grew only within an island's swampy interior and never covered the shore.

As he sailed on, his eyes darted about rapidly, repeatedly, and methodically, and the trolling line played out through his fingers toward its secured end. He wrapped the line to his lure around his left hand and began repeatedly wrenching the line forward then slacking it as he plunged onward into the melee ahead. As he chased the swirling, upwind *wūnaak*, he watched the lips of the butterfly fish gradually close as he continued his southwest course. The strike came a while later, coincidentally, just as he spied what he thought might be the stone village coming into view from behind the group of small islands on the reef that made up the lower lip of this mountainous butterfly fish before him. He released his sheet, let his secured oar drop into the water, and, as rapidly as possible, retrieved the small bonito tuna as his craft rose and fell and his sail thrashed furiously in the wind.

He allowed the tuna to slowly run the line through his fingers again, ducking below to recruit the hand-sized, T-shaped hardwood hook he often employed as a grapple to load much larger fish onto his deck. Then he resumed landing the bonito. But after removing his lure, he clutched the fish by the gill, inserted the hook into the thin skin between the tendons of its throat, and twisted its barb until it protruded through its belly. He tied the loop end of his thickest braided line through the fish's mouth and out its throat, onto and around each arm of the T-shaped shank beneath its jaws so that its gills would ride upon it and keep the fish straight in the water as it trolled through the waves behind him. He then allowed the crippled tuna to sink back into the sea as he sheeted in and burst off again into the flux.

This time, he held the played-out line unwrapped in his left hand as he steered with his right hand toward the direction of what appeared to be the stone village. It was just beneath the puckered mouth of the mountainous island with gray clouds atop that filled the horizon before him. The *wūnaak* had swarmed ahead more toward the south, and he followed it with the determination of a shark with the scent of blood in its gills. Would his crippled bonito attract one of these unlucky twisting monsters of the deep? He was hoping, of course, for something worthier and would soon find out. For the *wūnaak* held uncharacteristically together as it traveled south, parallel to shore. As he caught up and entered its midst, the din of the squawking birds grew louder, as did their numbers even as the ocean raged about them. Some flopped, some dove into, and others fluttered above the cresting, windswept waves. There was no joy, only apprehension, when a fish taunted his bait, took the hook, pulled the line taut, and all but stopped the lunging craft's forward motion. Ļainjin turned just in time to view the fish lift its spear from the surface of the sea and dance skyward in a valiant attempt to break loose from its captor.

In his mind, his grandfathers cried, "Your rigging, your rigging!" as he dropped the secured oar into the sea. He rose with one hand stingily burning out excess line and the other reaching for his halyard to drop sail before it backwinded and crashed down on him. He then managed to prop the lowered rigging with oar and sheet such that it no longer presented an additional distraction during his new pursuit. Now, without forward motion to arrest the powerful fish, it was up to him to struggle against it with his own might. If the fish succeeded in taking the thick braided line to its end, he feared it would break. He and those several coils of reserve line were all that stood between victory and defeat before the cove of the famous stone village of Pohnpei. Had he come all this way to debark and tell a story of a debacle at sea? What was he to say if forced to go ashore empty-handed? Then the great fish rose, glistening silver and blue in the sunrise for the second time as though to take a second look at its captor, and Ḷainjin drew a moment of encouragement that his catch might tire itself on the surface before attempting a deep dive that might run his line to its end and break it. He knew that, once the line had survived the initial vitality of the fish, his chance to land it improved, but alas, he had never seen a fish rise a third time, and this one was no different.

Luckily, the *lōjkaan*[21] was a beautiful creature that sometimes fought by instinct closer to the surface, and therefore, the smooth backward or forward drag of the boat — the smaller the better — became a prime factor in wearing the beautiful creature down. To that end, Ḷainjin's next task was a slow and deliberate attempt to get the belly of his still-unfurled sail out of the water, where it dipped periodically into the churning sea. He sensed that any part draped there in the water would increase his surface area, reduce the boat's mobility, increase its drag, and allow his catch more opportunity to break its tether. Hence, he began to steal a moment now and again from his opponent. Calmly, quickly, deliberately he hauled and secured the wet and weighty part to its lowered, hanging spars, and before long, he had accomplished this first critical task.

Then he began the long give and take of retrieving the line the fish had taken. He relied on his shark-catching experience, giving two hands as each wave crest passed and then swiping back three as his craft dipped into the trough that inevitably followed. His arms, his hands, his fingers became as flexible as tree branches in the wind, compliantly remitting to a tug whatever was required to prevent his line from breaking but not a smidgen more. The battle between the huge fish and its buoyant, ever-yielding captor thus became a struggle determined by the give and the take of small, frail measures. The rolled and twisted fiber twine had a natural springiness to it, a flexibility, he knew, that naturally multiplied along its length. The braiding tripled the strength and the pliancy of these lines, allowing them to float flat in the sea as the bait trolled behind. Once the fish had struck and changed its course in any direction, such a line created drag from the sea itself that hindered the fish from pulling it taut enough to break. Finally, there was the angler's instinct to give in freely yet begrudgingly, to prolong the battle as a

[21] Marlin.

confident warrior would want to do to tire his opponent until weakened to the point where the battle was all but won.

Now the time had come to cajole the great fish toward him. As the morning progressed and the heat of the day dried his salt-encrusted locks and burned upon his ever more determined brow, Ḷainjin's darting glances noticed other boats fishing among the rough seas shoreward. Did they suspect he was in trouble? Would one come to his aid? As slowly as the tide turns, he gained the upper hand on the *lōjkaan*, and by noon, after much give and take, he had pulled the long, magnificent fish, striped with black and silver blue, to the boat. As it came close, he saw what he expected: the barb of his thick hardwood hook protruding cleanly from under its pointy jaw. Now that he had nearly exhausted his foe, he had not a moment to lose. The fish, this close and if given a chance, could easily snap such a short leash. Ḷainjin had tied a large loop of cordage into a slipknot, which encircled the line leading to its mouth. Eventually, he planned to use this to ensnare the fish's tail. Then he draped the cordage over the outrigger deck and secured its end to the yoke of his canoe. Patiently, he spoke to the fish as he strained to pull it nearer.

"There you are. There you are, handsome *lōjkaan*! What are you up to there? We usually don't see you in this season! What do you have to say? You don't like that hook. What's that? It makes your mouth sore? Grandfather, he says he has a sore mouth." He snickered aloud as he dropped the noose that encircled the line to the fish's mouth into the water and eased it over the fish's spear-shaped nose.

Then he deceptively gave the fish line with one hand, allowing it to swim into the collar he had prepared as he held tight to the snare line with the other. The loop of the slipknot closed from the pressure of the fish swimming through it but quickly became too small to pass over its large tail fin and so closed tightly at the small of its tail, where the long dorsal fins jut up and down. As the fish turned to swim away, Ḷainjin allowed the line to run through his palm. The fish stopped abruptly as the snare line caught at its tail, the line ran taut, the deep hull cut firmly into the sea, and the boat itself became the final, fatal anchor to its freedom. The fish was unable to escape, but there would be no moment to celebrate until it was safe from the sharks he imagined were circling. He eventually snugged the completely exhausted fish, now on a short leash, against the outrigger side of his hull by tying the mouth end to his bow and the snare line to his stern.

Wasting not a moment, he hoisted his sail and burst once again into the onrush of wind and waves. He headed dead downwind toward the stone village where it seemed to rise from the reef at the edge of a cove off what he knew to be the island's eastern shore. Only this time, the drag of the fish next to his hull slowed his progress, stole his boat's natural buoyancy, reduced his mobility amid the following swells, and, more than once, caused a crest to crash upon his stern and threaten to swamp his unhatched hull. Quickly realizing that, to carry the fish, he would have to change his point of sail drastically from dead west to a better course on the opposite tack, he decided to shunt. Once again, he swung his craft into the wind and released his sheet. With much effort and care, due to his craft's now-reduced buoyancy in the tumultuous seas, he switched stern for bow, sheeted in, and headed back on an opposite downwind tack to the northwest, directly targeting the passageway into the mouth of the butterfly fish that opened into a broad inland bay. This course had the advantage of getting his catch out of the open ocean and away from predators as quickly as possible.

On the outrigger side of his hull, he was still shouldering the enormous fish, fin forward now. This was tricky, as the bottom half of its giant dorsal fin was acting a bit like a second tiller — in front of the boat. But with strength and endurance, he held his downwind reach, surfed the enormous swells, and avoided their crashing over his stern deck and sloshing water through the open hatches of his hull. His plan was now to enter the village through what his grandfathers had referred to as its "back door." Rather than approach the village from its natural opening to the sea through its partially reef-protected cove or the oblong lagoon that fronted the village, he would instead enter it by crossing over the reef that bordered the south edge of the bay that formed the butterfly fish's mouth. During high tide, that side of the reef led directly into the canals that separate its man-made islets.

Then, all of a sudden, the Chief himself came into view, gliding swiftly in a large arch to his left and then hanging in a breeze that allowed him to settle gracefully. His eye was no doubt concentrating on his nemesis, the diagonal outrigger stay that held the mast to wind at his place on the outer booms of the outrigger. As Ḷainjin sailed on, each islet in turn cut off his vantage to the village. His attention turned to the northeast coast above the upper lip of the butterfly fish's mouth. More so than the coast below, it appeared surrounded by a jungle of mangrove. He could see smoke rising from several spots inland but not a single roof amid the lush growth that blocked all view of villages. Then it came to him. No foreigner carrying treasure, particularly one accustomed to viewing an uncluttered village from the wide beach of an open lagoon, would likely venture into such a swampy shore. It's no wonder that villagers wanting to attract trade from coral islanders would want to stick their trading center out upon an open reef. He noticed the white clouds that had first attracted him the day before the day past and deceptively encircled darker ones lingering low between the valleys of the interior. These collected moisture from the lush foliage and redistributed the freshwater wealth back down onto them again, creating the legendary streams and waterfalls that had so captured his imagination as a youth. Would he dare venture inland among those mountains and find them more satisfying than he had dreamed?

As he sailed toward the mouth ahead, the stone village to the southwest again came into view between the two islets, and he caught a glimpse of the full length of the elongated, deep blue lagoon that fronted the village from a new vantage. Again, the proas came into view. He could see them anchored there in the comfort of relatively calm water along the eastern edge of the lagoon, protected by the reef he had since passed. This view of the village was his closest yet. Regardless of what he had viewed from farther at sea or the stories he had heard, the scale of the village slowly began to impress itself upon him. His first thought was that it must have been constructed in ancient times by giant men. Now, at low tide, it was higher and more expansive than he had imagined. Streams of smoke wafted rapidly inland. He guessed these were from cooking fires, too many to count, and immediately wondered where the firewood had come from. Transported from inland along with everything else, his reason answered.

Then he realized they had somehow constructed a wall or breakwater all along the front of the village to protect the various islets behind it. The breakwater was particularly high at the far corner of the lagoon, where the swells were rolling into it through the passageway and crashing there on the edge of the reef flat. From his vantage, he saw one narrow entranceway through the breakwater wall. It was clear that, at high tide, he could sail through it onto the reef, behind which he saw multiple, angular stone walls piled high with massive stick-like stones.

He also noticed paddling canoes fishing along the northern edge of the passageway ahead. Although he was concerned for the safekeeping of his prize in the passageway, likely shark infested, he should not enter the bay without politely acknowledging one or the other of these men first. Once he had entered the passageway and the safety of the inland bay, he would clearly have to wait until the tide returned to cross this reef. Then he would enter the village though its back door.

To avoid swamping in the passageway, he continued sailing on his downwind reach across to its northern edge, where he planned to *diak*.[22] He changed his plan again when he discovered an inlet there beneath the upper lip with surprisingly still water suitable for anchorage. To one side of the inlet lay a small cove nearly surrounded by coral and completely protected from the waves entering the passage. This cove, he realized, was where the two were fishing. The fringing reef that bordered the fish's upper lip and forehead curled around the island as far as he could see northward to encompass a long, narrow, and jagged lagoon, no doubt all the way to its legendary great eye of blue water at the top of its head. The two friendly anglers began waving incessantly from their respective craft as he approached the inlet. Their fishing canoes had little freeboard and were probably unsafe for the high seas of the passageway through which he had come. Sailing into the calm water and lowering his sail, he felt immense relief. He was exhausted and felt great fortune that the voyage had gone better than expected. What would happen next was the one unexpected thing he had worried about and for which he was, of course, unprepared.

"*Kaselehlie*!"[23] When the men greeted him, Ḷainjin realized he had no way to communicate with them.

---

[22] To tack or, more specifically, shunt. The tack of the sail is transported from one end of the canoe to the other, keeping the outrigger to windward.
[23] Pohnpeian for "hello."

One of the fishers whose boat lay anchored in the reef-protected little cove dove into the water and swam toward him. He popped up a few feet off Ḷainjin's bow and jabbered something he didn't comprehend. Using mime, the fisher finally made it clear he wanted Ḷainjin to toss him a line. Ḷainjin tossed him the end of the extra line he had used to snare the *lōjkaan*, and the man took it. As the other shouted orders, the man swam to the shallow water and tied the proa to the reef.

It must be their way of welcoming him, thought Ḷainjin, ducking below to retrieve his log of jāānkun. As he raised himself, he found the men still engaged in serious discussion, with the one in the water using his arms to measure first the length of the fish and then the dimensions of Ḷainjin's canoe. Ḷainjin cut a slice of jāānkun and extended his hand toward the swimmer, who accepted it with a smile and a nod of his head, thanked him in his language, and immediately swam the gift to his companion. Ḷainjin cut another slice and motioned for the man to return and retrieve his portion. The man returned with two freshly husked coconuts as a gift from the other, then accepted the jāānkun with a smile.

"*Kalahngan en komwi*,"[24] said the man, and Ḷainjin mimed back to him as best he could.

"Rālik or Ratak?" asked the man in the water.

"Rālik," Ḷainjin pointed to himself. "Ratak," he said, pointing to the jāānkun. He pricked open the mouth of the coconut, tilted his head severely back, his salt-heavy locks wafting in the breeze, and loudly suckled the sweet juice from the soft, immature shell. As the two watched him intently, he broke the shell open with one tap on the bulwark of his hull and began scooping the white, immature meat from each half of the shell with his thumb.

They proceeded to bombard him with numerous questions that the language barrier between them left poorly understood and only partially answered. It was clear that they had one main concern. Had he come to trade? If no, he should accompany them down the inlet to their village. If yes, he must first enter the stone village once the tide was right. Ḷainjin mimed that he had things to trade, he was sleepy, and his intention was to rest while he waited for the tide.

---

[24] Pohnpeian for "thank you."

Then the man in the water began to laugh and pointed down, circling his finger. "*Pako! Pako!*"[25] He laughed.

Ļainjin stood on his outrigger deck and looked down to find several sharks circling the small cove below. He was surprised the word was the same in both languages.

The Pohnpeian dove under his canoe and feigned a chase after the sharks, which disappeared back into the inlet. He popped up, still laughing, and then he and his leader proceeded to yammer back and forth at each other about the situation. One was still treading water; the other was anchored on the other side of the cove. Both were eating the jāānkun as they talked, with each pointing and laughing hysterically at the other's loss of teeth as they became gummed and covered with the sweet but sticky brownish substance. Finally, they decided how to proceed and made it understood, mostly using gestures, that the older leader with the shallower hull would paddle across the reef to the village and announce Ļainjin's arrival. The other would stay in the water and ward off the sharks with the blunt end of the older man's ray-barbed spear while Ļainjin rested.

Though still worried about the safety of his fish amid the sharks below, he felt too exhausted not to accept his new friend's commitment to protect it. He would leave its well-being to fate, and so far, fate had been good to him. What more could he have asked for? He had crossed the ocean! Not only had he arrived at his destination, but he had caught a *lōjkaan* to present first fruits to the *irooj*[26] of the stone village. Even his unamenable grandfathers would be impressed. He lay across his outrigger platform, resting in the luxurious warm sun and grateful for the calm amid the torrential winds of *añōneañ* that he had challenged and fought to a draw. He rested there, pleased and proud but mostly just thankful for a moment of rest. Yes, he had proved to himself, to his grandfathers, and to all that he had what it takes to traverse a great distance at sea.

A moment later, Ļainjin slumped down into the quiet shelter of his hull, put his face in the shade, and returned to his fitful, nightmarish struggle with the sea as he slept. But this time, he experienced a sense of dread. He had left

[25] Shark. Ļainjin's nickname: "man shark."
[26] Chief.

something critical to his voyage behind. This something was the tool he would need to explain who he was. How was he to ask about his mother? The unexpected had occurred. He indeed had not anticipated a new life where he would find it nearly impossible to communicate his needs or understand those around him. In the end, would he find he had crossed the ocean at much risk and hardship, with his grandfathers' help, to accomplish nothing? He dreamed he was in a storm outside the walls with waves crashing over him, struggling to find an entrance. He sensed they were in a panic on the other side, trying to contact him, but he didn't understand what they were shouting. Then he was awakened by urgent slapping against the outer side of his hull.

Ewalt

Ḷainjin's dreams were still spiraling about him as he slowly climbed and then rushed back into the life he had left. His companion, face in the water, was frantically slapping to get his attention. He passed Ḷainjin the blunt end of the spear he was using to poke the sharks. A shark had crunched off a good portion. Ḷainjin grabbed the spear, stood in the bright sun drenching his outrigger deck, and immediately saw the dark menace circling about the blue water of the cove through its windswept surface. He glanced at the single stingray barb fastened to the sharp end of the spear and found it well attached. His companion lifted his face from the water shortly and mimed, pushing the flat of his hand up to his nose and then biting and twisting his head. He had attempted to poke the shark in the nose with the blunt end of the spear, but the shark had bit onto it.

Ḷainjin began his deep, heavy breathing as he watched the shark circling deep below, perhaps discouraged by his companion's spear thrust yet utterly enticed by the enormous meal there for the taking. Finally, it turned, swung its body and began to rise. Ḷainjin dropped his kilt to the deck, exhaled all the air from his lungs, and then, toes pointed, dropped himself into the cove with nary a splash. He sank to the level of the shark and stood, not swimming but swaying in the current like an eel ready to strike. It was not clear to him in the blur of action whether the shark had become aware of him or had kept its attention on the meal above. He waited patiently as the shark slowly rose and twisted to bite into his fish. In that instant, he deftly poked the ray barb into the vulnerable soft spot directly beneath its lateral fin. At that point, the brute became painfully aware of Ḷainjin's threatening presence and shot away like a frightened bird into the inlet, dragging the remainder of the barbed spear like a suckerfish attached to its side.

Both men laughed uncontrollably at each other across the stern hull as they dangled in the water. The Pohnpeian had a perpetually gleeful expression on his pleasant, round face. His hair was modestly short cropped, like Ḷainjin's. After catching his breath, Ḷainjin scrambled to lift himself up onto the craft. His companion mimed back that he would release the anchor but first swam to his boat, removed a string of fish and a basket of husked coconuts, and swam back with first the fish, then the other. He placed both on Ḷainjin's outrigger deck. Then he swam to the anchor, diving for it and holding fast to the end of the line as Ḷainjin pulled. That done, the boat was set adrift. The man mimed that he wanted to board Ḷainjin's boat to lead him over the reef, leaving his anchored until later.

Ḷainjin stood and looked back across the wave-swept passageway, watching the incoming swells breaking along the reef.

"*Kanakan*,"[27] cried the man through the wind, as though he understood what Ḷainjin was considering.

Ḷainjin wasn't so sure the tide was quite high enough on the reef, given the depth of his hull. Though the great fish had reduced his mobility, it was clear the wind would carry him over the reef's edge with great momentum. There was danger of mishap. His boat was drifting quickly in the wind, and the tide was certain to bring more sharks with it. Better stranded there upon the too-shallow reef with his fish safe than anchored here vulnerable, without a spear.

"*Kanakan*, I hope," he warily repeated, bracing himself, extending his hand, and raising the man from the water. The two quickly shunted the yet-unraised sail. Then they hoisted it in the stiff wind and launched themselves through the inlet and across the passageway toward the reef on the opposite side of the bay. Ḷainjin was carrying the marlin spear forward again, so its tail was assisting as a second tiller, leaving his paddle feeling more normal in his grip. He studied the swells that rolled through the passageway to their left, parallel to the reef at the edge of the bay ahead. The swells could easily

[27] Pohnpeian for "good."

slap them broadside just as they reached its edge. Not a problem normally, but he worried that the marlin — though its belly had started to swell with gas — might still subtract enough from his craft's buoyancy to swamp them or worse as they surfed onto the reef. Again, he doubted that the tide had come in sufficiently to allow his deep hull and thick keel to pass unobstructed. Yet his companion, obviously more familiar with the area than he was, had measured his craft straight out. The spirit of the moment was such that he had no choice but to trust the competence of his Pohnpeian friend.

On his part, the man had already spotted Ḷainjin's *rajraj*[28] and had borrowed it to slice portions of his catch for their meal. He tossed the head to Ḷainjin's watchful bird, which deftly caught it, raised his head skyward, and swallowed it in a gulp. Then, like a child at play, the man gleefully repeated this self-appointed task until the bird lost interest and allowed the heads to fall into the bay. The man was directing them on a diagonal course across the bay toward a point farther inland than Ḷainjin had anticipated. By the time they were halfway across, they had finished eating, and he felt relieved somewhat when he noticed numerous smaller craft paddling over the reef closer to the mangrove-covered shoreline ahead. As time passed and they approached the reef, the swells began to lessen, absorbed perhaps by the edges of the bay. And the waves from the wind likewise became cut off by the edges of the reef itself as it curved away from the passageway to the sea. Then there was only the strong wind that filled their now dry and lighter sail and tilted their *kubaak*[29] on the surface of the water as they began to cruise more swiftly upon the surface, even with the humongous fish strapped beneath, to the side of their hull. Yet Ḷainjin was not without worry. The fish could tear if they collided with sharp coral on the reef. His keel could catch and tear loose, or worse still, his hull could crash and tear the stitching between its lower and upper halves. But then the longer course set to the farther point had given the ocean a little more time to rise.

His agile companion was still in great humor and enthusiastic about their progress. Perhaps to better judge the water's depth, he stepped through the forward hatch and dropped his feet into the hull. Standing there, he began

---

[28] A knife or sword-like weapon uniformly edged with shark teeth.

[29] Outrigger float.

directing Ḷainjin along the reef. Ḷainjin noticed more paddling canoes scattered upon the reef along the edge of the mangrove shore ahead and saw various other boats. They appeared to be rafts traveling in formations back and forth between the three obviously man-made islets on the reef ahead and the many others in the village across the reef to the south. The purpose of the rafts he could not guess, as he was concentrating his attention on his companion, who was frantically directing him. The still-gusting wind was uncontrollably propelling them on their downwind reach out of the deep blue water of the bay diagonally toward the dangerous light blue border of the white-frothed reef edge ahead.

His companion was obviously searching for some particular point along the reef and, with one hand clasping the lip of the hatch, was directing Ḷainjin with his free hand to windward or no. Then impulsively, he suddenly directed him to cut sharply onto the reef even as he viewed a small swell rising over his left shoulder. Ḷainjin's throat tightened as he maneuvered as directed. They crossed the white water at the reef's edge just as the swell touched the bottom of the outrigger float, broke, slapped them sidewise, and washed over them as the craft plunged onto the narrow, coral-free path across the reef edge that the Pohnpeian, still ecstatically laughing, had miraculously found. Their exuberant faces were still dripping with seawater as they sailed onto the reef flat and jovially glanced at each other. If it hadn't been for the confidence in the face of the Pohnpeian before him, Ḷainjin would have released his sheet. But exhilarated by the prospect of cruising breathlessly on a reach tack with but a hand's freeboard above the reef flat below, he held it fast with one hand as he steered them forward with the other. Gripped in the throes of another unexpected turn of events, Ḷainjin found himself screaming down a narrow channel, cleared of all the usual coral formations he would expect to find, directly toward the first of the man-made islets on the reef ahead. The tidal flat had calmed the swells, their outrigger had skimmed upon what waves there were, and their fish had not smashed. They had apparently cleared a path over the reef flat free of all obstructions to allow passage at neap tide. He was undoubtedly careening down the elusive, legendary back door into Nahn Madol.[30] If only his grandfathers could see him now.

---

30 A Pohnpeian village on the reef.

Before long, Ḷainjin realized that the path they were on met another channel at a knee angle. Another path from a second point of entrance onto the reef farther west than their point of entry had been cleared. The paths met on the reef a little ashore of the first man-made islet. The base of each of these man-made islets had been bordered with what appeared to be gigantic, flat-faced stones that rose into the surrounding walls. Each stone was horizontally angled though of a different size and length. A conch shell sounded from atop the wall of the islet facing them. A conch blast repeated from atop the next and then the third islet of the string. His companion stood again, motioning with his hand that he would have to steer them onto the other path between the islets and the shore.

As they approached the islet and Ḷainjin prepared to sheet in for his turn to the south behind it, his mouth was agape at the historic significance of the structure composed of monolithic stones before him. When, during the past hundreds of seasons, had these islanders moved these gigantic, flat-faced, shaft-like stones to build such an islet here upon the reef flat? Then it dawned on him that the very coral rubble they had cleared from these various channels must all have gone into backfilling the islet's base behind these horrendously compiled islet walls. Behind the walls was a village like any other, but the walls! They were awe-inspiring, rising sea-mossed green from the now green reef, more magnificent than he had ever imagined. These islets and these various paths upon the reef — all this constructed by some unimaginable workforce. Or had they perhaps been placed here by some race of giants, long since flown away on the wings of Mānnijepḷā?[31] To view these massive, angular shafts emerging from the water was to worship them in awe at their grandeur. Surely, this was the center of the ocean. Surely, this was the apex of his water world. Why had his grandfathers allowed him to linger so long in the backwaters near his birth? Wordlessly, he questioned them as well as himself.

As Ḷainjin pondered, he was simultaneously busy receiving acknowledgments and waving and nodding in response. Men, women, children — all stopped their tasks, stared, and waved at them as they approached and sped by. Once they had turned down the second path that led them between the shoreline

[31] A mythic bird that flew passengers from one island to another.

and two additional islets like the first, they encountered too many outrigger canoes to count. Each canoe, none rigged with sail, floated its shallow hull in the calm water, anchored to its islet in the broad channel ahead. Children sat on the stone steps at the water's edge and dove and swam in the calm water. All heads popped up to view their passing. Was it the fish or the proa that they viewed as an oddity? The leeward shores of these islets lacked the higher walls of the windward sides that faced the ocean, and the neatly thatched village structures and surrounding courtyards within came into view through broad entranceways. The scent of smoke from cooking fires filled his nostrils with its comforting odor. Rafts were anchored among outriggers stacked with wood for cooking or perhaps house building, as they appeared to be topped with bundles of thatch. That was when the thought came to him: the people were like voyagers on these little islets. They needed to float all the essentials for their village life from the mainland, and that must be the purpose of the rafts he had seen.

Ḷainjin and his Pohnpeian companion sped along the path behind two more of the man-made islets, which brought them close to the mangrove-covered shore to their right. He saw amazingly massive trees stretched out over the water, their black roots atangle at the edge of the swamp-like water. As they passed the third islet, he had to sheet in on a windward tack as the channel cut back to the southeast toward a fourth. The moment he made his turn, yet another conch blast sounded from the islet ahead. This one, centrally located in the middle of the reef, appeared to be a halfway post between the bay to the north, the village to the south, and the oblong lagoon to the east. Large rafts were anchored there, and the islet appeared covered with workers at the water's edge, as though waiting for the tide to turn. As they approached, he could see four immense rafts anchored in cleared pools to lee of the islet, each deeply loaded with one or two of the same large, flat-sided stone shafts that made up the walls of the islets they had just passed. "The village is still under construction," he thought.

As they cruised past, there was much friendly acknowledgment between his companion and the others, as well as with Ḷainjin himself. As they reached the southwest corner of the islet, the path angled abruptly to the south, directly across the remaining reef flat toward the center of the many islets and tideways positioned behind the great break walls. Yet another conch sounded from deep within the village ahead.

"Pahn Kadira," his companion shouted back triumphantly.

Ļainjin took this to mean the name of the islet from where the sound had come. He came to realize that lookouts were tracking their approach and that they had just summoned him to the islet of the *irooj* — or Saudeleur, as they called him.

They were sailing parallel now to the oblong lagoon that fronted the village, and from this vantage, he could view the tens of proas anchored along its eastern edge, protected from the ocean's swells by the reef he had now circumnavigated. He pointed to the vessels and questioned his companion. "Pohnpei?"

"Ei Pohnpei!" he responded, making a circle with his hand.

Ļainjin took this to mean that the proas were local but from the other side of the island. "Their village must attract traders from around the island as well as over the ocean," he thought. Everything they needed came to them. Now he understood what he had heard: that men of Pohnpei sailed not over the ocean. He would later find that indeed, they had no fleet. They bothered not to construct ocean-going canoes, although they admired them greatly, but the islanders from outer atolls with whom they shared their language constructed them and sailed to Pohnpei often. He would soon learn that the men of this island excelled at making fishing canoes and great rafts. They punted and pulled these rafts all about the island with great seriousness, like boys at play on the reef back home, but ventured not into the open ocean. They worked the stones. No matter what they did, he would learn, be it fishing or tending taro or harvesting breadfruit, they supported the stonework through their unique system of trade. Construction of the village, combined with the trade it fostered, had become their way of life. He would learn that no ancient giants had built these walls. Simple islanders had built them patiently over hundreds of seasons, using their own ingenuity. They had no need to travel to trade. Word of their magnificent village had carried everywhere over the seasons, and their system of trade set a standard duplicated probably nowhere else in their ocean world.

Ļainjin was amazed by the impressive thick walls of the breakwater. The wall heights on some of the islets ahead loomed from four men to six men high at the corners where lookouts stood. They had apparently constructed these thick walls by stacking the flat-sided stone shafts in alternating parallel and perpendicular rows, like placing the closed fingers of one hand on those of the other. In his imagination, these islets had the likeness of gigantic birds with uplifted wings about to take flight from their scraggy nests. Again, he wondered whether an ancient race of giants had placed these long ago. Who else could have cut the stone faces flat and set them in place? These cut faces appeared so ancient. Neither this generation nor the last had cut them. Who had and how? How had they gotten here onto the reef, and where were they from? Tales told that the Pohnpeians had done this. He had just seen their rafts loaded with stones. Yet how to explain these massive corner stones at the base of these walls? Who had placed these, and how? These were his thoughts. These would be the thoughts of any other newcomer unfamiliar with the mysterious stones of Pohnpei, yet all this would soon become clear.

As they proceeded down the path over the reef into the village and passed over a crisscross of now tide-filled channels between the walls surrounding the many islets, their momentum suddenly slowed. The high breakwater walls to the east began to block the torrential winds, and their progress became stunted and irregular for lack of wind. Ļainjin imagined defenders of these walls hurling projectiles down onto any invading force just as their initiative lagged, their sails began to luff, and the village's nimbler paddling canoes began to circle. Thus, the defensive purpose of the high breakwater and surrounding walls became evident to him. These walls were easily thicker than a man is tall. He could see this from the very few, small entranceways that they passed. The walls swept outward as they rose, making them seemingly impossible to scale. The smooth sides and flat ends of the stone shafts provided no cleft for a man's hand to grasp. What wealth must these walls protect?

The numbers of canoes paddling here and there amid the tideways were many. There were rafts like others they had passed, and they came upon small crews of men who appeared to be intently engaged in moving a stone into place here or rethatching a steep triangular roof there. Busy with their endeavors, the men waved not, nor did they otherwise acknowledge their arrival. On some of the islets where the walls were apparently still under construction, one corner sloped ramp-like down onto the reef. Ḷainjin recalled the friendly crews they had passed at rest on the reef and was impressed again that, after how many hundreds of seasons, this village was still under serious construction.

Patterned like the rectangular courtyards of coral stone surrounding the various homes in the villages back home, the islets appeared individual and distinct. Each had its own name, which his companion announced as they passed. They appeared to number nearly a hundred. None was round. Corners were everywhere, and the watercourses separating them were bare of coral rubble and easily passable at current tide.

They glided forward in fits and starts as the fickle breezes swirled about their surroundings. His companion appeared to gloat among the canoe paddlers they met, pointing to the large fish in tow as though he were responsible for the catch. Ḷainjin chuckled several times at the man's puffy manner. He was grateful, though, for the man's assistance and cared not what reward he sought from the situation. Besides, Ḷainjin was concentrating on the architecture of his surroundings. What did they use to cut these stones? Why did they cut each stone to a different measure? How did they place them together so perfectly? Thus, he mused, turning in awe to the left and then to the right as they slowly proceeded southeast down one of the more shoreward of the watercourses. They passed tens of man-made, sea-mossed green islets toward the massive seawall that bordered the southwestern end of the village.

A conch shell sounded ahead as they passed between a series of three smaller islets closer to shore on the right and two much longer, much more substantial islets on their left. "Pahn Kadira," announced his companion, pointing to the lookout at the southwest corner of the entry-less, upswept walls. Long and high, they bordered the shoreward side of these gigantic twin islets, separated by a narrow channel that led to yet other islets between them and the seawall bordering the southeast edge of the village. His companion immediately waved at the lookout, who seemed to be signaling for them to cut sharply to the left at the corner below him. When they reached the corner, Ḷainjin sheeted in. They were now sailing parallel to the southwestern seawall on a close haul to the southeast, moving toward yet another islet. Surprisingly, it was bordered on its leeward side by a string of anchored proas, many larger than his.

"Kelepwei,"[32] announced his companion.

Was this their destination? The walls all about them cut off their wind at that point, so Ḷainjin had no choice but to strike his sail and paddle. There was cooking behind the walls of Kelepwei, and smoke and the smell of food wafted from over the walls and through its single entrance. The walls of this islet were lower. There was a walkway at the waterline along its western border where they anchored their proas. Yet his companion's attention turned suddenly to the left, down yet another tideway that separated these two islets as though they had cut the smaller Kelepwei from the southeast corner of the other. There, a grand entranceway at the indented corner of the channel between them rose from the water's edge. His companion's counterpart, who had preceded them, stood there with a small contingent of men casually armed with spears and apparently awaiting their arrival. The conch shell sounded yet again, and Ḷainjin paddled down the channel to lee of the anchored seafaring proas. Various men attending the proa greeted them in a variety of languages. Rather than trying to emulate them, he responded in his own tongue — "*Iọkwe*!" — as his companion responded with "*Kaselehlie*!"

As they approached the entranceway, a man of high stature, probably the *irooj*, appeared from within and nodded to Ḷainjin as he paddled. All the others bowed to him except for a second man at his left. Ḷainjin's companion bowed low, and Ḷainjin, still struggling at the stern to push the canoe with the large fish attached and align its direction down the watercourse, nodded back. As they arrived at the entranceway, his companion jumped into the water. Several of the others stepped down into the channel, onto a sort of stairway that led upward to the water's edge, and spun the canoe's kubaak outward to allow Ḷainjin to gracefully debark from the stern and approach the Saudeleur.

"Raipuinlañ,"[33] said the Saudeleur, formally introducing himself. He clenched Ḷainjin's right arm above the wrist, inviting him to do the same.

---

[32] A man-made islet across from Pahn Kadira used to house visitors.

[33] The wealthiest chieftain; the Pohnpeian Saudeleur.

"Ḷainjin," he responded hesitantly and modestly, unfamiliar with the pomp of introductions. The Saudeleur placed his left arm around the shoulder of the man next to him and introduced him as Ewalt.[34]

"*Iọkwe,*" responded Ewalt, and he proceeded to converse with Ḷainjin in his native tongue. "The Saudeleur has appointed me to be your *ribwinbwin.*"[35]

"Count what?" Ḷainjin was surprised and immensely relieved that there would be someone with whom to communicate, someone who could provide answers to his many questions. In truth, he had never been so happy to speak to someone before. He wanted to grab Ewalt by his arm, but with the Saudeleur holding him tight in his grip, Ḷainjin pointed at the fish with his free hand instead.

"Please, I'd like to offer my first catch off Pohnpei as tribute to the Saudeleur." They all seemed to understand Ḷainjin's gesture without interpretation.[36] Ḷainjin's companion proudly handed his basket of fish to the Saudeleur, smiling and nodding his head as though adding his catch to Ḷainjin's to share in the Saudeleur's indebtedness.

"Let me add that, if this man had not chased off all the sharks at the passage, there would have been nothing left to offer," Ḷainjin said. At the end of the interpretation, there followed much good-humored response from the group as his companion beamed at one and then another, appearing to bask in the recognition.

At the Saudeleur's request, one of the attendants removed the shell knife from the belt of his kilt of inner bark and gave it to him. After the canoe had been spun back around, the Saudeleur stepped down into the water and untied its tail. The attendants spun it again, and he cut the throat and removed Ḷainjin's hook. The rest of his attendants carried the fish through the water and laid it on the landing of the entranceway above the highest step. A female attendant offered Ḷainjin two freshly husked coconuts, and yet another placed a headband of flowers upon his head. He set the other coconut on his outrigger deck, broke away the immature husk left just above the mouth, and began to drink as he watched the Saudeleur slice open the

---

[34] Ḷainjin's interpreter.

[35] Literally, "person who counts."

[36] Interpret: to provide an oral translation.

swollen belly of the marlin from anus to throat. The gas from the belly released like a fart and made the group chuckle. He removed the guts, rinsed them in the water to eliminate their stench, and placed them in the basket, commenting to his attendant. Reaching up toward the head, he pulled out the heart, sliced it open, and rinsed it in the water. He began chewing half as he directed his attendants to take the fish.

Turning back to Ḷainjin, he addressed him as he chewed and held up the remaining half before him. Ewalt was at his side, interpreting into Kajin Rālik.[37] "The Saudeleur comments that this fish must have been why your approach was delayed for so long."

"Then the lookouts *had* been watching me out there," Ḷainjin thought. Strange that he had felt them observing him.

"Yes!" he said, laughing. "That fish was very stubborn!"

The Saudeleur, as though reading his thoughts, pointed up at the guards atop the corners of the walls and countered. Ewalt interpreted. "They miss nothing and report everything. No matter your delay. You overcame the sea and brought your catch to shore."

Ewalt continued as the Saudeleur went on, again wafting his palm — this time toward the proas anchored to lee of the islet across the channel. "That is more impressive than beautiful sailing. They all do that. You showed determination. You are a brave young man to sail all the way from Rālik with only that bird as crew. To my knowledge, no one else has come alone for many seasons. You are self-confident and smart. You must have a lot to trade and care not to share your proceeds with a crew." The last sentence, spoken as a joke, brought laughter from the group when first spoken.

That was not true. Ḷainjin was not greedy and did not want anyone to think so. He had tried many times to form a crew. No one would follow him on a quest such as his, but how should he respond? Now that he had someone to interpret, he wanted to get right to his real agenda — finding news about his mother — but he sensed that the Saudeleur didn't mean his comment as an insult. He said it as though greed were a good thing, so Ḷainjin, after a moment of consideration, simply answered his question.

---

[37] Language of the Rālik Islands, now the western chain of the Republic of the Marshall Islands.

"I have a few shark teeth," he responded modestly.

On hearing Ewalt's interpretation of this, the Saudeleur sent one of his attendants off for something.

"Shark teeth are most valuable! We have few sharks here. Our fishermen kill the small ones and sink them to ward off others."

Then the Saudeleur said something that must have been very funny, because the group broke out in laughter.

Laughing, Ewalt continued interpreting. "He says he has assigned me to assist you with your trade. He says I must make you a wealthy trader, or he'll feed me to Nahn Samohl[38] — the *dāp*."[39]

Ḷainjin smiled at what he took as a joke and was surprised to recognize a second term, for "giant eel," common to both languages.

The Saudeleur spoke again, wafting his palm again toward the islet across the channel.

"I will teach you the simple rules of the trade, and I will notify him when you are ready. In the interim, I will take you to Kelepwei," Ewalt continued. "He says you are smart and brave. Learn the rules well and you will prosper."

The attendant returned with a *rajraj* fighting tool with shark teeth edges and gave it to Ewalt. "Are your shark teeth big enough to make one of these?"

"Yes."

"Then they are very valuable," Ewalt interpreted. "The Saudeleur promises that you will return to Rālik with more wealth than you now hold. He wants you to trade what you gain from us there, and then return to us and trade again!"

The Saudeleur nodded and commented that Ḷainjin must be tired from his voyage. "Go and sleep now. Once you have rested, we will drink *sakau*[40] together and talk about Rālik and Ratak. It has been a few seasons since he has heard fresh news from those atolls," Ewalt said.

Ḷainjin's companion and his counterpart — who, with the modesty typical of both cultures, had yet to introduce themselves — requested to

---

[38] An eel.

[39] Moray eel; marine eels of the Muraenidae family.

[40] Kava; a drink with anesthetic properties made from the mashed roots of the propagated *Piper methysticum*, or pepper plant.

board Ḷainjin's craft, as their canoe was apparently one of those anchored across the channel to lee of Kelepwei. Ewalt also accompanied them. Upon Ḷainjin's request, Ewalt introduced the men as Jeilañ[41] and Uerik.[42] Ḷainjin asked Ewalt if Jeilañ's house was at the shore of the inlet where they met. It was. He asked whether Jeilañ could please take his bird and care for it until his trade had been completed and he was able to retrieve it. After considerable discussion between the three, Ewalt interpreted Uerik's words. He would see that Jeilañ took diligent care of the bird. Jeilañ, on his part, was still eager to serve him and seemed overjoyed at the prospect. Ḷainjin knew that the Chief was happy enough to be handled by the last hand that fed him.

They found a spot between the other proas anchored in the shallow reef pool bordering Kelepwei. The spot was just wide enough to tie his boat to the walkway that ran along the wall. Ḷainjin dropped an anchor stone to secure the stern end to prevent drifting into the other craft. His angler friends seemed anxious to paddle home, and the Chief was easily bribed into the exchange with a fish head cut from Uerik's catch that had remained in his boat. They paddled off, one at the bow and the other at the stern. The bird sat tied on the outrigger deck, peering into the basket of fish in the hull below him.

Finally, Ḷainjin found a moment to ask how they had cut the stones. From the first moment he had laid eyes on the village, the size and shape of the stones from which it was made had amazed him.

"Let's go ashore," said Ewalt. They stepped onto the walkway, and he ran his hand over the edges of the geometrically shaped header stones. "Do they feel like they were cut?"

"No, they look and feel like they've always been this way."

"That's because they have. Some of our mountains, like Sokehs,[43] have flat faces. These *takai*[44] have broken away and fallen to the base, where we collect them. It's as simple as that."

---

[41] The Pohnpeian who looks after the Chief.

[42] Ḷainjin's Pohnpeian friend who estimates that "six men could paddle a takai down the mountain."

[43] An island with a mountain cliff on the north side of Pohnpei.

[44] Pohnpeian for "stones"; essentially the same word as in Kajin Rālik: "dekā." Takai are hexagonal basaltic crystals that date back to the volcanic origin of the island.

Ļainjin was surprised that his word for "stone" was nearly the same as theirs but went on to his question. "How can a mountain crumble like that?"

"When Nahn Sapwe[45] speaks, these takai break off. That's all I know."

"Nahn Sapwe?" Ļainjin hadn't heard that name before.

"The spirit of thunder."

"These were not cut like this?"

"No," Ewalt said. "These takai are hard and very heavy. You can't cut them. This is just the way they are. They were born from the mountain like this. Each has a distinct size, shape, and length. We say they're like women. Each is different in her own way."

"But how did they get these flat, angular sides?"

"Do you ask a woman why her children look this way or that? Can you expect the mountain to tell me why she bore them like this? All we know for sure is that Nahn Sapwe has a hand in this. He dwells here in these mountains. Yes, sometimes he roams out over the ocean. I know you hear him in Rālik, but here is where he dwells, and here, he is most powerful. He breaks these beautiful takai off the face of the mountains. We bring them here and build islands with them. That's the way it's always been from the olden days of Oljipa and Oljopa."[46]

"Who were they?" asked Ļainjin.

Ewalt laughed. "I'll let my mother tell you that story."

"How do you move them? Here, look at this one. Twenty men could not move that takai! I don't understand how they brought them here or how they placed them."

"They were moved one finger at a time. Our ancestors placed that takai. They built most of these islets hundreds of seasons ago, but as far as we know, the various chieftains traded with the men of their clan to bring and place one takai at a time — just the way we do today."

"Traded what?" Ļainjin was interested in trading.

---

[45] Pohnpeian spirit of thunder.

[46] According to *The Book of Luelen*, these men came to Pohnpei on the seventh voyage of settlement. They came from a place referred to as Kataupaitl and were instrumental in the construction of Nahn Madol.

"Well, tomorrow we'll see what you have, but probably the easiest way for you to understand our system of trade is one for you, one for the islet. Think of it this way. One man borrows another man's boat and goes fishing with it. When he returns, he counts the fish — one for him, one for the boat."

"When I trade my shark teeth, I give one to the islet for every one I trade?"

"No, traders give nothing to the islet, but buyers do. It costs nothing to offer a trade, but it costs to accept one. You can trade all your shark teeth and leave and pay nothing to the islet. But if you aren't satisfied with the items you received from your trades and you still want items not previously offered in exchange, you must pay the islet its share for what you buy."

"That's very complicated!" Ḷainjin said.

"Think of it this way," Ewalt said. "You sit on your outer atoll for seasons grinding your hooks, fishing lures, sinkers. Making your weapons and twisting your *ekkwaḷ*[47] — rope is in great demand here. When you disembark to trade your items, the Saudeleur doesn't want you to have to pay a share to trade. He wants his share from the buyers, who most likely will be lesser chieftains, perhaps with rights to one of these lesser islets here in the village."

"Why are these chieftains so eager to pay his share?"

"They need these items to trade with their clan members for takai," said Ewalt. "They need the takai to continue to build their islets. Their islets attract the people to trade. They come to see the takai they or their ancestors laid. They come to trade their dogs, mats, kilts, and whatever else, and those who buy pay them the islet's share. But to think anyone is eager to buy is a mistake. To answer your question — no one is eager to pay the share! To understand the system is to understand this: to be successful, you must not be too eager. The chieftains will gladly show you their items of trade. They'll try to entice you to buy with your items first and let you pay the share. Many traders that come here fall into that trap. You must also keep in mind that the Saudeleur doesn't want you to return home without trading everything you brought. That would be wealth lost. At some point, if the chieftains tarry, he will buy the lot of what remains in a fair trade. He has eyes and ears

[47] Sennit; coir fiber line made from processed coconut husk fibers.

who will study your trade, and if he believes in your potential, he'll offer more because he wants you to return. We all know returning is the hard part. We all love the *pali*![48] Do you have any questions?"

"What does *pali* mean?" Ḷainjin hadn't heard this word before either.

"That is their word for 'navigator,' one who seeks adventure. Men like yourself who don't fear the sea."

"Tomorrow, I'll have more questions. I need time to think."

"All right, one final thing. When they bring you your food, they'll give you baskets similar to those you call *alele*[49] for your items of trade. You must put your mark on them to distinguish from the others."

"Mark with what?"

"They'll show you," Ewalt said. "I will count and remember the numbers of all the items you brought with you, as will a second *ribwinbwin* appointed by the Saudeleur. We will be responsible for these items upon punishment of death, and you won't get them back until you decide to leave. This is our way to assure no trading occurs outside the walls. That is the rule all traders must obey. The Saudeleur's trading will begin tomorrow at Kariahn,[50] the islet at the easternmost entrance at the lagoon's passageway to the ocean. You are free to trade from your alele on any of the islets, but if you're smart, you will realize that Kariahn offers you the best trades."

Ewalt continued. "I must go now. The Saudeleur called me away from tasks at my home on Temwen,[51] and I must return there. But I'll arrive early tomorrow, and we'll get you to Kariahn at the sound of the conch. We'll count the items there, and you'll be ready to get started."

Then Ewalt got into his canoe and paddled off into the yet-incoming tide before Ḷainjin got a chance to ask him more about the takai or to ask him about his mother. It was clear these people took their trading seriously. His words "I will count and remember upon punishment of death" were still

---

[48] Alternative spelling for "palu." "Traditional navigator" in the languages of what are now the Western Caroline Islands of the Federated States of Micronesia. Wisim is "the palu."

[49] A flat purse- or pouch-like basket plaited with processed pandanus leaves and used for valuables.

[50] A Pohnpeian islet where trading takes place.

[51] The island inland of Nahn Madol whose surrounding reef supports the city.

swirling in Ļainjin's head. He was too tired to determine what it all meant. Should he go inside and meet the other traders? Maybe someone else spoke his language and could answer his many questions. Later, he thought. He was too exhausted and needed more rest.

He pulled on his painter to draw his boat up to the walkway, boarded, and lay down in his hull. He should thank his good fortune. He had ingratiated himself with the highest man on the ocean and now found himself safely anchored here among some of the best navigators. Yes, he did need to learn how to speak to them. Ewalt could facilitate that. He went over the words he had learned as he drifted to sleep. And he slept long and hard before she awakened him with her cold, wet toes, teasing the hairs of his shin as he lay, one leg sprawled against the inside hull of his stern.

Talupe

Ḷainjin had been sailing amid mountainous waves, down channels between high walls, tacking one way and then another, looking desperately for an exit into the calm lagoon he knew was on the other side but couldn't seem to find. He gasped amid his heavy breathing in response to her tickling him. Then she nudged him playfully with her foot, where he had propped his knee. His manhood was embarrassingly erect, and he glimpsed her unblemished legs beneath her skirt of breadfruit bark as she scrambled back from the opened bow hatch. She was sitting on the outrigger deck and glancing down through the stern hatch, through which he was now peering up at her. She sat with her back straight. Experienced woman that she was, she flicked her curly black hair onto her back and looked away, allowing him to inspect her lovely face with impunity. She was the woman who had placed the flowers on his head earlier. As if to remind him, she playfully tossed the wilted flowers she'd found discarded on the deck onto his chest with a chortle and began speaking to him in her language.

He recognized the word *mwenge*[52] as she mimed it. The word sounded similar in his language. Suddenly, he remembered what Ewalt had instructed him to do. He propped himself up on an elbow and listened to her intently asking him several questions until she must have satisfied herself that he understood her not. Then, just as quickly, she ceased and smiled. Inhaling sharply through her nose, she resigned herself to just sitting there, kicking her feet in the water and looking embarrassingly inviting.

---

[52] Food; to eat. Similar to "ṃōñā" in Kajin Rālik.

Ḷainjin roused himself and sat across from her at an angle, with his thighs on his stern deck and lower legs dangling over the lip of the bow hatch into the hull. The light in the sky about them was fading. He glanced westward to see the new moon, but it had already set behind the mountains. She must have boarded without his permission by puckishly pulling his painter to the walkway. She was older than he was. She had dusted her face and upper body with a yellow spice. "It's as though she prepared herself to be eaten," he thought rapaciously. Her skin appeared flawless. Her tattoos, though pleasant and like the rest he would see, lacked the complexity he would expect on his home islands. The heat of the afternoon sun had long passed, and the breeze circling amid the village had cooled the sweat from his nightmare below. Her dark, elongated nipples told him she had children, and the yellow dust that had settled into their tiny crevices begged him to put them in his mouth. To look at her was to want her. He wondered how such an attractive woman could be without a man.

Other attendants were unloading food baskets from paddling canoes and carrying them through the entranceway of the islet. She had left his basket on the stern deck behind him after she had boarded. She sat with two large alele across her lap and a ball of black-dyed hibiscus strips and a bird-bone needle in her hand. "So that was what Ewalt meant when he said he was to put his mark on them," Ḷainjin thought, accepting the ball of hibiscus. He reached for his *rajraj*, cut four pieces of equal length, and on the top purse on her lap, laid them out in the shape of the *wapepe*[53] symbol. She turned her head this way and that, peering first at the symmetrical design and then curiously at him. With a little smirk, she nodded and enthusiastically began her handicraft.

"*Mwenge*," she said, motioning him to eat from the basket. She pronounced the word slightly differently than he did.

"It must be another common word," Ḷainjin thought, reaching behind and grabbing the basket. He could barely tear his eyes from her and sat the basket on his lap as she worked. It was full of husked coconuts, breadfruit, taro, concoctions baked in leaves, and a long, cooked slice off the belly of the marlin he had caught, wrapped in a banana-leaf pouch. He tried in vain to

[53] Literally, "boat floating." The symbol represents the four swells, one from each quadrant, converging upon an island in mid-ocean.

get her to eat a piece of it. He even playfully offered to feed it to her as she sewed, but to no avail. In his culture, if he could get her to eat from the same basket, it was a sign she might agree to lie with him. Her response was to frown, shake her head quickly, then giggle as she kept sewing the *wapepe* pattern attractively onto the cross-patterned plaits of the alele. She held it up for his inspection, and when he approved, held out her hand for him to return the ball of hibiscus and his *rajraj*. She sliced the hibiscus into equal strips as he had and sewed his pattern onto both purses as he ate.

"What entertainment," he thought, intermittently gawking at her mature beauty. He bent his head back periodically to suckle the sweet water from one coconut and then another. Glancing up, he acknowledged his white wind-cloud companions as they passed rapidly below the gradually darkening blue sky above the stone walls about them and seemed to merge with the dense clouds covering the mountain.

But Ļainjin had no inkling of the dream-like events about to transpire that would most likely, by the Saudeleur's crafty design, frame his fond memory of this place as surely as these very takai secured this stone village from the ravages of the sea. First from inland, deep beyond the mangrove-covered shore, and as if on cue, came the sound of stone ringing out against stone from one and then another of the village islets. It was as though there was a great calling out that the events of the night ahead were about to begin. How different from the quiet murmurs that peopled the evenings of the villages back home.

From around the corner came a procession of canoes that stopped at the entranceway across the watercourse to fetch the Saudeleur himself. It then proceeded to transport him across to where they were. As he stepped onto the walkway, the stones rang out from behind the islet's walls, and as if on signal, the woman before him finished marking his alele and motioned for him to pull his canoe shoreward. She playfully disembarked from the outrigger deck into the tidewater, wetted her skirt, and beckoned him to follow. Enthralled, he stepped into the knee-high water, and she took Ļainjin's hand in hers. His throat swelled as he accepted her clutch. Then she led him up into the entranceway behind the Saudeleur, who turned to acknowledge and beckon them as if they were to be part of his contingent.

Ḷainjin could see from the entranceway that the surrounding walls were about as thick as a man is tall. The walls to the north and west, though less high, were comparable to those of the Saudeleur's compound across the tideway. But those to the east and south were half as high, and he saw the breakwater walls that enclosed the southwestern and southeastern quarters of the village towering above them in the distance. The ocean breeze gratefully swept over the eastern walls and swirled gently about the interior of the enclosure to cool the sweat on his brow. From the vantage of his canoe, he had previously viewed the peaks of several large and open pole-and-thatch structures. One in the middle was the center of activity. At the open end under its eaves, men were sitting around a large flat stone, pounding their pestles in awkward rhythm with similar sounds ringing out from elsewhere in the village and beyond. These men faced the interior walls, which sheltered three connected platforms fronting each wall, making a claw-shaped structure where other men sat on pandanus mats facing each other and talking in tongues foreign to him. They wore kilts of various fabrics and designs, and all acknowledged their entrance with polite nods of their heads. He had seldom felt so observed before, and he hesitated and squeezed his companion's hand until she responded with a confident smile, pointing with her eyes as if to say, "They are acknowledging the Saudeleur." Then she lifted her head high as though entitled to walk behind the great chief, and so Ḷainjin followed suit.

They entered the long house from its easternmost entrance, stepped onto a platform covered with soft pandanus matting, and sat there at the hinge of the claw, next to the Saudeleur, facing the foreign groups on each side. The rhythm of the pestles changed. They were now intermittently crushing what he knew from legend to be sakau roots. Attendants were setting lighted shells of oil about the long house. A young woman knelt before the Saudeleur and anointed his shoulders, back, and chest with coconut oil. Another sat down before Ḷainjin and did the same. She smiled and rubbed his muscular frame with no embarrassment, looking up into his eyes as a woman does when she wishes to break all formalities. His companion squeezed his hand and distracted his attention by placing her foot gently on his and scooting a bit toward him. He turned to her and she smiled broadly, with that same look of a woman with interest in her throat. So far, he liked everything about this enchanting place.

At another time, he would watch them mash the sakau roots with water and squeeze the ceremonial liquid through the twisted strands of freshly stripped hibiscus bark into shell cups passed to participants. This first time, he noted only that the first cup went to the Saudeleur. The second was passed to Ḷainjin as other visitors on the mats below them received theirs. These first cups, he would learn, contained a mildly bitter slime from the inner hibiscus bark used to twist the water from the crushed roots. The later ones would have the consistency of plain muddy water and would go down much easier. This night, he found this first cup disgusting. The later cups were tolerable. Everyone seemed to participate, his companion guzzling twice the number of cups as him. First, his tongue became numb, then his mouth and face. A feeling of relaxation overcame him, and the remainder of the evening became gradually more dream-like. He gathered that most of the traders there were from Truk[54] and its surrounding atolls. The Saudeleur seemed to speak their language well enough to joke and converse, and there was much laughing between them, although he had an attendant at his side to interpret in-depth communications between them. Unfortunately, the Saudeleur didn't speak Ḷainjin's language, nor did his interpreter. Though polite and friendly with Ḷainjin, he spoke to him not. If only Ḷainjin had Ewalt by his side!

The leader of the Truk Islanders was a burly man with immense arms and straight hair drenched with scented oil, piled high on his head, and held with a broad turtle shell–comb. He had a wide, nearly perpetual smile on his face. At one point, perhaps heavily influenced by the sakau, he plunged himself down between Ḷainjin and his companion in what seemed an overly friendly manner, grabbed onto his hand and shoulder like an octopus, and held on to him as he jabbered without interpretation for an uncomfortably long time. He introduced himself as Wisim,[55] and in the manner of a high person, asked Ḷainjin for his name and then repeated it often as he spoke. He wore flowers around his head and neck, as did his crew, and he seemed

[54] The next island and language group west of Pohnpei.

[55] Aka "the palu."

to be complimenting Ḷainjin on bringing in the marlin and on something concerning the design of his boat. As the evening wore on, Ḷainjin became more at ease with not knowing what people were saying. He learned to attune his ear to grasp a word here and there, in one language or another, that seemed to have a similar meaning in Kajin Rālik. He then tried to recognize and repeat it in mimed conversation. He considered again how fortunate he was to have met Ewalt, who could answer his many questions, and began committing the new words to memory so he could ask Ewalt about them when they next met. These thoughts provided comfort and hope that he could, at some point, climb the thick invisible walls that seemed to separate him from the others.

Later, after many cups of the numbing liquid, his companion motioned that they should leave, and he followed her back to his boat, where she seemed happy to drop her skirt and pass the remainder of the evening intertwined with him in the cramped privacy of his hull. She told him her name was Talupe but asked him not his name. After, they sat on his proa in silence. He wanted to ask her many things. Would she return the following night? He lacked the words to ask. Later, he watched her wade back across the shallow tideway with the rest of the Saudeleur's contingent as though nothing had happened.

Ḷainjin slept less fitfully, dreamed of calmer seas, and awoke the next morning, ready to resume his adventures. During the early morning, he occupied himself by eating from his basket, emptying his proa of its treasure of shark teeth, and counting them into his two alele. He wondered about the equivalent of a tooth in trade and thought about his friends for life on Namorik. He wished they were with him now, sharing in his adventure and trading the fruits of their shark-hunting endeavors. But most of all, he thought about the night before and the wondrous woman who had pleased him and left without a word. Had the Saudeleur sent her to him as some sort of welcoming gift? Or had she come to him of her own design?

Finally, he climbed the walls and walked the periphery of Kelepwei. The view from the top of the highest walls was most interesting. Each corner of the enclosure offered its own unique perspective, although taller structures on the surrounding islets obstructed the spectacle of the entire village. "The walls of what Jeilañ called Pahn Kadira, across the channel, would offer a better vantage," he thought. He could see glimpses of the southwestern and southeastern reefs through seawall entrances here and there as well as the remarkably high corner lookout between them. And he could see the islet of Idedh,[56] though he was not yet aware of its great mysteries, its purpose with respect to the Pohnpeian system of trade, or the opportunity it presented to accumulate wealth.

Soon the tide would withdraw again. The tideways and surrounding reef would no longer afford passage for their canoes and would become puddled pathways between the islets' impressive retaining walls. However, long before the tide would ebb to that extreme, Ewalt arrived in his canoe and suggested that Ḷainjin climb down and sail them to Kariahn, where the day's trading would take place.

As they boarded Ḷainjin's canoe, Ewalt was eager to see the trade items he had placed in the two alele. Ḷainjin lifted one of the heavy baskets.

"*Wōt jeej*!"[57] Ewalt was surprised by their number and size. "I had no idea…" He quickly stowed the baskets below.

The other visitors were also in the process of rigging and making their way around the corner between Kelepwei and Pahn Kadira. There was barely room for two boats to maneuver in the narrow channel between the islets.

The leader of the Truk Islanders, Wisim, the sakau-drinking navigator of the evening before, began prattling at them in his native language as, sail hoisted, he held his much larger craft adrift in the light air. Ewalt, although apparently not conversant in their language, understood his meaning. He explained that the man and his crew were from Satawan.[58] Ḷainjin later learned that the various languages of Truk shared more words in common with Pohnpeian than either did with Kajin Rālik.

"He is a great *pali* and admires your vessel," Ewalt continued.

"*Palu*!" interrupted the large man, laughing. He twisted his long hair into a bun and secured it with a hardwood dagger.

---

[56] One of many man-made islets on the reef off the coast of eastern Pohnpei.

[57] The same as "jeej." An idiom used to express surprise that translates as "heck" or "darn it." Demonstrates more deliberation than "wōjjej."

[58] One of the outer atolls of the Truk group.

"Palu," repeated Ewalt, nodding in deference to the good-natured navigator. "They say the word differently in his language. He wants you to go ahead so he can follow and judge your cut into the wind. I think he said he wants to see if your boat is worthy to race his."

These words caused an immediate reflexive reaction from Ḷainjin as he pointed his head down, raised his eyebrows, and peered at Ewalt from beneath his overhanging brow.

"Tell him the man with the longer canoe always wants to race." With a chuckle, Ḷainjin directed Ewalt to raise sail.

Ḷainjin had studied the Satawan canoe and the other canoes of the Truk group as well as the lay of the islets ahead during his morning sojourn. The hull of his canoe, in the tradition of Rālik and Ratak, was deeper and narrower than theirs. Navigator that he was, this man from Satawan no doubt realized the advantage Ḷainjin's craft would have in a close-hauled race and wanted a chance to judge this advantage before challenging him. Their progress required them to tack in the channel between the inside corner of Pahn Kadira and the northwest corner of Kelepwei, and Ḷainjin, encouraged by Ewalt's alacrity on the bow, let him take the helm into the channel. This allowed Ḷainjin to concentrate on assessing the competence of the Satawan crew as they shunted. He found them flawless. Ewalt suggested they tack again and follow the others down the cross channel that led along the northwest wall of Idedh, so they executed a second shunt, and Ḷainjin was back at the helm, steering them down the cross channel on a northeast tack parallel, and on the opposite side of the islets they had passed the day before. Idedh, the islet to windward, was narrow and rectangular like the others, but its walls were high enough to cut off their wind, and the boats ahead were making little progress in the light air once they made the turn into the cross channel.

"*Kiberikrik kōjatdikdrik*,"[59] Ḷainjin chanted, sheeting in as much as possible, flattening the belly of his sail, and skirting the walls of the islet to

[59] "Steer into wind and hope to win"; a sailing axiom when racing an outrigger canoe. The lateen sail takes a remarkable cut into the wind, rarely gets caught in irons, and in a smooth-water lagoon environment, does not always require a "belly" to perform competitively.

port. There, the air swirled heavier and allowed them to maneuver past the canoe that had preceded them. He noticed the Satawan canoe behind copy his maneuver. Shortly, as they came to the northwest corner of Idedh, the boats ahead sheeted in on a diagonal course off the northwest corner of Darong, on a course across an open stretch of reef that seemed to separate the upper and lower parts of the village. "They intend to pinch their way eastward toward the seawall that leads to Kariahn," he thought. He knew his boat could work its way forward through the group on a course like that, but he also realized there was a more definitive way to beat the lot of them. As immediately as they cleared Idedh, he would call for yet another tack. A third channel separated Darong from an islet to the southwest. Darong would cut off their air, but if they cut a similar course close to the wall of the islet parallel, he could emerge from the channel between them, tack into a reach run, and arrive at the seawall long before them.

"*Diak*!" commanded Ḷainjin.

Ewalt, who had expected him to stay the course of the boats ahead, was surprised but immediately executed his call. They shunted and successfully crossed the bow of the vessel they had passed along the wall. Ewalt's eyes met Ḷainjin's as if to say, "That was close!"

Ḷainjin laughed and motioned with his head back to the Satawan vessel to stern. He had forced the Truk navigator to decide to tack or no. Now, due to a moment's hesitation, he had to wait out of politeness for the boat that had followed him to pass before completing his shunt. He laughed again as he imagined the chagrin on this competitor's face as he tacked and headed, closely hauled, along the north edge of Idedh, now many boat lengths behind. He was no doubt watching him disappear down the watercourse to the southwest of Darong. By the time Ḷainjin cornered Darong, tacked, and headed northeast on his final loose-hauled reach, his competitor had just entered the channel he had exited. Once the palu finally emerged from the channel, however, it was clear that his Satawan vessel, racing toward Ḷainjin, had the advantage. Its protracted length, larger sail, and greater number of crew combined to grant it superior speed that Ḷainjin's much-smaller boat could never hope to match. There would be no quick shunting to surprise them but just the long, straight course that should allow the faster boat to catch up and surpass them.

But before reaching the beginning of the seawall that led uninterrupted northward to Kariahn, they had to cross the two wide passageways upon the open reef on either side of the fortress-like lookout isle that lay between them. In the first strait, he observed that the retreating tide met the waves that were forcefully sweeping the reef from its edge at the sea, where buñtokrear swells curled and crashed. These opposing forces churned up a nasty chop that streamed through the two openings to impede their progress. Halfway across this first passageway, Ḷainjin turned and viewed the Satawan canoe closing on them. He judged by its progress that it would pass them somewhere in the middle of the second passageway ahead. He watched the waves as each broke onto his kubaak, plunged it briefly beneath the surface, rocked their craft, and repeatedly deterred their progress. As the Satawan canoe crossed the passageway to stern, though, he noticed that this effect was even more pronounced, due to the fatter, less sleek design of its kubaak. From this, he knew he had them! As they entered the lee of the islet between the passageways, he allowed his sail to luff ever so slightly and spill enough wind to allow his competitor to catch up all the faster. His grandfathers' words came to mind: "There's nothing more disarming than lulling your opponent into a swagger as he comes in for the finish."

"They're going to catch us," said Ewalt in resignation.

"Please take the two alele from below and hold them high in the air," commanded Ḷainjin. They progressed beyond the lee of the islet to starboard, felt the full force of Tūṃur in their sail, and began to cross the second, wider passageway. Ewalt, after several words of objection, lifted the heavy alele, one in each hand, as high in the air as he could, and Ḷainjin waited a few moments until, in the corner of his eye, he saw an opposing crew member — apparently under his helmsman's direction — raise one of theirs.

They were so close that Ḷainjin imagined he could hear them laughing at the prospect of beating him, but of course, his face turned to windward. The wind's call rushed into his ears and carried all sounds from the craft just behind swirling off in the opposite direction. A bright, salty haze blew through the passageway; the whitecaps glistened in the morning sun, leaving shimmering, effervescent foam in the wake of each passing wave. He hauled in on the sheet, dramatically putting their craft at heel and raising their outrigger a calf above the waves cresting to starboard.

"Ḷainjin!" cried Ewalt, worried perhaps that they would flip and spill his items of trade into the tide churning beneath them.

In response, Ḷainjin just laughed at the worried expression on his face and, like a child gleefully at play, motioned over his shoulder. His opponent either could not or would not dare to replicate this technique, and their smaller craft, no doubt to the surprise of all, began spurting headlong through the passageway such that, by the time they reached the lee of the seawall ahead, they now had a toss-up chance of winning the race. By the time the larger craft had struggled across the passageway and reached the lee of the last stretch of seawall, Ḷainjin was already a third of the way along. Then, reaching the breakwater, the larger craft again began to gain on them and continued to gain on them until they simultaneously reached Kariahn. At the last, Ḷainjin left his tiller as his craft swung to into the wind before the wall. He dropped a secured anchor from his stern, then gracefully sprang past Ewalt and stepped casually onto the walkway at the edge of the wall just as the bow fluttered up to it and abruptly braked, the stern anchor line taut. Although he was undoubtedly the first to step off with his bowline, he looked not at the others and resisted the temptation to gloat, laugh, or make comment. Instead, he simply ordered Ewalt to strike, flake their sail, and prepare to debark.

Wisim, renowned palu from faraway Satawan, could not leave the results of such a race unheralded. First off, without interpretation, he offered his alele as a prize. Ḷainjin refused to take it. His intention had not been to bet his alele. In the heat of the moment, he had just wanted to point out that he was so certain of his skill he was willing to risk all if he flipped turtle in the gusts. Then Wisim began loudly announcing his defeat to the other traders of his Truk group and continuously slapped Ḷainjin on his back as he chattered away excitedly. He finally satisfied himself by seizing Ḷainjin's hand and clutching it in such a relentless display of friendship that Ewalt found it difficult to untwine the two even after explaining his need to begin the all-important inventory of items. He had to call for his Pohnpeian counterpart assigned to the Satawan Islanders to explain the need for the two to separate.

Unlike the other islets Ļainjin had viewed earlier that morning from atop Kelepwei or those they had passed by that morning or the day before, Kariahn lacked any sign of normal residence. There was no shelter there even for the several men assigned to lookout from the gigantic, upswept corners of its massive walls. Its purpose was simply to implement the trading culture of Nahn Madol. To this end, there was one entrance only, and what an entrance it was! Who could have imagined an entrance constructed beneath a wall of massive stones such that a brave man would cringe as he passed beneath its lintel of five massive stone beams, any one of which could crush twenty men if felled? Surely, the question of how they had built such a thing would linger on the shoulder of any man who entered. Inside was an enormous courtyard covered with coral beach pebbles surrounded by a gallery, nearly the height of a man, where traders sat in small groups with their items of trade. At the center of the courtyard was a square, flat-topped house built completely of stone beams that he came to learn was the perpetually guarded vault that would house a man's trade items until he departed the village. Atop the vault sat two guards shaded by the overhanging thatch of a lightly constructed pole-and-thatch canopy.

The islet built at the end of the seawall — and at the edge of that southern portion of the oblong lagoon that was open to the sea — was under constant broadside this time of year, from the mountainous buñtokrear swells that had swept him there. Despite a wall as thick as the length of two men, the sounds of these swells crashing on the east and north sides echoed throughout the structure as the very winds that bore the waves swirled about and cooled the bright, open interior. The smell of the ocean and salt from its winds filled the nostrils of every man and woman, and a damp coating of salt covered every stone.

Indeed, the origin of nearly every item traded that day, except for a few neck-strings made of dog teeth, was a treasure snatched up from the ocean's depths. Fishing lures, hooks, sinkers, sling stones, throwing stones, and pounding stones ground from the shells of giant clams. Shark teeth — and cutting tools and weapons made of them. Stingray barbs. Pearl-shell cutting tools and ornaments of pearl and turtle shell. There were no plaited mats or sails, no dogs or other food items, no coils of sennit. Items such as these,

Ḷainjin would learn, traded in plenty at centers elsewhere in the village. The Saudeleur and high members of the other clans, he would learn, valued these former items from far away that represented dangerous adventures and days of labor to fashion. They liked to trade and to bestow these items upon their workers, in conjunction with various titles, as rewards for the placement of building stones.

Ewalt led him directly to the center structure, where he formally introduced him to another Pohnpeian man who was to be his second. The three had to wait their turn to enter. His eyes glancing in all directions, Ḷainjin saw from features, dress, and language that many different island groups, in addition to the Truk Islanders he knew from Kelepwei, were present in the courtyard. Each group seemed to have its own local leader or counter-interpreter assigned to it by the Saudeleur. Those with the most items seemed to be Indigenous traders, perhaps from other islets in the village, who came to lay out their items atop the gallery for all to view as they passed by. Many of the non-Indigenous barterers were going from one trader to another, alele in hand, offering to trade for the items displayed. Ḷainjin recalled that those foreigners trading in this manner were paying double, due to the share required by the Saudeleur.

Ewalt confirmed his recollection. "Perhaps they should wait their turn at auction when the trading partner who offers to buy pays the islet's share." Ewalt clarified a distinction they had spoken of, that the share was paid to the islet Kariahn, not to the Saudeleur.

"Doesn't the Saudeleur own the islet?"

"Yes, but the trading creates a complicated tree of tribute."

"Why aren't their Pohnpeian counters advising them to wait?"

"Counters" — Ewalt used the Pohnpeian term this time — "are not allowed to offer trading advice."

At this, Ḷainjin pulled a particularly large shark tooth from his purse. "You mean you can't tell me what to expect this to trade for? How many of these for a good fishing lure or stingray barb?" Ḷainjin remembered that he owed Uerik a stingray barb.

The eyes of Ewalt's second grew large as Ewalt encouraged Ḷainjin to return the large tooth to its purse.

"Sorry, counters are not allowed to interfere. The Saudeleur doesn't care, but the other local traders will press their case to him. I could end up on Idedh!"

"The islet we passed on our way here? What's so bad about Idedh?"

At this, Ewalt's second laughed, and several others turned in interest when Ḷainjin questioned the name of the islet.

"I guess I should have taken you there first. That's the custom, but you seem to be an honest person and intelligent enough without having to visit the islet of Nahn Samohl."

"Who is Nahn Samohl?"

"She is the biggest eel of them all!"

Ewalt confirmed that the term *dāp* was the same in both languages.

"What about the eel?"

"It's the way we enforce our system of trade. Anyone breaking the rules must submit to her."

"What do you mean, 'submit to her?'"

"The well is very narrow, and Nahn Samohl is kept hungry. She'll twist off your appendages first!"

"*Wōt jeej*!" cried Ḷainjin as they all laughed nervously. But then it seemed to him it was not a joking matter. "Okay, teach me how to avoid that."

"It's simple. Just meet your commitments, and don't trade outside the walls! Also, remember this one rule of trading: no recast! Once you agree on a trade, that's it — no changing terms in any way without prior agreement between both parties. Keep that in mind, and you will have no problem. He and I have the problem."

Turning to his second, Ewalt said, "We must remember the count and recite it exactly when asked.

"Let's say you come tomorrow, Ḷainjin, and we count the contents of your alele and come up one shark tooth short. I must immediately report that to you. With your permission, I tell the Saudeleur in private what the count should be. Then he asks my second, and his count should agree because we counted them together at the end of the previous day. Then the Saudeleur replaces what is lost but begins watching the guards. A guard caught stealing or even falling asleep could end up at Idedh. If we" — Ewalt nodded at his second — "don't agree, one of us has a problem. If the problem is big, one of us could lose his title or even end up at Idedh."

"When was the last time someone ended up there, and what did he do?"

Ewalt turned to his second and spoke in Pohnpeian. There was a long pause. They honestly couldn't seem to remember. Then he said, "It has been many seasons — probably someone who accepted payment to deliver a stone and failed to deliver at the appointed time. Receiving payment before you deliver is always risky because of the law of no recast."

"What is the law of no recast?"

"You know when the *ri-kwōjkōj*[60] casts your lot, he sees your destiny. Once a trade is cast, both parties are bound by the trade. There is no recast!"

"Either you perform as agreed or go to Idedh and face Nahn Samohl!"

"That's the idea," confirmed Ewalt.

Ḷainjin was still asking questions when their turn came to enter the stone house. They told him no talking, just counting. He had over sixteen hundred shark teeth, fourteen giant clam–lures, and over twenty hooks to trade. They separated the smaller teeth into one alele and the larger into the other and set out to see the items displayed around the gallery.

As soon as they stepped back into the courtyard, his new Satawan friend, Wisim, clenched his hand and began giving orders and leading him about like a father would a beloved son. Ḷainjin got what the palu said from Ewalt, who interpreted it from the palu's counter. He was to save his items for auction, but in the interim, the palu would buy him whatever he wanted. He would show Ḷainjin how to bargain because he knew they never bargained where Ḷainjin came from. This was true. So Ḷainjin complied and allowed himself to be led here and there. He saw many items he needed: trolling lures, hooks, stingray barbs… A man cannot possess too many of these things because the sea inevitably recaptures them. The palu wanted to buy him a neck-string of puka shells and pearl-shell pendants for "the Pohnpeian woman with him." This brought many laughs because he and his company had, of course, seen him leave with his new companion Talupe the night before.

Ḷainjin, not wanting to be in the debt of the stranger, refused to allow Wisim to buy him anything. He simply wanted to see a fair trade for his

[60] Literally, "bones that cast fortune"; fortune teller.

small shark teeth. With Wisim's help, he settled for trading eighteen small shark teeth for a good-sized stingray barb. He paid the share of an additional eighteen to Ewalt. The Pohnpeians all wanted to offer in lots of twenty for a small barb. A large one was a separate matter, but his Satawan friend, whose single alele contained tens of such barbs, assisted in driving the bargain by showing all his barbs and reminding the Pohnpeian traders that, where he came from, a stingray was easier to catch than a shark. Ḷainjin also learned in the process that most of the shark teeth already in the traders' collections had holes already drilled into their base and that these were worth twice as much as his. Very few large shark teeth were displayed, and none were the size of Ḷainjin's, so he asked Ewalt to sew up the alele that contained them for another day. He would trade his small ones first.

When Ḷainjin's turn to offer items at auction came, he deferred his turn to Wisim, who successfully traded many of his smaller stingray barbs to the Indigenous traders for other items. His counter conducted the auction quickly and efficiently with a minimum of discussion between the counter and the navigator. It was clear the Indigenous traders had a set price for most items and instead of bidding against each other, took turns. This was their way of life. They did this nearly every day. They gave the impression they would buy anything at their set price. By accepting only stingray barbs as payment, Ḷainjin received immediate payment of some of Wisim's stingray barbs for his shark teeth in lots of twenty per barb. This saved them both from paying enormous shares had he purchased them directly from the palu. Ḷainjin also accepted trades for one- and two-digit fishhooks and trolling lures of five fingers and more, although these trades wouldn't finalize until he'd had a chance to inspect their quality. All occurred in the span of a few moments, such that Ḷainjin commented laughingly to Ewalt that he could have sold one of his own teeth if he could have extracted it quickly enough. At any rate, he had most of his treasure of shark teeth still in carry and many other days to better judge the market, so he paid close attention to the remainder of the day's trades to better learn what the market had to offer and at what price. By the time they finished, the afternoon tide had turned and had again begun to flood the reefs. Each man completed his trades with the assistance of his counter, and the alele were stored in a guarded, thatch-covered stone house that stood, vault-like, at the center of the courtyard. The Saudeleur sent baskets of coconuts and other provisions, and the men sat in small groups about the gallery, eating and socializing in their various languages.

Ļainjin concentrated on learning Pohnpeian from Ewalt. Except every time he turned, Wisim, the friendly navigator from Satawan, cornered him, wrapped his big, muscular arm about his shoulders, and spit his language into his face. Sometimes he had an interpreter, sometimes no, but he always seemed to assume that the more intensely he spoke, the easier it would be for Ļainjin to understand. He began to get a headache from it all. At one point, he thought, "What is he talking about?" Turning away as politely as possible, he escaped and, seeking a moment alone, found steps to the top where the guards stood. His face ached from politely smiling and pretending he understood what he did not, so he turned to his old friend the wind, which had no questions, required no answers, cooled the blush from his face, and calmed his soul as though its rushing sound was a woman's intimate whisper in his ear.

Ļainjin looked out across the lagoon inlet at the ferocious, whitecapped ocean from whence he had come and to which he knew he must one day return, and a sense of peace and purpose overcame him. True, he had failed to anticipate the difficulty overcoming this wall of language, but what about the opportunity he would pass up if he allowed it to cripple his ambition? Out there, he and he alone determined his destiny. In the village, destinies mix — others take charge, and he must be wise enough, ambitious enough, to allow it. He would learn Pohnpeian by day with Ewalt and by night with Talupe, and he would learn Satawan or the language of Truk or whatever it was the palu was speaking — and any other language he needed to master to accomplish his goal.

Walking the periphery of the high walls, he found them heavily fortified with hardwood spears and baskets of large, egg-shaped hurdling stones of polished giant clam–shell. With a guard's permission, he lifted one of the heavy stones. "This is too heavy to throw laterally, but if tossed down from this height, it could kill a man quickly or even damage a canoe," he thought. "Then after the battle, they could be easily spotted and collected from the reef." Looking down, he noted that the outside wall was concave, making it nearly impossible to scale without a rope, and it was too high for a man to easily grapple. "If a grapple did come over the wall and catch here, a stone like this could easily crush it — let alone the hand or arm of a man seeking to pull himself over." Then he turned back to the single entrance. Its height was so low it required a man to bow as he entered, leaving him vulnerable to attack from within or from anything flung or dropped onto him from above. He noticed the conch shell where each man stood. That confirmed to him that a lookout's primary duty was to warn of approaching vessels. He imagined reinforcements arriving from the neighboring islets to guard the entire length of the wall that led to the structure's single entrance. Without question, it was the most defendable place he had ever been. The vault, the walls, the guards… Everything gave the impression of a secure foundation for their system of trade. He thought about his shark teeth in the vault and realized for the first time that he was a wealthy man. It was no wonder this place was successful! For how many seasons had it been so?

Then he completed his walk. Returning to where he had started, he found Ewalt climbing the steps after him. Surprisingly, he was carrying Ḷainjin's two alele, filled with his items for trade.

"You're like that bird of yours — in love with the wind! It does feel good, doesn't it," spouted Ewalt, losing his breath. When he had reached the top, he turned his face into the onrush, his handsome face and close-cropped hair pressed by the wind. "We need to change something." Then in a separate comment, he said, "You must be lonely. You're quite a distance from your home island." He carefully placed Ḷainjin's two alele between the takai and then dangerously flopped onto a stretcher stone at the edge of the wall. He hung his legs over the edge with no fear of the height, as though he were merely sitting on the deck of a proa and dangling his feet to dip his toes in the ocean now far below. He nodded for Ḷainjin to do the same.

Ḷainjin paused as he stood back from the edge of the wall.

"What, you're surprised? Don't forget I grew up on these walls." Ewalt nodded for Ḷainjin to join him and talked on without waiting for him to comment. "I have never crossed such a span of sea. I can't even imagine having the bravery to try, and you did it all by yourself. You have certainly caught the eyes of the Saudeleur. You people of Rālik and Ratak are so self-reliant and at ease on the ocean, it amazes him. My father was the same way — every day out to sea. He fished for the prior Saudeleur and earned a title for his work. Myself, I am a man happy to plant my yams and taro there on the island behind us."

"You mean that's a separate island?" Ḷainjin turned behind him and, from the heights of the wall, visualized the outline of an island separated from the mainland by the bay he had entered the morning before.

"Yes, it's called Temwen. My mother is from there. She jokes my father came from the sea and grabbed the first woman on the first island he came to!"

"Is your father from Rālik or Ratak?"

"His mother was from Namorik and his father from Epoon.[61] Have you been to either?"

"Yes, both lie south. Like Pohnpei, they get lots of rain and are very lush."

"But no freshwater streams, I'm sure!"

"And no falling ones either! You must take me to one. I've heard you have many. I want to bathe under the falling water before I return."

"Well, maybe we're cousins! I will certainly take you, but you can't stand under the waterfall." Ewalt laughed. "It falls into water too deep to stand, and the force pushes you down."

"Can I bathe behind it?"

"Yes, and the falling water will cover your nakedness!"

"Good! Modest man that I am, I worried about that my whole trip here," Ḷainjin paused. "What about Talupe? Is she from Temwen too?"

"No, she's from a mainland village on the other side called Metalanim, closer to the waterfalls," Ewalt joked. "You like her?"

"Oh, yes."

"Myself, I don't like older women," said Ewalt, "Too ambitious! Take an old man's advice — choose a woman who is young and reckless."

"Old! You aren't much older than me!"

"I'm talking like my father," continued Ewalt. "He is older than Mother. That's the advice he always gave me. I know I'm older than you are now, but don't worry, you'll catch up to me quick if you chase that woman. She has much ambition. She's already placed many takai and is on her way to earning an important title from the Saudeleur."

---

[61] A neighboring atoll seventy-three miles south-southwest of Namorik.

"Placed takai? Where? How could she…?"

"Don't let her girlish smile deceive you. She would do anything for the Saudeleur, and she competes with some of the strongest-handed men on Pohnpei. You might as well cuddle with his eel, Nahn Samohl!"

"*Jeej*![62] Ļainjin recalled what Ewalt had said about the eel twisting off the appendages. "In Rālik, we compare men to eels and women to the holes in the reef."

"*M̧ōm̧aan m̧aj*![63] Yes, I know my father is always saying that, but a *m̧aj* is smaller than a dāp! You should talk to my father. He loves telling stories."

"I'd like that. How do they bring those takai that break off the face of the mountain?"

"That's not as hard as it seems. They use an ancient system of ladders passed down from the ancestors."

"Ladders, how do they help?" Ļainjin asked.

"I'll let the attractive one show you."

"Jeej! You don't like her, do you?"

"It's more jealousy than anything else — all men want her. I was no different," admitted Ewalt. "She's warm and flattering when she needs to be but cold as a deep-water fish when she doesn't. You'll see. She's just like everybody else, only more so because of her extreme beauty and cunning. We Pohnpeians are a strange circle of fish. According to my father, our system of trade captivates us, and we lose our sense of self. We seek fortune and title and lose sight of more satisfying elements in life. Let's just say Talupe isn't the type to jump on your boat and return with you to Rālik. She has too many plans. Do you remember what I said about choosing one young and reckless? That is the type for a *pali* like you, but you decide for yourself.

"We need to change your symbol," Ewalt continued.

"Why?"

"Someone else is using the same pattern on their alele."

---

[62] An idiom used to express surprise. Translates roughly as "heck" or "darn it." A short form of "wōjjej."

[63] Literally, "a man is an eel," which means that he always develops a relationship with a hole. "M̧ōm̧aan" means "man"; "m̧aj" means "eel."

Raipuinlañ

"Who?" Ļainjin was shocked, his curiosity piqued to the extreme.

"Obviously, someone else from Rālik," replied Ewalt. "It probably belongs to one of the *pali* we call the Seekers."

Ļainjin corrected him. "That symbol doesn't belong to anyone. The understanding of what it means belongs to only a few. I would like to meet this *pali*."

"He or she is still out at sea."

"She? Who is she?" Ļainjin was getting visibly excited now.

"There is a woman among the Saudeleur's Seekers. I don't know if this is her symbol or not."

"What's her name?"

"They call her Rojak."[64]

"How old is she?"

"My age," Ewalt answered. "Maybe a little older."

"Okay, so it's not my mother." Ļainjin was despondent. His mind raced from one thought to another. "What are Seekers?"

"There are many ways to earn fortune and title here in Pohnpei. One is to seek and bring back the large trees that float out there. The bigger the better — we need them for our rafts. Seekers are always from the outer atolls. These Seekers are from Rālik also. They came many seasons ago and now speak our language, so I don't interpret for them. They return to sea each

---

[64] The female Seeker; Lañinpo's sister; aka Lirojak.

season to seek the kājokwā[65] our people use to transport the largest stones, the foundation stones, from the face of the mountains. They use the wind to tow these things to us."

"Doesn't Pohnpei have large trees?" Ḷainjin asked.

"Not like these, and not as buoyant."

"Where do they seek the kājokwā?"

"You should ask my father about that," Ewalt said. "He used to take them their favorite foods and spoke with them often when he was younger. They prefer to stay at Kelepwei as favored guests of the Saudeleur. Half refuse to trade the kājokwā for the Saudeleur's titles, so half have amassed great wealth, and they keep it here, in the vault below. Now, how can we change this symbol to identify these as yours?" He removed a bird-bone needle and a small ball of black-dyed hibiscus bark from one of the alele.

Ḷainjin couldn't answer. He was so intrigued and had so many questions to ask that they clogged his thoughts, and he sat dumbfounded by Ewalt's story. The ocean before him shrank in that instant, and he transported his spirit back over the sea he had crossed to the fire that night but a few tides ago. Burned like a scar into his memory was the comment "Surely, any survivor of Tarmālu's fleet would tarry there, where a man could earn a fortune, before returning to Rālik." Surely, his long journey had suddenly ended. These Seekers might give him, or lead him to, the story he had for so long been seeking!

"When are they expected back?"

"Definitely, they'll be back before the wind dies. They can't paddle far with something like that in tow."

All of a sudden, Ḷainjin's present seemed to him quite arbitrary. He must wait for them and hope they return swiftly. He envisioned himself scaling the walls each morning to look out for their arrival. "Perhaps I should join the Saudeleur's guard?" He laughed to himself at the thought. "It's that or I volunteer as a worker for the intriguing Pohnpeian woman!"

"Ḷainjin, how can we change this symbol?" repeated Ewalt, forcing him to set aside his neck-string of thoughts and bringing him back to the wall where they sat.

[65] A tree trunk adrift in the open ocean or washed up on the shore.

"How many of these Seekers did you say there were?"

"Four, I believe, in the Rālik group — each with their own canoe, just like yours. I believe they constructed them here with the patronage of the Saudeleur."

"Haven't they chosen Pohnpeian women and men?"

"They have taken many and have fostered a child, but because they refuse to live in our villages, our women lose interest as they grow older, and the woman…"

"The woman?" Ļainjin was curious.

"Hard like a man. She lacks the softness of most women. The story goes that none of our men could please her or impregnate her, though many tried. What about the symbol?"

"Here, give me that, please." Ļainjin took the needle and began sewing a small X shape in the center of the *wapepe* symbol as his thoughts came one after the other like the swells breaking against the walls below. He quickly completed the task. "Is that okay?"

"Yes, that's fine. Let's go down and get something to eat. Aren't you hungry?"

They descended back onto the gallery, where the traders were telling stories, and Ewalt left him for the vault. Wisim spotted him immediately and called him over to eat from their basket. Ļainjin, in a better mood now that he realized he was making progress in his quest, was happy to join him. He sucked on a coconut and ate among the palu's crew.

They were engaged in lively talk, of which he understood little. This time, Ļainjin overcame his fear of blindness and loss of control as though he was stepping into a dark room, knowing his loss of sight was but temporary until his eyes adjusted. He began concentrating on the men's words, and they, in turn, stopped ignoring him and began politely looking at him now and then as they spoke, trying their best to include him in the conversation. Their interpreter chimed in from time to time to relate what they just said in Pohnpeian as though that would help. Ļainjin stopped trying to keep track of the different languages and began thinking of both as simply not Kajin Rālik. That made the task easier. If he could only stop himself from grinning and pretending to understand, his face would stop aching. Where was Ewalt now that he could really make use of him? Once Ḷainjin learned how to ask the meaning of a word, he gradually stopped pretending he understood and began interrupting the speakers in midsentence to ask the meaning. Finally, by simply repeating the word, he could stop them in midsentence, and together, the group would mime the meaning for him. This slowed the conversation down, and he found that someone in the group could quickly come up with a like word from his own language. It was easier to converse with the group rather than with any one individual. Once he realized this, his spirit soared carefree like a seabird that took solace and direction from joining one of the swirling flocks.

By the time Ewalt returned to join the group, Ḷainjin had successfully turned the point of the conversation to learning the different pronunciations of the same word among the three languages, and all took part enthusiastically. It became a game to find a word that was the same or similar in all three. The words for "dog," "mountain," "shark," and many other things seemed to be similar. They became so engrossed in their game they seemed not to notice that most of the others had left for neighboring islets with the tide. They continued even as they embarked and set sail beneath the new moon high in the still-blue, late afternoon sky. They even shouted words at each other as they made their way back and anchored at Kelepwei. Strangely, the Pohnpeian word for "moon" was the word the Rālik Islanders used for "light." They even continued during sakau. Though having great fun, Wisim must have noticed Ḷainjin's head constantly turning about, watching the entrance and turning back, bravely hiding his disappointment that the Saudeleur had not joined in the sakau and Talupe had not come to cheer him. Ḷainjin had begun aching for her, and it must have been evident.

"You must come to Satawan and see our women for yourself! Forget racing. You'll be sitting your entire time staring between knees in the pandanus patch!" Ewalt was interpreting for Wisim and laughing with the rest of the group. This was where Ewalt expounded upon the women of Truk, their famously swollen clitorises, and the details of their seemingly painful efforts to enlarge them.

"Jeej!" Ḷainjin cried out in surprise as the men of the Truk group sat, nodded their heads in assent, and beamed with pride as though they were the brave beneficiaries of their women's efforts to enlarge themselves by using captured *kallep*[66] to bite their sexual tissues.

Ewalt interpreted for another of Wisim's crew. "You will be wiping all the girls' runny noses with the middle knuckle of your forefinger! It will get as calloused as the palu's."

At this, Ḷainjin glanced at the palu's huge hands as though such an accusation could be true. The palu, for his part, quickly placed them out of sight under his armpits, causing his enormous breasts to hang like those of a woman over his cupped arms. Ḷainjin, the palu's crew, and the others all rolled on their sitting mats in uncontrollable laughter.

Later, after much sakau, and with the new moon long gone behind the mountains and the retreating tide threatening to trap their interpreters, he and Wisim stumbled their way to the landing to cast them off. The palu raised his hands wide and bowed to the entrance of the Saudeleur's islet. "No cheating," he said in Pohnpeian. Then he made his offer before the two appointed counters that tomorrow, he would trade two neck-strings to Ḷainjin for a few of his "tiny" shark teeth. The men laughed, but it was clear the palu was serious and saw a neck-string as a solution to Ḷainjin's problem.

"Women of Pohnpei," the palu said, "make nice neck-strings but tire of wearing the same old styles their mothers wore. The neck-strings the women of Satawan make are different, so they make a woman stand out, and they carry a little magic to make them remember who gave them."

After much laughing, the men all agreed to implement the trade the next day, although Ewalt didn't seem as enthusiastic as his counterpart. Ḷainjin fell asleep that night greatly encouraged by the progress he had made studying two languages and the art of Pohnpeian trade. He had even formulated a way forward in his quest, and all in a single day! Unfortunately, due to his youth, he had not yet learned that capturing a woman's throat was a more perplexing task than buying a neck-string to snare it.

The following day stayed the course of the one before — except that the lag in the tide gave the men a little more time to mime before their interpreters arrived. They set sail for Kariahn a little later in the day, but instead of racing against each other, the goal of the helmsmen was to sail

---

66 Trap-jaw ant: *Odontomachus simillimus.*

as close as possible without bumping, to continue their word games. The word for "clitoris" became the rage of the morning. The word in Kajin Rālik was *puti*, the same word used for "pimple." In Pohnpeian, the word used was *tohl*, or "hill," yet this was the word used for "mountain" in Kajin Rālik. That amused Ļainjin, but then they found that Pohnpeians had a second word, *kaneng*, for having an exceptionally large clitoris. "Larger than a mountain!" he exclaimed, comparing the word in one language to that in another. Ļainjin and Wisim were laughing so hard they were crying like small boys playing along the shore. Their laughter was so loud it reverberated against the high walls of the tideway and drew much curiosity from the other traders. Completely incapacitated by his laughter, Wisim nearly backwinded his sail at one point and would have embarrassingly lost his rigging if not for his crew.

Once they had anchored, the word games continued and progressed into the galleries of Kariahn. They seriously affected trading that afternoon as the games spread among the traders and the infectious laughter and uproarious, good-humored joking continued. At one point, when one of the Pohnpeian traders offered many shark teeth for a few of Wisim's stingray barbs, Wisim commented that the shark teeth they offered were no larger than Rālik *puti*. But he would agree to the trade if the Pohnpeian could answer the following riddle: How could a mountain in Rālik be smaller than a Pohnpeian *kaneng*? The Pohnpeians took the riddle very seriously, consulting with the interpreters and others and finally answering. "There are no mountains in Rālik; therefore, all *puti* there and in Pohnpei must be larger than nothing. And in addition, it's well known that the women of Truk don't need to exaggerate the size of theirs." After a pregnant moment of awkward silence, Wisim and the others broke into more uproarious laughter.

Later that morning, Wisim offered his two neck-strings at auction. They were somewhat different from each other, each incorporating uniform beads of sun-bleached coral and uniquely shaped pendants of pearl shell. The men passed them, one to another, around the gallery. Ļainjin, in the thrall of the word game they had all been enthusiastically playing, immediately offered to trade one *kaneng*. Again, there was much good-humored laughter among the men around the gallery. Then they waited for him as he partially unsewed his alele and withdrew one of the many large shark teeth it contained. The laughing suddenly ceased, and there was a hush as the men turned their attention to the size of the tooth, which was larger than most had ever seen. There were no other offers as no one, apparently, had anything that could compete. Wisim gleefully accepted. Ḷainjin didn't offer to trade any of his others, setting the impression that he considered them too rare to trade and that anyone wanting one would have to offer dearly. The remainder of the trading session broke into discussion about the size of the tooth, how to incorporate it into a weapon or cutting tool, and how Ḷainjin could have caught such a shark.

Ḷainjin gave Ewalt another of the large shark teeth for the islet's share and, in addition, gave him one of the neck-strings as a gift to the Saudeleur. He also asked if he could remove one of the stingray barbs from his inventory. He wanted it to replace the barb he had lost to the shark the day before and give it to Uerik. Wisim interrupted, taking the neck-string back from Ewalt and tying it around Ḷainjin's neck. Then Wisim stood back, hands on hips, admiring Ḷainjin's look. Wisim asked Ewalt to explain that, for binding effect, the woman must see Ḷainjin wearing the neck-string before he removed it as a present to her.

After interpreting for Wisim, Ewalt responded that he would seek the agreement of his counterpart and, if he agreed, would return with the barb. Ḷainjin told him he would wait for him in the wind. Then he climbed the steps to the top of the wall and sat in the same spot as the day before, where he'd first learned about the Seekers. The sun was in the western sky behind him, illuminating the transparent blue belly of each successive swell as it curled and then thumped onto the edge of the fringing reef that spread out before him and to his right. To his left was the dark blue, lagoon-like bay that stretched north. Oblong in shape, the bay's southeast end was punctured by enormous swells breaking through its passageway to the ocean and crashing against the takai walls of the structure beneath him. Across this expanse was a small natural islet that headed the other side of the break in the reef. This islet — across the bay from Kariahn, also fortified with takai — seemed to serve as an encampment for traders visiting from other parts of the island. Theirs were the small proas he had observed anchored upon his arrival.

"Was that only the day before the day before?" Ḷainjin wondered. He sat on the cool takai stretcher at the edge of the wall where Ewalt had sat the day before. He dangled his legs, leaned over into the force of the wind, and cooled the sweat he carried from the sheltered gallery below. Over the past day, he had been wondering why the guards had been able to observe his approach the day he caught the marlin when he only felt but couldn't observe their presence atop the walls. At this height, they must be above the salty haze that thickened the wind blowing over the surface of the ocean beneath. "My view must have been clouded by the salt spray," he concluded. Then Ḷainjin noticed the wall beneath him, shaded from the sun. Sea grass grew on the lower stones under the water line and completely covered those at the base, obscuring the view of the foundation stones the ancestors had originally placed on the reef. Other swells entered the passageway and rolled across the deep lagoon. They crashed diagonally upon the north corner of the structure where it invitingly met the very edge of the bay and where they had constructed a breakwater to allow a single line of canoes to surf between the walls and enter the village at high tide.

"I have another question for you," he asked Ewalt when he joined him a few moments later, stingray barb in hand. "This place seems so impregnable! When were the last times boats came from afar to attack and plunder?"

"I don't know — not during my lifetime. There are legends of great battles in ancient times with people of the south who came in great canoes of forty men or more. They say, during and after the time my father arrived, the people of your islands came here in such large numbers of canoes that the battle alarm was sounded and men covered the walls, ready for an attack. But each time, they came only to trade. Their trade was very profitable for the prior Saudeleurs. Your people brought beautiful shell jewelry, giant clam-shell hooks and lures, and they wanted dogs to breed and mangrove, taro, and banana cuttings to plant. As the story goes, they seemed backward to us, but my father says the opposite is true. He claims his people had more time in their lives because they weren't busy building stone islands. Not that he doesn't love this place. He does, but not because of the takai. He loves to fish the barrier reefs. He stayed for that, I guess, and for my mother."

"All our reefs fringe the islands and have the lagoon at their center," Ḷainjin replied. "There are no lagoons on the ocean sides of our islands. I can see why a fisher would love these barrier reefs. The one I viewed to the north provides so many coral chasms and crevices, so many opportunities to catch fish. We have nothing like them. By the way, do you know any of their names?"

"I know a few. Every inlet and cove of these reefs has a name, but you'd have to ask a fisherman."

"I meant the names of the people from my islands that came."

"No, that was before I was born," replied Ewalt.

"Have you ever heard the name Tarmālu?"

"Yes, I have. As the story goes, she was their leader."

"She is my mother. Do you know where she is?"

Ewalt turned silent for a moment, obviously thinking.

As the wind rushed between them, Ḷainjin felt Ewalt's eyes examining him. He started to speak several times, then stopped himself.

"I can't answer your question," Ewalt said, "but I know someone who can. I must speak to the Saudeleur. Is it all right if I tell him who you are?"

"I don't see why not. Does he know my mother?"

"I'm not sure. I must allow you both to speak for yourselves. Can we go now?"

Below, they found the men kicking words around their circle like men back home kicking an *anidep*. They were waiting for the meal that always came with the tide. Ewalt spoke to the Truk interpreter, and Wisim pinched his own neck as if to compliment Ḷainjin again on the look of his neck-string.

As they bent low to exit the structure, Ḷainjin repeated the word *mahi*, one of those that had been tossed about.

"That means 'breadfruit,'" Ewalt said.

The word in Kajin Rālik was *ma*. Ḷainjin marveled that so many words were similar across the three languages. He noticed that some Pohnpeian women had frizzled hair while most of the women of Rālik had hair that was long and straight. Yet the opposite, to a lesser degree, was also true. There were women in Rālik with frizzled hair, and there were many women in Pohnpei whose hair was straight. According to legend, the people of both island groups claim their ancestors came from somewhere else — from the west. Like so many hermit crabs scampering about the shore, they all must have come from the same stock. They had just housed themselves in separate shells they found along the way.

The tide had only half-flooded the reef, and they were the first boat to leave Kariahn. Ḷainjin expressed a little apprehension, but Ewalt suggested they start along a course close to the wall, where the water was mostly deeper than elsewhere. Ḷainjin's throat was tense as he followed Ewalt's directions over the reef. He was at the mercy of Tūṃur. With such strong wind, he could do little to slow down, and with so little separation between reef and keel, one coral outcrop on the reef could damage his canoe. But he was slowly coming to realize that all such outcrops, which were common on most reefs, had long since been dislodged by the islanders and used to backfill the islets about them. Miraculously, under Ewalt's direction, they arrived at the Saudeleur's islet of Pahn Kadira without incident, but because there was no anchorage there, they had to tie Ḷainjin's canoe at Kelepwei and wade through the waist-high tide in the watercourse between.

Two Pohnpeian paddling canoes were just leaving as they arrived. Crewed and loaded with provisions — no doubt for the men they had left — they gave Ewalt two coconuts, one of which he shared with Ḷainjin. He had watched Ewalt send a message for the Saudeleur with one of the men guarding the entrance, and while they waited for a response, they sat near the water on the stone steps and sucked the sweet water from the soft, husked shells. The smell of cooking fires that had long since expired and the pleasurable smell of smoke from unearthed ovens and cooked food wafted through the entranceway from inside the high walls that loomed above them, teasing their hunger.

The guard returned and offered a few words to Ewalt, who turned to Ḷainjin and invited him inside. As they entered, Ewalt pointed to a thatched structure open on four sides that sheltered a fire atop a three-tiered rectangular mound constructed from takai. Ewalt referred to this structure as the resting place for the thunder spirit, Nahn Sapwe. The islet seemed populated by a host of the Saudeleur's attendants, two of whom rushed up to them with new, bushy Pohnpeian kilts, one for each. Ewalt placed the second neck-string and the shark tooth on the ground and wrapped the new kilt about himself. Modestly dropping his old one from beneath, he wrung the water from it and carried it folded against his side like a purse. Ḷainjin did the same. He was surprised to see additional fortifications within the walls, one of which surrounded the beautifully thatched residence of the Saudeleur. It was about half the size of the enclosure and surrounded by a courtyard of bleached-coral beach stones like those of his home islands. The house inside the enclosure was of the same design as the sakau house of Kelepwei, except the squared-off, U-shaped sitting platform was higher — so high above the height of a man's waist it required a step to reach. The tall, thatched roof slanted down over the single room to the height of a man's shoulders. They had constructed the walls of the pole house from slats of a material that he wasn't familiar with and had covered the floor with plaited pandanus mats. In the center lay a square fire pit, behind which sat the Saudeleur. He invited them to climb up and sit to his left. His actions appeared more formal than his friendly manner the day before, as though he expected the requested meeting to be a matter of trade.

Ḷainjin glanced about the well-made, comfortable-looking structure. The best exterior view was to the left or right of the fire pit, at the corners of the low-hanging thatched eave that stretched outward from beneath the front gable and provided shelter for the large, flat sakau stones exterior to the fire pit. The interior of the shelter was private, due to the slat walls. Though from his point of vantage, the Saudeleur could look out through these same slatted walls into the courtyard and see all as they passed by.

Ewalt presented the neck-string and the shark tooth to the Saudeleur, who dropped his head and thanked him for the neck-string, which he took in his right hand. Ḷainjin watched him focus immediately on the shark tooth in his left. Ewalt spoke to the Saudeleur without interpreting. He mentioned Wisim's name.

At that point, the Saudeleur's head bowed, and he peered over at Ḷainjin with a sparkle in his eyes, holding the shark tooth between his thumb and index finger. "*Sho wihn!*" he said.

This was a mixture of both their languages, with *sho* meaning "no" in Pohnpeian and *wihn* meaning "profit" in both languages. Ḷainjin understood, yet out of politeness turned to Ewalt for explanation.

"The Saudeleur thanks you for the gift but wishes to point out that he values a shark tooth of that size more than two of those neck-strings," said Ewalt, talking with his fingers to allow his chief to follow his words. "He respectfully suggests that next time, you demand more for a tooth of this size."

"But the value of this neck-string is enhanced by Satawan magic, as promised by the great palu. Surely, it will bind the throat of any woman he gives it to," Ḷainjin responded.

The Saudeleur laughed then countered, this time speaking directly to Ewalt as he held the neck-string. Ḷainjin heard Talupe's name mentioned and must have started to blush just as the Saudeleur turned to him again with an amused sparkle in his eyes.

Ewalt said, "He thanks you for the attractive neck-string. He will keep it to remind himself of the Rālik youth who braved the ocean in his quest for adventure but recommends you offer any other neck-string in your possession to one of the many beautiful women out there in the courtyard."

"My neck-string is for Talupe. Is she spoken for?"

Even without interpretation, the Saudeleur laughed at the thought. Then he jabbered in monologue to Ewalt, who then interpreted it into Kajin Rālik. "No man speaks for Talupe, not even the Saudeleur. He did not send Talupe to you. She used her cunning to replace another he had sent. She is very willful and is in big trouble. She is mistress of her own destiny now, and she will not value a neck-string from Truk. She already wears Ḷainjin's name as well as the names of other newcomers around her neck. She has littered the island with men cast by her spell and left broken and discarded like so many children's toys along the shores. She currently toils in the mountains to make good on her many commitments. She will never agree to accompany you to Rālik. You must choose a seabird who will want many children and require you to return here to nest. You can amass a fortune in the process. You would be happier walking into the courtyard and grabbing the hand of the first woman who does not look away."

Ḷainjin clearly had not expected to hear this from the Saudeleur. Then he heard his mother's name as Ewalt diplomatically transitioned the topic of conversation. Now, the Saudeleur was taken aback, suddenly speechless. He motioned for one of his attendants standing in the corner by the sakau stones to bring food.

After much questioning back and forth, the Saudeleur looked remorseful. Ewalt interpreted his words. "Now that he knows who you are, the Saudeleur understands why such a willful, ambitious woman attracts you."

"Can he tell me where she is?"

"She's at Sokehs trying to meet her takai commitments."

"No, Ewalt. I mean my mother."

After more talk back and forth, Ewalt related that the Saudeleur had advised he wait. Ḷainjin should wait for the Seekers to return and relate what had happened to her.

"Is she dead? What has the Saudeleur heard has happened to her?"

After more discussion, Ewalt told him that all the Saudeleur knew was what the Seekers had told him. Her fleet had set out to save itself from a great storm that drove them to islands west and south where islanders attacked them, and the Seekers were the only ones to return through Pohnpei. Others may have ended up elsewhere. The Saudeleur cannot say whether she is alive or dead. But if she were alive, would she not have shown up by now?

"What islands? How many days west? How many days south?"

The Saudeleur's responses were interpreted.

"Only the Seekers can answer that!"

"When do you expect them to return?"

"They always return before the wind dies."

"Tell me more about Talupe's takai commitments," Ḷainjin said bluntly.

After a back-and-forth discussion in Pohnpeian, Ewalt paraphrased. Talupe was too aggressive in her approach to wealth. She used a tactic many, mostly ancestors, had used before, often to tragic end. Most deliver the takai, receive the agreed-upon reward, then distribute some of it to their workers. After successfully delivering several takai as agreed, she started taking rewards before delivery. This allowed her to expand her operations and enter into commitments with more raft owners, who in turn, traded for bigger rafts. She has become a major supplier of takai for one of the islets still under construction. Now, she has missed — by several days — a delivery of one takai that is holding up construction and has not started delivery of a second due by the full moon."

"Why doesn't she just pay back the payments she was advanced?"

Ewalt answered this without posing the question to the Saudeleur. "Don't forget the law of no recast! I'm not sure she still has the payment, and even if she does, they need the stone! The master builders require a takai of a very particular size. You have climbed the walls. You've seen how big and small and in between all fit together to build the wall and give it strength."

"Why is she missing her agreed-upon deliveries?" Ḷainjin asked.

Ewalt interpreted this question for the Saudeleur, who laughed and responded.

"Because she thinks I don't have the throat to feed such a perfectly beautiful woman to Nahn Samohl! She's threatening our trading system! Every day or two, someone comes to me to complain!"

"I mean, why is she late?"

The Saudeleur explained to Ewalt, who interpreted. "They left one of her rafts unattended in a storm at high tide. As usual for her, the raft was too small for the takai, and it flipped in the storm waves. The stone lies at the bottom of some lagoon somewhere."

"Where does she find these takai?"

"They can be found in several places around the island," answered Ewalt. "She's from Sokehs, so that's where she gathers hers."

"Where is Sokehs?"

"On the far side of the island."

Attendants brought two baskets of food and they ate. Would Ḷainjin accept the Saudeleur's advice? He would follow some of it, yes. But all of it? No. He would wait for the Seekers to return. That much was clear. In the interim, he knew he wanted to talk to Ewalt's father to get more insight into who these Seekers were. He would avoid the young women in the courtyard as he would breadfruit on the lower limbs of the tree. He would rather climb high into the mountains to search for Talupe even as he would climb to the top of the breadfruit tree to fetch the hard-to-find, the perfectly ripened, and those the others had missed. Once he found her, he would do whatever it took to take her again. If he must humbly submit his strength and skills to whatever task she had at hand, then that is exactly what he would do. He'd offer his life rather than a trinket he had traded for.

Regarding his mother, nothing the Saudeleur said surprised him. After all, though no one had said it outright, everyone Ḷainjin had ever talked to thought she was dead. But until he found someone who saw her die, he would continue his search. That was his destiny, and he accepted it as he did his name. He was not likely to become the trader the Saudeleur wanted him to be, but he would bury talk of that in his throat.

As they exited Saudeleur Raipuinlañ's compound and crossed the courtyard carrying their baskets of food, seeing the women in the courtyard, Ḷainjin immediately changed his mind. He decided to take the Saudeleur's advice after all and began glancing here and there at the attractive women at work around them. Ewalt, always observant and wanting to assist, sought the help of an older woman among them who seemed to be in charge.

"She can present the neck-string to whichever one you choose," explained Ewalt, perhaps wishing to avoid Ḷainjin any embarrassment.

Many of the women appeared to pretend they didn't notice him. Others seemed to be joking with each other yet offering him glancing smiles.

Ḷainjin set down his basket, with some difficulty removed the neck-string himself, and handed it to the woman.

"I honestly find them all so attractive I can't choose. Ask her to present it as an award to the girl she feels works the hardest for the Saudeleur."

Once Ewalt had completed the interpretation, the woman smiled, showing missing teeth. She held the neck-string on her own neck with both hands and began an amusing little dance that incurred great laughter and much attention. Ḷainjin, who had picked up his basket and was prepared to turn away, found himself compelled out of politeness to watch her dance her way among the girls. After much pretending to place the neck-string at this throat or that, she stopped behind a tall young woman who held baskets of firewood in each hand and was standing before the first tier of steps to the fires of Nahn Sapwe. The shy woman divulged a furtive smile at him, bowing forward at the insistence of the old woman and allowing her to tie the neck-string around her neck. Ḷainjin nodded to thank the old woman, who followed them through the entranceway to the water's edge.

Ewalt interpreted. "She says when you're ready for the girl, to give her a day's notice so she can prepare her."

"Okay, thank you," said Ḷainjin in Pohnpeian.

"She says not to wait too long, or the girl will be embarrassed because the others will say you don't want her."

Ḷainjin looked back through the entranceway at the woman still standing there, fondling the necklace he had given her and still glancing furtively toward him. Again, he heard the Saudeleur's words swirling in his memory: "Walk into the courtyard and grab the hand of the first woman who does not look away."

"Typical," thought Ḷainjin. "At sea, you hand another fisherman a coconut, a container shell of water, or a basket of something to eat, and he nods his thanks and sails away. On shore, you give something away, and there is no end to the entanglements that ensue!"

Yet such entanglements, he now realized, were in truth the basis on which the Saudeleur ruled his village.

Paddling takai

This thought reminded Ļainjin of the stingray barb and his unspoken commitment to replace it, and he wondered how his bird was faring in the care of Jeilañ. He watched Ewalt remove his new kilt as he stepped down into the water and tucked it, folded, beneath his chin as he wrapped his old one about him. Ļainjin followed suit, and the two of them waded shoulder deep, back across the still-flooding reef, holding their fluffy new kilts above their heads.

"Ewalt, can you take me to Idedh? I want to meet this creature called Nahn Samohl!"

"Is it all right if I paddle my own canoe there so I can leave directly for home?"

"Perfect!"

By the time they arrived at Idedh, evening had set in and the sakau stones were ringing out in all directions. They anchored their canoes by the single entrance to the Idedh compound through the northwest wall. The wall was a little higher than those of the surrounding structures, so it appeared the stone fitters had backfilled the islet to a greater height. There in the abandoned courtyard, directly in front of the narrow entranceway for all who passed by and glanced in to see, stood the sturdy rectangular scaffold. It spanned two X-shaped trestles on each side, with the hanging-spar dangling ever so slightly in the breeze that blew over the walls and swirled about. The spar was to be placed under the arms of a man whose hands were tied behind his back.

Ļainjin approached the hardwood frame, its legs thicker than a spread hand. He peered down into the well. It was square and of little more than a single arm's length on each side. Someone had pushed a stout line through a hole drilled in the middle of the wide spar and knotted it. The line had been haphazardly coiled and set to one side, and he couldn't help but recall Ewalt's words of the day before, "No recast!" Then he realized he had passed by four times previously and failed to notice this famed symbol of Pohnpeian justice.

"We've passed this islet so many times! Why didn't you point this out to me?"

"Well, you were either racing or talking or playing games. Who am I to interrupt you? Besides, I don't care for this place."

"Given what you have told me, I can see why. What's that over there?" Ḷainjin pointed at an open thatched cookhouse.

"That's where they prepare food for Nahn Samohl."

"Why do they cook its food? I'd think an eel like that would prefer to eat its fish raw."

"I'm not sure how often they feed her, or if they feed her the guts of the animals raw or cooked. As you can see, no one is here this evening, but I know they don't feed her fish."

"Her?"

"She has had many babies. They know because they appear in the pool over here."

Ewalt led him to a large, deep pool of water that must have been a natural feature of the reef before they constructed the islet around it. "A natural coral tunnel runs between this pool and the well over there. They constructed the well walls over a second, much smaller pool in the reef by crisscrossing takai to span that pool and build the well before the backfilling. Nahn Samohl, as is her wont, always lies in the tunnel between the two pools, but they feed her through the well. Her babies swim in this larger pool until she eats them."

"Jeej!" cried Ḷainjin.

"Well, the idea is to keep her hungry, no?"

"And the eels that father her babies?"

"She eats them too!"

Ḷainjin laughed. "Well, don't you think she'd have a happier family life if they fed her fish occasionally?"

Then Ewalt motioned back toward the spar that dangled from the scaffold above the well, and Ļainjin realized there was a good reason why they wanted to keep Nahn Samohl hungry for the taste of flesh. He peered again into the black well more out of pure curiosity than anything else. The light was fading quickly, and he was hoping his eyes would adjust enough to glimpse at least the walls of the well. He felt that something down there was calling him to his destiny, but then Ewalt jerked him back by the waist, giving him a fright and a laugh simultaneously.

"The walls of the well must span and partially seal a second pool below all this," explained Ewalt.

Ļainjin peered back down into the well. "I wonder what it would be like down there." Then he looked over at the surface of the adjoining pool and estimated the walls of the well must be at least two ñeñe[67] deep. The tunnel between the pools at least four.

Ewalt spread his arms. "To build up this ground, they must have brought all this crushed coral and fill from the surrounding reefs. Or maybe transported it through the swamps surrounding Temwen."

"So, the walls of the well are made from the same takai they used everywhere else?" Ļainjin looked at the walls surrounding the islet.

"Yes. They realized they had these two pools on the reef with a coral tunnel adjoining them. And they constructed this islet around them both with the plan of creating this execution pit!"

"Incredible," Ļainjin said. "How long did that take them?"

"That's part of the mystery of this place. An exceedingly long time, obviously. This must have been one of the first islets built to solve the problem of people not living up to their commitments."

The men left the eerie, abandoned islet and quickly boarded their waiting craft. The tide had nearly reached its extreme. The sun had long set, and the western sky above the white clouds, tinged yellow and orange earlier, had turned dark blue. The moon looked like the nail of a finger backlit by the light of the sun, destined to ever so slowly set behind the sea, behind those ever-mysterious mountains in the foreground. The ringing of the sakau stones pierced the quiet of the watercourse and prompted the thought that

[67] The length across the breast from fingertips to fingertips; one fathom.

he might answer the call of one there in the distance. He withdrew the stingray barb from where he had placed it earlier and held it up to Ewalt, who was paddling backward into the channel.

"I think I'll return this to Uerik. Then when I return, I want to visit Temwen with you and meet your father."

Ewalt studied him warily, as though he was stealing his thoughts despite his every attempt to conceal them. "Of course. Just remember the Saudeleur's advice to you!"

"I will," responded Ḷainjin in a serious tone. He stowed the stingray barb, hoisted his sail, and began to make way in the direction opposite that of his new friend. Paddling canoes crowded the village. The canoes paddled between the stone islets, and each paddler acknowledged his presence whether up close or from afar. He would have just enough light to cross the reef and the bay and then enter the coral-bound, wave-protected cove behind the barrier reef where he had rested and fought the shark the day before the day before. From there, he planned to home in on the ringing of pestles pounding on the famous flat sakau stones to lead him to their village. Something about the authority in Uerik's voice when he had volunteered Jeilañ's services led him to guess his stone would ring the loudest.

Once Ḷainjin had passed the first islet on his left, he cut back downwind to the point where he could reverse the course Jeilañ had set for them the day he entered the village. Then he came upon an islet that had one wall that didn't rise vertically. Was that one of the islets still under construction? Its northeast wall slanted down into the water like the broken wing of a bird squatted there on the reef. Was it a ramp to carry those shaft-like takai to the top of the walls? Perhaps they didn't haul them vertically with ropes as he had assumed but pulled or pushed them up that ramp-like wall. He wondered about the ladders Ewalt had mentioned. How did they come into play? He became confident the mysteries of the stone village were about to reveal themselves to him, but not from within the village itself. He must see for himself the famous mountain with a flat face. He must scale it and watch as the great roar of Nahn Sapwe himself caused the takai to cleave off and drop to the shore.

Ḷainjin waved to the guards as he passed the great walls. There were no blasts from their conch shells to announce his escape. Only the clean, ocean breath of Tūṃur to starboard as the eldest son lashed the flooded fringing reef beneath him with his harsh whisper and filled his ears with an incessant rush each time he turned his head from the ubiquitous sounds of sakau pounding to port. In this light, with the tide as high as it was, he had no need to follow the paths on the reef as they had done the other day. Here and there, a star appeared and then disappeared behind one of the many graying clouds rushing between the darkening water beneath and the quickly darkening blue sky above. He wondered, Were the Seekers still sailing with their prize in tow, or had they stopped to fish and take their rest for the night? In which case, did they still have their kājokwā in snare? If so, they may be resting for the night, themselves in tow! Do they snuggle together into one or two craft to keep warm, or does each man or woman sleep in his or her craft alone? He had no doubt that such a kājokwā, with its surrounding circle of fish, could easily sustain them for the entire season of *añōneañ*, but what did they drink? When would they arrive, and what news of his mother would they relate to him?

Once he had left the village, he was surprisingly alone on the reef. Most of the islanders who spent the day in the village, like Ewalt, had most likely headed straight for shore within the protection of the great seawalls that fronted Tūṃur's fury. As Ḷainjin passed behind the islets on his way to the bay, the islanders — and especially the children — again acknowledged his passing as, surprisingly, they still played amid the various rafts and other craft at the water's edge as though no days had passed between. He realized these children took for granted the very takai that appeared so mysterious to him. Yet curiously, these were the very stones, according to Ewalt, that would mesmerize them as they grew older, into a life of endlessly seeking fortune and title by moving them from one place to another. These thoughts captivated him in the gradually dimming light as he spirited his way between the buñtokrear swells that had entered the bay and, with gray-capped spray, were darkly curling upon the edge of the reef fringing the more turbulent waters of the open bay. At the very edge, a curling wave caught his kubaak, but he avoided its headlong crash over his bow by turning it deftly downwind and allowing the wave to merely wash down an angle along the length of his starboard hull instead. This slapped up a deluge of water mostly trapped beneath his outrigger platform, but some flew into his face from between the outrigger booms. He chanted good-naturedly and proudly, "*Wa tutu! Wan eman,*"[68] as his grandfathers had taught him to do whenever that had happened to him as a boy. He laughed up into the darkening sky as Tūṃur's rush chilled the water on his skin but hardened his spirit's response.

Now clear of the fringing reef, Ḷainjin came upon flocks of white fisher birds hovering here and there, with one and then another flopping onto the dark surface of the bay. He decided to test his luck, dropping his lure into the wake at his stern and rapidly unfurling one of his lighter lines from the forearm-length plank upon which it coiled. He wondered what fish were circling beneath him. As he reached the center of the bay, he had his chance to find out. "*Ikabwe*! *Ikabwe*!"[69] he murmured confidently to himself in answer, raising from the water a frenetic fish of modest length. He held its unarmored mouth and quill-less gills close against the bulwark by the taut of his line with one hand and carefully laid back the slippery spines of its dorsal fin with the other before grabbing it in his palm, raising it — still taut — to his face, and crushing its skull between the teeth of his large mouth.

"It will be a very modest gift, but a gift no less," he thought, chanting, "*Wa jab depet āne.*"[70] Flipping his lure back into the water, he guided his line as it naturally played out of his hull with the fingers of his free hand. However, his fishing done, once his line had completely played out, he began winding it back with his foot pressing his spool against the bulwark and his free hand coiling the line as he headed for the inlet behind the barrier reef where he had met his two friends the afternoon of his arrival. No one was fishing that night. He released his sheet, turned downwind, and followed the island's jagged fringing reef to his left until he could hear the ringing of sakau stones coming from the inland shore.

Then he saw the fires of the small village through the blackness ahead. He passed a dark natural islet on the fringing side of the reef to his right.

---

[68] Boat spray; the bath of a man.

[69] Mackerel.

[70] Literally, "boat does not pierce islet." This proverb means that a canoe's hull does not pierce the sand of an islet without bearing gifts.

To his left, the mangrove had encroached upon the reef, fringing the island all the way to the edge of the inlet's deep water, where its gnarly roots lost their toehold. As the inlet turned shoreward, the swamp to his left cut off his air. He could no longer hold his point of sail so had to lower it and paddle. The village lay on higher ground above the narrow shore. There, a welcoming patch of sand and stones lay between the entrenched mangrove swamps, both left and right, that had otherwise intruded on the little cove. Upshore, he saw what appeared to be open boathouses sheltering fishing canoes. He beached his proa, placed his broad shoulders beneath its outrigger platform, and, with his powerful legs and broad feet, nudged it firmly upon shore. The tide had ebbed, and he judged it wouldn't return to this height until well into the morning.

Ḷainjin removed his wet kilt and wrapped himself with the new kilt he had received earlier. Then he took the fish and the stingray barb and proceeded toward the sound. There, he saw Uerik sitting at the center of a raised floor amid a group of male sakau drinkers who were sitting and facing each other on either flank. Ḷainjin was pleased that his impromptu plan was, so far, a success. Then he stood politely, holding the small fish in the firelight. The sakau was being prepared under a frontal canopy that slanted down from beneath the home's high gable. Uerik immediately left the group and came outside to greet him in the traditional arm grasp of his people.

Ḷainjin gave him the stingray barb and held out his catch. "*Wa jab depet āne.*"

Uerik, not knowing the meaning of his words, of course, thanked him profusely, making more of the gift than necessary and handing the fish to his niece, who had suddenly appeared with her hand extended. He invited Ḷainjin inside and had him seated in the front of the group to his left.

A woman approached Ḷainjin with a shell of coconut oil and proceeded to rub the oil onto his shoulders and chest. She spoke to him in Pohnpeian, and when he didn't seem to understand, she grabbed hold of Uerik's arm and then pointed to herself, meaning Ḷainjin was her man. Apparently, she very much admired his tattoos. The overall motif on his front was that of a triangular-shaped canoe prow that began at his shoulders and ended at the navel. This prow consisted of two parts: an upper true triangle and a lower one shaped like a shark tooth tapering toward its point. Yet ending not in a point but at a blunt mast two digits wide that rose from his navel to his breastbone. In the upper triangle, each side of the mast consisted of a column of inward-pointing hash marks extending down to his sternum. Across this mast were perfectly horizontal rows of dots making up the triangle itself but, at the outer edges, outlined by two rows of V-shaped hashes running from shoulders to sternum. Breaking the horizontal pattern of dots that made up the triangle were inward- and downward-slanting columns of hash marks.

These elaborate patterns had caught the woman's eye, and she flicked her finger admiringly down the columns of hash marks in the upper triangle and then across the rows of dots, each shorter than the one above. Then she rubbed the oil across the zigzag lines that radiated evenly down and outward from the lower part of the mast across the muscles of his stomach — each line shorter than the one above — each line completing the lower triangular pattern ending with the blunt end of the vertical mast just above the navel.

Of course, Ḷainjin was proud of the tattoos his grandfathers had commissioned, but they were those of a commoner where he came from, and he had never thought of these admittedly elaborate designs as something to marvel at. So, he felt some embarrassment watching Uerik watch his woman's fingers explore him admiringly. Perhaps sensing his embarrassment, she reluctantly turned away to fetch a shell of sakau for him.

Then he sat there among the joyful, talkative crowd, sipping his cup of dirty water from a coconut half shell. He was grateful he had arrived late. Earlier, he would have had to drink one of the first cups filled with slime from the inner hibiscus bark that they used to twist the juice from the pounded sakau roots. He liked the way they raised the floor of their homes. "It was probably necessary because of the slant of the land," he thought, "but then it became customary. So, when they built houses on the islets, they continued the process, though no longer necessary." He began to study the tattoo motifs of his hosts. Neither the men nor the women had tattoos across their breasts or stomachs, so it was clear why his tattoos had caught their eye. They were more intent on decorating their arms, hands, and legs. The women weren't as modest as the women of Rālik, who bundled their thighs in dual, matted skirts. These women didn't hide their legs as carefully and displayed tattooed rows of dotted Xs up the sides of their thighs as though enticing a man to see the rest, which they seemed careful to show not. He liked seeing as commonplace that forbidden in his culture.

However, he was busy contemplating the wall of language that separated him from his companions, a wall he set himself to patiently dismantle. He could view what those around him were doing but found himself separated from their intentions. He was alone amid the group. They had each other and needed him not, yet from their strength as a group, it was easier for them to befriend him than vice versa. He didn't know what they were saying and could easily misunderstand something said or done. After the events of the preceding days, asking the names of things had become natural. He began questioning those around him, and the responses were enthusiastic. He learned to say the numerals one to ten, among other useful terms. Wishing he knew the question words "how," "why," and "when," he resolved to ask Ewalt when he saw him next.

Later that evening, his shark-chasing friend Jeilañ suddenly appeared. Ḷainjin greeted him warmly, and Jeilañ's precocious daughter rushed to sit beside him as though she expected Ḷainjin's affection for her father to append to her. The father shooed her away. This time for good.

"How is the *kasap*?"[71]

"The *kasap* is good — always hungry," Jeilañ mimed, arching his neck back, patting his stomach, showing the sizes of the fish, and then feeding the bird with the fingers of his hand.

"*Kalahngan en komwi,*" Ḷainjin said. He had practiced the formal method of saying thanks.

Later still, after the numbing effect of the sakau was well under way, they brought food for all to eat, and this became another opportunity to learn words and mime questions and answers. He learned that yams, which he had never eaten or heard of, were roots that grew in the ground like taro but not in the mud. The plant's leaves grew from a vine that could clutch on to a rope tied to a tree that the vine would climb in search of light. He learned that Sokehs was on the exact opposite side of the island and that he could get there by sailing inside the barrier reef through a series of lagoons surrounding

[71] Pohnpeian for "frigate bird."

islands that lay between the barrier reef and the mainland. They always brought the takai around the north side behind the protection of the barrier reef that protected the lagoon from the ocean swells this time of year.

Of course, the question burning in his mind was, assuming the raft was large enough, "How do they get the takai down from the mountain and then back up to the top of the wall?" At one point, Uerik asked for a few heavy sticks of dried mangrove firewood as props to aid the discussion. After much back and forth, the gist of what he had gleaned from the men was that it was no different from launching and paddling a boat. It required rollers and levers, but no matter how many times they mimed their way through it, he could not picture how they accomplished this. If you put one of those huge stones on rollers and tried to launch it down the beach, the weight of the thing would push the rollers into the sand, and they would prove useless. If you tried to push the thing with levers, they would either dig up a lot of sand or crack.

Ḷainjin wanted to know how many men it would take to move a takai. He showed the potential size of the stone he was asking about by circling his arms in front of him, leaving a big space between to demonstrate its girth. He had learned to say "how many?" from the counting exercise earlier in the evening.

"How long?" one of the men questioned.

"Two men long!" Ḷainjin answered.

"Eight men to move," suggested Jeilañ.

"Six men," suggested another.

They settled on two men for each arm's length of stone as the standard.

"No!" Ḷainjin was no fool when it came to launching large craft or how many men it took to lift large weights like the trunks of coconut trees used as corner posts.

That was when Uerik settled the matter, stating definitively that though it might take eight to ten men to roll such a stone uphill, six men could paddle a takai down the mountain.

Ḷainjin was incredulous! How could these men sit there and lie to him? True, he had no experience with mountains. Did they think men from Rālik were so stupid they would believe you could paddle a stone down a mountain? "Ridiculous," he thought, looking each man in the face and seeing not deceit but perhaps merely overconfidence and pride staring back at him. The only thing they all seemed to agree on was that he had to sail to Sokehs to see such things for himself. Very well, he would leave immediately and sail for Sokehs. He would watch, count everything, and return with the results of what he had observed.

Uerik, though, appeared offended at such an announcement and insisted he stay with him for a few days to first rest. Ļainjin remembered the Chief and compromised by agreeing to spend the night and leave in the morning.

Despite Ļainjin's refusal to believe him or accept his hospitality for an extended period, his host remained extremely gracious. Uerik gave Ļainjin a soft mat to sleep on. It was so new it still smelled of the leaves from which it was plaited. As Ļainjin lay there curled up in his mat, protected from the cool ocean breeze that swirled through mangrove swamps below, amid the soft light and sweet smell of the hardwood embers, he could not help but be thankful for his first opportunity to sleep with solid ground beneath him. From the moment he had received the sleeping mat, he was ashamed of himself for intimating that the men were lying to him about moving the takai. It could have been due to the sakau. Perhaps they were just so proud of their stone village they were just innocently pretentious. Somehow all this blended together, leaving him to wonder if he had entered another world where reason failed him. He covered his head, curled up in a comfortable world of his own, and slept.

He dreamed he was racing against Pohnpeians, straddling a large takai that magically floated. Among the others, he paddled it down mountain streams that kept branching off into dead ends, searching frantically to find the one stream that led to the shore. He was reluctant to follow the others, assuming they would trick him into choosing a course that led to falling water. He needed to win the race to save Talupe, who somewhere amid his dreams was waiting anxiously for him. He awoke the next morning to the reality of a meal with his friend but with an enduring longing to find her and an unspoken vow not to rest again until he did. Many of his new friends were there to see him off, and they brought more food in a basket with fresh coconuts to drink on his voyage. As they helped him launch, he remembered what his kind host had implied about the takai process after much mime the night before, that it was as easy as launching your canoe and paddling across the reef. Surely, that had been the sakau speaking and not his friend, but was he not about to find out which?

On his way to the lagoon, Ļainjin crossed what was clearly yet another path they had cleared to allow passage for takai-laden rafts. Just to be safe, he decided to lax his sheet and follow this new path to the blue water. This was not the first time on his trip that he had wished the winds of Tūṃur were less insistent, allowing him to proceed at a more leisurely pace. He found himself impelled on a course through a fisher's dream, where he would rather tarry. He spotted reef pools here and there, as though some spirit had punctured them into the fringing or barrier sides of the narrowing lagoon, and wondered what types of fishing they fostered. Then up ahead, the reefs on either side narrowed in to trap him like a fish in one of his boyhood friend Kalbōk's[72] stone reef weirs back on Namorik. He held his breath as he again glided into a short reef path just inland of a narrow spit of sand where an island wanted to form. Past the sand spit, the blue lagoon opened again and appeared dotted with what seemed like giant, colorful mushrooms of coral. He found himself cautiously swaying his course around or in between them even though the receding tide was still high enough to carry him over.

Here and there along the way, wherever the mangrove swamps parted before the shore, a small village came into view, with its canoes and people going about their chores. In another spot close to the mangrove-covered shore, he saw what appeared to be a team of six or eight men paddling a takai-laden raft. Gradually, Ļainjin began to view the mangrove as a menace that the islanders had to fight and overcome to seize their share of the coast. Had they built their islets out on the reef to avoid its imperceptibly creeping grip? It was not greedy, in that it grew where nothing else wanted to grow, yet it had — over how many hundreds of seasons — innocently, almost inadvertently, conquered the entire coast! To him, an island with a mangrove swamp had always been something to praise as a source for spears, booms, poles for house building, and, yes, the best and hardest

[72] Ļainjin's fishing, shark-fighting friend for life.

firewood. Not to mention a place for crabs and fish to spawn. Here, it overcame a man's view of the ocean. It prevented him from beaching his canoe at will. It interred him within its perimeter like a fish caught in a weir, henceforth destined to look out at the sea through the battens of his trap. Yet it was a handy place to defecate. He would concede it that! Looking seaward, he found the reef erratically perforated with more pools calling to his fisher instincts. He knew of no such pools on the reefs of Rālik. Truly, he had reached an island like no other.

The lagoon narrowed and later that morning, widened again, and then the first of the multiple ocean passageways through the barrier reef that they had told him to anticipate came into view on his right. It was thin and it wound through the barrier reef like the tail of a gecko. To Ḷainjin's left was a small, low islet like one he would find in Rālik, except that the mangrove, with its shiny and incredibly green saltwater-tolerant leaves, had nearly covered it over. Still farther to his left, beyond the islet, he saw an inlet that appeared to flow deep into the island's interior. He found both borders of the inlet fringed with a meandering morass of submerged reefs, the layout of which would take an angler's lifetime to master. He noticed the tide was receding rapidly, the lagoon emptying and the current flowing ocean bound. He set his course across the passageway accordingly. The current was swift. The passage was pouring water into the already-receded ocean from the area he had traversed, from the inlet to his left and from the large bay ahead that made up the fish's eye, which he was about to enter. He knew from his atoll life that the fewer and narrower the passageways into the ocean, the stronger the currents. Luckily, or so it seemed, he could cross into the bay by using the force of the wind against its oncoming, ocean-bound current by simply holding his course into the swift current of the passageway. He wondered whether the current would have spit him out into the ocean on a day of lesser wind.

The bay, or eye of the fish, contained a series of eight variously sized high islands with peripheries suffocated by mangrove. The heights of these islands were quite impressive. The first cut off Ḷainjin's view of two others, but he saw the fourth in the distance and knew he was to sail around its ocean side, between it and the barrier reef sheltering the relatively calm waters ahead. This first island was so high and long that when he had first distinguished its tip back in the narrow lagoon before the passageway, he didn't recognize it as an individual island separated from the mainland. It wasn't until his vantage reached the point where he could look inland to his left down the coral-strewn inlet that he realized it was a separate piece of land that jutted out, haplessly clawing upon the fringing reef like the knuckles of a severed finger. He had never imagined an island that size — so high or so deeply infested at its shores by mangrove. In many places, the width of the seemingly impenetrable surrounding swamps was wider than the island itself. He marveled at all this as he gazed at all the light-absorbing shades of green to his left and sun-blazing, eye-squinting shades of bright blue ahead and to his right. Now that he had an open bay before him and could see his course clearly, he decided to troll a line and test his luck.

He wasn't disappointed. By the time he passed the tip of the finger to his left, he had caught an *ikabwe* like the one he had hooked the night before and given to Jeilañ. By the time he reached the submerged reef on the ocean side of the next two islands, he had caught two more. Then in the distance, between the ridge of the island he had just passed and the shores of the next island to the west, he was surprised by an irregular plateau that progressively jutted into view in the distance, far above the green of the low rolling hills of the mainland before it. From his view, the plateau was the highest green plane on the otherwise light blue horizon, scattered with white clouds. It ended abruptly where he imagined it met the sea, dropping flat faced from a height of what must be a hundred men straight down to where its famous quarry of stones must lie. This must be the promontory at the end of the peninsula they called Sokehs. That was his destination, and his course was clear. He must pass lagoonward of one more winding passageway into the ocean and then sail to the northwest corner of the barrier reef and along its western edge, past a series of westernmost ocean passageways to his journey's end.

He glanced at the position of the sun glaring through the puffy, pure-white clouds and imagined where it would be on his arrival, and then a fish struck again. He released his sheet and listened to his sail's pervasive flutter as he carefully retrieved his lure, which had attracted yet another fish of the same type. As the afternoon wore on, he refreshed himself by repeatedly digging into his basket of food and drinking from coconuts. He continued his course toward the northernmost bend in the barrier reef, the top of the butterfly fish's dorsal fin. There he shunted to catch the wind from the opposite end of his proa and continued to troll the lagoon just inside the reef. The ocean smoothed on the lee, ocean side of the barrier reef as he preceded westward.

The closer he came to Sokehs, the less it appeared to be the end of a plateau and the more it appeared to be the largest of a series of rocks tossed onto the ridge of a peninsula. He couldn't help but recall the stories of the spirit who — according to legend — had torn holes in the reef of Majuro and tossed these rocks about, creating islets where they landed. The corals of the sea grow quite naturally, but how does a rock grow up like a wart on an island? He didn't believe in the supernatural feats of such stories but understood their purpose, to teach the children the features of their environment. There must be stories among these islanders to explain this feature. Had he heard them growing up, he would perhaps view Sokehs rock as an old friend he had often slept next to rather than the looming and perhaps dangerous mystery confronting him. He was struck by the light and deep brown vertical lines, which he imagined were the faults made by Nahn Sapwe's cracking thunder. Its sheer cliffs thrilled him, and his excitement grew as he approached the broadest passageway so far and snagged a much larger fish than the ones before — a jack of magnificent blue and silver colors that fought hard and required clubbing.

Once below the Sokehs headland, he had but two choices of progress due to the broad reef projecting outward toward a second broad passageway and to the level of tide, which was low. He must either stay his course and sail around the reef, approaching the peninsula from its western edge, or turn down an inlet between the peninsula and a low island on the opposite side and cross the reef from the east. He could see a village on the eastern shore, so he figured there must be another path through the reef to provide access to the lagoon. He turned into the inlet, and as he approached the village, it became obvious he had chosen well. Canoes and rafts were anchored by the shore, and he spotted the path over the reef to take him there. He anchored among several paddling canoes in a pool of shallow water on the reef, next to a small landing made of takai. Next to these, he found three well-built rafts. They were also anchored but stranded on the reef flat due to the still outflowing tide. Somewhat coincidentally, three men sat in the shade of mangrove forest, which threatened to overgrow the landing. They acknowledged his arrival with the obligatory *kaselehlie*, which he repeated back, and then he motioned toward the rafts with a nod of his head as if to ask permission to approach them. One of the men motioned in a friendly manner with the back of his waved hand for Ļainjin to go ahead.

Each raft was a different length proportional to the width of the two logs of relatively equal size that served as twin keels and provided its buoyancy. The logs of the largest were greater than the girth of a man's arms. The men had flattened the tops and slightly dug out the interiors with adzes. The ends of these logs exhibited an effort to sharpen them for faster transport. Had he come across such logs in his homeland, he would have assumed they were roughly hewn hulls ready to transport to a boat builder's shelter. Ļainjin wondered why they had not gone the next step and finished them. A finished hull would certainly be more buoyant! On top sat a platform of overlapping crosspieces, each the diameter of a man's outspread hand, lashed to the logs beneath. In turn, the crosspieces were secured together by diagonal pieces of comparable size that were grooved and lashed uniformly beneath for further strength and support. He wondered how large a takai such a raft could safely deliver to the other side of the island. Wouldn't a hollowed hull carry a larger takai? The men, perhaps intrigued by his interest, perhaps as owners of the rafts, slowly waded into the pool at the side of the landing, then splashed their way up and across the reef to join him.

Ļainjin used gestures to ask the men his question. He pretended to hack at the hull, pointed to the interior, and then held both palms outstretched before the men as if requesting they fill them with knowledge. They appeared to understand and, turning to each other, laughed good-naturedly. One of them bent low to the water — still draining from the reef — cupped his hands together, and filled them. When he bent down a second time, he plunged his cupped hands below the water to the reef. Ļainjin's thoughts lightened, as a torch would light a dark reef. They didn't want the hull to fill with water because if it did, it wouldn't merely swamp the raft but would sink it due to its heavy load. One of the others launched himself onto the raft, mimed that it was his, and appeared to offer it to Ḷainjin by mimicking the way he had held out his palms. Now Ḷainjin laughed at the man's antics, and the others joined too.

Having successfully initiated contact, Ḷainjin decided to feed his new friends. He motioned for them to stay while he retrieved something from his boat and waded back into the pool by the landing. One of the three accompanied him and, using gestures, suggested that he anchor farther lagoonward to avoid being in the way of the rafts awaiting loading. The man pointed to the broad path that appeared to lead up the mountain, suggesting that, by the time the water reached his chest, they would bring the stones. Ḷainjin understood but remained uncertain, skeptical that large stones would appear so quickly. He gently paddled his proa backward until the man motioned he was good. Then, taking three fish he had cleaned and cut open to bake in the sun from his outrigger platform, he put them in his basket of food and coconuts and presented the basket to the man who had just directed his anchorage. He accepted it with a broad smile and motioned for Ḷainjin to join them. He passed out the remainder of his catch to the men, and they climbed the takai, conveniently placed as steps up the landing, to sit in the narrow band of shade along the edge of the mangrove on the north side of the jetty.

In turn, the men offered Ḷainjin coconuts from one of the baskets that had made up their afternoon meal. As he held his head back to suck the sweet water, the height and beauty of the gigantic rock rose straight up, flat faced above them. Illuminated by the afternoon sun, its green, forested base — which he thought must hide its repository of treasured takai — compelled his attention and left him without words. Shrubbery in many shades of green grew on top of the massive rock and crept down its face, bringing life to the ancient, weathered stone. Although the striking landscape was like nothing Ḷainjin had seen before, he tore his gaze from it and watched his new friends as they hungrily stripped the half-raw flesh of the *ikabwe* from its skin and bones.

They chattered in Pohnpeian, sat cross-legged on the large takai, mimed questions about his catch, and obliged him to respond. He replied that he had caught the fish trolling and pretended to jerk an imaginary line held over his shoulder. This precipitated a great deal of discussion among the men regarding the characteristics of the Rālik proa, which they seemed to hold in high regard. At first, he suspected they were just humoring him out of politeness or perhaps gratitude for the fish. But they appeared to be saying, motioning with their hands as they spoke, that the design of the deep and narrow hull gave the proa greater speed, a better cut into the wind, and less lateral drift than any of the others that visited their island. He wondered how these men, whose rudimentary craft had no sails and no true hulls, obtained such intricate knowledge of sailing. Clearly, appearances were not what they at first seemed and he would be further surprised — or rather, amazed — at what would come next. The sight of men paddling takai!

The empty quarry

Gradually at the start, and nearly imperceptibly at first, came the sound of men working from around the bend leading up the mountain trail to the base of its cliffs. The others temporarily ceased their talking to listen for a moment and then resumed their conversation. It became clear they had anticipated these sounds, but Ḷainjin was intrigued and couldn't resist investigating. He pointed in the direction of the sounds and motioned that he was going there to watch what was going on. After a round of thanks, he left the men sitting in the shade and began hiking up the path. "These workers are chanting," he thought, climbing the well-worn, ancient trail in long strides. He marveled at the thick foliage on either side. This plant life wasn't found in Rālik, and he stopped occasionally to examine a leaf. He also followed a few of the many shallow side paths to see where they led. In each case, they dead-ended at a nearby campsite where food had been prepared. The chanting grew louder as he proceeded up the trail. Then he stopped motionless, and tears filled his eyes as he realized that Uerik had told the truth. Ḷainjin had simply not understood the way he'd used the word "paddle."

There on the path before him, he counted exactly eight men amid a small crowd of bystanders and a takai that was as large as or larger than the example he had posed the night before. Four of them were standing on top of the takai, their legs spread wide for advantage. And yes, each had a stout pole in his grip, using it as a lever to move the stone in a way that he could very well describe as paddling! What hadn't occurred to him was that the ladders they'd referred to were not in any way used vertically. The men laid them down on the ground, one to slide on top of the other. Their rungs created points of advantage for the ends of the poles used to nudge the one on top, the "boat," over the other, its skid. The process was just as they had described. He had simply not envisioned it. The men acknowledged him briefly as he broke their chant with his approach and watched them at work.

They had tied the stone securely to the boat on top, which matched, of course, the length of the stone. This boat slid on the longer, ladder-shaped skid beneath it as though it were a raft with its twin keels floating upon water. The "raft" reminded him of those on the reef below. The ladder-shaped skid on which the boat slid was made from freshly cut mangrove. It appeared light but strong and flexible. Still, each skid took four men to carry. They had two skids that they alternated from back to front. The crowd accompanying the "paddlers" carried other skids in various states of repair. These paddlers, as Uerik had referred to them, stuck the pole ends diagonally behind the horizontal "steps" of the ladder-shaped raft on top and in front of the steps of the ladder-shaped skids below, crushed by the weight of the stone into the pathway beneath. The men simultaneously lunged with their shoulders, lifting the lever ends from high upon the stone and nudging the raft forward a hand's length or so with each chant as they pushed their levers vertical. There were two men with levers on the ground in front and two in back. Their jobs were to keep the raft in the middle of its course by leveraging its twin keels between the long, lengthwise poles of the skid as though they were guiding a canoe down the shore on coconut fronds. They all chanted in unison and moved as one — as gracefully as the legs of a centipede.

The accompanying onlookers were apparently part of the team. When the paddlers moved the boat from one skid to the next, the onlookers were quick to seize it and just as quick to transport it forward. The women's tasks were to provide drink and other sustenance from baskets they carried as they followed, watching the sweat streaming down the paddlers' muscular, nearly naked, and fiercely tattooed bodies. Ḷainjin looked up but couldn't see the sun for the forest. Then he wondered how many days it took from top to bottom and how many such teams were yet above. He marveled at their progress. The men exuded an aura of gallantry and vehement strength. They rested not, and their downhill momentum appeared as insuppressible as the seasonal winds that had brought him there. Then, on signal, the men whose task was to paddle stepped down and were energetically relieved by the four whose job had previously been to guide the boat upon its skid. The smooth, routine movements reminded him of *jebwa* dancers at battle. He would later learn that these paddlers, from Kosrae,[73] had been hired for the occasion by titled Pohnpeians.

Ļainjin accepted a coconut that was graciously offered by a member of the group and continued his way up the mountainside. He quickly encountered a second, recently abandoned takai. Nearly identical to the first, it was sitting on two similar ladders at the side of the path. Spotting a third ladder braced against a large tree he was unfamiliar with, he rushed up to run his fingers along the length of one crosspiece, or rung. The immense weight of the endeavor had torn its bark here and there toward the center, where the fresh mangrove was weeping and slick to his touch. The undamaged bark beneath the wet lashings had swelled and held them firm, like those on the outrigger booms of a proa. He then inspected the raft-like ladder beneath the takai on the path. He noted that the men had lashed the twine they used to bind the many crosspieces to its two well-crafted keels into indentations so as not to wear as the heavy load slid on the slippery hardwood rungs of the ladders beneath. He smiled at the thought that the islanders utilized the very mangrove forest that attempted to encircle them to break free and launch their village oceanward beyond its sluggish embrace.

Then he heard more chanting from above and hurried to observe even as the smell of a cooking fire in some unknown direction filled the air. The well-worn trail had been rocky from the start and much lower than the dense forest on either side, as though rainwater throughout the seasons had washed the indigenous mud into the fringing reef below and left only those stones too heavy for the water to sweep downward. His legs began to ache as he climbed, as though he were mounting his tenth coconut trunk or wading through the surf, dragging a basket of lobsters on the reef. Hiking toward the base of the rock cliffs towering above, he heard hollow chanting ahead from

[73] An island about 300 miles southeast of Pohnpei that is now one of the Federated States of Micronesia.

different teams in the distance. They were coming from different directions, and the reverberations tricked him into thinking he was closer to them than he was. He had begun to wonder if one of the side trails he had passed held one or more of the sounds he was searching for when he finally came upon another group. This group was larger than the one below, and the stone they conveyed heavier. Yet their progress down the rising trail was equally as swift. This group numbered six men on the stone and again, two in the front and two in the rear. The weight of the raft sagged and then audibly crushed the flexible rungs of the ladder beneath into the contour of the trail. The uniform distribution of the stone's weight apparently inhibited their breaking although he noticed several onlookers carrying replacements.

He plodded onward, searching for Talupe and wanting to see the stupendous pile of takai he anticipated he would find at the base of the cliffs. Sweat poured from his body, but the cool breeze from the ocean swirled about the mountain and fanned his damp skin. The unfamiliar sound of chirping island birds filled his ears as he climbed. At last, he entered a clearing where the horizon opened, and there before him was the sight he had sought, though not the one he had imagined. Instead of the high pile of stones he had expected, he found an open crater of picked-over takai. Had Nahn Sapwe stopped thundering them loose from the cliffs above? Was Nahn Sapwe actually just another disappointing spirit conceived by old men late at night while coaxing their grandchildren to sleep on their mats? Where was the tumultuous jumble of recently fallen takai that the ancient stories implied?

Yes, he was disappointed that he had yet to find Talupe, but he had solved the mystery of the giant stones. He turned back down and was again facing his old companions, the seasonal winds of *añōneañ*. He lolled in their welcome coolness against his sweaty body. Now and again, the overspreading treetops opened to the ocean's breeze and allowed him to glimpse the deep blue of the sea and the many shades of azure outlining the reefs and lagoons beneath as he carefully tramped down the mountain path. He would bathe in the high tide off the landing below, swim to his canoe, cross the great western passageway by sunset, and return safely before the low tide could threaten his keel. The various stone crews he had met on the way up must already have reached the shore, save the one with the largest stone, which he encountered resting in a relatively clear area where the entire reef below opened before them. The men appeared dauntless though tired by the strain of the day and sat upright as they rested. He was about to speak to them when, glancing out over the reef, he saw a crowd of men at the landing, apparently loading a takai onto one of the rafts. He saw the other two, anchored high upon the incoming tide, but something else that was supposed to be there was not — his boat!

He flew off in a panic down the trail, no longer careful with his step, his eyes still searching the reef until his view was covered over again by the dense forest about him. How could he have been so trusting? He should have charged somebody with looking after it! Had he anchored it properly? Had he searched the beach to see if it had washed up there? Had someone taken it? They could never retie the lashings, so it would be useless within a season or two! Everyone knows this, or do they? Did they even stop to think? Boys could take something without thinking! These were the thoughts that swirled in his head as he lurched down the trail to the trees obstructing the horizon. That was the hard part. Knowing it was gone, but not able to see. He wished he had not flown off so quickly. He should have climbed a tree to get a better view of the beach. No, that was silly and wouldn't have helped! In his haste, he stumbled repeatedly, scraping skin from both knees and the palm of one hand.

He reached the beach panting and in bad temper. He rushed to the landing, leaping one after the other over the lines securing the raft. Suddenly, he felt great relief when he saw his craft tied to the landing just seaward of the raft, now surrounded by a crowd that had hidden his boat beyond his vantage. Members of the crowd eyed him strangely, perhaps surprised by his heavy breathing. On his part, he fixated on the people frolicking on his boat as it bobbed in the reef waves that slapped the landing. There were three of them: two boys and a man. The boys were wet. They must have swum to the boat, raised the anchor, and paddled to shore. The small paddle was there, lying unseamanlike on the foredeck. They had reanchored the bow closer to the landing and tied a stern painter to one of several rocks there for that purpose.

The man had Ḷainjin's large paddle and was using it to fend the boat from the stone wall of the landing. It was not clear to Ḷainjin if they were about to launch or embark. The boys took one look at his face and appeared scared out of their wits. He was out of breath and in no mood for mime. He jerked the craft toward the landing with one forceful yank on the painter. Both boys glanced fearfully at each other, then jumped headlong into the water and began swimming toward the single raft still anchored away from shore. Ḷainjin stepped onto the craft, taking the painter with him and pushing hard with his last step forward to ease the craft from the landing. He would leave no noble landward exit for this thief.

The man stared at him from the stern as he leaned against the backstay, holding the paddle in the water with one hand. His eyes glowered curiously into Ḷainjin's as no man's had before. It may have been contempt, almost amusement, perhaps resignation — as though he had expected what was to come and had resigned himself to the punishment. Ḷainjin lifted the smaller paddle from the foredeck and leapt onto the outrigger deck. When their eyes met again, Ḷainjin saw no fear there, as though the man welcomed the blow. Attacking, his paddle in both hands, he leapt again, landing his forward foot on the aft deck and swinging with all his might. Instead of paring his blow with the larger paddle as Ḷainjin had expected, the stranger foolishly tried to halt his mighty swing with his outstretched hand. The result no doubt crushed its bones and toppled him into the water.

To Ḷainjin's surprise, the men at the dock rushed to the thief's aid and began shouting at Ḷainjin as though he was at fault for clearing his decks of the rats that had crept aboard. Then he saw the green, freshly plaited coconut-leaf basket of food lying deep within his hull and choked as though his opponent had landed a blow to his throat. There in the middle of the basket, lying above the husked coconuts and freshly baked food wrapped in browned breadfruit leaves, was a hand-sized *wapepe* tied with miniature twine and made from coconut-leaf midribs. He looked up at the angry crowd and the handsome man with the hanging arm being lifted from the water and wanted to cry but did not. Surely, they knew the code of the navigator, not to lay a hand on another's boat without invitation! Why would she have instructed these boys to do this? One part of him wanted to hoist sail, reach across the reef, and return as planned. Another stubborn part insisted he stay and face what revenge the men of the island decided to take. He anchored his boat a few arm's lengths from shore and stared defiantly at the men in the crowd. Some returned his stare with anger in their faces. Others, probably the Kosraeans, returned to the task at hand, loading the takai still lashed on its boat ladder onto the water raft secured at the landing's edge.

Ḷainjin momentarily distracted himself from his embarrassment by deciphering their movements. The trick to loading the takai, he observed, was to end the skid ladder on which the boat ladder slid at exactly the end of the landing. The men accomplished this, as he later learned, by measuring and cutting the poles for this final skid from the adjacent mangrove swamp next to the landing. The transfer from land to raft depended on the height of the tide and was limited to four times a day, depending on the extremity of that day's tide. They had to secure the raft tightly against the landing to prevent the stone from pushing the raft away from the landing as they paddled the stone outward. They accomplished this by tying spring lines to stout trees at the edge of the swamp. He watched the men accomplish this venerable task, passed down to them over the hundreds of seasons that it would have taken to diminish Nahn Sapwe's pile of takai to the depleted open pit he had visited earlier that day, but his throat was elsewhere and his thoughts soon returned to the predicament at hand.

Had he moved too fast, jumped to conclusions, missed obvious signs? He questioned himself as he lifted the oar still floating in the water at the stern. It was still tied to the boat, so the man could not have used it to defend himself. Yet he could have quickly untied it or broken it loose as Ḷainjin himself had done many times. Why had he just stood there and taken the blow?

He searched the crowd for signs of Talupe but to no avail. Once the men had completed their task, he watched them withdraw from the landing in twos and threes. Eight of them took their place on either side of the stone and began paddling the now-loaded raft with its roughly hewn hulls head-on into the waves that capped shoreward across the reef.

The waves broke over the foredeck of the craft. Ḷainjin saw that its bow had no rise, and the waves crashed over its solid hulls. It was clear from the start that the stone was too large for the raft and placed too far afore, probably because the men had implemented no mechanism to prevent it from sliding aft and breaking the tiller. These were not men of the sea, yet their mettle was unmistakable. Each timed his stroke, digging for all his might into the swell rather than the trough. Collectively, they were making way but barely. He searched the shores of the islet across the inlet and wondered, would they round it to north or south? Regardless, they would never make it by nightfall. At the rate they were progressing, they might not make it by dawn!

"What a hapless enterprise," he thought, but then recalled their ingenious method of transporting the stone on land and admitted he had to respect that. He had to respect their tenacity regardless of their lack of seamanship. Truly, he could hardly blame them for losing such knowledge. There were plenty of fish for them within the protection of the barrier reef. They had no need to venture seaward, no reason to escape such a magnificent island!

"Siss!"

Ḷainjin turned to see where the sound had come from, and there he saw Talupe, standing in the wind and holding the hands of restless children in hers. She looked up with a furtive smile then back down to the children, jabbering with them as they tried to pull her in one way and the other. They were by themselves on the landing, all three preoccupied with one another. He teetered his way to the stern, then straddled the deck and dangled his feet in case he needed to fend off with his foot. Slowly, he pulled the painter of the bobbing craft as close as he could to the landing before feeling the tension of his bow anchor. The boy was naked and of that age where he would play all day on the shore when his mother let him. The waves were crashing diagonally against the landing and splashing as they swept by. The children began to get wet as they drew closer. The boy giggled gleefully while his sister squinted and turned her head away, as did her mother. To Ḷainjin's surprise, the boy broke loose from her and sprang at him. Ḷainjin reached out as the boy lunged forward, caught him under the arms, and spun him around to the deck. Off in a moment, the boy sat himself politely in the middle of the outrigger deck, glancing naughtily back at his mother as he inspected his new place to play.

Ḷainjin was unsure why Talupe had approached him. At first, he assumed she had come to scold him. But how was she to do that? Neither of them spoke the other's language. She could have thrown a rock instead of sissing him. She could break off into a tirade in her own language. He was expecting that. Was it possible she wanted him to transport her somewhere?

He pointed to the smoke rising from the cooking fires of the village across the inlet. In her language, he asked, "There?"

"There!" she said. She was pointing, he thought, to the raft that had just launched. A short distance away, it continued struggling to make way in the waves.

That was the worst idea he had ever heard, but at least, she wasn't throwing rocks at him. And once he'd gotten her on his boat again, he might be able to change her mind and take her wherever she wanted. He reached out to help her aboard, but a discussion emanated between her and her daughter, who obviously objected. To Ḷainjin's great surprise, Talupe left her daughter on the landing, took his hand, and climbed aboard. The girl untied the painter and threw it to him.

"There!" repeated Talupe, pointing again to the raft. The wet crew was paddling hard into the wind and the waves.

"Why would she want to expose herself and her son to the elements on a craft like that?" he thought, weighing his anchor stone and paddling his bow out onto the reef and clear of the landing.

Talupe grabbed the spare paddle he had used earlier as a weapon and began paddling from the bow. Her son sat at the seaward edge of the outrigger deck, each hand clenching the first lateral beam that crossed the outrigger booms beyond the platform. It wasn't long before they overcame the raft, at which point she began shouting orders at the men on board. Before long, she got them to throw her a line. She then looked at Ḷainjin as if questioning what to do with it.

"Pull it in?" he mimed.

Talupe mimed back, "No, I want to tie it." She pointed to his propped, unfurled sail and then to the top of his mast.

He thought for a moment and concluded that she wanted him to raise sail and tow the raft. Tying the line to the yoke of his proa, he hoisted his sail and set off into the wind. He stood in his hull, straddling the towline as he sheeted in to trim his sail to a close reach. The raft slowed his progress, but it appeared to make its way through the waves with greater momentum. The wind in his ears, he heard the muffled, comforting sound of laughter coming from the very men who had earlier cried their disdain for him.

Talupe retreated from the heavy splash inundating the foredeck and, now drenched, took a place next to her son. In turn, he took the opportunity to stand in her shelter and straddle her back. She pointed to a spot on the opposite shore of the island across the inlet, meaning that it was their destination. The evening sun glistened off the wet of her bare, brown shoulders, and the graceful curls of her drenched hair had been bundled and stuck in place with a long weapon-like needle of mangrove. Her bright eyes — as if judging the length of the day remaining — flitted between her daughter returning to the village along the shore, the men on the raft, the setting sun, and the destination ahead.

Ḷainjin could distinguish a large village with many canoes on the shore down the islet, on the mainland. The going was slow, but he judged that the combination of the wind's force in his sail, the tapering waves as they gradually entered the lee of the island to eastward, and the continued aggressive paddling of the men in the raft might easily triple their progress.

By the time they reached the edge of the fringing reef, the evening sky had darkened, and the swelling sliver of moon, now above the sheer cliffs behind them, shone a little brighter than the night before. The distance across the deep water of the inlet was but a quarter of the distance they had traveled. When they reached the reef on the other side, the water was so calm and the wind so light in the lee of the high island that the raftsmen began making way on them. At that point, Talupe discarded the towline, making it clear they had completed their mission. She wished to turn back and directed Ḷainjin in her language to do so. The men in the raft waved and nodded their thanks as they watched him fall off, shunt his sail, and waft off on a downwind glide.

Her son, now tired from the adventure, required a nap. Talupe made use of her intimate knowledge of Ḷainjin's hull below decks to lay the boy out on his mat and lie down with him there. Then, much to Ḷainjin's pleasure, she flopped on her back, exposing her thighs in the dim light of the setting moon and sunset glow through the forehatch. After a tantalizing while, she spread her knees, one against each hull, reminding him of how she had passionately invited him to pleasure himself the night they were together. She purposefully parted the fibers of her skirt to expose the light skin of her inner thighs, their four porpoise-shaped tattoos swimming upward on either side, leaving only the minimum strands necessary to cover her mysterious cove of pleasure, which had captivated his every thought from that first nights.

There in the deep waters of the inlet, hardly able to tear his eyes from her to the sail above, Ļainjin hardened as she thumped her foot impatiently against the hull below. He wondered what she expected him to do. What did she expect him to do? They cruised quickly back across the reef, but then — almost too late — she came to him from beneath the yoke and up through the hatch. Pressing her breasts against his and with her leg against his erect manhood, she announced that her son was sleeping. Then she turned, parted her skirt, and exposed the smooth, light skin of her arched rear. Standing on the balls of her feet, she invited him to enter her wet pocket from behind.

They glided swiftly across the reef toward the landing, sinking through the shallow troughs and rising on the whitecapped swells that rolled past them and crashed ahead into the entangled mangrove swamp on their right and the rocky shore to the fire-flicked village on the left. "Quickly," she implored.

Given their location when they started, they would grow rapidly into a potential embarrassing spectacle for onlookers. The expedience of the moment was such that Ļainjin released his seed long before he would have liked and even as she mumbled, "Faster!"

"Why now and why this way?" he wondered.

He reached below for his anchor stone. Following his instructions, she moved first to the halyard to lower the sail and then to the bow with his painter. He dropped anchor from his stern, and she jumped ashore and tied them to the landing. The end of their adventure came all too abruptly. The boy had awakened and must return to the village for his supper. Ļainjin must stay by his boat and reanchor away from the landing. She had her own plans, as he would find out, and made him pledge to stay until morning, when she promised to return. Then, standing on the yoke of the hull, she took the spare paddle and poked him with the handle. She opened her eyes wide, feigning surprise, as if to question why he had struck her messenger. He had no words, no answer to mime. She slowly twisted her neck and tilted her head as if puzzled, then went below to boost her son from the hull. He followed her sleepily to the bow, where she lifted him to the landing. With no parting word or gesture, she carried the boy away on her hip, leaving a depressing transactional feel to all that had occurred.

Ḷainjin watched them slowly progress along the shore, searching for an excuse to rush after them, perhaps to carry the boy. Then he was fully awake and restless, so she put him down to walk next to her, and they continued deliberately toward the village. Ḷainjin flaked and propped his sail for the night, ate from his basket, and gradually turned his attention to the last of the three rafts teetering in the waves that crested over its bow. "Surely, less roughly shaped hulls would serve to raise its platform higher in the water and give the craft more rise into the waves," he thought. At minimum, they must place the stone further aft to accomplish the same thing. A wider tiller would also stabilize the craft and reduce leeway.

These musings would prove useful the following day. Talupe had absorbed all his concentration the evening before, and he had missed critical weather signs in the sunset. He awakened to the sound of men calling orders as they secured the last raft to the landing. His legs ached from the doings of the day before. He raised himself and peeked out into the gray morning, then sank back gleefully into his shell. Again, he covered himself and imagined he was burying his face between her breasts — her clinging to him like an octopus surrounding its prey. He became mesmerized by the first sounds of chanting in the distance, then lulled by its comforting cadence, then pleasurably captivated. He was ready to allow her to crunch through his shell and enter the most intimate corners of his soul. Why had he not let fly with his sheet and let drift to wherever on the reef their passion took them? He longed to redo what had occurred with more time to savor their moment of intimacy as he fell back asleep, wishing she were there with her legs wrapped around him.

Finally, the heat of the late morning sun began to stifle him within his burrow, and he unwrapped himself and looked lazily up into the forenoon sky. Much had changed from the days before. His friends the low, white wind clouds were still there, but instead of clear blue above them, there was now dull menacing gray. He saw that the men had already loaded one stone on the raft at the landing and were in the process of loading a second. During the undertaking, he saw Talupe motioning as though giving orders. He didn't see the man he had clobbered the day before.

"Were they in danger of overloading it?" Ḷainjin wondered. He wanted to advise them to place the center of the stones slightly abaft of mid-raft but hesitated for a moment, not wanting to wrest control from Talupe or the owner of the raft he had met the previous day. He decided he would go ashore but mingle in the background and study the terms they were using. Not to his surprise, she didn't address him immediately, and he didn't approach her.

After a while, she drifted over to him, and he expressed his suggestion by way of demonstration with stones and sticks. He held his hand level and angled it upward. She understood and directed the men with the poles to lever the stones aft. She returned. Speaking in Pohnpeian, she pointed to his boat, then the raft, and then inscribed a semicircle in the air with her hand. He distinguished the words "Nahn Madol." Others hushed quiet and turned attention their way. She seemed to be asking if he would help her deliver her stones to the other side of the island. She had caught him by surprise.

Ḷainjin glanced at the others around them, who were listening ears up, their faces looking as though they had knowledge of what she would ask and what his answer might be. What could a man say but that he would try?

He began by inspecting the thick, multitwisted coconut-fiber lines used to secure the raft against the landing, then walked closer to the raft and began to study it in earnest. It was obviously overloaded. One of the two stones was slightly smaller than the other yet sat the same distance from the edge as the other. This gave the raft a slight list that he would have to correct by moving the smaller one closer toward the edge. He motioned for nine men to board the raft. Their combined weight, he judged, was that of a third stone, and the raft was, in truth, large enough to carry only one. He asked the men to debark two by two. When he was down to four, he remembered the difficulty six men had had paddling into the wind the evening before and looked up at the clouds streaming westward. The steady, intense winds of the past days had increased and, by the looks of things, might increase even more. In these conditions, Ḷainjin judged that the impact of paddlers was not worth the burden of their weight. He would need a tillerman, and he would need a much larger rudder. He jumped onto the raft, pulled the paddle-like rudder from the raft, and motioned to the raftsman that he needed a fatter, deeper blade. Motioning that he and the owner would undertake the transport alone, he folded his arms to show that these would be his conditions.

Talupe's men adjusted the smaller stone as well as the lashings that tied the stones to the raft to his satisfaction while two of the men brought a different rudder borrowed from a much larger raft. They loaded a second basket of food on Ḷainjin's canoe and a third onto the raft, and the raft was ready to begin their passage. He measured the line he would need to tow the raft at five times its length — with an additional two times in reserve — tied the towline as the day before, and hoisted his sail to beat wildly in the wind. Then he sheeted in and glided off over the reef like a big bird taking flight. He allowed the towline to unfurl into the water from its coil on his outrigger deck until it reached its end, at which point his flight came quickly to taper. As the line drew taut, the raft turned toward his stern, left the landing, and began to slowly move across the reef.

Clearly, they had designed the raft and its gear for one stone and not two, for paddling in light winds and not being towed by another craft. This was the sort of not-tried-before, untraditional sort of scheme his grandfathers would have argued against. Glancing shoreward, Ḷainjin saw the crowd still standing and watching, and he spotted Talupe in its midst. He kept recalling the Saudeleur saying she had only until the full moon to deliver her stones, and the vision of the spar at Idedh hanging from the scaffold above the well flickered among the dark thoughts that swirled in his head. What was he to do? He mustered his senses to battle!

If the waves out there — anywhere — turned the raft broadside and its drag caused his proa to lose its momentum, his rigging could backwind and collapse. During the time it would take him to recover, all could be lost on a reef at low tide. Yes, they had built the raft well, but even under these moons of neap tide, it would surely break up if pushed by this wind and these waves onto one of the many reefs ahead. And the tide was retreating. By midafternoon, the reefs would have but an arm's length of water on them that would drain to even less as the momentum of each wave sucked them shallow before it thundered down upon them and rolled onward. He would need all the fortune he could cast to get this raft to Nahn Madol in the seven days left before the moon was full.

How had she planned to do this before he arrived and accepted her plea for help? Ḷainjin wondered how many days it took to paddle or punt such a raft there on the fringing reefs along the in-and-out, irregular coastline of the island. Alternatively, did they manually pull the craft, or more probably try a combination of all three, depending on the variables of tide, wind, the shape of the coast, and its fringing reefs? Surely, she had been destined to be late to meet her bargain before she hatched this scheme. She stood precariously at the edge of the well at Idedh either way. These thoughts sharpened his senses and honed his determination like a coral file against the dense shell blade of an adze. His life, this woman, and his story were all at stake here. He began to slowly make his way across the reef to the calmer waters of the deep inlet and on to the even calmer waters to lee of the island on the other side.

He looked behind for the hundredth time to the old raftsman at the tiller. "You good?" he cried in Pohnpeian.

"Me good!" shouted the noncomplainer, laughing and pointing upward. White clouds streamed below higher gray ones that were unusual for this season. He nodded his head in affirmation that he accepted the risk of what was coming.

They would avoid the passageway ahead, if possible, by crossing the still-flooded tangle of reefs in the lagoon west of the island to starboard, but eventually they would have to face the waves again and beat into them. Ḷainjin imagined the waves building as they crossed the northeast section of the lagoon he had viewed from the hilltop. They would be larger and would crest more forcefully onto the raft. At some point in the early afternoon, the ocean would sink and expose those same reefs they would have crossed. "If the waves on the other side impede the raft's progress and push it back onto those reefs, all could be lost," he thought, but he took solace that there was no better companion than a man who knows the risks and laughs in the wake of them.

He wondered if Talupe would climb the mountain to watch their progress. He remembered how quickly she had spread her skirt and puckered her alele for him. She had spurred him on — "Faster, faster" — much as Ewalt had the day of their race. What was everyone's hurry about? The quarry was almost empty. "What would happen to Raipuinlañ's village when the last stone was placed?"

The palu

By noon, they had rounded the island and were about to cross the morass of reefs fringing its northern shore. Lucky for them, the moon had reached its neap cycle, which would continue until it swelled three-quarters full. This was the period of *iedik*,[74] when the ocean didn't bulge as high and the tides on the reefs wouldn't reach the extremes, as they would during *iielap̧*.[75] During the period of *iielap̧*, the ocean's swells swept over the barrier reef surrounding the island and into the lagoon. Now, during *iedik*, these swells were breaking on the barrier reef to the east, protecting the lagoon inside from the worst of their incursion. Ļainjin was hoping this would work to their advantage and allow headway against the waves and the current ahead. What he hadn't been counting on was the fresh increase in the velocity of the wind that was about to fall from that menacing gray above. As they crossed the first such reef and passed north of the island's lee, they met its force for the first time. As he looked out at the surrounding haze swept from whitecaps in every direction, he began to doubt that it was the right combination of conditions for success.

The passageway into the ocean ahead was one of three entranceways into the lagoon along the northwest portion of the barrier reef that ringed the island. It was the only one that angled directly into oncoming wind and so the only one where the waves combined with the receding, outflowing current. They had reached a point that required a decision. Yes, he was worried about that current, but his alternative was to tack and head inland. Shunting in that direction, between coral reefs with the raft in tow, would be

---

[74] Literally, "small time"; neap tide.

[75] Literally, "big time"; spring or extreme tides during full and new moons.

nearly impossible. Besides, should the current ahead prove too strong for them to pass without sweeping them oceanward, the tide would eventually slack, reverse, and allow them to reenter the lagoon. That seemed to be the safer course. Ḷainjin got the attention of the raftsman at the tiller, pointed to the course ahead, and got his nod in agreement.

The lagoon had changed markedly from the day before. Its inviting face had turned to a scowl. The smooth blue water of the passageway into the ocean was now gray and whitecapped. The magnificent multicolored coral ledges that fringed the passage had turned pale aqua with white surf splashing upon the edges. Swells were still tumbling on the ocean side of the barrier reef, but now the waves whipped up by the slightly northward shift in this even stronger wind were breaking on its lagoon side as well. There, in the distance, he saw transparent rain slanting toward the southwest. That meant the rain wouldn't be thick, but it would hit them diagonally, and the wind wouldn't diminish but gust beneath the cloud.

Once the raft behind him had crossed the reef and entered the deep passageway, Ḷainjin knew he had a problem, the one he had anticipated. The level of the lagoon — plus all the water in the various inlets of the irregular coast of the mainland — was still higher than the ocean on the other side of the passage. Thus, the outflowing current would stay strong until the tide turned slack later in the afternoon. In the interim, this current would be strongest toward the opening in the barrier reef to the left. His goal was to head toward the northernmost pair of islands to their right, which lay safely across the passageway and out of its current.

His problem was this: as they crossed, the current had a greater effect on the raft due to its greater surface on the water. Both craft were drifting in the current, but the raft was drifting faster toward the ocean to the north while he was pointing northeast into the wind. As he made his way across the passageway, the raft kept dragging him northward of his target. Eventually, the towline no longer pointed astern from the yoke at the center of his hull but began to creep laterally. If this continued, at some point, he would be sailing parallel to his tow.

Ḷainjin found himself caught amid forces that were totally out of his control. He contemplated cutting the raft free and then retrieving it later from out in the ocean, where the current would draw it before it dissipated a short distance oceanside of the passage. However, there were dangerous barrier reefs with which to contend. If cut loose, the raft would turn broadside to the wind, and the wind might blow it onto the reef at the west edge of the passage. If it missed the reef, a strong westward current that likely bordered the north edge of the barrier reef might catch the raft and make it difficult, if not impossible, to retrieve before nightfall. While he struggled to analyze his situation and search for a potential solution, the clouds darkened the sky. The first wave of rain slashed suddenly, pelted his bare skin, shished the water about him, and pattered relentlessly upon the deck of his canoe.

What had he gotten himself into? He chuckled to himself as he immediately heard his grandfathers' response.

"He strayed from the tried and traditional! These people have been moving stones for hundreds of seasons. Learn from them, how they do it."

He resigned himself to the fact that there would be much hardship ahead. There was no way around it. He decided to join the raftsman — to hunker down, hold his course, and face the developments as they came. He hoped for the best, but the worst was next to come. They were no longer making way across the passage. His sail remained full, but his canoe, caught in the outflowing current, drifted slowly sideways, toward the barrier reef at the west edge of the passage. He laughed at himself as he remembered the story of the little boy who made a kite so big that when he let it fly, it caught in the currents of the wind and took him sailing away through the sky.

Through the rain and haze that had long since enveloped them, Ļainjin looked at the raftsman over his shoulder and saw him pointing to the reef behind him with a look of panic on his face. Behind the innocent-looking aqua that bordered the edge of the barrier reef was the sharp live coral leading to the reef flat itself. Too exposed to drift over, that portion of reef had waves crashing upon it from two sides. Ļainjin was about to shout to the raftsman to cut one of the lines, tie it around himself, and then cut the other. He would haul him aboard his canoe and let the raft drift or crack up where it may. This man's very life was now at stake!

Then the man pointed back over Ļainjin's head toward the islets to his right. Lainjin turned his face into the gale and there, close by and blowing before the storm, was a large proa with full crew, sail puffed at full tilt, advancing like the wind itself straight toward them. He knew the boat well. He had raced against it but two days before. There sat the palu, Wisim, his long, wet hair clinging to his back like that of a woman. One hand was clasped to his mast, and the other pointed here and there as he commanded his crew. He looked not at Ḷainjin but straight at the raftsman, motioning with his arm swinging over his head for a line. By the time the proa reached the raft, its owner had secured his last two lines, tied their ends together in a twist, and prepared to hand off. The palu reached out from the leeward platform of the proa and grabbed the knotted end tossed to him just before he called for his crew to shunt. The crew members swirled about the boat like a flock of birds as the giant, wind-puffed wing of the craft flipped magically from one end of the proa to the other. As the sail passed over his spot, the palu gingerly stepped first in front of the mast, then behind it. Then he flopped his bare thighs back down on his lee platform, hauled in his sheet, and trimmed his sail to return on the same tack as Ḷainjin's. He sailed upwind toward him until his towline pulled taut and brought them to a parallel course. It was not till then that Wisim turned his broad grin toward him, laughed heartily, and, miming, challenged him to a race! Ḷainjin understood not the remainder of the palu's jabber, but whatever he said turned his crew into hysterical laughter and brought tears to Ḷainjin's eyes that, unnoticed, gratefully washed down a face drenched with cold rain and warm sea.

The lift from the second, much larger sail was more than enough to save him from his folly and haul the raft from the brink of mishap. Just across the gap between their boats, the palu sat half reclined on the forward edge of his lee platform. He appeared oblivious of the elements, calmly darting his eyes lovingly about his boat — now barking commands like someone's pet dog defending its master's courtyard, then preening like a waterbird safe in its nest. The cold seemed to stream off his body like the beads of water rolling off his bare, well-oiled shoulders and back. His proa was his domain, the island where he felt most at home.

At that moment, Ḷainjin envied his stamina, as he was shivering and powerless to prevent it. The scare from the straits he had narrowly escaped seemed to have played havoc with his resilience.

When the palu next turned his bird-like glance toward Ḷainjin, he must have noticed his impairment but turned first to the raftsman. His next command was for his crew to fetch yet another line from below and swim it back to the fellow. He decided to replace him at his tiller with a crew member and ordered the raftsman to be hauled forward, like a caught fish on his back, with a loop over his chest and under his arms. Then the palu dispatched the man into the hull, no doubt to warm himself beneath pandanus matting.

With that accomplished, he turned back to Ḷainjin and jabbered something to one of his crew, who immediately dove headlong from the bow into the lagoon. The boy grabbed onto Ḷainjin's towline, followed it to the yoke, and hove himself out of the water onto Ḷainjin's craft. All this without requesting permission to board, and now beckoning him to surrender his paddle. For an instant, Ḷainjin was ready to swing it and knock the boy back into the brink. Was this cunning Satawan Islander intending to steal the takai or somehow lay claim or get a reward for them? Ḷainjin glanced over at the palu but found his face innocent and grinning proudly as he squinted up into the elements and broke into some song. Then he looked back at the boy, also grinning, smooth chin dripping, leaning forward and wiggling the fingers of his right hand to show his eagerness to take the helm. Then back at the palu, who made a diving motion with his hand, a sleeping motion with his head and shoulder, and a rocking, cradling motion with his arms as he sang, indicating he wanted Ḷainjin to go below and sleep like a baby in their care. Ḷainjin nodded and surrendered his steering paddle. Spirit spent and obedient as a child, he opened his forward hatch and crawled through. Then he adjusted the hatch over himself and retreated from the harsh rainstorm into the dark, tossing hull of his craft.

Wisim had rescued him. There was no doubt about that. The sensible thing was to give him his trust. Besides, he had caught Ḷainjin shivering. He calmed himself with this thought, crossed his arms over his chest as Wisim had done in such a silly manner, and rocked himself to ward off his chill. He laughed a bit at the thought of the palu singing him to sleep. It had been a long time since he, too, had had a crew to do his bidding. He lazed in the comfort and savored the simple pleasure of having a roof between him and the elements he would otherwise be facing.

Then it struck him. What had the palu been doing out there? What was his destination? He couldn't have known that Ḷainjin was in distress. Was his rescue due to more than happenstance? Had the Saudeleur sent him? Had Ewalt had a hand? These questions churned in his thoughts as the hull in which he lay methodically rose and fell and rocked back and forth. Gradually, the inviting, damp warmth of the cramped, dark hold overtook him and he slept.

He turned his head against her warm breasts as he did so often in his sleep and felt her breathing down on him. He basked in her smell, which would linger in his throat until his dying breath. The scent of the loving arms he had fallen from… In his dream, he was cast like a leaf falling through a stormy sky. He looked up from the dark and saw her looking lovingly down at him from her proa as he fell and as she blew away like a bird into the sky. He landed in a prickly pandanus patch. The thorns scratched his tender skin, and he cried and cried until his grandfathers retrieved him and brought him up in their patient, manly ways. To replace his mother's breast, they gave him a pandanus nodule to chew. Instead of milk from the warm nipple he craved, he sucked *jekaro* from the mouth of a coconut shell. That had been his recurrent dream from childhood, and he turned to it now as he rocked in his cradle and the wind continued to rage. They lumbered on past the islands of the lagoon toward the eastern edge of the barrier reef that surrounded the mainland and increasingly sheltered them from the storm's waves as they approached.

Ḷainjin saw his mother's face again, looking down at him through the storm. She called his name, as did the lad who had taken his tiller and was trying to awaken him from his deep slumber. They had arrived at the barrier reef. He rose, lifted the hatch, and gazed at it sleepily. The rain had thankfully stopped, but the wind was still bellowing in his ears. The tide was out as far as it would go, given the neap stage of the moon. Huge ocean swells were curling upon the reef's outward edge, thundering enough to make Nahn Sapwe jealous. The sky was dark but less threatening, and the clouds above were white again and streaming westward beneath an upper sky of gray.

Ḷainjin quickly drew the attention of Wisim, who cocked his head, grinned broadly, and, with an exaggerated expression, feigned approval at his appearance.

"Good!" he cried in Ḷainjin's language and then circled his finger in the air to indicate it was time to shunt.

At Ḷainjin's nod, his companion released the sheet. His sail burst and then convulsed violently, overtaken by the wind. Ḷainjin crawled onto his foredeck, half concentrating on the movements of the other craft. Unanimity of movement could prove important, considering the cargo in tow. He untied the forestay and the strap that secured the *bal*[76] to its hand-sized platform at the tip of the bow. He lifted the sail by its *rojak*[77] and carried it — still suspended from the mast above as it progressively tilted vertical — back toward the yoke of the boat, where he handed it to his companion. Finally, once the mast had begun its slant forward as his companion moved the sail to the alternative bow, he adjusted and resecured what was now the back stay and took his place at the stern. There, he retied the paddle he would use as a tiller. The towline tied to the yoke remained to leeward, and the kubaak remained to windward, but before sheeting in, he waited for his sister vessel to complete the same process.

The palu had done nothing but duck the lateral boom of his sail as it passed over him, and he maintained his position on the leeward platform, which unlike the outrigger platform on the windward side, angled upward to reduce weight and prevent it from dipping into the sea when the craft heeled over. He had sent another of his crew members to swim to the raft to relieve the man there, and he waited patiently for the one returning to climb out of the water before turning to nod at Ḷainjin and haul his sheet. Ḷainjin did likewise and they were off, giving him a moment to reflect.

They had found that the word for "boat" — *wa* — was the same in all three languages. Yet each island group had added its own twist to the basic outrigger design. A larger Rālik proa — or even one the size of his — might also have a leeward platform where the navigator sat, held the sheet, and had access to the lines that ran the length of the mast. But Taknol, the craftsman who had built his boat, had decided against it because of the added weight.

---

[76] The foot beneath the clew of the lateen sail where its vertical gaff and horizontal yard join.

[77] The individual booms of the lateen sail. Vertical boom: rojak m̧aan; lateral boom: rojak kōrā.

He had wanted a boat any one of them could nudge ashore no matter how low the tide. Besides, in Taknol's view, the most efficient place to add weight was the decking. Most Rālik canoes, like the palu's, had open hulls with high, upswept, protective bowsprits. Taknol had rejected the design of a dramatic rise at the pointy ends for a more gradual rise conducive to decking. That, combined with its narrower hull, was a major difference between the two boats that had attracted the palu's eye. The width of the palu's hull compared to its length was much wider than that of Ḷainjin's. This meant his craft sank deeper in the water, and its comparatively deeper keel gave it the cut into the wind that the palu envied. His deck compensated for the lesser freeboard and offered a multitude of additional purposes, not the least of which was shelter.

The larger boat pulled ahead until its towline tightened, at which point the craft were sailing parallel along the inner aqua-colored edge of the barrier reef where Ḷainjin had fished the day before. He noticed that the design of the outriggers was another difference between the craft. The distance to the outrigger was supposed to be half the length of the boat. In that regard, the palu's outrigger extended the same as his, but on the palu's craft, the kubaak itself, though comparatively heavy, was shorter and stubby looking. While Ḷainjin's outrigger platform was rectangular, the palu's was nearly triangular and extended all the way to the kubaak. His crew looked comfortable and stretched out in the added space. Ḷainjin judged his lighter boat to be comparatively less comfortable on deck, especially on long voyages, and less able to transport passengers or cargo, but that was not its purpose. He would soon learn that the palu came from a long history of traders who traveled to distant islands and navigated by the stars. He regularly stopped at isolated atolls to load his boat with sea turtles of immense size and weight. They had designed their craft accordingly, and while his afforded more secure shelter below decks, theirs also had boards above their bilge that allowed them to lie in their hull beneath matting that provided some protection from the elements. Still larger versions of either design could support a light, makeshift hut on the outrigger deck to provide privacy and additional shelter for women and children.

This stretch of their journey would be a much easier sail. Gone now was the earlier headwind and the combative oncoming lagoon waves it generated.

Though the wind remained strong, no waves were this close to the interior of the barrier reef. The raft behind them cruised more quickly in the smoother water, and its drag on their progress lessened. He wondered how the paddling crew he had helped the night before was faring in the headwinds along the north coast. Were he by himself, he would surely stop first at Uerik's village to apologize for doubting him. Yet who would have believed it possible to paddle stones like a boat down the mountainside?

Ḷainjin knew he was in an adventure far greater than the sharking escapades of his youth. This was truly a story for the ages. How much wealth could he amass delivering such stones? he wondered, though he realized his craft was far too small for the task. He could hardly wait for Talupe's reaction when she arrived to find her stones safely delivered and her life safe from the clutches of Nahn Samohl! Then he lost himself completely — contemplating the fleshy details of exactly how she might reward him.

The tide turned as they progressed rapidly along inside the barrier reef. The sky remained overcast with white and gray clouds streaming in the rainless wind. At this point, the timing seemed perfect. The tide should rise for the rest of the evening, and by the time they arrived at the fringing reefs by Uerik's village and beyond, they should be well flooded. He could probably proceed from here alone, but somehow, he knew the palu would act offended, and his charisma was such that Ḷainjin found himself curiously fascinated and relieved by his commanding presence. The palu sat there as attentive as a mother bird happily tending her chicks, patiently training this one to flap its wings, feeding that one, preening the one over there. He shouted not, yet his crew hung on his every word, and his good-humored joking never stopped. They were like children playing in the sand, except one was secretly and very seriously scanning the horizon, keeping his laughing eyes on every detail of their surroundings and relentlessly watching out for the welfare of the others. To meet this man with his lively smile was to like him, and to watch him in action was to emulate him without trying.

When the crew member on Ḷainjin's bow finished the last of their coconuts, the palu ordered a line thrown to them. They accomplished this by using a device like an *anidep* — perhaps a rock plaited over with pandanus tied to a light line tossed from one boat to the other. Then the palu tied this leader line to the stouter line, and as soon as the crewman on Ḷainjin's craft clasped the second line firmly, the palu gave him a nod and released the basket of coconuts into the lagoon. The forward momentum of Ḷainjin's boat under sail combined with two or three arm pulls quickly brought the basket from the stern of one boat to the stern of the other, and they had more drink aboard. The palu's every movement had a utility that he executed with concentrated deliberation as if dancing his own *jebwa*. His every thought was for the well-being of those in his midst. He was the type of man others crowded around in battle to draw inspiration, courage, and ferocity.

The palu burst into song again even as the wind and the thud of the buñtokrear swells falling to windward echoed down the barrier reef and drowned the sound of his voice. They sailed on beneath the gray, tumultuous skies, passing the islands, the mangrove-infested coasts, and the tiny villages fighting for their place on the shore he had viewed but the day before. They crossed the passageways with their tides now incoming, and he found the dim light of the cloud-covered crescent moon as it gradually appeared through the darkening gray sky. Once the darkness overcame them, each of the many village cooking fires they passed cast its beams of light to lie and flicker at them on the wind-rippled surface of the lagoon. They began to pass over the multifarious reefs that led to the back door of Nahn Madol. Once again, Ḷainjin's lack of familiarity with their depths caused a lump in his throat as they crossed them one by one and amazingly without incident — whether by the knowledge of the palu or the direction of the raftsman, he was uncertain. But the raftsman apparently didn't want to proceed into the great village on this night, and so they anchored his raft at one of the islets at the village border close to the mangrove-covered mainland. His thanks to Ḷainjin, and especially to the palu, were simple yet ardent eyed.

After they had departed and begun the last short leg of their journey through the village, Ḷainjin saw one of the palu's crew pointing along the way to a dark wall rising at an angle out of the reef waters to the top of one of the rectangular structures. He had wondered about this "broken wing" the day before. There it stood, clearly out of place amid the other walls about it in the dim light of the moon. This night, after the adventures of the past days, it stood clear in the blackness as what it was: the ramp that Talupe's stones were to traverse to the top of the structure. Now he knew how she would do it, and he had confidence she could accomplish this in the time still allotted.

As he followed the palu's proa through the strangely deserted tideways back to Kelepwei, he vowed to himself — out of the respect he now had for him — never again to set his craft across the bow of the great navigator. Ḷainjin anchored his boat next to his, so close he could contemplate the sound of every word he spoke to his crew, and vowed never again to anchor anywhere else. So, that was how he entered the palu's care and how he felt himself the luckiest of men to have cast himself into his presence.

Ewalt showed up early the next day, eager to resume the trading, and quickly cleared up how the palu knew Ḷainjin might be in trouble. "The Saudeleur, after hearing the palu's prediction of the storm, told him he worried you might get caught helping Talupe transport her stones."

"But how could the Saudeleur have known that?" Ḷainjin hadn't even known himself that he would try to transport them.

"Talupe had bragged to him you would search for her and help her before she left."

Ḷainjin wondered how she could possibly have known he would search for her, find her, and offer to help.

Ewalt drew his thoughts from his face and concluded, "She is known to use magic to guide men to fulfill her objectives. Her stones have ended up being anchors about the necks of many paramours."

Ḷainjin spent most of the afternoon wondering about this as they traded. Distracted by thoughts of her, he found himself beginning to rely increasingly on the trading advice of the palu. At the end of the day, he was quite pleased with the trades made.

Without appearing ungenerous, the palu had a way of pretending to have a vulnerable lack of experience when among the native traders. He would ask simple questions in a seemingly naive way that upset the strategies of his negotiating opponents and left him with an advantage. For instance, he questioned the traders in the markets about adze heads and why they valued the sharpened adze heads by weight equal to the value of the coral files used to sharpen them. True, the files were light of weight, but in his view, still not equal in weight to the value of the adze heads they sharpened. Their calculations were leaving out the value of the time it took a man to sharpen them. Perhaps the island traders had gathered a large supply of unsharpened adze blanks, or perhaps their surrounding lagoon lacked a good supply of the tree corals needed to sharpen them.

Annoyed at his impertinence, that the palu would question how they had valued the markets, the traders joked that it was easy to gather giant clams, but the coral files came from a great depth that a fat man like him could never hope to reach. Laughing heartily with the crowd, as was his wont, the palu responded that, if that trade held, he would commit to trading for every adze head they had. Then he would return to Satawan, have his wife cook a batch of *mpwein tenek*,[78] and have the boys on the island retrieve the corals for it. He committed himself either to return with a fleet of coral files the weight of the adzes they'd given him or to feed his fat rear to the enticing Pohnpeian female in the well. He slapped the bare side of his rear for emphasis amid a roar from his crew that was followed by silence from the local traders and no adzes offered in trade. He ended up trading stingray barbs for the adzes at a ratio of two to one. He knew what the Pohnpeians coveted and drove a hard bargain for those items they needed most. He also had them convinced the magic of his neck-strings was infallible, and he teased Ḷainjin that had he simply taken his advice and given the neck-string to Talupe, he could have avoided having to paddle down mountains for her.

That evening, Ḷainjin relaxed on the palu's outrigger deck as he sat in his spot on the lee platform. This deck was made of slats while Ḷainjin's was made of boards laboriously hacked by adze. The slats, probably easy to gather, gave way under a man's weight and were surprisingly more comfortable. The tide had been out until early evening, so they had returned late from Kariahn, where they had supper and sakau. The weather had cleared that afternoon. That evening, they sailed back by way of the broken wing slanting up to the walls under construction. Partway up the sloped ramp of smaller takai and lighted by the still-swelling moon sat, it appeared,

[78] Pohnpeian for the sweet, spongy endosperm of the newly sprouted coconut. It can be eaten raw or cooked into a dessert-like dish with arrowroot and coconut milk.

the two takai — one after the other — they had delivered the night before. Her workers had no doubt been busy moving them that day. Ḷainjin had been wondering if she would stay at the Saudeleur's compound over at Pahn Kadira and if she would come to him. His eyes drifted repeatedly to its entrance across the tideway, but as the night wore on, much to his chagrin, she did not appear.

Ewalt was still there with them, waiting for the tide to rise a bit more to return home. Through him, Ḷainjin asked the palu how he'd known he would be in trouble.

"Because of the fighting star, the shape of the moon, and the four clear preceding days," he answered. To a man, the palu's crew took notice he had transitioned into his teaching mode. They sat motionless and spoke not.

"Fighting star?" inquired Ewalt.

"Mailap.[79] When Tūṃur is there at dawn" — the palu pointed a quarter of the way up the eastern horizon — "Mailap rises and fights for five days."

"Fights?" asked Ḷainjin in the palu's language. He was surprised to learn that the palu knew about Lōktañūr's[80] eldest son, Tūṃur, and his wrath at the start of *añōneañ*, which Ḷainjin would later learn was called *lefung* where the palu was from.

"He battles for five days." The palu spread his fingers as Ewalt interpreted his words.

"Mailap was obviously their name for the second brother, Mejleb," thought Ḷainjin. According to his legends, the palu expected a storm during the first five days of the new moon. When the first four days were clear, he knew to expect something extreme on the fifth day. But if he had expected a storm, why put his craft at risk? For the interim, Ḷainjin was happy to learn more about the mysteries of the sky. They talked more about the cycles, and it became clear both navigators kept track of them the same way. They both tracked the same stars rising in the east under successive moons. Tūṃur began the dry, windy season, and five stars later, Jebrọ[81] — the group that

---

[79] Mailap and the Trukese pronunciation Mājlep are both names for the star Altair.
[80] Tūṃur's mother. The story of Lōktañūr and her twelve sons, who became stars, is the cornerstone of Marshall Islanders' knowledge of seasonal weather.
[81] Aka Pleiades; constellation.

the palu called Maragar — began the wet season of plenty. The neap tides under each star were the "fighting times" vulnerable to storm, sometimes during the swell of the moon, sometimes during its wane. This was like the time of "bitter waters" that his grandfathers would mention as a reason not to go fishing. Ḷainjin was familiar with all these things, but then the palu tracked other stars as they rose and fell at all points on the horizon, and he used these to set his course from one group of islands to the next. He had his crew recite the stars one after the other, pointing to their spots in a circle around the horizon where they would appear, slowly drift, and dip back below the sea.

Ḷainjin very much enjoyed the comradery of joining the palu's circle, the language learning, and the unfamiliar perspective of a learned man from a different area of the vast expanse surrounding them. However, he was disappointed at evening's end when Talupe did not appear, and a covetous hunger for her grew in him that night. It grew as they traded the next day and as they saw the takai moved nearly to the top of the wall when they sailed back beneath the ever-swelling moon the next night. Yet she came to him not and sent not a token of gratitude now that she was safe from all thoughts of the horrible well. Images of her tormented him such that, after a few more days, he lost interest both in the palu and in the trading.

Wottok's story

Ḷainjin turned then from the pleasant comradery with the palu, where teasing over his distraction had become commonplace, to his friend Ewalt, with whom he felt he could speak openly and who lacked a teasing nature. He left his canoe in the care of his new friends and accompanied Ewalt to his home on Temwen Island.[82] His little village was on a hill a long walk above the mangrove swamps that crowded the shore. His house was just like the others Ḷainjin had seen. It stood high on a platform of stones with walls of mangrove slats and thatch of pandanus leaves. The woman he had chosen had a kind smile and was well adorned, and his two boys followed him everywhere.

Perhaps out of custom, Ewalt escorted Ḷainjin to the dwelling of his father. Like the other structures he had viewed, there was a deep fire pit built into the stone base of the house, and Ewalt's parents, both elderly and very devoted to each other, made that their center of activity. Ḷainjin knew they had known his mother, and they knew the Seekers who could tell him of her fate, so he was excited by the opportunity to talk with them. The couple sat before the warm hearth, heating their *nen*[83] tea slowly on hot rocks in a wooden *jāpe*,[84] sipping it from decorated coconut half shells, and taking turns reminiscing of times past. They worked as one, very deliberately, very

---

[82] The island inland of Nahn Madol whose surrounding reef supports the city.
[83] Fruit from *Morinda citrifolia*, a small tree prized throughout the islands for its medicinal properties; a tonic thought to promote health. Also called "noni."
[84] A wooden, trapezoid-shaped vessel carved from breadfruit wood and used to knead breadfruit; the constellation Delphinus, the dolphin.

slowly. They each had an opinion about what the other said but always left a pause between so they never interrupted each other. Ewalt had left him alone with them temporarily while he completed a few chores and his woman and children worked the pandanus patch with other neighbors. His parents were a pleasure to be around and no doubt normally took an active role instructing and raising their two grandchildren. Ewalt's father's name was Wottok,[85] and Ewalt had already told him and his mother that Ḷainjin was searching for the story of Tarmālu.

"We knew her before she had children," began Wottok. He had the dignified aura of an orator.

"She was unusual. We women of Pohnpei had never imagined a woman so strong." Ewalt's mother laughed and divulged for the first time that she spoke Ḷainjin's language as well. She asked if he would like tea, and he wheezed his assent.

"He taught me, and spanked me when I mispronounced his precious words," she added. Twisting and crunching the shell cup, she embedded it firmly into the coral stones that separated the takai of the hearth from the pandanus matting on which she sat and poured the warm tea into it from the corner of the trapezoid-shaped bowl.

"I can still spank you, and don't think I wouldn't enjoy it!" dared Wottok, smiling bawdily first at one and then the other.

Her name was Kiton,[86] and her appearance was immaculate. She had tied her long, gray-streaked hair in a neat bun and encircled her head with a fragrant headband of flowers. Her skin was moist with coconut oil and clung to her petite bones with dignity and sagged not. She was an attractive woman who wore her age with spirit and smelled as though she had just come from a bath despite her location poking the fire, the smoke from which rose to the ceiling and drafted through the open gables of the house.

Perhaps to prove to Ḷainjin she was the one in charge, she pretended to stab Wottok with her fire stick. "Dogs like to bark" — she raised her brows — "among other things!" Her eyes twinkled as she laughed at her own joke, but Ḷainjin held back for Wottok's response.

---

[85] Pohnpeian elder; Ewalt's father.

[86] Ewalt's mother.

He veered his head away from her with a laugh and a blush and ignored the temptation to respond directly, as if from experience he knew he was unlikely to get the best of her. "Do you know they eat dogs here in Pohnpei?" he said with some disdain, separating himself from her way of life.

"No," said Ḷainjin in a matter-of-fact way, trying not to show his disgust at the thought. Dogs were rare among Rālik Islanders, and his people did not eat them.

"I like dog. Delicious," said Kiton. She put her hand on Ḷainjin's kilt. "I'll kill one dog so you can try."

Ḷainjin was at a loss for a response. Wottok saved him. "They eat people too!"

"Not us Pohnpeians," Kiton snapped back. "The people here before us, the *liet*.[87] They live in *nanwel*,"[88] she added. "We people of *nahnsapw*[89] have never eaten people, and he" — she pointed her nose at her mate — "knows it! We aren't descendants of *liet*. Our ancestors came to Pohnpei in seven voyages from downwind Kataupaiti.[90] The two brothers Oljipa and Oljopa came in the last voyage. They were the ones who taught us to ride the takai down the mountains and use them for foundations to build islets on the reef."

Although Ḷainjin had not heard about cannibals in the mountains, they looked so vast and mysterious he wasn't surprised. But he wanted to talk about his mother. "Was my mother blown here in a storm?"

"Your mother came here deliberately many times," Kiton said. "The last time we saw her, she left with many items of trade."

"They tell me she was lost in a storm."

"That isn't what the Seekers tell us," said Wottok. "They say they fled on the edge of that storm. It blew them into a great calm stream with no islands, where they ran out of water and nearly died of thirst. Finally, they came to an island they called Papua, so large it must take three moons to sail about its shores. Many *jowi*,[91] each speaking a different tongue. People with black

---

[87] Pohnpeian for "cannibal" or "cannibal peoples."
[88] Pohnpeian for "the mountains," or the area outside human authority.
[89] Pohnpeian for "coastal or cultivated land."
[90] Legendary origin of the first voyagers to settle in Pohnpei.
[91] Clan or tribe.

skin and frizzled hair. That's the meaning of Papua — 'frizzled hair.' They survived the storm. The storm didn't kill them. It was a rogue *jowi* from that island who eventually ate them, or so the Seekers say. You need to get the story directly from them. They should return soon."

Ḷainjin was not surprised at this tale. He had heard many times that they had probably drifted up onto some cannibal isle and been eaten. It seemed to be the most logical explanation, and he had long ago prepared himself for this eventuality. "Which stream?" he asked Wottok.

"The Seekers tell us there is a great stream just south of Pohnpei, running eastward through the middle of the open sea in the direction opposite to the swells. They're probably fishing there now, searching for a great kājokwā to snag out of the stream." Kiton dropped another coconut shell onto the hot coals of her fire and adjusted it with her fire stick.

"You mean kāleptak?" Ḷainjin said it more as a statement than a question.

"I guess that's what they call it," said Wottok.

"Like a current?"

"I think so." Wottok squinted and turned his head as the shell began to smolder.

Ḷainjin laughed. "Well, that is kāleptak! They showed me how it forms a swell that rolls onto the western side of an atoll. In the open ocean, it rolls under the opposing swell from the east and counteracts its strength in such a way that, when we pass east of an atoll, we notice a change as we enter its shadow."

"Well, anyway, they crossed the stream to the other side, and that's where they were eaten," Wottok added.

Kiton took the breadfruit leaf stub she'd been using and fanned the smoking shell until it burst into flame.

"Then how did the Seekers escape?" Ḷainjin asked. "Why didn't they get eaten?"

"I think they were lookouts. You'll have to ask them."

"Maybe just late for supper?" Ḷainjin joked more to break the somber turn in their conversation than to make light of the potentially tragic news. He had been through this before and had long ago allowed himself to dispel any thoughts of rescuing his mother. It was her story he was after.

"Sounds like they looked out for themselves." Kiton fanned another smoldering, dried coconut half shell with her breadfruit-leaf stub, causing it to flare and light the dimly lit home.

"They talk about a place where mountain peaks are higher than clouds — streams of fresh water as wide as our passageways into the ocean and geckos that swim in them big enough to eat a man in one bite. Warriors collect the heads of their enemies and adorn their homes with them," warned Wottok. "Yet they say they trade with honor among themselves and with newcomers as well. If offended, though, they turn into dogs fighting over a scrap of food."

Kiton snorted. "They treat their women like spoiled fish."

"But the Seekers are honorable men," said Wottok.

"They seek fortune. Our men believe their stories, but we women see them for who they are — out for themselves."

"What's wrong with seeking fortune?" Wottok retorted. "They tease a man if he's poor but yell at him when he works! Leave it to a woman to find a flaw in any man."

"Our friend came too late in the day for me to start counting yours! Ḷainjin, next time come at sunrise. I might be done by supper." Kiton placed another coconut shell on the flame so as to prevent it from smoldering.

"What do they get for trading one kājokwā?" asked Ḷainjin.

"The Saudeleur handles those trades," Wottok said. "It depends on who bids the most. They offer land, titles, items of trade. Their value fluctuates with the buoyancy of the wood and current construction plans. New islets need the largest base stones. A second kājokwā the size of the first in a potential pair can bring a better offer than one without a match. This season, they're out there searching for a match to the one they last brought."

"It's the fastest way to earn a title and less dangerous than the way he earned his," added Kiton.

"How was that?" Ḷainjin asked.

"Fishing!" she responded.

"Fishing? What kind of fish?"

The old bird was silent for moment and puffed his feathers proudly as he looked toward his mate to answer.

"*Dāp*!" Kiton spoke the word in a way that was out of the ordinary, slowly squinting her eyes, creasing her nose, and reverberating the word with the tip of her tongue off the roof of her mouth. Her face expressed that the mere thought of the thing infuriated her.

The men looked at each other, half laughing at the curious face she made as she pronounced the word. Then, as though to emphasize her point, she dramatically clutched her man's forearm and forced it forward so Ļainjin could see the scars on his arm caused, he supposed, by the sharp teeth of the ugly beasts.

"But why do they treasure *dāp*? Do they eat them?"

"Never!" replied Wottok.

"Poison!" Kiton added with the same cryptic tone.

"Nahn Samohl is the Saudeleur's pet."

"They go right for appendages where they can clutch and twist! Lover's play." Kiton spoke softly, as though revealing a secret. "Like any woman, she knows where to go!" She showed her teeth and squinted her face amusingly again, then clutched her teeth on an imaginary appendage and pretended to tug like a dog with its master over a bone.

"Jeej!" Ļainjin laughed. "You mean the Saudeleur trades for them?"

"For Idedh!" responded Wottok.

"He would kill for them," Kiton said. "He would trade anything!"

"Why?"

"He has a big problem," she answered.

"What?"

"No babies!" Wottok said.

While Ļainjin was trying to imagine why this was such a problem, Kiton added, in the same soft voice, "Nahn Samohl eats all her mates!" She had the same disgusted-looking face. "Every ... single ... one he put in there," she whispered, poking a smoking coconut half shell with her stick, bursting it into flame, and lighting the serious look on her face. "She eats her mates, then she eats her babies! She's not fish, she's worse than the *liet*." Kiton said this not as a joke but seriously, as though she had come to this conclusion after much deliberation. She sat up and straightened her back as if for emphasis. "She ate every *dāp* he caught! Not even one left! The Saudeleur wasted his title."

"No," argued her man emphatically. "She's just hungry! She isn't this mean spirit. She's just a fish. The Saudeleur has the same problem they have always had. If they feed her, she won't attack when they lower the reprobate into the well for his punishment."

"What happens then?" Ḷainjin was curious.

"By law they must haul them back out of the well and set them free. They are exonerated."

"How long do they leave them down there?"

"From one tide to the same the next day."

"I would die the moment they lowered me into the well," said Kiton emphatically. She crossed her arms over her breasts as though to protect them and shivered her body to persuade the men that she was serious.

"Why are babies so important?" Ḷainjin asked.

"They wanted her replaced by one of her own. She is how old now?" Wottok looked at Ḷainjin as though expecting him to answer. "She has to have over one hundred seasons counting from the time Sareid en Sahpw,[92] the father of Raipuinlañ, took her as his pet. His idea was to fill the well with eels, and he lowered many false traders before every one of that generation learned to follow our custom of trade. Then there was a lengthy period when they lowered no one, and that's when Nahn Samohl developed her reputation and her taste for mates. Therefore, the Saudeleur continued to collect the biggest eels he could, and he stored them in his pool at Darong."

"Darong?"

"It's another islet close to Idedh," answered Wottok. "They built another small islet around a second, larger natural reef pool. They keep giant clams and use their babies to seed the reefs. They raise the eels with the giant clams. They constructed tunnels at the base of the island to allow fresh reef water to seep directly between the takai into the pond at high tide. They keep the eels fed so they don't bother the men who harvest the little clams. Other tunnels lead to the edges of the islet. These they filled with coral pebbles to filter fresh seawater in and out."

Ḷainjin was curious. "How did they transfer an eel from Darong to Idedh?"

---

[92] The father of Raipuinlañ.

"You can't easily transport those monsters. They secrete a poisonous slime and use it to squirm out of your grasp." Kiton spoke derisively, with the same humorous, disgusted look on her face.

"There has always been a natural crevice beneath the reef, connecting what was originally two natural pools. The eels can swim from one to the other below the reef."

"And turtles?" prodded Kiton.

"And they keep turtles there also," Wottok said.

"For what purpose?"

"Store them for the Saudeleur's feasts."

"And…?"

"To feed the guts to Nahn Samohl—"

"So…?" Kiton was dogged.

"So, she develops a taste for—"

"Guts," she concluded, answering her own question for him. "It's all about guts! It's all about keeping that *liet* in the well with the taste of flesh in her throat. Once she eats your manhood, there's nothing in her way, so she squirms in for the rest. Imagine them hauling you up! What you'd look like! Who would break the law after seeing something like that?"

Ḷainjin got the feeling she was no longer storytelling but releasing deep-seated feelings.

Kiton went on. "Let me tell you something. It is an eel after all. Someday the nasty thing will die! What will happen then?"

At that point, Ewalt returned and spoke harshly to his mother in her language. He had probably heard "Nahn Samohl" several times and worried she was too critical of the Saudeleur and the sacred eel. Then he told Ḷainjin he wanted to show him his garden and suggested they take a short hike into the hills.

"My mother was never happy with the success my father had in obtaining land and title by his eel fishing," he said as they left the village. "He was landless. He came here with a few hooks. My mother's land isn't much. How else was he to become successful than to use his fishing skills? I'm proud of him and the life and land he earned for us. She worried greatly over his safety and grew angry over the Saudeleur's constant insistence he find eels that were ever larger and more dangerous to catch," he continued. "It got so he had to sneak off in the night thinking she was asleep. That's when he caught those things, and he went by himself, not wanting the others to learn how he caught them. But she always knew when he was gone and sat up the whole night worrying he would never return. That's when she started insisting that she accompany him."

"I thought they caught them in traps. Your father said—"

"He tried that, but they squirmed out as he raised the traps," Ewalt said. "He ended up wrestling them out of their lairs under the moonlight!"

"Jeej, that little man must have the throat of a *ñiitwa*!"[93]

They walked up a path of dried mud with steps of thick tree roots through a heavily forested area. Ewalt chose his moves carefully, as though he was familiar with every plant, every footstep. Ḷainjin followed closely behind. Although he envied the greenery of Ewalt's land especially during this dry season — which he had come to see was not too dry in the distant mountains — he wasn't a planter. He enjoyed eating their roots and fruits, but laboring in the mud was not Ḷainjin's idea of adventure. He had come to learn, though, that being a man in Pohnpei was tending plants. Even the Saudeleur, he had heard, coveted his little patch of bananas and lime trees.

First, they came to Ewalt's taro patch, which he cleverly fed from the runoff of a tiny stream. He explained that even a quickly passing cloud would drop enough rain for the little stream to capture and flow into the swampy depression he had dug into the hillside. The plant's heart-shaped leaves — immense and dark green — glistened in the sun, and each had shiny new leaves unfurling at the center despite the dryness of the season. Ḷainjin looked back out over the ocean and realized they had climbed above the salt vapor that clouds its surface and covers and kills all but the hardiest of plants. The mangrove, of course, thrives in the saltwater at the land's edge like corals do at the edge of the surrounding reefs.

On the other side of a thick line of jungle, they came to an accessible area that Ewalt had obviously cleared by hand. His garden's layout was orderly: its boundaries were distinct, and its interior was well weeded and exhibited care and artisanship far and above its basic utility. This was where he spent

---

[93] Crooked-tooth barracuda; genus Sphyraena.

his days, keeping his heavily composted patches of bananas and his prized yams. He had staked thick ropes from the treetops to the ground, and his yam vines climbed skyward into the sunlight, which streamed down in splotches here and there onto their delicate light green leaves.

Ewalt knelt and uncovered the top of one of his large tubers. It was nearly as long as his forearm and wider than his outstretched hand. He stooped over the little hill into which he had planted his prize and looked up at Ḷainjin with pride as bright as the sunlight that splashed onto his sweat-wetted face. In truth, Ḷainjin struggled to return the admiration the poor man's labor deserved. His favorite food was a fruit that grew so large a man had to struggle to carry two, from a tree so hearty it grew right up the shore and didn't need rain because its roots, dangling from its sturdy trunk, sucked water from the air. It took but a sharp stick and a few moments to plant. Its textures and flavors came in a wide variety, cleaned his breath, kept his teeth, and exercised the muscles of his jaw such that he could crunch the skull of a small tuna or turn the hand of an enemy useless with a well-executed snap. True, he had never bit into the slimy head of an eel, but he had no doubts it would succumb to his powerful bite. It became clear in that moment that Wottok had taught Ewalt to speak his language well but had taught him not the life of an outer islander who could sail up to the lagoon shore, twist off a pandanus fruit, and be on his way with nails clean and little or no effort expended.

Once they returned to the house, Ḷainjin — so captivated by Ewalt's parents from his first encounter — settled himself before their fire for the remainder of the evening, as snug as a sand crab in its hole above the line of highest tide.

Wottok began. "The story of Pohnpei began with the construction of a proa by a forefather named Japkini."

Kiton joined in. "Two women, among others, helped him. Lipalikini hewed out the hollow of the hull, and Litorkini plaited the sail and threaded its head, foot, and leech with fibers from outer layers of banana trunks."

"Till this day," continued Wottok, "the various parts of the canoe are named after the people of this first voyage. On their way here, they met an octopus named Litakika in the middle of the ocean. He told them about a submerged reef, where they decided to build an island. It is said they called for stones for the island's base from far places. Then called Katenenior, the barrier reef, and Kaitanik, the mangrove tree, to protect what they had built from the forces of the sea."

No sooner had he paused than Kiton continued. "They named the stones *pei* and everything on top, they dedicated Pohnpei — 'on a stone altar.'"

They told of five more voyages from a place called Kataupaiti in the west. Jauiap, who was the chief of Yap, and Lijariap came on separate voyages. He introduced his kingfisher bird. He also brought many varieties of bananas and instigated the first sakau drinking. Lijariap brought the mangrove crab, which is so highly coveted it instigated much fighting among the early people. Apparently, there were many return voyages and many hundreds of people transported. They navigated by the stars as they rose and set on the horizon. And they, too, recognized the same twelve stars that crossed the sky from east to west and divided the seasons, starting with the selfsame Tūṃur and ending the dry season with Jebrọ, whom they called Muakeriker.

They went on and on, reciting more names than he cared to remember and explaining that their orators pride themselves on telling the stories of each voyage and naming the men and the women who took part and what each accomplished. On the seventh voyage came Oljipa and Oljopa, in a huge vessel with one mast and three sails like the other. These brothers taught them to paddle the stones down the mountain and raft them to construct the great village and tideways on the reef.

According to Kiton, Oljipa died first and Oljopa became the first Saudeleur.

Ḷainjin was proud of himself for having solved the mystery of stone paddling. Used to deciphering the meaning of these legends, he thought that, surely, the first people who'd come here passed on the story of the atoll from whence they came or, at least, passed through. No doubt, it was a place of many reefs but no stone. Later generations forgot that part and attributed the creation of these mysterious mountains to the newcomers preceding them. Whereas in his mind, they should have attributed their discovery — the true achievement — to the great *pali* from the low islands who'd had the courage to set forth and find this place.

Ḷainjin had seen nothing quite like the hillside view of the ocean he shared with Wottok that next morning. He saw with a glance at the proud man's face why he had lingered there for so many seasons. He supposed it took a man from the low islands to appreciate the simple act of viewing the dawn from such a height.

He spent a leisurely morning listening to more stories of Pohnpeian history while sipping shells of hot *nen* before Kiton's open hearth. Outside, the saltless wind rustled the branches about them. The sun rose bright and clear amid the onrush of white, puffy, and energetically evolving clouds as the tide slowly crept upon the reefs until the time was right to retrace the trail back down the hill into the dark green mangrove where Ewalt had tied his canoe. As they paddled toward the village, Ḷainjin tried to memorize the narrow veins of open water that meandered through the dense overgrowth of black, tangled roots and outstretched limbs that twisted toward the sunlight, but his thoughts kept returning to Wottok's story of the island called Papua, where his mother had been eaten. An island so large it took three moons to circumnavigate.

Talupe reciprocates

They arrived at Kelepwei around noon and found that Wisim had detached his enormous matted sail and wrapped it about its two spars, awaiting Ḷainjin's arrival. He motioned for Ḷainjin to do the same with his. Wisim's translator explained to Ewalt that the Saudeleur was holding a feast in their honor and had asked Talupe to provide them with new sails. They were to take their sails across the way to Pahn Kadira for measuring. When Ewalt passed on Wisim's words, he gave Ḷainjin a teasing smirk and a hearty laugh that summarized the elation Ḷainjin felt at that moment. That he would see her was more than enough to put up with the palu's annoying foolery.

He quickly lowered his sail booms, wrapped his sail around them, and, with the assistance of one of the palu's crew, loaded the booms onto the palu's boat. Then they were on their way, paddling across the watercourse. They entered the courtyard, where a crowd of women was waiting for them. It took but a few minutes to stake with twine the outline of the sails into the pebble-covered courtyard grounds. These were the boundaries where the women would sit and complete the work of expanding the square patch of plaited matting they had already begun. The palu knelt for a moment to run his fingers through the hundreds of narrowly cut strips of specially processed pandanus leaf. The women would continue to plait these in crisscross fashion up to the borders of the sails, edge them with banana stalk fibers, and finally tie them to the *rojak* with hefty coconut-fiber twine. Ḷainjin examined the crowd in search of Talupe or anyone else he might recognize who might know her whereabouts until Ewalt informed him that the women were to work under the light of the moon until they finished.

So Ḷainjin left his lonely-looking sail booms, shorn of their friendly, worn sail, and returned with the palu to Kelepwei, where they spent the rest of the day at their favorite pastime of word games. Ewalt sat with them. They started with the names of all the parts of each other's boats and were all surprised at how many of the words were similar or often different in the same way. They told legends that spoke of their ancestors arriving from the west and speculated they might have spoken the same language originally. Maybe even come from the same island. Maybe even shared the same forefathers.

"My ancestor was a fat cannibal," joked the palu.

Ewalt interpreted. "He was too fat to sail, so he sat under the breadfruit tree all day singing navigation songs and eating. He only ate young girls — before they bled while they were still tender. Then one day my grandfather said to him, 'Stop eating all the young girls! They will grow up and give us much pleasure!' So, my ancestor agreed, and now the women are all grown up and they own all the land and they tell us when it's time to rethatch their houses and when we can go fishing and where we can defecate. Now, we spend all our time fashioning pendants for their neck-strings. True, they give us much pleasure, but sometimes I long for the old days!" At this, the group burst into laughter and insisted he sing one of the navigation songs of his ancestor. So, he sang until it was time for Ewalt to paddle ashore. Then they turned to learning the names of each day in the moon's cycle and ended up falling asleep learning the names of the stars that each used in navigation.

When the next day came, Ḷainjin was so smitten he sat most of the morning at a single spot on the wall where he could see the comings and goings through the main entrance of Pahn Kadira. But mysteriously, despite the spectacle he'd made of himself, he saw her not! Ewalt appeared at noon and informed him that the Saudeleur would send them transport to prevent them having to rush off to attend to their boats in the watercourse during the low tide coming that evening. When the feast was over, they could simply saunter back across the mostly dry channel. After what seemed like an eternity to Ḷainjin, long after the sun had reached its zenith, several canoes finally rounded the bend of the tideway between the islets, invited them aboard, and floated them across the watercourse. Had the palu not been watching him like a papa bird, certain to tease, Ḷainjin would have waded rather than wait.

The Saudeleur, a gracious host, welcomed them at the entrance of Pahn Kadira. He stood surrounded by a team of women who adorned them to a man with flower headbands and *ṃarṃar*.[94] Soon thereafter, Talupe made her hasty appearance. She appeared as lovely as she had when they first met. She smiled politely and nodded to Ḷainjin but went to the palu, taking his hand and escorting him to the places laid out for them, immediately to the left of the Saudeleur and his contingent. The palu swung Talupe's hand like a boy dancing down the shoreline and glanced back at Ḷainjin with a broad smirk as though he was the child left behind. Ḷainjin followed, but this didn't make him jealous. The palu was the elder and had certainly saved the day and cut critical time delivering the stones. Ḷainjin was to sit next to him but left a place between them in case she decided to sit next to him. She did not and soon disappeared to fulfill her part in the festivities. This launched him into a snit that the palu sensed and immediately began to prick like a festered pimple.

He began by scooting next to Ḷainjin and draping his arm around his shoulders, but that approach failed when a young woman came with shells of flower-scented coconut oil to anoint the palu. He couldn't resist making himself the center of attention and deployed some of the antics he was famous for, like raising his arms into the air and shaking his tits at her each time the unfortunate woman reached with oily hands toward his chest.

Despite his mood, Ḷainjin couldn't help but break into laughter with the others. Distracted by the palu's antics, he didn't immediately notice the woman who had come and quietly sat back on her calves, knees bent before him. Oiled and fair, her skin blushed red with laughter as she turned from the ridiculous, self-deprecating palu to glance momentarily into his eyes before looking down into the cup of oil she patiently held in her lap. She wore the palu's neck-string. She was the woman chosen to wear it. Her laugh was shy and her smile warm but simultaneously sarcastic as she viewed the palu's ongoing foolery and turned her head modestly away. She caught Ḷainjin's attention such that he began inadvertently watching her reacting

---

[94] Flower leis.

to the jokester next to him. Why hadn't she started to anoint him? Most of the others had finished and turned away from their partners. Still she sat there, shyly giggling, until the palu's partner withdrew and bawdily pretended to flick the back of her fiber skirt in his beaming face.

After all the others had finished and retreated, she began to dab the oil on Ḷainjin's shoulders and rub it over his skin with her forefingers. Her touch was not sensual, as had been the touch of others performing the ceremony, but tender, as though she were handling an egg she feared breaking. Rather than distracting herself with his tattoos, she cast her eyes firmly into his, capturing his gaze as though she might imminently apologize for something she had done or neglected to do. If she felt embarrassed by her low status compared to that of Talupe, who she must know he wanted, she didn't show it. He realized she should have finished long ago. It was as though she longed to be sitting there and anointing him in the most dignified way she was able to and for as long as decorum allowed. Then the palu finally noticed his neck-string. He was about to slap Ḷainjin across the back when she darted a glance at him that threatened instant redress, as though releasing his sheet, leaving him adrift and powerless to proceed. She wouldn't allow an interruption by him or by others in the group who had turned their heads her way. Rather, she performed her duties seriously and, in her own time, turned away and gracefully retreated.

When she had left, the palu turned to Ḷainjin, etched the shape of the neck-string on his chest, and tipped his head in the direction she had gone. Then the palu nodded affirmation before raising his eyebrows and looking about to his crew as if to say, "It's working, only he gave it to the wrong woman!" This he followed with a hearty laugh and, straightening his back, he repeatedly lifted his chin, as if to reiterate his unspoken words: "When will my protégé come to his senses, follow the cultivated palu's advice, and trust in the magic of the neck-string he traded for?"

Next, the women returned with baskets of food for each of the Saudeleur's contingent and then for each of themselves. Midway through their meal, the muffled sound of softly blown conch shells could be heard in the distance. After a brief period during which a procession was perhaps forming on the other side of the temple steps, a line of men stepped forward, each holding a short hardwood fighting spear in the right hand and in the left, a few strands of fibers from the kilt of the man ahead. The muffled sound of the conch shells was continual as the men slowly walked toward them, adding a sense of ceremony to their procession. Behind the first few men who passed came others carrying what turned out to be their newly made sails, which they placed, bundled, before the palu. The procession of men with the short spears passed before them. Each had stuck wildly protruding *kino*[95] into their head leis. Coconut oil slicked their shoulders and chests. Then the women passed, their breasts glistening with oil. Each woman held a few strands of the skirt of the woman preceding her, and each wore her thick, curly hair wrapped atop her head and stuck with two hardwood daggers. The procession of women then traced behind the men, climbed to the third tier of the temple, and stopped behind a temporarily constructed rail atop several tripole supports, each standing on the tier below. The procession of men filled the second tier, the women filled the first, and finally, a fourth row of women sat on mats laid at the edge of the temple's tall steps.

When the procession ended and all was in place, Ļainjin counted twelve participants on each row. The *woo* of the conch shells ceased, and the eldest of the group, who stood in the middle of the top row, addressed the Saudeleur and appeared to recount some voyaging tale from the distant past. The group burst into song as the men rhythmically clacked their spears against the pole before them and swayed their hips and arms as they sang. Next the women, in unison, joined in the singing as they pulled the daggers, one in each hand, from their twisted hair and began clacking them against each other in time with the men. Their twists freely disentangled, and their hair was left to unfurl haphazardly down about them. The singing reminded him of that of his home islands and the clacking, of the *jebwa*. But the sounds he heard were of history and instruction, not battle. The women were a spectacle unto themselves with their shiny oiled breasts, red-flowered head leis, and graceful hand movements, which reminded him of the current-induced wave movements on the surface of the water in the ocean

[95] A fragrant, broadly lobed fern (*Phymatosorus grossus*) often used to spice earth ovens; grows at the base of trees.

passageways. The women sang several songs in exquisite harmony. Then the men began dancing. If only Ewalt had come to interpret all the significance being portrayed.

By midafternoon, the singing and dancing had stopped. Talupe appeared again with attendants, and they passed out food for the performers. That was when she addressed the group, and as far as he understood, explained how the palu and Ḷainjin had helped her deliver the stones. No sooner had the performers eaten than the group sprang into song and dance again. Later that evening, the sakau stones rang out, and the servers began by bringing the first half shell of the dirty, slimy drug to the palu. When the woman wearing Ḷainjin's neck-string returned the second time with his cup, the palu plucked her arm and gently guided her down between them. This broke the decorum of the ceremony but probably appeared to most as just another antic to laugh at. Ḷainjin watched as she looked toward the older woman who had presented the neck-string to her, asking for permission to sit and getting a nod of affirmation.

Neither of the three spoke the language of the other. The woman sat with a half smile, politely looking ahead. The two men sat sipping the sakau from their coconut half shells and listening to the stones ring out. They watched the pounders pile wet, crushed roots onto the strips of hibiscus bark and wring the dirty water repeatedly into the half shells, one after another, to be taken to the guests and others. To alleviate the awkwardness, the palu began to jabber at the woman in a soft, kindly voice, saying funny things that he laughed at. She didn't laugh or pretend she understood, yet she didn't ignore him. She turned a shy smile from one man to the other and then looked forward again with the same pleasant, self-conscious expression on her face. This presented an opportunity for Ḷainjin to glance at her and politely study her features at will. She was longer in stature and bonier than Talupe, her movements less graceful but agile. Her face looked less perfectly shaped. Her nose was sharper, her lips less puffy, and her face gaunter, as though less fed. Her skin was darker and her hair shorter and bushier. Her breasts were pointy and without child. Her eyes were what had attracted him from the start. They sparkled with life. She sat proudly like a bird at the edge of a branch, ready to flutter without notice yet staying as though happy to rest a bit longer in his presence.

As evening approached, Ḷainjin thought about exchanging names with her, but first things first. Feeling awkward but unable to resist the impulse, he asked her, "Where Talupe?"

She responded by jabbering something he didn't understand. Then she pointed with her face and tilted her head toward the other side of the temple.

He pointed to her and then himself and then in the direction that she had indicated. Rising, he looked in the direction of her toothless mentor, whom he had noticed watching them. She seemed to give the young woman a nod of approval. So, she rose, surprisingly took his hand, and began leading him, accompanied by much encouragement from Wisim, who sprang another joke, much to the amusement of his crew. Ḷainjin followed her to the single entrance of a long, thatched house facing the compound of the Saudeleur. The house had been built over a stone platform, and several steps of takai led to the entrance. There, as though by happenstance, emerged Talupe, carrying in each hand a basket filled with rolls of pandanus leaves and sail-making tools. It appeared she was about to take advantage of the remaining tide to depart the islet before dark. As was her habit, she took immediate control of the situation. She spoke in a commanding tone to the young woman wearing his neck-string, who immediately turned her back to them and stood as though guarding the entrance.

The light was dim. A single half-shell lamp filled with oil flickered in the corner just inside the entrance. The long house appeared to be sleeping quarters for the Saudeleur's attendants. There was no lingering smell of smoke, and no sign of a hearth. No cooking fires in the house, and no sound of anyone else about. Her face suddenly turned seductive. She reached out and wrapped the fibers of his kilt slowly around her hand, reeling him toward her. She playfully reached into his kilt for his manhood and touched his hanging parts gently with her fingers, springing him to action. At the same time, she rose on the balls of her feet to kiss him, but when he lowered his mouth to hers, she turned abruptly, took his hand, and led him toward the darker end of the long room. In the dim light, he found furled sleeping mats along each wall and pandanus pouches for personal items behind. The room appeared otherwise empty. Unfurling one of these mats, she sank to her hands and knees and spread the fibers of her skirt to expose her rear to his view. Then she arched her back, puckered her lips, and, looking over her shoulder, beckoned him to join her.

His eyes by now adjusted to the dark, Ḷainjin modestly glanced around to assure himself there was no one about. The woman with the neck-string was still guarding the distant entrance with her back to them. He sank to his knees behind Talupe, raised the remaining fibers of her skirt onto her back, and probed gently for the damp place she was inviting him to enter. He was still scooting himself into position when her fingers found his manhood, and she plunged herself down onto him, forcing him painfully back, thighs on heels, his fingertips bracing himself on the matting until he managed to stretch one foot forward, rest backward on his palms, and tuck the other beneath the outstretched leg. She shifted the weight of her body from one side to the other like a mother bird settling at nest. As he braced himself on his elbows, she sat back on him, relentlessly twitching her hips backward and forward, applying the sort of lubricious pressure that entices a man irresistibly to the point of release. He groaned. Upon which, to his surprise, she slipped her luscious haven from him, pinned his manhood against his leg, and wrung the seed from his body like so much sakau dripping wastefully onto the mat below.

No sooner had Talupe accomplished this than she crawled to his side, stared him in the face, playfully imitated his groan, and swiped the hair above his lip with her finger. Then she explained she wanted Ḷainjin to remain there, intimated she would quickly return by pointing to herself then the exit then back to him, and left him there to wonder where she had to go at such a moment. He listened to the sticky sound of her bare feet retreating on the matted floor and softly inhaled the smell she had left on his lip. He watched her take her baskets and leave without speaking to the silhouette of the woman who had guarded the exit for her. Surprisingly, that silhouette turned and began pacing quickly toward him. He stood and straightened his kilt. She approached, appearing upset and absorbed by the status of the mat they had engaged on. Embarrassed, he watched her bend to her knees and carefully clean it with the fibers of her skirt. Then she rolled it back the way it was as though it were hers. When she turned to face him, her eyes glistened in the dim light from the doorway, and he saw tears on her cheeks. She took his hand firmly again and led him, as if a child, somewhat hesitantly toward the exit.

But Talupe had told him to remain, so he inquired of the woman, "Talupe?"

He understood her to say, "Talupe bad! Come!"

Upon exiting, she took his hand surprisingly more firmly than before and hurriedly, angrily led him to a second entrance on the far side of the islet that opened into the narrow tideway running between Pahn Kadira and the islet to the northeast, nearly to Idedh. As they approached Talupe, she was in the process of loading baskets into the fore hull of a small paddling canoe. She left one basket on the steps of takai and boarded the canoe. She then held her hands out to his companion as though to request that the woman transfer the remaining basket to her. Ḷainjin watched as the woman overcame her anger, humbling herself in the face of insult and injury, and chose to comply with Talupe's request. The woman left him standing there at the entranceway and went forward, grabbing the basket and dipping her skirt into the waterway.

But Ḷainjin's eyes had long since darted to the stern of the canoe. There sat a man with a paddle in his hands, pressing gingerly against its shaft with a leaf-bandaged hand. He was the man Ḷainjin had wrongly attacked at Sokehs rock. Talupe arranged the final basket into the hull and motioned to the man to embark. Then, laughing and speaking to Ḷainjin's companion, she directed a sharp glance at Ḷainjin and muttered the word *kihng* to his companion. She elaborated not as the young man, a telling smirk on his face, quickly backed the canoe from the landing, pivoted into the channel, and paddled deliberately down the watercourse toward Temwen. That smirk was the same one he had given Ḷainjin when he had wheeled the blade of his paddle at him. Apparently, he wasn't the stupid man Ḷainjin had later felt sorry for but perhaps a cunning young competitor who had provoked his attack by purposefully not divulging Talupe's gift basket he had placed within Ḷainjin's hull that fateful day.

Ḷainjin stood stunned as the canoe turned down the cross channel and disappeared. His companion had turned her attention to him.

"What mean '*kihng*'?" he asked her in Pohnpeian.

She looked up at him with sympathy in her eyes and, without a trace of her earlier anger, said, "Bad Talupe!" Then she led him away without attempting an answer. She returned him to his place behind the rolled-up sail that Talupe had rewarded him with and sat down next to him as before. But this time her back was even straighter, and she had a more determined but still blushed appearance. Clearly, she was on a mission.

Ḷainjin decided to ask her name. "Call me Lipanmai."[96] She looked straight ahead as though not wanting to meet the eyes of those around her.

"Who was that with Talupe?" he asked her distractedly, in his language. Then realizing she was unlikely to understand, he mimed by pretending to paddle.

Knowing what Ḷainjin was asking though probably not understanding his words, Lipanmai faced him with both forefingers pointing in the air in front of her. She identified the first finger as Talupe and the second as the man paddling. She pivoted the finger she had used to identify Talupe. "Mother," she said, in her language. She pivoted her other finger and said, "Uncle." Then she crossed her fingers, making an X in the air between mother and uncle.

"They must be cross cousins!" Ḷainjin thought. The young man was perhaps the father of her children. It all fit together now like these takai about them. He understood this type of relationship well. The young man could not afford to be jealous. He, his father, and brothers would be her children's guardians one way or the other even if she took another man. She was the hull, filled with all the wealth and prestige her ambition had achieved. He was her kubaak, to utilize or replace as needed. The only question: Would he share her wealth? He would be a cunning competitor to all, and more successful for his patience. As her children grew among his household, she would become increasingly entwined with him. He held the commonplace advantage of family, culture, and location. It struck him now that he, Ḷainjin, was but a tryst in her otherwise ambitious though conformable life.

He found himself still pondering such things when, after a while, a messenger informed Lipanmai that she was to bring Ḷainjin to the

[96] A Pohnpeian name meaning "woman under the breadfruit tree."

Saudeleur. Again, she grasped onto his hand and towed him over to the Saudeleur's contingent, where she dropped to her knees and tugged him down likewise.

When the Saudeleur spoke, there was a hush in the crowd, and the incessant ringing of the sakau stones abruptly ceased. The chief made a short speech to the crowd and then presented Ḷainjin with a curious-looking mangrove ring. They had taken the large shark tooth he had presented to the Saudeleur before his trip to Sokehs and lashed it securely by fine drilling and strong, narrow cordage to a slot etched into the hardwood. The ring hung from a cord like the pendant of a neck-string, and the Saudeleur demonstrated how the cord wrapped about his wrist to prevent the ring from slipping off the middle finger when cutting.

At the wave of the Saudeleur, the contingent around him separated, giving Ḷainjin and Lipanmai space to sit down next to him. This was an unexpected honor for him, and when he turned to Lipanmai, it was evident from the blush on her face that she was certainly unaccustomed to such a position. He would later learn that her father, like many of the stone workers, had come from Kosrae to earn his fortune as a stone fitter. Her mother, also from upwind Kosrae, had died in childbirth when Lipanmai was a little girl, and her father had died from wounds when crushed by a takai mishandled on a wall. The Saudeleur had offered to take the foreign orphan into his courtyard as an attendant, where she was happy to find a surrogate family and where she demonstrated her Kosraean people's penchant for challenging work and her mother's devotion to feeding the fire of Nahn Sapwe. After a while, if only to make conversation, Ḷainjin turned to Lipanmai and asked her about the meaning of *kihng* again. She didn't respond but instead resumed her embarrassed, forward-facing posture.

The Saudeleur himself interjected. "*Kihng*?"

"Yes, *kihng*," Ḷainjin said.

"*Kihng*," repeated the Saudeleur. Cocking his head back, he went, "Ka-ka-rook! Ka-ka-rook!" and flapped his arms, giving one of the most hilarious imitations of a rooster Ḷainjin had ever seen.

Except he didn't laugh with the others, and Lipanmai, who no doubt now wished she had told him herself, laughed not. It flashed before him that if

Talupe or even her cross cousin had spread the accusation that he copulated like a rooster, it would now seem confirmed to all by the Saudeleur himself! Ḷainjin worried himself about her accusation for the rest of the evening. He sat like a speared and deflated puffer fish, nursing himself from time to time with sips of the mouth-numbing, dirty water. He peered down at the coconut half shell he held onto dispiritedly and recalled each of their two past engagements. Was it not she who had rushed and cut short their intercourse? Had the choice to discard him in favor of her cousin been premeditated? This implausible cause so embarrassing it would allow him no protest?

Lipanmai proved his sole source of relief from such thoughts. She squeezed her strong, bony hand into his and continued to do so even as she walked him to the landing. The palu's crew had already carried Talupe's gift for him in reciprocation — his new sail. Lipanmai stood on the takai steps, watching and acknowledging him. He turned from time to time to see her there as he carefully walked alone across the tide-drained reef of moon-reflecting puddles to his boat, anchored across the way at Kelepwei. There, as he had done so many nights before, he crawled into his hull, wrapped himself in his mat, and shut out the world in deep, comforting slumber until the new day was to arrive.

The legend of Jau Areu

Ḷainjin awakened at the sound of the first rooster. It irritated the *kihng* pang he still felt in his throat. He must show Talupe that he, too, could work to obtain a title! The bright, swelling moon had nearly slid behind the mountains, Tūṃur was high in the eastern sky, and the sun had not yet begun to light the horizon. The tide had risen and begun to ebb. He wanted to be on his way and, due to the tide, knew he must move now or stay till noon.

What was he to do with the new sail bundled onto his outrigger? He went to the meeting house and hoisted the bundle of sail and *rojak* to its rafters. Then he untied his painter, hoisted anchor, and silently backpaddled into the watercourse, as had the young man with the broken hand the evening before. Ḷainjin couldn't dispel the man's smirk from his memory. He craved the isolation of Ewalt's house high up on the hill and remembered his father telling him that the time to catch giant eels was under the moon during the time of spring tide. Did he remember the forks in the passageway through the mangrove to Ewalt's path at the shore?

Ḷainjin paddled slowly down the waterways, where he found a fisher here or there, like himself, making a distracted, last-moment attempt to escape the still-flooded reef in the outgoing tide. Light had come to the sky behind him by the time he reached the mangrove, counted the alternating turns properly, and reached the shore. By then the tide had receded too far, and his footing was too slippery to beach the heavy canoe. So, he decided to immobilize it by securing it on three sides to the mangrove swamp about him. As he climbed up the path, the wind cooled his back, and he turned from time to time to watch the sky, which dawned pink then yellow then blue, again marveling at this new perspective on the world about him. If he had trusted unwisely, behaved rashly, or made other mistakes, he would determine how to adjust course and rectify. He would regain his spirit here, where the air was clean with the smell of life all around and where the wound from that smirk could heal even if never forgotten and impossible to avenge.

When he reached the house, he stopped at the doorway, peered inside, and found the elderly couple sitting in their home before the hearth as though they had not moved since he left them last. They invited him inside and poured him a half shell of hot *nen* tea. He got right to the point.

"I want you to teach me to catch *dāp*."

"*Dāp*!" repeated Kiton, confronting him with the word and, as usual, overarticulating it to emphasize her distaste for the thing.

"Wait, please. I'm not asking him to show me but to teach me."

"Because you don't know him!" she responded emphatically. "He is the Jau Areu.[97] He'll make any excuse to cram his scrawny butt into any hole on the reef big enough to fit through. He's a fisherman and will take a challenge even when too feeble to walk down that hill."

Ļainjin turned from one to the other, looking for a clue. Was she mad at him for bringing it up or proud of the man about whom she was speaking?

"Besides," she added with a grin, "I have such taste for *kihr en eiwel*,[98] I'm ready to grab a pole and go fishing myself!"

She got up and pulled a nearly indistinguishable loop of twine from between the thatch of the house close to the wall. To the old man's surprise, out popped a *rajraj* nearly double the length of her hand. She tossed it onto the mat next to him.

"He's never seen this before! I kept my eye on him and carried that in my basket to cut off his arm if the tide threatened to drown him and that thing wouldn't let him go."

"Oh, yes," Wottok said. "I've seen that many times. I knew you carried it. Why do you think I was so daring?"

"Well, I was ready to cut off head or arm — whichever I thought best at the time!"

---

[97] Pohnpeian title: master fisherman.

[98] Pohnpeian for "red snapper."

It went that way, back and forth between the two of them, until Wottok began his instruction and Kiton commenced her plaiting.

"Everyone knows you lure a *dāp* with a dead fish you hold in your hand along with a stick and then prop its mouth open with the stick to prevent it from biting your arm. If that is so, then why do men — even those who are successful at catching it — end up losing their fingers?"

Ḷainjin guessed. "Because they reflexively pull back their hand when the fish bites?"

"I have no doubt that, many times, that's the case. To jerk back is a natural reaction, but what about the men who are successful at launching the stick and wrestling the monster into their basket? Many suffer serious injuries to their fingers and never try a second time."

"Is it because they don't venture their hand far enough into the throat of the thing?"

"If you push your arm all the way inside, the digestive juice in its stomach will burn the flesh from your finger bones." Wottok laughed gruesomely. "You see men go after these things for the reward without knowing much about them. Just as in Rālik, the *dāp* here are often poisonous, so the people don't eat them. They never cut them up and study them."

"Then what's the secret?" Ḷainjin asked.

"They have two sets of jaws, one inside the other. They have a big pair and a small pair. It's the small set that does all the damage once you're inside. They prop open the big mouth, but then the little one strikes. Fishers are surprised by what seems like a second baby *dāp* attacking from inside."

"But you said you shouldn't stick your hand all the way inside!"

"You don't have to," Wottok said. "The second mouth strikes forward to grab and tear."

"Jeej! What a monster!"

Kiton prodded Wottok. "Show him your hands!"

The old man held out his hands palm down, but his fingers were all there and relatively unscarred.

Ḷainjin was impressed. "So, what's the solution?"

"Most men try a stick that's too long. You use a smaller stick, and you prop open the little mouth!"

“Then what about the big one?”

Wottok glanced over to Kiton, who was busy plaiting. “She came up with the answer for that.”

She held up what she was plaiting. It reminded Ḷainjin of the material they had plaited to make his new sail, only thicker. She draped the patch, rectangular so far, around his arm to show how it would protect him from the top of his hand to his elbow. “The big teeth will get through and scratch you, but the matting protects and allows you to slip your arm out when you have to.”

“What if the big mouth clamps down, and the thing swims back into its hole dragging your arm?” Ḷainjin shuddered. “I’ve heard they can entwine their tails into their holes under the reef and refuse to come out.”

“I used to hear that too,” Wottok said. “It’s a woman’s tale — not true. The *dāp* can’t use its tail to hook itself into the reef. It uses it to swim backward. When we catch them on a hook and can’t bring them to the surface, it’s because they’re strong and can swim backward like a lobster. But it can’t drag you with it. The big mouth cannot clamp down on your arm with a stick stuck in its inner jaws. I don’t think it can because that thing has to contract when it closes its mouth, and trust me, it does not want to close its mouth.”

“Why not?”

“Because it’s gasping for air,” Wottok said. “It breathes water through its mouth, but now it has a fish, a fist, a stick, and a pandanus mat in there, and it starts to panic just like you would. And that’s when you guide it into your basket, release your hand, and pull the string tied to the stick in its throat. That makes it very, very relieved for an instant. Then it tries to slither and push its way out of the pouch, and it’s very strong, so you have to sew the pouch tight very quickly and tie it to your boat.”

Ḷainjin knew that a fish had to breathe water and that a shark had to keep moving or it would suffocate, so all this had the sound of truth to it. “Why the boat? I thought you did this at low tide.”

“Yes, but you still need your boat. You put the *dāp* in the basket, tie it to the boat, and leave it in the ocean. It’s a fish, not a turtle. It’ll die if you take it out of the water for long.”

"When do we get started?"

"Tonight!" Kiton turned to Wottok. "Don't think I'm staying here while you go out and get drowned!" Then she spoke to Ḷainjin. "Catch another fish — too exhausting at my age." Grabbing Wottok's arm, she said, "Better to hold tight to one I've caught!" Finally, she cautioned Ḷainjin not to tell Ewalt: "Too protective!"

After Kiton completed her plaiting that afternoon, the couple took a long nap, as did Ḷainjin. Earlier, Wottok had disclosed the area he intended to fish, and since it was near Uerik's village, Ḷainjin suggested they wait there for the moon to approach its apex and drain the reefs dry. He wanted to visit his bird. He also wanted to close their discussion concerning the takai. He still felt bad he had not accepted Uerik's description about paddling them down the mountain. When Ewalt heard about the fishing trip — without mention of eel hunting — he cut a stalk of bananas for Ḷainjin to take as a gift to Uerik.

Later, the swelling moon was high in the sky and still rising through the blue background behind the crowded clusters of white wind clouds floating toward them as they carried their fishing poles and baskets down the hillside to the mangrove-covered shoreline and to Ḷainjin's proa. As instructed, he paddled the waterways throughout the swamp and, upon entering the open reef behind the village, they raised his sail. They sailed down the wide canals just as the sun began to set behind the mountains and the sakau stones began to ring out.

Right off, Ḷainjin saw that this trip would be an adventure for Kiton. He had neglected to have her bring a mat to protect herself from the sea spray and the wind, and she refused to cover herself with his sleeping mat. She had obviously never glided across the reef at such speeds. Yet she seemed to be enjoying the experience. With her hands clasping each side of the outrigger platform, she hunkered down, dauntless as a shore crab on the rocks despite the dimpled skin on her breasts and arms.

They arrived at the beach below Uerik's village at dusk. Wottok suggested that the tide was already too low for Ḷainjin's plan to visit, but he wanted to get the stalk of the bananas out of their way. Sakau stones were ringing out as he delivered them, and it was good to see his friend's warm, welcoming smile. He excused himself to go fishing and promised to return with the incoming tide.

When they reached the pathway on the reef leading to the long and narrow lagoon ahead, the outgoing tide had reached the point where, out of caution, they decided to lower the sail and paddle. Once they had crossed the reef and reached the lagoon, they raised sail again and headed north. Their plan was to sail north as the tide continued to retreat and then check each of Wottok's favorite reef holes on their way back. When Wottok deemed the tide right, he directed Ḷainjin toward their first fishing pool to windward on the barrier reef, and they beached the canoe at the edge of the stony reef flat. Ḷainjin unsecured their three somewhat short mangrove fishing poles. Wottok sprang upon a reef crab too slow to escape his agile grasp. He tore off a shoulder and gave it to Kiton. She baited her shell hook, walked her tender feet carefully to the near side of the pool, and tried her luck. A red snapper immediately seized her bait, and the fishing portion of their little adventure began.

These were the big-eyed night fish that rose from their daylight slumber and nibbled not! They seized their baits with rapacious anger that such tidbits would barely whet their appetites amid their moonlit scramble to feed themselves. Ḷainjin felt good being back in his element again. Likewise for the old man, apparently, who laughed in competition with his mate. Her eyes shone happy, excited, and bright — as though the sea had revived her spirit and the wind had whisked seasons from her silver, wind-blown locks. The sounds of Tūṃur's buñtokrear swells thundered and swished across the reef as the cycle sucked the remaining tide slowly back into the ocean, and more and more of the reef gradually emerged about them. They moved from barrier reef to fringing reef on either side of the long, narrow lagoon that separated them, pulling tens of fish from each hole until the moon rose toward its apex and the tide reached its lowest extreme.

"Time to get serious," announced the old man. His expression was determined yet somewhat anxious. They returned their fishing baskets to the canoe and paddled a short distance to a spot along the barrier reef side of the lagoon, where Wottok began explaining the relationship between the tides and the eels. "When the water drains from the reef, the fish trapped in the smaller pools have already been attacked and eaten by the eels we're looking for. If the pool is their home, it's likely they have returned to their lairs. And they'll wait there until the tide returns to bring them fresh prey. Their appetites are enormous. Their eyes are small and cloudy. They strike by scent not by sight. They're unlikely to go for your foot or your leg or arm. They're attracted only to the fish in your hand."

Ḷainjin put his right hand into the matted protection device Kiton had plaited for him. It protected the top of his hand and covered his wrist and the circumference of his arm. It looped around his thumb but was open at the fingers.

"Hopefully, it strikes from within its hole. If so, keep him there if you can. Its lair prevents it from writhing and twisting about. Remember, the longer your hand remains in its mouth, the more the eel longs to breath. Pin it to its lair until it becomes desperate to escape. Make your basket seem like a new refuge where it looks like it could breathe. Once it's in the basket, you begin slowly withdrawing your hand. Its mouth may be open, but its teeth are long and sharp, and they all point toward its stomach."

Wottok had a surprisingly small mangrove stick with a line tied through a drilled hole toward one end. He threaded it inside the sleeve of Ḷainjin's pandanus armor, which extended halfway to his elbow and out to his fingers. Then he took a small fish from one of the baskets and slid it headfirst into the sleeve, with its tail extending into the palm of his hand. Now that he was ready, Wottok walked Ḷainjin over to a small, cramped pool and motioned for him to slide in. The corals at the edge were sharp, and he had to slide over them as Wottok cautioned him not to jump. He looked up and saw Kiton silhouetted by the moon above her. She handed Wottok the large, finely plaited eel pouch, which blew like a sail in the wind as he passed it down. Ḷainjin hung its strap over his head and treaded water, waiting for Wottok's final instruction.

"Ḷainjin, before you continue, you must ask yourself this question. First, are you a man with a plan, yes or no? Second, are you the type of man to stick to your plan once you begin to battle?"

Ḷainjin nodded and began to work his way around the pool as Wottok followed and continued his instruction. "Keep your hand close to the coral at all times. Stick it into any hole you find. When it strikes, keep your head out of the water. It will swim backward to drag you down, but you are stronger."

When they had circled the pool with no response, Wottok motioned for him to crawl out, and they moved on in like fashion from one pool to another. They tested some on the island's fringing reef and others on the barrier reef side of the narrowing lagoon between. Finally, within the ninth pool, he caught a strike. His first impulse was to pull his hand free. The next instant, when he sensed the strength of his opponent, he wished he were back by the hearth listening to stories about it. But remembering Wottok's instructions, he concentrated on his plan. The plan, he knew, was what would save his arm. In hindsight, it was Wottok who saved him. He flopped down in the shallow water on the reef at the edge of the pool as he would before Kiton's hearth and instructed Ḷainjin calmly through the nightmare, repeating the same instructions he had before.

"Turn your fist upright! Do you feel the teeth of its inner mouth? Hold your position! Do not give it downward momentum! Don't worry. You've already won the battle! It can' breathe! You're slowly smothering it. It does not want you! It thought it was going to bite a fish, and now it knows it made a mistake! Get your basket ready! Here, give me one end."

The thing, though still lively, finally tired. It stopped trying to swim backward and emerged into the pool. Then Ḷainjin could guide it as it clung haplessly to his arm, powerless to spit it out. When he finally had it inside the pouch, he raised it to Wottok, who quickly sewed it partially closed with coconut-leaf midrib. Then he stood, Kiton now securing him at the waist, and hoisted the basket halfway onto the reef.

"Let it go now! Release your fingers from the stick! Keep your hand vertical if you can, or you risk slicing your wrist veins with its teeth! They're too sharp to feel. Slide your arm very, very slowly now. Leave the arm sheath in its mouth! He'll wriggle it out later!"

As directed, Ḷainjin slowly slid his arm through the tough pandanus matting stuck in the eel's backward-facing teeth and removed his hand from the mouth that no longer wanted it.

Wottok continued. "Pull the string with a gentle jerk. Gently now, don't snap the line!"

Ḷainjin felt the stick give way and knew the line hadn't snapped because the eel's mouth closed on the stick and would not open.

"He'll spit it out later," said Wottok, standing triumphantly and trying to shake Kiton away from behind him. But she giggled like a girl and clung to him even more, as though he were a little brother needing to be protected from the slimy eel in the basket. Then they all laughed with her as she twisted Wottok back and forth from behind as though he were a *dāp* she was wrestling, and they were all relieved that Ḷainjin had survived his ordeal and had successfully trapped his prize. Kiton stopped her merrymaking to help Wottok sew the mouth of the deep, pouch-like basket, still partially submerged in the pool.

As Ḷainjin crawled out of the pond onto the reef, it became clear his arm was bleeding from several cuts. Soon thereafter, Kiton sat down next to him and began scrubbing the cuts and the slime from his arm with the fibers of her skirt and the clear, salty reef water. The slime was poisonous, she informed him. The long, speckled fish lay curled and safe in its pouch, no doubt relieved it could force water through its gills again. Yet he wondered, was it still trying to free itself of the alien matter in its mouth?

Later, the majestic beast rested in its new lair, hanging in the swampy water at the edge of the shore where Ḷainjin had reunited with Uerik. He begged Uerik's forgiveness and helped him build a large fire high up on the little strip of beach bordered by mangrove on either side. As the fire smoked and then blazed beneath the small, palm-sized stones they had piled on it, Ḷainjin went to feed his sleepy bird. The moon was high in the sky, and the Chief awakened easily in the bright moonlight. He did not, of course, acknowledge his old friend. He held his head high, undoubtedly maintaining his regal posture toward all who came to feed him despite the inconvenient line ingloriously tied to his leg and secured to the branch on which he sat. Though his appetite was short, perhaps for all the feeding, he appeared in good health. His foot had chafed not from his snare. Ḷainjin left confident he was in good health and filled to the brim with his usual self-interest.

He joined the group of men and women below, who had assembled on the sand to windward of the blazing fire. He flopped next to Wottok, whom he intended recruiting to interpret as much of the chatter about him as possible. All had gazed at the size of the eel curled in its pouch and shared comments on his bravery and posed questions about the evening's enterprise, though Wottok coyly omitted the secret parts about the stick and the protective device. Ḷainjin told the story of his trip to Sokehs rock, how he had seen six men paddling the takai down the mountain path, his trip back, and how the palu had saved the day. Later, each cooked their own fish on the hot stones amid the glowing coals beneath and between. They squinted at each other through the white, savory smoke rising and swirling in their faces from the hiss of fat spit from the roasting fish.

As the group began eating, their host began to speak. Uerik decided to tell the story of Jau Areu, the title the previous Saudeleur had bestowed upon Wottok. As he spoke, he held onto a pair of cooking tongs that he used here and there to manage the fire around which they sat. Here, he would adjust a hot stone to cover the bright red coals flaming in the streaming wind. There, he would grab onto a fish and flip it from one side to the other on the smoldering firestones as he explained that Jau Areu was the first master fisher. He was an expert at fishing with traps, and every day before he went to his traps, he asked his son to prepare a ground oven to cook the starch half of their daily meal.

As he told his tale, greedy fingers snatched at the cooking fish above the glowing coals until the tails cooked off. Then everyone inserted eating sticks into their fishes' charred, yawning mouths and held their stiff bodies to cool in the constant wind that breezed over the tops of the mangrove trees from seaward.

"One day, an evil spirit had gotten to Jau Areu's traps first and had transformed itself into an eel. The eel escaped the trap, turned tide on the man, and ate him, but it wanted the son too, so this was its plan. It would turn itself into the father that it just ate and deliver some of the guts left over from its meal and give them to the son to cook. Now the boy did not realize that an evil spirit had eaten his father and that it was, in fact, that evil spirit standing before him. So, the boy complied and covered the viscera in the ground oven. The spirit lay down to wait in the feast house, but it kept calling out to the boy—"

"Are they cooked yet?" interjected one of those around the fire who knew the story well. He was busying himself scraping away the large, thick scales from the chewy, tasty red skin of the big-eyed fish. He peeled back the half-cooked flesh from the bones with his teeth.

One after another of the small group of seven sitting before Uerik's fire chimed in. "Are they cooked yet?"

Uerik raised and inspected his tongs in the moonlight. Then he continued his story. "The boy uncovered the oven and turned the viscera with his cooking tongs, but the tongs spoke out to him and said, 'Surely, these are not the guts of a fish, and surely, that isn't your father calling from the feast house.'" As he spoke this last part, he snapped the tongs repeatedly at them as though to chastise them for thinking that such a commonplace tool could not inform them.

"That's when the boy responded back—"

"Not yet!" called out one of the women crowded by the fire. She laughed and juggled one of the fish from the fire, then flopped it onto a piece of banana leaf.

"Then the boy ran for his life, and after a while, the evil spirit called again. 'Are they cooked yet?' When the evil spirit heard no reply, it rushed to the oven, but no one was there. Greedy as it was, it stopped to eat the cooked organs, which was lucky for the boy because it gave him a head start. Later, the evil spirit had to sniff the paths to see which one he took, and that's when it had to turn back into an eel to accomplish this. The tenacious eel soon discovered the correct path and followed the boy blindly all the way up into the mountains by the river Letau. This is where the boy tricked the eel into entering the fresh water, where it could not breathe and where the current was strong and rushed it back down the mountain gasping for air. The only way it found to survive was to crawl between two mature coconuts it found tied together in a place called Poroj. To this day, we say 'tied coconuts of Poroj.' Meaning a man can float a long way by tying a pair of coconuts under each arm. The eel floated down into the ocean and across the sea to a place called Pontip, but he was homesick for the piece of land called Areu on Pohnpei, so they called that place 'Areu in Ant.'[99] And from that point on, the eel could no longer chase people on land but had to live on reefs or in pools of water by the sea."

---

[99] Ant is a coral atoll seven miles east of what is now called Pohnpei.

One of the men around the fire summed up. “And that is why Wottok’s title is so fitting, because he is a man from the low islands who wrestles the evil spirits of the reef.”

“But be careful,” advised another, speaking to Ḷainjin. “If the Saudeleur starts calling you Jau Areu, you’ll have to take a woman from Pohnpei like Kiton, whose grip you won’t be able to shake, and she’ll follow you up into the mountain as well as down onto the reef!”

At this, all laughed at Kiton’s expense. She blushed red in the moonlight as she accepted the man’s chide as a trinket she would gladly trade to see her Jau Areu safe.

Yes, that was but the first of what would be many adventures Ḷainjin would share with the fisher couple from one cycle of the full moon to the next. Their excited, firm voices cut through the sounds of the wind and reef— echoing through the water clogging his ears, always calmly instructing, teaching, and encouraging him on. He recalled the beauty of it all. The dark, mysterious mountains to the west— the swells curling in procession along the barrier reef to the east — the calm, deep lagoon, narrow and coral-encrusted, in between them. He recalled the caw of the kingfisher as it sat high in the mangrove swamp, peering down into the water and ready to dive like a stone thrown down onto its prey — the thrill in the moment of strike by the eel that became so intoxicating and the fortune and title granted by the grateful Saudeleur so captivating.

The Seekers

While Ḷainjin busied himself catching eels and delivering them to the Saudeleur's pool on Darong, his friend the palu occupied himself just as lucratively by delivering additional takai. The palu refused to accept any of the titles offered in exchange. He wanted only items of trade, and his stores at Kariahn began to grow remarkably. One moon cycled into another and then another, and all the while, *añōneañ* visibly shifted as the sun rose and set slightly more to the north with each passing day. Tūṃur began to tire, blow less forcefully, and the low wind clouds began to rise into the upper sky where only the *ak*,[100] like the Chief, could fly. Here and there, rain clouds began to appear and drift their slanted rain across the horizon. The salt in the air began to dissipate and the whitecaps to disappear, and the huge rollers from the east became less cresting, bluer, and less gray as they tumbled and frothed upon the fringing reef.

One day, a canoe nearly as large as the palu's arrived from Satawan. Apparently, the palu's woman, having long ago anticipated his return, had sent a rescue craft upwind to find out what had happened to him. Of course, as fate would have it, she didn't realize the peremptory weight this decision would have on the palu's own judgment as the story of his and Ḷainjin's simultaneous adventures continued to unfold and intertwine like double strands of coconut-husk fibers twisted into one destiny. After providing the crew ample days to rest, the palu sent them on a return voyage, fully provisioned, with two members of his current

[100] The frigate bird; *Fregata magnificens.*

crew and loaded down with the entirety of his earnings as well as a considerable additional payment received for takai he had now unwisely committed himself to deliver. In his throat, he had done the right thing and provided support to the families on his home island. In retrospect, he had left himself shorthanded — with no wealth and with commitments that might be difficult to meet, given the changes in the season already under way.

Then the dawn of the awaited-for day arrived. Ļainjin was sitting with Wottok and Kiton before their hearth, learning Pohnpeian and rehearing stories of days gone by, when they began to hear the muffled alarm of conch shells sounding from the walls of the stone village far below. From a spot just outside his door, with one hand outstretched to block the glare of the rising sun, Wottok pointed to yellow flecks on the sea before the horizon.

"There they are. Do you see them?"

"Are they sails?"

"Those are your Seekers. Your wait is over. Count the sails."

"Four!"

"Exactly!"

Ļainjin gathered his things and was off before Kiton could offer him his morning meal. The last thing he could hear her say as he began his descent down the pathway to the swamp was, "Don't drink so much you drown yourself."

"Why would she say that?" he thought as he big stepped, nearly leaping from one root-edged landing to the next on his way down the path. His decline reminded him of his rush to the shore below the rock of Sokehs moon cycles earlier, when he had looked out to find his proa missing and plummeted down that path to find it. He hoped this descent would lead him to a more gratifying end. If the Seekers could complete the ending of his mother's story, surely that would fill the hole she had left inside. He had thought much about how he would question them, and it was important he got to them before the news of who he was did. He wanted the raw, unsympathetic tale of what had happened. Ideally, he would catch at least one of them even before they got to shore. He arrived at his boat just as the heat of the day, the sweat of his rapid plunge, and the torpor of the mangrove swamp met to stifle his way through the seemingly endless morass that separated him from his objective. He cursed the tangled thicket as he paddled, twisted, and turned along the waterway, now well memorized but none the easier to traverse.

Drenched in sweat from head to foot, he finally emerged into the pleasant breeze, raised his sail in the fresh, cool air, and headed toward Kariahn and the narrow opening into the lagoon that he knew he would find there. However, he had not counted on the numbers of canoes that would be attempting to exit all at the same time. It became obvious that every canoe in the village wanted out into the ocean to engage in some sort of mission. He changed plan and sailed southwest along the seawall as he had so many times before. The tide wouldn't reach its full height until noon, but he judged it would be safe to cut back across the reef to the lagoon passage. There, he found it filled with men in canoes paddling aggressively into the oncoming swells — smooth, rolling, and deep blue. He glided past one and then another of the two-man craft racing toward the yellow sails barely visible on the horizon. A veritable procession of craft bobbed its way across the glossy crests of the swells pointing in the exact direction he intended to sail.

Then, from one of the craft ahead, came cries for help. Two men had put aside their paddles and were holding high bunches of netted coconut-water shells. The first thought that came to mind was from the story of Lōktañūr, when Tūṃur tells his mother to go along with one of his brothers. Why would he want to slow himself down with all that heavy water? But then it came to him — they may be dying of thirst out there! Bringing water to them, and perhaps getting there first, might be the perfect introduction for his questioning. Why hadn't he thought of all this and had his water-shells ready? He must take the time to alter course and, with the luck of Jebrọ, advantage himself. He approached their craft, released his sheet, and drifted, giving them time to maneuver their craft port to starboard, outriggers on opposite sides, his sail flapping in the breeze across their hull. Ḷainjin glanced at the water-shells they held up and was surprised to see some of them secreting putrid-looking white foam from their mouths.

He expected the men to offer him one of the several bunches, but one braced himself instead, looking at him as though asking permission to board his craft. That had not been part of Ḷainjin's plan! What to do?

Ḷainjin reached below for his trolling line with lure and offered it to the man as a trade.

No, motioned the man. "*Tuba*,"[101] he said, raising one bunch of shell containers.

Tuba was the Pohnpeian word for fermented *jekaro*. Why were they taking *tuba* to these people they called Seekers? Now Ḷainjin realized these men would normally accept such a trade as though it were a great windfall. Surely, out here, they weren't afraid of the Saudeleur or his counters and surely, such a trade would be exempt. He could run all that through Ewalt and make everything right, but as he considered the man's face, he sensed that something other than a simple trade was at stake. He remembered the luck of Jebrọ and the words of Kiton as he'd left the mountainside. "Don't drink so much…"

Ḷainjin motioned for the man to come aboard, and once they had loaded the entirety of the shell containers, he sheeted in and they were off. His companion beamed a grin of humble gratitude for the lift and offered Ḷainjin one of the shells. He accepted it, raised it to his nose, and sniffed the putrid foam bubbling out the small round mouth of the shell. It was obviously not ready to drink. He gave it back with a questioning look on his face.

His companion responded by miming that the shells were for the Seekers, who would drink them all with much gusto.

"Strange," thought Ḷainjin, but the better for his plan. He would take his answers drunk or sober, and once drunk, they were all the less likely to grasp who he might be and alter the answers accordingly.

They called it *jemañūñ*[102] back on Namorik. Ḷainjin remembered bouts of drunkenness that had broken from time to time among certain men, but Rālik women would not tolerate their men drunk and would soon entice the elders to squash any outbreak. They viewed drinking more as a sickness and

[101] Carolinian for "jekaro."
[102] Fermented jekaro; tuba.

not a legitimate form of celebration. His companion wasn't drinking and only seemed interested in getting the substance out to the Seekers before the others. He seemed to gloat increasingly as they tacked back and forth and, like Jebrọ, passed each of the canoes ahead.

The four Rālik proas, under full downwind sail, appeared to have formed a line, sailing ten or so ñeñe apart. But they were barely making way toward them due to the drag of the kājokwā they towed. It was an enormous tree trunk, its girth a man wide. Ḷainjin judged that, under a slightly lesser wind, they could no longer hold sail and would have to paddle. Given the imminent change in the season, they had timed their return perfectly. As he approached them, he avoided their course, intending to come about upwind of the northernmost craft. Its occupant stood at the stern and waved good-humoredly to acknowledge their presence. A worn and scanty kilt covered his lower half, and he wore a tent of plaited pandanus leaves tied at the neck to protect his shoulders from the sun. A sun-dried band of coconut leaflets draped around his forehead partially shaded his face and cut the ocean's glare.

When Ḷainjin's companion held up his bunch of netted shells, the reaction was immediate. The man appeared to unsecure his towline. He sheeted in and turned his boat into the wind. He quickly shunted, lowered the sail, and fetched his excess towline from below. Then he jumped to the bow and began hauling his boat against the wind to fifteen or so ñeñe from the kājokwā even as the others attempted to sail on, keeping it in tow. The added strain clearly slowed the progress of the other boats, which eventually succumbed to the elements and followed suit, one by one.

To Ḷainjin's surprise, once the Seeker had closed — dangerously next to the kājokwā as it rose and fell with the swells — he managed to coil his towline and heave it haphazardly over the root end of the trunk, as if to announce his part completed. Then, returning to his stern, he repeatedly dug deep with his paddle until clear of the whale-like menace now slowly turning broadside to the smooth oncoming swells and motioned for Ḷainjin to approach. He had likewise lowered his sail, but two Rālik canoes, each with outstretched sail booms, must approach each other very carefully in order to avoid damage. Ḷainjin decided to kiss him bow to stern. The Seeker interpreted the meaning of his movements and backpaddled at his stern accordingly.

As Ḷainjin closed on him, the Seeker good-naturedly began to praise his boat. A skinny man with sun-baked skin, his hair was thinning and his eyes kind and knowing.

"*Ejelok eṃṃan in wane,*"[103] the Seeker said, praising the boat beneath him as though it existed separate from either of them and belonged to neither. Of course, that was an impossibility in their language, where a boat, like a pet, demonstrates obvious possession. He spoke as though he wasn't sure Ḷainjin knew what he was saying.

"*Ebar ṃṃan wa ne wam,*"[104] responded Ḷainjin, revealing that he not only knew his language but spoke it fluently.

"Look at that jaw. He's a pandanus eater." Laughing, the Seeker spoke in Kajin Rālik. He stared at Ḷainjin's eyes, then ran his fingers and thumb over the evenly cropped stubble covering his own jaws to emphasize that they shared the same physical characteristic he should have recognized at a distance.

"*Riia*?"[105] The man's eyes were captivating and of many seasons — calm, friendly, and curious, yet physically tired and somewhat droopy.

"Namorik," responded Ḷainjin.

"I am from Epoon. I could be your uncle. What is your mother's name?"

"That was it," thought Ḷainjin, disgusted with himself. "Two statements to get myself trapped and turned turtle?" Not wanting to reveal who his mother was, he stared down into the water in a panic just as a fish jutted by. He pointed at it, and his new acquaintance twisted his neck from left to right and back again as though surveying the entire area.

The Seeker laughed. "Fish everywhere! Many sharks! It has been like this from the first day we tied on. They think the kājokwā is their mother," he joked, then added sympathetically, "Wherever we drag it, they just swim along like children."

Clearly, he was the kind of man others enjoyed talking with. Clever and amusing, though not sarcastic. Ḷainjin would learn later that he liked to cleverly turn most of his words into a joke.

---

[103] Literally, "there is nothing good about that boat!" An idiomatic way to highly praise the obvious.

[104] "It is also good, that boat beneath you."

[105] "Bones from where?"

His Pohnpeian companion, meanwhile, had scooted his way to the bow with both bunches of the netted shells in his left hand. Ḷainjin expected he was about to hand them, bunch by bunch, to the Seeker, who had carefully maneuvered the starboard point of his stern next to port of Ḷainjin's pointy bow. To Ḷainjin's surprise, though, the man rose just as the smooth crest of the oncoming swell was passing. He then leapt, unseamanlike and without requesting permission — but with an air of familiarity and much to his risk — headlong onto the stern deck of the other. Landing on one leg, he collapsed against the Seeker, the other leg dangling over the side and his bunches of netted shells haphazardly suspended between the two of them. Unfazed and apparently not surprised, as though accepting an inept child on his craft, the Seeker seemed more interested in determining which of the shells he would imbibe from first than in untangling himself or boarding the man's leg from the swirling, shark-infested waters beneath them.

Clearly, the Seeker was no longer expecting an immediate answer to his question about Ḷainjin's mother, as he was unstopping the plug of dried coconut husk from the mouth of one shell and then another to find the taste he was looking for.

"Ahh," he exclaimed finally, having drifted away somewhat and having found one that tasted the way he wanted. "I learned long ago never to drink this stuff as it foams." Shell in hand, he expanded his arms to imitate a bloated stomach and formed such a silly look on his face that Ḷainjin couldn't help but laugh. "It will give you that dead-fish look," he exclaimed, expanding his free hand outward from his lank belly amusingly.

He talked with his hands, as would a man used to speaking in fragments in other languages and miming the remainder. He pointed with his eyes at his new crew member and repeatedly nodded his head knowingly like a happy bird. "He didn't offer you any did he?"

Ḷainjin wheezed in affirmation as he smiled and looked at the man still struggling to get himself situated on the other's craft.

"It's his way. He brought these for me." The Seeker explained as though apologizing for the man. "Of course, he knows nobody trades as charitably as I do, and he's very loyal to me. After towing a thing like this for so many days at sea, I'd give my ear to a cannibal to chew on if he brought good *tuba* — and he knows it! He always brings the best. It's just not always ripe because who knows when we'll arrive?"

Ḷainjin was about to question the Seeker on the topic of cannibals when he continued insistently.

"Here, come forward, take one — take two. The fun is about to start. Wait until they get drunk and start falling into the water. The fat ones trying to lift themselves back into their boats are hysterical. Every season, one of them ends up swamping his boat trying to scramble from the water. The best thing from all this is that every fisherman will bring a share of his catch to Kelepwei. You'll hear many stories before this thing gets ashore."

Ḷainjin refused the shells as politely as possible. He did not like the taste of jemañūñ and hadn't developed the habit of inebriation.

"You should float out here for a while and watch things get crazy. I'm heading ashore myself. My daughter will draw a bath for me. I'm going to drink the rest of these on the way and sleep for three days!" He began to shunt. "You're staying at Kelepwei, are you not?"

"Yes!" Ḷainjin shouted back as their boats drifted farther apart.

"Okay, I'll find you there, and we will drink sakau together and tell stories under the stars to come. That is, if you can spare time from those Pohnpeian beauties," he said, laughing again. "Protect your life until we meet again." A moment later, he billowed his sail and glided off, like a cloud against the horizon on a light breeze, to complete his long-suffering voyage. His elbow periodically tilted outward as he guzzled the jemañūñ that Ḷainjin hadn't even known the villagers produced.

Ḷainjin had been observing the next two Seekers, who had each acknowledged their companion's departure with a nod and were now, on each canoe, simultaneously hauling and coiling their even longer towlines with corresponding movements. The towlines weren't of the same length. The two on the outsides were shorter, and these two in the middle were longer, affording their craft sufficient lateral spread from their tow.

Of course, the first thing he noticed about the younger two was their unusually long, slender bodies, which — unlike the older two of the group — were untattooed. From this, he surmised they must have left Rālik as children and never returned. Perhaps they were ri-Rālik[106] in origin only. Their culture and language might even be more Pohnpeian. Their features were handsome and nearly identical. Their long, black hair was tied in similar buns, and their burnished, muscular arms, torsos, and legs were of equal amber complexion. They grappled with the heavy lines and hauled their two canoes on a rising and falling course toward the kājokwā amid the rolling, glistening swells sweeping the surrounding seascape. Their features were almost the same except that one was a woman and the other a man.

"They look identical," he mused. "Except one has plump, unmothered breasts!" The male lacked hair on his face. He paddled close enough to see their kindred eyes and faces. Their smiles were proud but warm as they, in turn, stole fleeting glances at him and his canoe.

"*Iọkwe*!" Ḷainjin declared, making them aware, if they hadn't already guessed by the shape of his boat, that he was a fellow islander.

The eldest of the three Seekers, whose towline on the far side had been shortest and who had draped his line over the kājokwā in similar fashion, was the first to respond. "*Iọkwe*," he shouted back enthusiastically.

"*Iọkwe*," responded the other two simultaneously. The two remaining towlines separated Ḷainjin from the elder. He was obviously the *rijeḷā*[107] of the group, and the one most likely to know the details of his mother's story.

"Planning to fish?" The elder motioned to the first of the paddling canoes rapidly approaching and displaying its coconut shells filled with jemañūñ. It had by now dawned on Ḷainjin that fishing the kājokwā and not just towing it must be one of the reasons so many were heading toward them.

"No," Ḷainjin shouted, holding back the questions he wanted to ask and waiting for the Seeker's craft to close the distance. The light wind against his furled but still outstretched sail expedited the Seeker's progress as he paddled off wind toward Ḷainjin and swung his craft back into the wind to drift beside him and face the kājokwā he'd just left behind.

---

[106] Bones of Rālik, the western chain of what is now the Republic of the Marshall Islands.

[107] Literally, "bones that know"; navigator; captain; pali; palu.

"Coming toward you," responded the man, standing at the yoke of his canoe and pointing down into the water. Ḷainjin stared down into the water, which was turning bluer as the sun continued its path above. Tens of silver bonito raced through the water beneath them.

"You're right! That makes me want to lower a line."

"They'll still be there tomorrow and the next day. This one really attracts them." The man took hold of his halyard as though preparing to raise his sail again. "The Saudeleur gave us size requirements for this one. Wouldn't you guess? The only right-sized one has roots! I hate roots. Takes too long to drag." He looked eastward through the light breeze toward the endless expanse of ocean they had arduously crossed as though he had just remembered he'd left something or someone behind.

Ḷainjin remembered how alone he had felt on his passage and shared the feeling that that time, that experience, was eternally out there waiting for him to return.

"How do you find those things?" He pointed with his nose toward the kājokwā they were ever so slowly drifting away from. He wanted to keep the conversation going before the other man left.

"Well, you can see there are four of us. When we spread out, we cover a good swath of ocean. We head for the middle of the kāleptak stream, where the countercurrent is strongest, and then tack our way westward against the current until we find something. We focus our eyes mostly on each other. We have ways of signaling when one of us spots something."

Ḷainjin laughed. "Sort of like catching lobsters at the edge of the reef flat just as the incoming tide delivers them."

"Exactly!" Then the man changed the subject. "How long are those *rojak*?"

Ḷainjin dropped his paddle and clasped the middle of his forearm to show the other man that the length of his *rojak* exceeded the length of his boat by the distance from his fingertips to his midforearm.

"Perfect. I thought that was a big sail, but why such a fat kubaak?" The man was backpaddling now to keep sufficient distance between their craft as the swell rolled beneath them.

"*Kubaak en kapako.*"[108]

---

[108] An outrigger float for shark hunting.

"Perfect, you should join us next time. We would have been back days ago had you been with us! It's an important mission. What the Saudeleur is doing—"

"Where do these things drift from?" Ḷainjin interjected foolishly and would later regret not letting his elder continue. By custom, a rijeḷā seldom reiterates if not seriously listened to the first time.

"This one was a full-sized tree, probably swept out to sea by the massive waves out there in the west that are known to crash ashore from time to time." The rijeḷā answered as if not annoyed that Ḷainjin had cut him off yet eyed him curiously as the two paddled to and fro to keep their craft adjacent, as if trying to figure him out.

"What happened to the rest of it?"

"The sea grass, the fish, the waves combine to break off all limbs eventually."

"Islands to the west?" Ḷainjin led him back toward his mission.

"More than you can count on your fingers and toes. Bigger and higher than Pohnpei — tens of them. Hundreds perhaps. Canoes with and without sails of all shapes and sizes."

How, amid such a conglomeration of islands and languages, was he to know where to search for her? What was he about to say about the Saudeleur? Ḷainjin was angry at himself for being less than polite with the one man who held all the answers, a man of an ilk that was legendary for turning silent upon the first instance of impoliteness.

"We left a lot of good kājokwā drifting out there this season, many already trimmed down to hull size. They're sucked offshore by waves or lost in trade transport from one island to another," the rijeḷā continued graciously. "They transport canoe logs out there from high island to low the way we trade our atoll-produced goods here on Pohnpei."

"You were about to say something about the Saudeleur, but out of impoliteness, I cut you off."

"I was going to say he's a visionary. As the people proliferate here in the east as they have in the west and as the need to trade grows, the stone village they're building will attract much commerce and wealth. They'll sing songs and tell stories to commemorate our part in its construction. Trade is the only thing they've developed out there that has served to stop the fighting and bring peoples together in peace."

"I'd like to hear all your stories of what you saw out there," Ḷainjin said. "Is your task finished now?"

"Oh, yes. They will take the kājokwā from here and harvest the fish as they paddle it ashore. They'll make a real *kaṃōḷo*[109] of it! As you know, the women forbid their men to drink *tuba* on the island, so the men take advantage of this situation to drink out here. They usually sober up over the time it takes to paddle back, but some will stay the whole night here sleeping it off."

"Are those two brother and sister?" Ḷainjin backpaddled as a swell lifted one craft, then the other.

"Yes, born the same night. Both parents dead now. We are their guardians, and we've taught them the best we can."

The twins finished coiling their lines and likewise slung them with little care onto the kājokwā, leaving them for those who would retrieve them and complete the final leg of their mission. The siblings maneuvered their craft concurrently and paddled toward Ḷainjin and the rijeḷā, who turned to watch the first paddling canoe arrive and head toward the craft of the tall brother. With much eagerness, he politely accepted two clusters of the netted shells of jemañūñ. With little effort, he immediately tossed one of the clusters a full boat's length over the rolling sea toward his sister's craft. In turn, she snatched it from the air like a weightless trinket and, seemingly without effort, held the entire bunch above her face as she began unplugging with her free hand and tasting from one and then another.

Ḷainjin could barely tear his eyes from the muscular thighs and rear that occasionally peeked back at him through her scant and badly tattered skirt. He was amazed at her strength and, with surprise on his face, looked back at the rijeḷā.

Sensing Ḷainjin's admiration, he responded, "Like creatures of the sea, they have had a diet of mostly fish since they were quite young and developed the endurance of those bonito below! I have seen them sail for days at a time with no rest and not complain of the cold even as I lay in tow and shivered under my sleeping mat."

---

[109] A newcomer celebration.

Other canoes began to arrive and started to fish. Their catch was immediate and high spirited. There was much to watch. Another canoe arrived with a woman paddled by her grandsons, perhaps, and it headed straight for the female Seeker. The woman had brought grated coconut to her for bathing and a new fiber skirt. The sister invited her aboard and later lowered herself into the ocean to discard her tattered one and scrub herself with the grated coconut.

"She's not afraid of sharks," observed Ḷainjin.

"No, never. She does that all day long. She was born first by a few moments and would never hang her rear over the side and let her brother view her eliminating."

"What about the Pohnpeian men? She isn't embarrassed swimming there naked before them?"

"If one approaches her, she'll chide him to be a man and come down into the water to see her close up," the rijeḷā said. "She hates the men here — has no respect for them and even refuses the Saudeleur's titles."

And vice versa, Ḷainjin was sure. Everyone knows a man won't respect a landless foreign woman and will always take a second local woman as well to provide security for his children.

The sister remained there naked, treading her powerful long legs, lifting herself high from the sea, and sucking jemañūñ from her nearly empty shell as her companion squeezed coconut milk over her long, straight hair.

Men paddled up to them offering their netted shells. The rijeḷā declined and so did Ḷainjin.

"Myself, I am too old to *kaṃōḷo*," the rijeḷā said. "I'm looking forward to a little sakau and a lot of sleep."

"You must be exhausted. Will you be staying at Kelepwei?"

"Yes, stay for the fun. I'll see you there this evening." He raised his halyard, drifted downwind a bit, and then headed his craft off toward shore.

Ḷainjin watched as he expertly filled his large sail and shouted after him. "Maybe I'll catch a fish for us."

"Don't bother," the rijeḷā shouted back. "They'll bring us many fish for many days."

Ḷainjin turned his attention toward the male twin, who had long since turned to windward and set his boat to drift close by. Perhaps he had politely waited for their leader to finish his conversation and depart.

He was the first to speak. "So, you're not celebrating with the rest?"

Ḷainjin paddled hard to close the distance between them. "Believe me, meeting you people from my home islands is celebration enough!"

"Well, we aren't from there exactly, although my sister believes we are. We left when we were young. Most of the language and customs we learned from Ḷōbwilñawa[110] and Ḷōbwedi,"[111] the brother said, revealing for the first time the names of the men Ḷainjin had just spoken with. "They teach us and we repeat like parrots, but we don't really understand all we memorize."

"Parrots?"

"Birds in Papua. When you take them as pets, they try to repeat what you say."

"Papua?" Ḷainjin had already been introduced to that place by Wottok so was making conversation.

"The big island to the south and west."

"Bigger than Pohnpei?"

The male twin pointed toward the islands Ḷainjin had passed on his trip to Sokehs. "Compared to Papua, Pohnpei would be like one of those little islands there inside the reef to the north."

His sister, eyes on her brother — who was facing Ḷainjin — lifted herself stark naked from the water and wrapped herself quickly and apologetically in her puffy new skirt. Ḷainjin politely lowered his eyes as she rose, though acknowledging to himself that he had never seen the naked body of a woman her age so well formed. Like most men of whatever age, he found himself attracted yet intimidated by such a strong, shapely woman.

The brother saw Ḷainjin lower his eyes. "Don't be intimidated by her," he said, loud enough for her to hear. "She's very unlucky at love."

"As opposed to my brother, who has stuck his thing up every crevice on that mountain and can hardly wait to get started again as he speaks."

---

[110] A Seeker; aka Bwilñawa; the rijeḷā. "Lō": the male prefix, used to emphasize respect.

[111] A Seeker; aka Bwedi.

Her brother closed his eyes and slowly, methodically nodded as she spoke. Their brother-sister relationship was not like anything Ḷainjin had experienced back home. They were more like cross cousins, but then she hadn't grown up in any village, so how was she to know how to act?

"I'd say more unbowed than unlucky," offered Ḷainjin in her defense.

"Jeej! I like our little brother from Rālik. He speaks well." As the older, she exercised the privilege of asking the name of a younger. "What is your name, brother?"

"They call me Pako."

"So why didn't you attack me in the water?"

"I have more respect for you than any creature below or on the surface of the ocean," Ḷainjin said.

The sister looked at her twin. "Listen and learn from him, brother. A man should talk that way to a woman. Jeej, I forget you never talk to them! You just stick it in, wiggle a bit, groan a bit, and then fall asleep like a baby."

Her brother went back to his closed-eyed nodding. "My sister speaks as though she isn't the only woman I have seen since the rising of Tūṃur! May I go now?" he asked her impatiently.

"Yes, you can go now, but you know which crevices to stay out of?"

"Yes, I know!"

His sister continued. "Should I recite their names for our new friend to memorize and be forewarned of?"

"Not unless you want him to know how imperious and incredibly overbearing you can be."

"Okay, go! Nobody wants you here anyway. The man shark is about to tell me stories of how many women he has eaten!"

Ḷainjin and the twin sister floated and sculled their boats together for a moment as they watched her brother hoist his sail and take the helm. He sheeted in to turn his boat to wind and then sheeted out to puff his sail like a gently moving cloud. Finally, he gave them a handsome, mischievous farewell smile and cruised away on the same path as had their leader.

"His name is Lañinpo,"[112] offered the sister.

---

[112] A name: "heavy weather requiring the striking of sails." A Seeker; Rōjak's brother.

More paddling canoes arrived. Some of their crew had retrieved the towlines from the kājokwā. Others were fishing successfully.

"Sweet mouth, you are the only Rālik man left to defend this quiet and deft maker of pandanus thatch."

Ḷainjin smiled at her. "So, you know the story of Lenkar?[113]

Lenkar turn about Jebrọ,
sewing pandanus thatch — ten at a time!

"Well, I doubt if you need defending!" he said. "Moreover, I doubt that these men don't know it! Somehow, I assume your reputation is well engrained among them."

She turned her head toward the men at the kājokwā. "I have seen much worse than these! Yes, I know all about Lenkar and her duty to sit quietly and look beautiful. To shut up and make pandanus thatch for the *irooj* while Jebike chases down the thunder, and I've wondered why a woman's place in the Rālik neck-string was always to sit and look beautiful. Why do we women never get to be the hero of our own stories? I don't believe in these tales, and believe me, Ḷōbwilñawa and Ḷōbwedi — the two who just left, who raised us — have done their duty. I have heard it all. When raised by storytellers, you can't help but memorize every word of every tale and every song, but in my opinion, they're just a way for our ancestors to prevent us from breaking out and finding our own way."

"How did it come about that you were raised by those men?"

"They were chosen because of their knowledge, I suppose. Ḷōbwilñawa is a natural leader and Ḷōbwedi, his natural follower."

As she spoke, the woman she had taken aboard began to stroke her long, now oil-soaked hair from behind her with a large turtle shell-comb. The twin sister grimaced each time the other broke through one of her many knotted strands.

"This is my Pohnpeian mother," the young woman explained with a quick flick of her long neck, turning her head slowly and respectfully

[113] The stories of Lenkar and Jebrọ are told in *Man Shark*, the first volume of this series.

westward. “I have many others out there. We never would have survived without them. I love them but do not aspire to be like them.”

“And your mother from Rālik…?”

Just then, her adopted mother’s grandsons, who had been fishing close by, landed a dolphin fish that they hauled into their hull without first clubbing. The fish battered itself frantically and released its soul with loud, erratic drumming against the hull of their craft that attracted attention and some laughing from the more experienced fishermen. Under their grandmother’s direction, they paddled over port to starboard, and the twin lifted the large fish by its gill, clubbed its head, and laid the wide, dead fish onto the enormous blade of her paddle. From somewhere, she produced a shell knife. Standing in her hull, her knee bracing the shank of her paddle to secure all, she began slicing the fish’s top and bottom periphery, head to tail.

Looking up into Ļainjin’s eyes, the twin answered. “Killed, I suppose, along with the rest. Probably raped. Maybe even eaten.”

“You suppose?”

“I was that tall.” She held the knife out over the water to demonstrate how tall she must have been. “All I know is from what others said.” Then she took the knife and began peeling off the skin at the end of its tail.

“All I remember is this wall of green mangrove jungle close to the shore of a narrow passageway. All the members of our fleet were wading through the low tide toward the islet where we had beached, and then the Black men came out of the mangrove, grabbed her, and dragged her feetfirst back into the jungle. She was screaming to the others for help. I never saw her again.”

After several big swigs from her coconut shell, she bent over the tail of the fish and bit onto the skin at the end. Holding it down at the tail with one palm and at its gill with the other, she began ripping the rainbow-colored skin from its light red flesh with a swing of her strong neck. Like a hungry dog bent over its bone, she ripped at it in one piece until the skin from the fish’s upward half was dangling down her neck. She dropped it into the water, caught her breath, and washed her chin and neck with seawater from one quick splash from her hand. Then she took several more swigs from the shell.

They both watched the discarded skin for a moment as it sank slowly in the clear, incredibly blue water. The first of a small circle of small blunt-headed sharks, wriggling its tail fin at top speed, hit it and dragged it off in an instant.

"When they heard my mother's screams," she continued, "all the men reversed and turned back toward her, but that's when the arrows started hitting them one by one. Long arrows from bows taller than a man stands that puncture so deep no man can survive, and their aim was perfect. Many of our men dove into the deep water to protect themselves and later formed a search party, but they never returned. Cut down, they said, in the tall grass. Their bodies taken. Eaten probably. The Sigaba[114] Islanders we stayed with told us they heard reports from growers returning from their yam plots that they carried them up into the hinterland like dead pigs lashed to poles. In fact, that's how they referred to them: 'long pig.' They have ugly people and terrible customs over there."

"And your father?"

"He was behind them all and never emerged from the jungle of mangrove, and they never found his body either."

Ḷainjin realized now that there should be more than one version of his mother's story. Each of the four could only contribute her or his perspective. Like four birds eyeing a *wūnaak*. One might be concentrating only on the baitfish below. Another more cautious bird, not wanting to dive into the mouth of a shark, might be watching their movements as well. Still another might have his fill and be eyeing the bigger birds to make sure he keeps his meal in his gullet.

Ḷainjin did not want anything held back, so he wouldn't ask about his mother's name until he had heard each version of what had happened that day. He remembered he had to move quickly now as the Saudeleur might be waiting for Ḷōbwilñawa to come ashore and congratulate him, and one or the other might speak of him.

Why had he meekly lowered his eyes as she emerged naked from the sea? He upbraided himself. She was bold. She must require a boldness from

[114] Later called Sio Island, a "place of mixing." A precontact trading center located off the Kunai coast of the Huon Peninsula of southeastern New Guinea.

her men. He should have stared right at her and quenched his throat with her nakedness.

She began flaying the flesh from the bone and flung a long strip directly at his face, as if he was a bird she was trying to tease. She gave others more gently to her Pohnpeian mother for the boys and began conversing with her in Pohnpeian.

This was exactly what he had been searching for: a raw report of what happened. And he was getting it from the tallest, most magnificent woman he had ever seen. Yet he knew he dared not tarry.

"That proa of yours looks slow," he offered slyly.

"Easy to say when your proa is obviously longer," she answered.

"You're right. It wouldn't be fair for me to challenge you to a race ashore. You have a shorter proa with just women aboard."

That got her eyebrows raised, and she appeared as though about to come back with some sort of tirade when perhaps, by the expression on his face, she realized he was just taunting her. She formed the haughtiest face of a woman challenged he had ever seen. The expression seemed to negate her natural beauty in a self-deprecating manner, but it was followed by a girlish laugh as she slung the fish headfirst into his arms and barked something in Pohnpeian to the older woman. She hoisted her sail and was catching wind before he could stop laughing, wash the fish smell off himself, and calmly prepare for the journey back. She would beat him easily in the downwind run with her bigger sail and lighter craft, and he would be happy to allow her to arrive respectably first.

Women love to talk

So, this was how his journey would end, Ḷainjin thought. With a race back to the stone village of Pohnpei and a quiet story told beneath the stars about his mother's demise under the weapons of western cannibals. It would end, or at least he thought it would end, just about the way he'd expected. Surely, the twin's older companions would provide more details leading to the certainty of his mother's death. Once he knew her story and could tell its details well, he would be free to pursue his own destiny, follow his own adventures, and continue to create his wealth amid these new laws of barter amid these mysterious, cloud-entrapping mountains.

The Seeker turned now and then to glance back at his nonthreatening course. He munched on the strip of fish she had given him, sitting in the meandering shade from the tip of his sail as the sun continued its late-afternoon passage before him. The white half-moon rose slowly through the light blue horizon above his wake, and the light wind kited his craft upon the smoothly rising and falling swells.

The tide had turned during their encounter at the kājokwā, and the incoming tide was high enough for him to follow the impressively valiant woman over the reef and into the canals leading to Kelepwei. Once there, having proved herself the winner of their race, she pressed on toward shore, no doubt to deliver her adopted mother. The man called Ḷōbwilñawa had anchored and was bathing in the tide next to the landing. The palu and his crew were chatting with him in their language. Ḷainjin lowered his sail and sculled his canoe in the channel. They had left a space between his canoe and that of the twin's brother, so Ḷainjin left that spot empty in case she wanted to take her spot in formation and anchor between them. The man called Ḷōbwedi and his canoe were absent. Seizing the opportunity, Ḷainjin slowly paddled his canoe next to that of the rijeḷā, dropped a stern anchor, and slipped off into the cool tide to secure the canoe to the landing.

Not wanting to waste the remainder of the beautiful fish, he brought it inside the compound walls and delivered it to a circle of women preparing food for the evening meal. Amid their giggling and chatter, he recognized the name Lipanmai. He assumed they were teasing him and suggesting he deliver the fish to her instead. He laughed politely, feigned confusion, and returned to the landing. The rijeḷā had just finished his bath, and he and the palu were engaged in animated conversation.

"We were Wisim's guests on Satawan for many cycles, many seasons ago," the rijeḷā told Ḷainjin. "He was very kind to us," he said as he climbed onto his proa. "He fed us lots of turtle!"

As he used the Truk word for "turtle," the palu and crew all laughed proudly.

Then the rijeḷā dropped into his hull and wrapped himself in a new hibiscus bark-kilt that someone had presented to him. He flopped onto the yoke at the center of his proa, on the closed stern hatch of his hull. With his chest slanted backward, his back against his mast, his legs crossed and folded, and his feet locked beneath him, he no doubt intended to rest and slowly water himself from a netted, very large coconut shell in his lap.

Ḷainjin sat at his stern facing him, ready for the right moment to continue his questioning. He was determined to be polite and not to address the other until he spoke first. He would have a long wait. Despite the rijeḷā's awkward posture and obviously uncomfortable resting place, without lifting even once his water-shell, Ḷainjin soon realized he had fallen asleep. There was nothing for him to do but rest and wait. He lay back in the late-afternoon sun on the stern deck of his canoe, where the mild, erratic breezes that wafted about the islet lulled him to sleep.

When he awoke, the rijeḷā was gone. The palu sat a distance away, on his leeward deck like the proverbial bird at nest, carefully observing all that passed. The sun had nearly sunk beyond the mountains, the sky was still clear, and the tide had turned again and begun its retreat. But there was still no sign of the impending celebration Ḷainjin expected. He used gestures to inquire about the rijeḷā's whereabouts. The palu mimed back that he had retired into his hull. Fair enough. Ḷainjin remembered how tired he, too, had been on arrival how many cycles ago, and he had been at sea for a mere three or four days. How he, too, had grown irresistibly sleepy upon anchoring despite his fear that the sharks would attack his fish. How he had slept again a few hours later, and again after lying down with Talupe. He felt a pang in his throat when he thought about her again, but his spirit rose when the proa he had raced arrived suddenly at the mouth of the channel and headed toward the empty spot between the brother's proa and that of the rijeḷā.

The palu, uncharacteristically not waiting to acknowledge the young Seeker, jumped from his proa to the landing like an agile youth, hand outstretched to receive the painter she somewhat hesitantly tossed to him. Something about the grin on his face and the way they encountered suggested a strained intimacy. They met as though meeting for the first time after many seasons — he, the older, strangely uncertain, and she with an expression of certainty on her face. He addressed her in his language, apparently knowing that she spoke it well. When Ḷainjin heard him speak the Kajin Rālik word *rojak*, he realized that must be her name.

She began shouting at the palu to such an extent that Ḷainjin felt a responsibility to his friend to intervene. He quickly disembarked and approached this Rojak in the middle of her tirade that, from the look on the palu's face, had the obvious intention of emasculating him.

"What's the problem?" he asked her. "Has my kindly Satawan friend managed to offend you in some way?"

"No, he didn't offend me at all. He just smoothly enticed away a young girl's virginity, that's all! After the little frizzy heads killed her parents, he guilefully tricked her into thinking he would take care of her, but once he uncovered the treasure he wanted, he summarily dumped her for the chubby little cousin he knew he was destined to take all along! Now he wants to have a reunion. Where's a *rajraj* when I need one? I would love to have a reunion with that stinky fish of his. I'd love to cut it off and relieve his woman of the misery of being crushed by all that fat every night!"

She turned to yank her proa toward the landing. Ḷainjin looked at his friend, who appeared embarrassed, upset, and at a loss. Clearly, events were out of his meticulous control, and he was in unfamiliarly vulnerable territory. He looked back at Ḷainjin in silence with such pain in his eyes that Ḷainjin knew every word of what she said must be true.

"What says he?" Ḷainjin asked, taking a chance and lightly seizing her elbow on behalf of his friend.

She pulled away her arm. Turned and stared at Ḷainjin as if he was a traitor for even suggesting there might be another side to her sordid tale. At this point, he realized he might be putting his whole mission at risk and realized he should have kept his mouth shut. Was he next? Then the tears welled up in her eyes, and he felt relieved that, just perhaps, he had blurted out the right response.

"He says he has wanted to apologize for seasons but came and left before we returned from our hunt because until now, he lacked the courage to apologize. He says they forced him to take his cousin to continue his navigation apprenticeship. Now that he has accomplished all this, he comes here to vomit his puke in my face. But honestly, the stink of it all is too much for any self-respecting woman to bare."

Then, ignoring Ḷainjin, she let into the palu again in his language even as her voice became louder and angrier. His crew began to assemble from inside the compound onto the landing behind him, and even some of the women who had been cooking appeared in the entranceway. The palu stood like a rock on the reef— pummeled by the breakers, moving not, complaining not, and speechless in his defense. Soon enough, she tired and abandoned him there, humiliated and speaking not to his companions. He stood there for a long time despite her entreaties to hide himself from her sight. Ḷainjin slid his hand ever so slowly over his shoulder to express his support.

The fewer his words the better. He returned to his craft. One by one, the onlookers left until he was the only soul on the landing. Ḷōbwilñawa, apparently undisturbed, continued to sleep in his hull. After a while, perhaps to further demonstrate her disgust for him, Rojak wordlessly disembarked and tested her legs by wandering into the compound. She emerged shortly thereafter, walking like an old woman and scowling at seeing him still there as though it was his fault she had sea sickness in her legs. Then she decided to visit with Ḷainjin, who quickly paddled forward to approach the landing and allow her to board.

He retreated to his place at the stern. She sat before him on the outrigger deck with her new skirt fluffed out, hiding her thighs and knees. She nervously watched, her long legs dangling down and her unusually large feet splashing in the water, which must have felt cool from the incoming tide. Her face, now turned away from the palu — who had since sat in the water at the edge of the landing — broke into a burst of half laugh, half snicker that must have caught the palu's ear, as his eyes darted to Ḷainjin's, expressing the same pleading message for help.

She changed her tone and spoke softly, head down, probably to prevent Ḷainjin's good friend from hearing. "It wasn't as though I was a lobster that he chased and trapped on the reef! More like a crab that sidled up to him with claws outstretched!" She looked up with laughing eyes as a naughty girl would to a friend. When she looked back down again at her feet, Ḷainjin darted a nod and a quick flick of his eyebrows to notify his friend he was making progress. At which point, tears welled up in his friend's eyes as he sat there like a little boy whose toy proa had sailed irretrievably away.

"He was quite handsome back then and … my time had come."

Ḷainjin wasn't sure what she meant by this. But she wanted to talk, so he was listening carefully.

"We had spent the rest of the season among the islanders, hoping my mother, or maybe one of the others, would reappear someday. I had witnessed firsthand how they treat their women. They make you feel so inferior! Whether they're Black or Brown or in between, they all treat their women like poison fish. They hate us! They claim to be afraid of us! They think we are witches who will pollute them when we bleed. Can you imagine a young woman with no true mother taken and kept away in a blood house the first time she becomes a woman? Told day after day that everything down there is poison? Satawan was the first island we came to where all that changed. I loved it there. I felt free, like a woman is supposed to feel. We stayed I don't know how many seasons. We sailed among all the atolls of their group, catching turtles and all. I knew all about his cousin. The women are fantastic there. Do you know what the women like to do to themselves?"

"Yes, Wisim has told me," Ḷainjin said.

"Well, the men — naturally — think they do it for them, but they do it for themselves. With a thing like that to play with, who needs a man?"

"Did you adopt their custom yourself?"

"Their custom is for a woman to feel and for a man to wonder how much! His cousin may have had a big one, but she was a land crab. As soon as we sailed for turtles, I showed him what a woman's legs looked like and felt like wrapped around him."

She raised her wet feet and bent her knees, admiring her own strong and very shapely legs to the point that Ḷainjin wondered if she was flirting with him.

"I wrapped my legs around him and squeezed the last drop out of him like he was so much spent grated coconut. Look at him. He remembers and can never forget what that felt like!" she said, braving now a glance back at him — seeing him for the first time, his head turned away, crying on the landing.

"Did he not please you?"

She darted a questioning glance back at Ḷainjin as though, for an instant, she was accusing him of already knowing more than he should.

"His people also made me sleep in their blood house when my time of the cycle came, though, and they made me stay in a cramped pandanus-leaf hut they built there on the lee platform for me so I wouldn't pollute their navigation when we sailed off to gather turtles! They turned the turtles upside down with legs agape. Then they slept next to their yawning sexual parts, but they had to hunch me over in a hot pandanus hut until we got to shore. Men and their customs!"

As though a bit embarrassed, almost as though she had girlishly decided to flirt with Ḷainjin, she began to enticingly flutter her long feet in the water, glancing at them admiringly and at him and then back down again as though to entice him into dreaming what those tender heels would feel like pounding on his back.

"When did you come to Pohnpei, little brother?"

"I came with Tūṃur."

"Just you and Tūṃur?" She laughed. "Nobody else?"

"I brought things to trade."

"What to trade?"

"Shark teeth."

"How many?"

"Many, many."

"How big?"

Ḷainjin laughed loudly, catching a grimace from the palu on the landing. "That's for a man to know and a woman to wonder about!" As she laughed, he saw his opportunity to turn the conversation casually back to his mission.

"Do you mind if I ask you a question about that day they captured your mother?"

"No," she said. "I realized earlier today that I feel better talking about my story. Most people avoid bringing it up out of sympathy. I was so young! I've avoided talking about it for too long. What part do you want to know more about?"

"You said something about walking on the reef between two islets?"

"Sigaba sits in the passageway into a little inland lagoon that's surrounded by mangrove. The passageway is shallow and narrow. We always anchored in that lagoon. It's off the coast of an island so large you cannot even imagine."

"You say you always anchored in that lagoon? How often?" Ḷainjin asked.

Rojak smiled. "As often as we stopped at Sigaba. Under every other moon, at least. We liked it there. They're easy to trade with."

"So that's what you were doing, trading with cannibals?"

"Well, why not? Cannibals don't eat the people who trade with them. That would be stupid! Right?"

"Right, but you said..."

Rojak shook her head. "I said *we* traded with the people of Sigaba. We never saw them eat anybody. They were our friends. It was the people of the hinterlands, with whom *they* traded, who killed my parents and everybody else."

"What are hinterlands?"

"Look up there at those ridges on the way up to the mountains." She pointed and moved her arm horizontally, back and forth. "Those are hinterlands, where the people can look down on the coast and see who is coming and going."

Ḷainjin was puzzled. "They saw an array of boats coming, and they attacked to steal your trade goods?"

"No. Not to steal. They probably took the women as decoys. According to Ḷōbwilñawa, they knew who we were and didn't like us, but they don't fight honorably like we do. They shot our men from afar and carried them off like pigs. He says that was one way of sowing disrespect. Eating them, if that's what they did, was the ultimate act of disrespect."

"Men… What about the women? How many women were in your group?"

"Several women sailed with their men." Rojak splashed her feet in the water. "Ḷōbwilñawa can tell you how many. She believed that men make mistakes when they rush against the weather to get home, so she allowed us to sail as families. But so far, we were the only children. They say we had to leave a few young ones behind when the storm started. By Sigaba, only two women were left. The others were lost in the storm."

Ḷainjin felt his heart thump in his chest and leaned forward. "Who are you referring to as *she*?"

"They called her Tarmālu. She was the leader, and according to Ḷōbwilñawa, that was a big part of the problem. Even the people of Sigaba were afraid of her. They thought she was a witch and, at first, didn't want to trade with her. They preferred to trade with men. They didn't know how to deal with a group led by a woman."

"What changed their minds?"

Rojak smiled as though proud of Tarmālu's accomplishments. "She had learned exactly what they wanted and when they needed it most."

"And what did she trade for?"

"Blackstone,[115] mostly, and other items they made locally that we could trade elsewhere for blackstone."

"Blackstone," Ḷainjin repeated. "What is blackstone?"

---

[115] Obsidian; volcanic glass.

"I don't know. When their young boys grew up, they cut their foreskins with it. The men shave their face with it. Ask my brother about blackstone. The fool let them initiate him," Rojak sputtered. "Who knows what that involved? Big secret among the men. Instant death if he tells his sister about it. Men are fools! And you're probably wondering why I didn't bring back babies, are you not?" She scooped water with her dainty, narrow toes and flicked it toward him.

Ḷainjin didn't want to ask the next question. "This woman Tarmālu. Did you… Did you talk to anyone who saw her killed?" He held his breath.

"No, but we saw them kill lots of us. We four were the only survivors."

"Why didn't they just shoot your mother? Why did they drag her off?"

"I've always assumed they wanted to, you know, stand behind her first and pretend she was a dog! They probably injected their disgusting goo into her before they slit her throat. They have a male-dominated culture. They pass the land from father to son. The only thing that encourages equality between the sexes — women make things for their men to trade. Was it not for things they make, I doubt they would even trade for what their women need. They treat them the way they treat their dogs, and they have intercourse that way. They won't touch a woman down there. They believe the water in a woman's well is poison to them. Men don't talk to women over there in the western islands. They might get bewitched!"

"Didn't these men from Sigaba help?"

"Don't forget I was small. All I remember is we stayed on Sigaba for a long, long time, and they took good enough care of us, and they inquired on our behalf with those people of the hinterland. It's better if you ask Ḷōbwilñawa."

"Was this it?" Ḷainjin thought. Had he finally found someone who was there and presented a credible story of his mother's end? Did he now have to add rape to the list of calamities that had certainly befallen her? Suddenly, he felt nauseated and didn't want to continue talking. He had heard all he could.

He looked over at the palu, sitting out of place like the rare sighting of a flabby sea dog and crying to himself without a mate in sight.

"Would it hurt too much to walk over there and listen to the rest of what he has to say?"

"Ḷainjin, there is a quiet battle out there to which you are oblivious. A struggle that we cannot fight with hands, though you men might prefer it that way since you're the stronger. Their whole way of life, their whole way of thinking about woman must change! If he wants more words, I'm glad to spit them out at him!"

She went to the bow, lightly tugged on the painter to glide the boat to the landing, and disembarked. As she walked toward the palu, Ḷainjin, accommodating their need for privacy, sank down into his hull to absorb all he had heard.

Later, though awakened from the ringing of the sakau stones inside the compound, he decided he was in no mood for sakau. He was no longer in the mood to talk. He told himself he had accomplished his mission. Yet he felt no triumph. He was now free to pursue life as a normal man. Why had he turned morose? What does a normal man do with his life besides fill it with triviality? He had always told himself his life would have an extraordinary story. He napped. Woke up. Napped again, despite the sound of others coming and going on the landing. Finally, perhaps due to a wind shift, he heard his hull bump the edge of the reef pool that bordered the landing, and he rose to reset his stern anchor stone. It was long past the middle of the night. The sky had turned black as the moon had long since set.

Ḷainjin waded into the pool to reset his stone. Returning to his craft, he grabbed his kilt, stepped up onto the reef, and stood there for a moment, naked in the starlight, knowing what he wanted now that the tide permitted. He tied his kilt and splashed through the knee-high water of the canal to Pahn Kadira. There, he awoke Lipanmai at her window flap, and she led him to their spot along a secluded section of wall where the takai were the perfect height for her to sit, spread her legs, and allow him to enter her in such a way that, even if seen, they would appear as though talking.

She always smelled of smoke from Nahn Sapwe's fire and tasted of the limes she brought to freshen her breath before allowing him to kiss her.

"True? Women want talk to their men?" asked Ḷainjin in his broken Pohnpeian.

"Oh, yes!" She handed him one of her limes to cut with the new weapon the Saudeleur had given him. Then — before she squeezed the lime juice into her mouth, puckered her face, and shuddered at the taste — he understood her to say, "We want our men to talk to us, but we wait for them. Our grandmothers teach us not to demand or we will lose our men to easy women."

"Okay, talk to me now."

"Kiss me first!"

He kissed her. Tasting the lime as he had many times before, he hardened and entered her.

"Talk to me now."

"Right now, while doing this?" She giggled.

"Why not? Men and women need talk."

"Okay, this takai always bruises my rear!"

"Of course." He thought about how rough this position must have been for her in the past. He lifted her up, spun her around, and held her with one hand on each buttock under her fiber skirt. Her arms around his neck, she stood with her tiptoes pressing on each of his feet, swaying her weight from one foot to the other, slowly teasing his manhood within her.

"How does this feel?" she questioned him softly, boastfully in his ear as she danced slowly on her tiptoes, swaying her hips and shoulders right then left. He massaged each buttock as she writhed on his manhood inside her.

"Too good! Too good! No can hold!"

"Hold!" she commanded him softly, distractedly clasping onto his ear with her teeth and biting down increasingly firmly as her writhing accelerated. She continued to muffle the word — insistently at first, then frantically in his ear for much longer than he thought possible, and then shuddered exactly as she had after drinking the lime juice. Relaxing, she sank exhausted into his hands, and he had to hold himself no more. He sat back on the takai, and she, as though hoping to keep him inside her, leaned forward against him and pressed her breast against his mouth.

"Talk to your mother," she whispered jokingly as he played with her partially erect nipple with his tongue.

Then she inspected his ear. From the feel of the wound as she fingered it, he realized she must have drawn blood.

"Sorry, I forgot to tell you that my grandmother was a cannibal." She giggled.

"*Kinjen emman*, we say in Kajin Rālik."

"What does that mean?"

"Cut of a man."

"I want to learn Kajin Rālik. Teach me more!" She arched her back to adjust her hair comb, using both hands to remove her curly hair from her face and pushing her breast before his face again.

"*Ninnin*," he said, pretending to suckle her.

"*Dihdi*!" she repeated in her language. Then she laughed softly and so did he. They smiled at one another in the starlight as though, for the first time after many sexual encounters under several moons, they were proud they had learned to talk to and know each other in this new way.

Challenging him, she wiggled her rear to reignite his manhood, but it slipped from within her.

"*Dundun*," she said in her language, flicking the limp, wet tip of his manhood with her index finger.

"*Kawko*," he responded in his.

"*Wihl*," she said, grasping her forearm with her other hand and clenching her fist, miming an erect penis.

He laughed. "Same in Kajin Rālik."

"We must have had the same grandmother!" she exclaimed as they laughed together and contentedly clutched each other as lovers and friends and relatives all.

Over her shoulder, Ḷainjin saw Rojak's brother very tentatively crossing the moonlit courtyard. "Who is that?" He pointed at the unmistakable image of Rojak's twin.

"Your brother from Rālik. He's been cavorting."

"I need talk him. Should I go?"

"Okay, go. But come back and talk!" She smiled at him as he departed.

Hurrying, Ḷainjin caught him as he stepped down the takai into the ankle-deep, star-shimmered water covering the reef flat. "I have been talking to your sister, and she said I should ask you about blackstone."

"Do you really want to talk about blackstone, or do you want to ask me about who I was with? *Ṃōṃaan ṃaj*!" The taller man put his arm around Ḷainjin's shoulders, revealing the smell of jemañūñ still heavy on his breath, and drew him awkwardly close, reminding him of the way the palu liked to grab hold of him.

"This must be the way of western men," Ḷainjin thought.

The tall, handsome man laughed profusely at his own joke until Ḷainjin expected his sun-cracked lips to bleed. He drew Ḷainjin even closer, as if to see into his eyes despite the dim light, and announced, "My name is Lañinpo. What's yours?"

"They call me Pako."

"Ḷōpako,[116] to understand my sister, you must know that our mother taught her constantly that she could do anything better than any man, which, of course, my sister always took to mean me. My mother taught her never to depend on anyone. Now we both know, had Mother lived, she would have had to modify her advice to fit growing up. My sister still treats me like a little boy. However, our mother died before she started to bleed. There you have her now — overzealous, overbearing, overconfident."

"What is your sister's plan?"

"She doesn't have a plan. She insists on taking my plan. All I want is my place on the mountain and a title to go with it, so I always trade my share of the kājokwā reward for title. She trades hers for wealth. She wants me to settle down, but only with a woman she likes. She insists I make a lot of babies to take care of me, but by that, she means to take care of her!"

"Doesn't she plan to have children?"

"I doubt it. She's older than me, so how do you criticize your older sister? If you come up with an idea, let me know."

"That's a tough one without an ally," responded Ḷainjin.

"That's it! You and I will be allies. Together, the two of us will outmaneuver these wild, controlling women! If only she wouldn't bully every interested man she ever meets. What about you? She likes you — take her, please!"

Ḷainjin stopped walking and stared at the other man in the starlight.

"Does a brother not talk about his sister this way back in Rālik?" Lañinpo asked. "I guess not. I'm sorry. We are so isolated out here. Ḷōbwilñawa

---

[116] Aka Pako; Ḷainjin's nickname. Literally, "man shark." "Ḷō": the male prefix; "pako": "shark."

teaches us, but we don't understand our own customs. Out there — can you believe this? — men trade sisters the way they do pigs. They talk about how many pigs a woman is worth. In their culture, if I like your sister, I offer you mine, regardless of age and regardless if you may already have a woman. The only discussion among the family is how many pigs must be exchanged!"

"What about fish? Can a man give fish?"

"Asked by the man who, according to legend, arrived here with a *lōjkaan* in tow. Typical thinking for a man of Rālik or Ratak, I guess. But no. Pigs, only pigs! These people are meat eaters! Yes, they eat fish all the time, but they have to eat pig — or something similar — to celebrate anything."

"Something similar?"

"There's not much difference, they say, in the taste of a freshly baked man when it comes down to it."

Ļainjin quickly decided to let that answer stand on its own. He would refuse to turn judgmental until he got all the answers he wanted. They walked slowly and nearly sideways at times, the taller man obviously still inebriated, his arm hanging over Ļainjin's shoulders. Stepping tentatively but deliberately, they walked like crabs across the tideway. When they arrived at their anchorage, all was silent. All appeared asleep. Each went to his own craft and succumbed to the night.

The next morning, at the break of dawn, the tide was low but rising and the weather fair. The periodic shade from his white and puffy wind-cloud friends was now completely absent. The air was sticky with only a slight refreshing coolness rising from the fresh incoming tide. The palu's boat had apparently departed during the night. Had Rojak accompanied him? Ļainjin saw her not, and she had sealed both hatches on her canoe. The others slept as Ļainjin went ashore and climbed to the top of the wall to catch a breath of air. He could see craft out in the ocean waiting for the tide to rise a bit higher before attempting to cross the reef. The weather had turned listless. A faint breeze cooled the sweat that had emerged from his hairy scalp. All this was unusual, as Jebrọ had not yet poked his head before dawn. It was as though *añōneañ* had come surprisingly to an abrupt halt. "Too abrupt?" he wondered.

Ḷōbwilñawa's story

As Ḷainjin sat, his thoughts continued to swirl around and around the news of yesterday. Absolutely every word he'd heard had fallen into place pretty much as he had feared and expected. There was one question, though, that he was unable to resolve. Why had the group lingered so long in Pohnpei? Had they no family back in Rālik? Clearly, they had business here, but these were men of the sea. A journey back to Rālik would be but a few days' sail for them. Had they no regard for all the families who longed to hear what had happened? Had they been afraid they would seem like cowards? Who, after hearing that story, would accuse them? Clearly, the parents had charged them with taking custody of the children. There had been no opportunity for them to rescue anybody without putting the children at risk. No, he sensed that either there was some outstanding secret they were yet to resolve, or they were afraid some other survivor might show up with a different or conflicting story. Perhaps he was just unwilling to surrender his search and begin a new life.

After a while, from around the bend came Ewalt, paddling hesitantly in his two-man fishing canoe. When he had anchored, Ḷainjin acknowledged him and motioned for him to climb the wall.

"Father sends his regards," said the sweaty man, clearly pleased to feel the ever-so-slight breeze gently wafting at that height. "I bring good news. Tomorrow, the Saudeleur will prepare a feast for the kājokwā and present you with the title Jau Areu. He is pleased with all the pet eels you've captured, and he's pleased with Father for instructing you."

"Isn't that your father's title?"

"Yes, and the Saudeleur has granted Father land rights to a strip of land wider than what we have cultivated, from the south shore of Temwen across the island to the shore opposite. The title will be yours too, and he has decided to grant you rights to Idedh! If you refuse the title, as is your right as well, he will add wealth to your store at Kariahn for you to trade or take as you wish."

Ḷainjin wanted to make the right decision. His inclination was to go for title. A little voice somewhere was whispering that that was what Talupe expected. "What do you recommend?"

"Wealth is for your life only. The title is for your posterity. Father chose the totem kingfisher for the clan that, for generations, will share his rights. The land will pass from mother to eldest daughter. The title from father to eldest son. Some will travel afar, but all will remain brothers and sisters and be proud to be kingfishers. Half the Seekers have chosen title, Ḷōbwedi and Lañinpo. The workers on their lands provide for their every need. What say you?"

Ḷainjin looked over and beyond the islet in between to the corner of the wall surrounding Idedh. "Okay, I'll while the rest of the day over there and make my decision. Is the Saudeleur likely to speak to the Seekers today?"

"He will give them another day to rest while he prepares for their *kaṃōḷo*."

"Good, I haven't had the opportunity to fully question them about my mother's end. I don't want them to know who I am yet. As far as they're concerned, my name is Ḷōpako. Are we clear?"

Ewalt agreed and together, they descended the takai and went to their respective canoes.

"Here, take this for your meal over there." Ewalt took a fresh catch from the kājokwā someone had given him and presented it to Ḷainjin.

With that, each departed in a separate direction. The tide had risen and the fishermen, who had cleared the reef, appeared here and there as Ḷainjin leisurely paddled down the canal past the only islet that separated Kalepwei from Idedh. He beached his canoe at the entrance to the islet, knowing he would have to return repeatedly to rebeach until the peak of the neap tide had passed. Truly, the islet needed a caretaker. *Kōṇṇat*[117] bushes had

---

[117] A short, sprawling tree that grows next to the shore; beach cabbage: *Scaevola taccada*; "naupaka" in Hawaiian.

sprouted everywhere. Should he accept the title, he wondered. Would it be his task to lower any defaulted trader down into the well? He must make it clear to the Saudeleur that, although he respected his trading traditions, he didn't want that responsibility. He was an outsider and should not be responsible for such things. Or was it because he was an outsider with no relatives on the island that the Saudeleur wanted to entice him to take it? What was the fortune for anyway, now that his search for his mother was at its end? As it turned out, the desire to show Talupe he, too, could gain a title became a major factor in his decision.

He stood at the lip of the pool and stared down into its surprisingly clear water. Though he had come on many occasions, Nahn Samohl had never appeared. "Perhaps she comes out only at night," he thought. He would have to enter the water of the pool to view the entrance to her natural tunnel amid the corals below.

The pool was like many others he had been in. He saw that it extended laterally underneath the reef. The builders had backfilled the islet, like all the others, and the coral stones used sloped down beneath the water to the reef at the pool's edge. They had also surrounded the pool with takai placed on the reef before the builders backfilled with stones. *Kōṇṇat* had grown at the edge of the pool and partially blocked his view. The well just south of the pool had been built with the same crisscrossed takai used for the base and walls. Supposedly, according to Ewalt, these takai straddled a second, smaller pool connected to the larger one before him by Nahn Samohl's tunnel. The water in the pool, like the water in the well, must rise and fall with the water on the surrounding reef and within the canals, Ḷainjin decided. According to Ewalt, an islet had been built in the same fashion around a second natural pool at Darong, directly across the canal, as well.

He had an idea. He went back to his boat, dragged it farther ashore, and brought back the large fish Ewalt had given him. Tying it with separate twine through the gill to the spar hanging from the rectangular scaffold over the well, he lowered the spar until the fish rested on the bottom. He sat and sweated for the rest of the afternoon in the humid, stagnant air, holding the rope as though fishing as the tide ebbed and trapped him there and then flowed back. Finally, the smell of cooking food wafted from Kelepwei, and his hunger got the best of him. He left the fish unretrieved, promising himself to check later. Then he submerged himself in the cool incoming tide of the canal before paddling back to eat his dinner with the others.

He was still dripping wet though pleasantly cooled from the heat of the day as he turned the corner and entered the anchorage. The palu's proa was still gone, and so was Rojak. Ḷōbwedi was not around, and Lañinpo and Ḷōbwilñawa were eating on the latter's craft. Except that the rijeḷā looked different. He had pulled all the hair from his face. They signaled for him to join them. Ḷainjin entered the breezeless, smoke-clogged compound and claimed the basket of food they'd prepared for him. He was glad to see the last rays of that hot afternoon sun descending behind the mountains.

"The four of you arrived just in time. This has been the first day without wind," he offered as he sat on the breadfruit planks of the rijeḷā's outrigger platform.

"We knew we were running out of time. We were down to a quarter night's sleep and a midafternoon nap. You're right we just made it. When I see the Saudeleur, I'm going to tell him to have his men stop fooling around out there and get that thing to shore before *kapilak*[118] blows it away!"

"But Jebrọ hasn't even—"

"Ḷōpako, always remember! The stars are one thing. That ocean is another. We have been out there watching kāleptak creep north over the sea for days now. When it slaps that hard this far north, even before the wind stops, you know vast areas of sea out there are listlessly baking in the sun. The ocean doesn't know about Lōktañūr and the rest. When it bakes in the sun like that, eventually that warm air rises and forms some sort of monster — ready or no! Stars or no! The star is only a sign of what should come based on the cycles. The ocean decides on its own what will be."

"So, where is the palu?"

"That's another worry! Fat rascal ran off with the girl again! Good man has a weakness for stubborn women. He's likely to find she's no longer the girl he knew. Likely as not, he'll come back castrated like a tamed pig. That is, assuming they're not blown off the face of the sea first."

---

[118] A gale sometimes associated with the first morning's sighting of the constellation Aries.

"Before the round moon?" Ḷainjin asked.

"Definitely! Let us see what tomorrow brings."

"Lañinpo, you never told me what blackstone is."

The rijeḷā shot an annoyed glance at Lañinpo, whose return look said, "So what?"

"The blackstone," answered the rijeḷā, "is a secret we keep from the Saudeleur. We're afraid if he knows about it, he'll force it into his trading system. We keep a little here and there. It's a big item of trade in the west. We want to keep it. It's one thing a man can't collect too much of. And none of us wants to go back for more — at any price."

"You can trust me to keep your secret," promised Ḷainjin.

The rijeḷā reached under the mat he was sitting on and produced a smooth and shiny chip of transparent stone that was black in color. Ḷainjin had never seen anything like this before. It was sharper than a sharpened shell, thinner and sharper than a shark's tooth.

"Give it here," said Lañinpo. He took the chip from the palm of the rijeḷā's hand, grabbed him by the wrist, and used the flake as a tool to shave a strip of hair from the top of his forearm.

Ḷainjin glanced at the broad smile of the rijeḷā. He hadn't pulled the hairs from his face. He had shaved them off with blackstone! "What is this?"

The rijeḷā spoke quietly. "They say it's beach stone melted in the fire mountains."

"Fire mountains?"

"Oh, yes. In the west, days away at sea, you see them belching smoke like clouds. It was the first thing we saw once we'd crossed the kāleptak current and how we held our course."

"What course?" Ḷainjin assumed that the rijeḷā was talking about their course from the *ḷañ eḷap*[119] that had blown them southwest but wanted to draw him into telling that story.

"Okay," began the rijeḷā. "We had been blown by the tail winds of the *ḷañ eḷap* for ten days! We were heading southwest, right?"

"Right. You could have headed south to stay clear of it, but I assume the wind would have blown you over on a reach." Ḷainjin understood their strategy.

[119] "Big wind"; typhoon.

"Yes, that would have put us safely in the kāleptak current much closer and sooner, but no matter how often we tried, the wind was just too strong for a reach run like that. We beat just a little off wind. We blew our conch shells at night to sail tight together. We nevertheless lost half our craft to who knows what. Ten days, night and day, on that southwestern heading until the storm finally dumped us in the middle of it, but upstream and much farther to the west than we had ever before been. Of course, it turned very calm, as you would expect in the middle of the kāleptak stream. We had collected plenty of water and found kājokwā to fish, but we couldn't sail. On the third day, Tarmālu ordered us to take down our sails."

At hearing his mother's name again, Ḷainjin bit hard on his tongue to control his mouth. Then he started eating to prevent the excitement he felt from rising to his face and revealing his intentions.

The rijeḷā continued. "I mean, we lowered masts and all! We tore up our platforms to make more paddles. We overloaded our lee platforms and even paddled from the outrigger floats. We paddled and kept our course to the southwest, toward the smoke. We had heard the stories, of course. Head southwest and eventually you will come to the cannibal isles, and we'd heard that the cannibals wouldn't eat the traders they deal with. So, we continued with confidence. Eventually, we paddled out the stream and entered the south sea, where everything turns backward. The seasons change. Jebrọ brings strong, rainless winds from the southeast. Tūṃur brings rainstorms and still air. We caught the last breath of Jebrọ's windy season, hoisted our sails, and cruised toward the smoke from the fire mountain. Before we got there, we arrived at what seemed to us at the time this incredibly long island. For comparison, it wasn't as high as Pohnpei but just as wide and probably five times as long. Naturally, we were reluctant to go ashore. We sailed around the island till we saw what we were looking for — their proas. They had long, skinny hulls, with long outrigger booms."

"And can you believe it? Two rectangular sails," said Lañinpo.

"Two?" Ḷainjin was having trouble imagining a canoe with two sails.

The rijeḷā began speaking again. "Two rectangular sails and two masts, one a little afore of the outrigger booms and another smaller a little aft of them, but neither yard rests on the deck like ours do. Only the masts do. The yards just hang out there on the mast. They fly the sails like kites. The hulls are so narrow and so long… The boats move fast on the reach, but we were never afraid they would overtake us because they can barely sail them into the wind."

"They must spend a lot of time waiting for fair wind."

"We noticed they do. We only approached them on windy days. We followed them from place to place and decided they were traders. They rarely went ashore, though, and only stopped at these little villages built on the reefs off mainland lagoons or to lee of small islands."

"How can you build a village on a reef or in a lagoon?" Ḷainjin couldn't imagine such a thing.

"That's another thing we wondered about. I guess they lack the seas that we see here. The ocean is calmer down there. Although to listen to them, it gets very rough during storms, but in our experience, all that rain kills the wind. They refuse to sail during their rainy season, and they were surprised when we did. I think they use the storms as an excuse. I don't think their boats adjust well to variable winds.

"Anyway, they build their houses on pilings on the reefs. They make their homes of thatch just as we do in Rālik, but they sink the corner posts and all the rest right down into the reef. It seemed to us they were landless. We studied them from a distance, and these village people did go ashore all the time. They seemed to trade with the people of the mainland, but we realized they seemed afraid of them just like we were. Sometimes, they would dump their goods and go away, and come back the next day to pick up what the mainlanders had left in return. Sometimes, they would meet them in the open on the beach, but they seemed afraid to venture far into the interior."

"So, did you make contact with these traders?" Ḷainjin asked.

"They are called Mwanus,"[120] the rijeḷā said. "Oh, yes. We became good trading friends."

"How?"

"We did what we do best." The rijeḷā laughed. "We went fishing! We trolled for tuna. The fishing was good, and we caught many tunas. When the

---

[120] The people living in villages who build on the reefs of Manus and the other islands of what is now called the Admiralty group.

tide was retreating, we piled them on one of the numerous sandspits ahead of their course, and then we sailed on an upwind course toward them and pointed to the place where we put them. They, of course, wanted the fish, so they stopped, and they left us coconuts, bananas, and *buai.*[121]

"What is buai?"

"It's shaped like a little coconut, and it grows in bunches on palm trees," said Ḷōbwilñawa. "The people of the west seem preoccupied with it. It keeps your teeth clean, like pandanus, but it is not sweet and is not food. It's bitter and very habit forming. They chew it wrapped in a leaf, with a sprinkle of baked, powdered coral."

"Preoccupied?" asked Lañinpo. "More like obsessed! It turns your whole mouth red— teeth and all. Rijeḷā, I used to watch you so seriously negotiating with them. This fellow has something to trade with us. We have something to trade with him. It's hard enough for one of you to understand what the other is trying to get across, and here's this fellow grabbing one nut after another from this basket around his neck. He splits each nut with his red-stained teeth. He puts half back in his bag. You can see he's counting how many he has left. He wraps the half nut in a leaf, sprinkling just the right amount of white powder from another container also hanging around his neck. Then he pops the whole thing, wrapped up just so, into his mouth and starts to chew with this look of absolute pleasure on his face, and you get the feeling he's not comprehended a word you have said or a motion you have made. That all he is thinking about is how many he has left, how long they will last, and what he must do, where he must go, to get more. I tell you, they're obsessed! They wake with buai on their mind, and they probably sleep thinking about it, as do their spirits once they're dead."

"Feigned disinterest and disengagement are characteristics of a successful trader," responded Ḷōbwilñawa.

"They don't seem to care if they get a good trade," Lañinpo said. "You have said many times they seem more interested in establishing partners to trade with than accumulating wealth. They're very generous traders, especially if you fatten the trade with buai. That always encourages them to

[121] Areca nut, often chewed wrapped in betel leaf *(Piper betel)* with a sprinkle of slaked lime: calcium hydroxide, $Ca(OH)_2$.

give more than they get. I've watched them trade with each other, and all they do is sit and chew that stuff. When they finally get up — red spit everywhere."

"Most of the time, the Mwanus spit in the ocean and you know it," retorted Ḷōbwilñawa. "It's true that to be a 'big man' in their way of life is to have many 'trade brothers.' It's also true that, because we did not value the buai nut, their trade for it seemed very generous. That was how it started. We followed them around. We fished, and they traded the fish they got from us to the islanders ashore, and they started giving us other stuff they thought we needed: eggs, twine, coconut oil in containers, caulk for our canoes, stuff like that. It wasn't until we followed a couple of these canoes all the way back to their home village that we got a chance to see all the stuff they obtained on these trading trips of theirs. We had anchored a respectable distance away, and one afternoon, under the bright sun, they brought us food in these beautiful hardwood bowls, baskets and strings of shells and dog teeth, and this single blackstone knife. It was black, actually, or it appeared black. Anyway, when we found out about this blackstone... What it could do. How it keeps its edge. Where it comes from — cooked and spit out by the fire mountains. That was it. We were hooked on one idea."

Like an expert storyteller, Ḷōbwilñawa stopped here to take a coconut from one of the leaf baskets on the boat. He punctured its mouth with his thumbnail and began sucking the water from the nut even as he kept his eyes on Ḷainjin, apparently waiting for him to finish what would be the first episode of his long story.

"Blackstone!" exclaimed Ḷainjin. "I get it. Why return from a trade with a basket of their buai nut when you could fill it with useful blackstone instead?"

The sky had dimmed as they talked. The orange-tipped gray clouds behind the mountains had faded, and the first stars of the night sky had appeared here and there amid the fading light blue sky. What afternoon breeze there had been now disappeared into the listless night air. The tide was still rising and slowly cooling the warm, thick air about them. He hadn't returned to his food despite his hunger. He had consumed every word and hardly noticed the fishermen returning from the kājokwā with their catch.

Ḷōbwilñawa wheezed his assent and belched loudly.

"Tell him about the Bar Nor!"[122] said Lañinpo.

"Yes, now who are they?" Ḷainjin was eager to know.

"The Bar Nor are the most hospitable people we traded with."

At this, Lañinpo began gyrating his hips and stomach, pantomiming the act of sexual intercourse.

"That's his very poor imitation of the Mwanus phallus dance," Ḷōbwilñawa said sarcastically.

Ḷainjin laughed. "What is that?"

"It's a silly dance Mwanus men perform with great seriousness. They cover their penis with a gourd, gyrate the thing back and forth, and swing it up and down to the beat of a slit drum."

Lañinpo added, "Young boys practice it all the time, without the gourd, much to the amusement of their elders. My sister hates it! To her, it typifies the male centeredness of their way of life."

"In what way?"

"Ask her! It's her favorite thing to talk about!"

"The Mwanus led us to the Bar Nor. They live two days across the sea in fair wind, but we had no idea. We were in awe the whole trip. They were taking us to a place that was bigger than anything we had ever imagined. They call it Papua."

"How big?" Ḷainjin asked.

Ḷōbwilñawa pointed at the mountains. "Can you imagine those mountains ten times higher? Can you imagine an island bigger by more than a hundred times?"

"No, I cannot."

"You are correct," said Ḷōbwilñawa. "There is no way to imagine it! Yet there we were near the base of a river they say came down from the mountains, and it was three times as wide as the passageway into the lagoon in front of Kariahn."

"The river contains gecko as large as your boat that swim and have teeth bigger than sharks," added Lañinpo.

---

[122] Melanesian peoples inhabiting the Murik Lakes region of what is now Papua New Guinea; a coastal, intertidal area characterized by connected inland lagoons seasonally flooded with overflow from the Sepik River.

Ḷainjin laughed. "Jeej! How big are the inchworms?"

"Don't laugh!" Ḷōbwilñawa cautioned, holding his hands wide. "They say they have worms that long! They say some of them have poison mouths!"

"*Ekūtañtañin eṃṃaan!*" chanted Ḷainjin.

They all laughed at his joke, but not in a light-throated way. They seemed to have lost any enthusiasm they'd once had for the place.

"This Papua sounds like an island of bad dreams!"

"Exactly," replied Ḷōbwilñawa. "Sometimes bad, sometimes good. You've only heard the beginning of our story. Bar Nor means 'mangrove man.' They live on a lagoon surrounded by mangrove just inside the coast, just north of a river they call Sepik, in houses like those of the Mwanus. Over the water, only not on reefs, right off the shore. They're so hospitable they provide their women for your entertainment."

"Tell him the story of Andena[123] and he'll understand," interjected Lañinpo.

"The Bar Nor tell the story of two brothers. The elder is Andena. When the younger brother, Arena,[124] and his age group are ready for initiation into the men's cult, Andena sails off to trade for the necessary number of pigs, leaving his woman Mwed in Arena's care. One day, Mwed decides to go fishing and paddles down the river close to where Arena is pounding sago pith."

"What is 'sago'?" Ḷainjin asked.

"It's starch from a palm tree they plant along the banks of the river, like taro," Ḷōbwilñawa said. "It tastes like arrowroot, but it doesn't take as much work per pouch, although it takes more steps to process.

"Anyway, when Arena gets tired of pounding, he picks up a section of white sago bark and begins to scratch his design onto it. After a while, he discards it into the water, and it floats down to where Mwed is fishing. She covets the design and asks Arena to tattoo it on her. 'Where?' he asks. She tries to fit the piece of bark in several places on her body and decides the best place for it is between her legs, so she spread her legs for him. When elder

[123] The elder brother in "The Two Brothers," a folktale told by the Sepik area peoples.

[124] The younger brother in "The Two Brothers."

brother returns and sees the tattoo, he's jealous of younger brother but starts building the men's house for his brother's age group. He allows each young man to carve his design into the center post. When the design of younger brother matches that between Mwed's legs, elder brother has his proof and decides what he must do. When they ready the hole for the center post, he gives his younger brother the honor of entering the hole and guiding the post into place, but in anticipation of what was to come, younger brother has already dug a wide side tunnel for his survival. He feigns injury by spitting betel juice at the base of the pole. Once it's set, the older brother accuses the younger of raping his woman and orders the hole filled in on top of him. That night, Arena climbs out and sets to work making himself a proa in which to leave the island.

"A few days later, Andena is out hunting for pigs when he comes across Arena constructing his proa. Thinking his younger brother dead, he disregards the resemblance and asks him to make a proa for him. Arena responds, 'Okay, but you pound sago so we can go to the offshore islands and trade for pigs.' Andena agrees and plants all the sago in the swamps of the lower Sepik River. When the proas are ready, the two men load them with sago and sail out into the ocean, but Arena has tricked his brother. He used a weaker vine on the lashings of his brother's proa, and it breaks up in the waves. And when Andena calls for help, the younger brother refuses, announces to his brother who he is, and sails away, never to return.

"Andena eventually made it to shore, constructed another proa, and set after Arena, distributing gifts wherever he went. He gave the coastal peoples the tools and trading skills they needed to become wealthy. He taught them to treat the visiting off-island trader as their long-lost brother, and so they treated *us* everywhere we went. They taught us their language and customs. They fed us and gave us women."[125]

"When I was young, they didn't pay me much attention. In later seasons," boasted Lañinpo, "a line of young women was waiting for me outside in the rain. There was my sister, who was livid over it all! Then

[125] The story of Andena and Arena has been borrowed from *Mangrove Man* by David Lipset, page 73 . (See bibliography for full citation.)

there was our host, insisting I sleep first with his wife, and finally, there was Ḷōbwilñawa, cautioning me to be polite. It was a crazy experience to say the least. And—"

"Misunderstand us not! They're as jealous as the next man!" Ḷōbwilñawa interjected. "They fight over women all the time. They will kill a man they don't like, boil his head, and adorn their house with his skull, but they treat offshore traders like long-lost little brothers who can do no wrong."

"But obviously something did go very wrong, right?" Ḷainjin asked.

"Trade is always a shark tooth," Ḷōbwilñawa said. "It has three sides. We didn't understand this and never took the time to understand the people of the bush with whom our partners traded. The bush-beach trade is starch for fish. The bush people pounded the sago and raised the taro and bananas and all that, and the coastal people caught the fish, but they treated the bush people with disdain. They considered them poor and ignorant. The Bar Nor sent their women to trade with them. That would be an insult anywhere else on the coast, and the Bush Murik, as they called them, treated the Bar Nor as spoiled children and always let them get the best of the deal. Then when off-island traders came, the Bar Nor were able to pass on the generosity of the bush people as their own."

"So, what happened?" Ḷainjin asked.

"Nothing happened for a long time, but at the same time, something else was going on. Look at it this way. You go to Kariahn to get an item you need, and you have things to trade. Are you going to announce to everyone what you want?"

"No, that wouldn't be smart. If they know I need it, the price will be higher, and I would end up with a poorer trade," responded Ḷainjin.

"That's right!" Ḷōbwilñawa congratulated him. "You would practice deception. You might pretend you're interested in something else and only casually ask about the thing you want — and maybe include it as part of a larger trade. You might even end the day and return home without anyone knowing what you needed. What I'm trying to say is that not only did we not understand the third side of the triangle, but even the people we traded with didn't always understand they weren't getting what they needed. Nor did they understand, nor even care to understand, what resentment was building.

"The Mwanus left us there in Murik[126] amid the Bar Nor just in time for the rainy season. That took us by surprise. At that point, we didn't understand how upside down the weather was. We were expecting dry winds of our *añõneañ* and got rainstorms of *añõnrak*[127] instead. You can't imagine the rainstorms they have there. It rained under the next three moons, but we fished and traded the fish for sago. When Jebrọ rose, their dry season came with southeast winds, and we followed the Bar Nor to islands off the coast to the north that were part of their trading circle.

"We traded the sago we collected from the Bush Murik for the pigs the Bar Nor wanted. When we returned to Murik, they gave us baskets for the pigs, and we traded the baskets to the returning Mwanus for blackstone they collected from an island called Lou that was part of their circle. We fished every day while the Mwanus rested and traded the fish for sago, and we followed the Mwanus back to Lou to trade for blackstone. But then the Mwanus, when they realized it was blackstone we were after, told us about still another trading circle farther south along the coast of Papua centered on Sigaba. Across a channel from Sigaba lies Siassi.[128] The people of that island traded blackstone in abundance to the islanders of Sigaba for the *pwentang*[129] they made. We returned to Murik and fished and traded for these things while we waited for the Mwanus to do the same off their mainland. When they returned to Murik, they traded their sago and buai nut to the Bar Nor for baskets, and we followed them to Manam,[130] the fire island, on the way to Sigaba. There we traded baskets and sago for almonds and pigs. These we brought to Sigaba and traded for the

---

[126] The Murik Lakes lie just north of the mouth of the Sepik River. The Bar Nor live in five or so villages along the banks of its mangrove swamp. It was a precontact maritime trading center similar to Sigaba.

[127] Call of the south"; the northern solstice, which annually coincides with summer in the northern hemisphere.

[128] A volcanic island (Umboi) between the mainland of Papua New Guinea and the island of New Britain. It was a third center of precontact trade concentric with Sigaba.

[129] Titan word for "cooking pot."

[130] Known locally as Manam Motu, Manam is an island located in the Bismarck on the northeast coast of mainland Papua New Guinea. The island was created by the activity of the Manam volcano, one of the country's most active.

blackstone they had received from the Siassi for their pwentang. It's a circle of trade, get it?"

"Sago, buai nut, almonds, pwentang… I have no idea what those things are," Ļainjin said. "But never mind, they are things of the Mwanus, Bar Nor, Siassi… And now what did you say these people of Sigaba are called?"

"Like most off-island people, they came in proa from somewhere else, and they call themselves 'beach men,' " Ļōbwilñawa said. "But the mangrove men call them 'grass men' — Kunai[131] — after the grass that covers the coastal plain they plant with yams."

"They're planters like Ewalt?" Ļainjin asked.

"Yes, but like the Mwanus, they're also fishermen. They trade pwentang to the Siassi for their great proa and sail a bit up and down the coast, but the Kunai are known, like the Bar Nor, for their hospitality and generosity to traders. They're famous as middlemen and pride themselves on having many trading brothers."

"Tell me about these pwentang."

Ļōbwilñawa cracked open the unripe coconut he had been drinking from and held it before him. "Imagine fashioning something of this shape, only larger, from the thick red mud you probably slipped on coming down the mountain from Ewalt's house. Imagine it having a lip around the base so it wouldn't tip and spill. Now imagine firing it by continuing to pile dry grass on top until it bakes hard as stone. Now you have a container to pour water and boil food. You have a pwentang, which is a Titan[132] word. There are other names for it. Titan is the language of the Mwanus, who introduced these things to us."

"Except that men don't make them," added Lañinpo. "Only women make them. A man would never make a pwentang. It's women's work. Men dig the mud and deliver it in baskets, but only the women know how to fashion the pwentang, and trust me, they're not telling the men! They tell the men that, if they make pwentang, their balls will grow as big as the pwentang they make, and the men believe them! It's a woman's only advantage."

---

[131] "Grass men"; also, the New Guinea pidgin English term for "grass," or *imperata cylindrica.* The edges of this grass are narrow, serrated, and very sharp. It catches fire easily and is between two and ten feet high.

[132] The language of the Mwanus.

"Let me get this straight," Ḷainjin said. "These Kunai women of Sigaba are the only ones who know how to make these pwentang?"

"No, women up and down the coast make pwentang, but only the Kunai trade their women's pwentang," Ḷōbwilñawa said. "They, like the Saudeleur, have developed a culture to welcome people with a fair system of trade. Like the offshore lagoon homes of the Mwanus and the homes on the water in the Murik lagoon and like the stone village here, their little island off the coast offers a readily accessible onshore lagoon to traders seeking refuge. What trader wants to chance running into an arrow or spear foraging inland on an island previously unknown to him?"

"But isn't that exactly what ended up happening?"

"Yes, but not the way you think. It was more complicated than that. Every story has its beginning and end. The why of the end? Therein lies the purpose of the tale. Yes, our story ends in violence, but it was not the result of our arrival that terrible day. It was the result of many seasons of complicated interchange without regard to the needs of the people of the bush. We continued to trade even during the seasons the Mwanus, the Bar Nor, and the Kunai — even the offshore Siassi — shivered in their huts. Ultimately, what ended up happening was the result of our greed for—"

"Blackstone!" Ḷainjin said.

Ḷōbwilñawa grinned. "Good lad. Now you're looking through the details to the why of the story. The bush people, as the Kunai called them, were their traditional trading partners. They were their enemies as well as their trade friends. They traded with them out of necessity. The moon the Kunai call *sulu*[133] is their hungry time. It corresponds roughly to the end of our wet season when theirs is about to begin. By that time, they've exhausted their supply of yams from the previous season's crop. By the time of *sulu*, they would have planted all their seed yams during the dry season just passed. These seeds would grow large during the upcoming wet season, but the Kunai must survive to harvest them. The southeasterly winds of trade would have died out, and they couldn't expect their Siassi friends to return at least until the moon they call *ṃaj*,[134] the moon before

[133] Kunai word for October.
[134] Approximately April.

Jebrọ. Their enemies, the hinterland people whom they call the Komba,[135] may have killed a few of their planters who ventured too close to their hills beyond the coastal plains, but the Komba know they're hungry, so the time is right to bring their mountain taro down to trade with their 'friends' for their blackstone and pwentang.

"Everywhere up and down the coast of this great island, people base all this trade with the bush people on personal relationships. A western man boasts of how many trade brothers he has — even among his enemies. These trade relationships supersede cult-initiation killings and provide unconditional protection to trade partners. No man would ever consider killing his trade partner. Therefore, you can trade with him even though, if truth be told, he would rather eat you than chase down and risk attacking a wild boar. They say there are maybe hundreds of tribes, cultures, and languages in the Papua bush and hinterlands, and they're all enemies of each other because the one thing they share is the belief that you're not a man until you have killed one. Yet they make this exception for a man who arrives in their midst bearing items to trade."

"You make noise with your mouth, tattooless one, but you have no opinion! Who have you killed?" shouted Lañinpo. "I got so sick of hearing them taunt me like that! I let them bleed my penis."

"You mean you let them circumcise you?" Ḷainjin asked.

"The Kunai do not circumcise." Ḷōbwilñawa laughed at Lañinpo's expense. "They circumnavigate!" He took the sharp piece of blackstone and pretended to cut the skin all the way around his thumb.

"Jeej!" exclaimed Ḷainjin, looking at Lañinpo.

"Yes, I had them do that too," he said. "Women like it. It's exceptionally clean. But that's not what they call bleeding. That's a ceremony you do first along with your age group. It's secret, and if I tell you about it, they say I'll die!"

"Nonsense!" exclaimed Ḷōbwilñawa. "I know exactly what they did to you, but it's not worth talking about. I'm going to finish my story!"

---

[135] The mountain or hinterland villagers inland of Sio (Sigaba). They live on the Huon Peninsula of New Guinea and were both enemies and trading partners of the Kunai.

"Ḷōpako," continued Lañinpo, as though this was a point of honor, "first you let them bleed you. Then you kill a man. Then you get circumcised. That is the order of manhood."

"Now, the Kunai use blackstone for circumcision," continued the rijeḷā, "but some of them also love to shave their faces with it. As you can see, that's one custom I found comfortable to adopt. They shave the heads of their boys from the time they climb down until they conduct the bleeding ceremony. The Komba use the blackstone for some of the same purposes, but their age-group boys must kill a man and boil his head first. The same for the trading partners of the Komba all along the hinterlands above the coast. However, the Kunai, who trade their pwentang to the Siassi for the blackstone, started trading their blackstone to us instead, for the sago we brought to them despite the severe weather."

Lañinpo interjected. "There's one thing you need to understand about blackstone. It's so handy you start using it to cut everything, but that's a mistake because, once it loses its edge, it does not sharpen well."

"It's the hardest thing out there, so what are you going to sharpen it with?" questioned Ḷōbwilñawa. "Pumice stone?"

"Why not?" Ḷainjin asked.

"Because pumice stone is basically ash that floats from the fire mountains, but this was baked in the fires of the mountain. It was turned hard and brittle like the baked mud that makes the pwentang."

"I have to see one of these pwentang to understand completely," Ḷainjin said.

"Ask the Saudeleur. We gave a few to him when we first arrived," Lañinpo said. "He is careful with them. Oh, yes! The other thing you need to understand is that these pwentang will break if you drop them or even knock them over."

"Can I continue now?" asked Ḷōbwilñawa, as though piqued by the interruption. "After several seasons of sailing and up and down the coast, our boats were starting to sit low in the water with all the blackstone they were carrying, and we had transported most of the pwentang offshore. The Komba had a large crop of young men needing to take heads, and they were all waiting for fresh blackstone flakes for their cult-circumcision ceremonies that would follow. At the same time, their women were annoying them for more pwentang."

"So that's why they attacked. To steal your blackstone!" Ḷainjin said.

"Wrong. Western men do not steal! They would rather die than have it said they stole from someone. They didn't touch our craft. They were mad we were taking all the blackstone, but they came for our heads."

"Well, what did the Kunai have to say about all this?" Ḷainjin asked. "You said they were their enemies."

"The Kunai said, 'Don't follow them! That's what they want.' That's why the Komba took the women, so they could hide in the grass with their longbows and stop our men in their tracks like pigs. And unfortunately, that's exactly what happened, based on reports we received from the Kunai who were returning from their inland gardens.

"They call themselves 'trade brothers' because a man inherits his father's trade relationships. Some of these relationships are hundreds of seasons old, and we decided to trade everywhere based on greed. Who could blame the Kunai if they were silently relieved? Every head of Rālik the Komba took was a head they would not take from the Kunai. Killing our people probably didn't even affect these long-established trade relationships with them. By now, there has probably been peace for many seasons, and there is only the story of what happened that's passed on as a lesson to the boys in the men's house."

At this point in his story, word came from the Saudeleur that they would drink sakau together the evening next. He had commanded the kājokwā retrieved by then, and he would offer wealth-or-title rewards to all involved. Ḷainjin realized his new friends had much to decide. They expected the Saudeleur to contact Ḷōbwedi. How were they to contact Rojak? Where, by the way, were they? Were they perhaps retrieving a stone from Sokehs?

"Well, rijeḷā," commented Ḷainjin, "that was an amazing story. Fire mountains, geckos as long as proa, and cannibals with longbows. I can't wait to hear more, but I just remembered I forgot something at Idedh, so I must return there. Tomorrow, we will drink sakau together and talk more."

With that, he excused himself. He took his basket of food back to his boat, lifted anchor, and retreated into the night. Stunned, yet he paddled.

Exhausted, yet he guided his craft down the tideway. His throat cut. His life's blood seemed drained from his body. He craved thoughtlessness. Solitude. He was thinking not about wealth or title. He had heard his mother's story, and yes, it was more exciting than he had imagined, and yes, he got its meaning. It was greed. They hadn't been rushing to return to Rālik, yet what a triumphant return that would have been. Over all these years, he'd had no idea they had purposefully stayed so long. Had she not been thinking of him? Yet she had been a leader of men, and a good leader doesn't lead based on what she wants but what her followers want. It must have been a group decision. Indeed, Bwilñawa's story spoke in terms of *them* not her. It had been a lot to take in. Little did he realize the biggest twist was still to unfold.

Ļōbwedi's story

The half-moon, though setting, was still high in the evening sky when Ļainjin beached his canoe a third time and walked over to the perfectly still pool at Idedh. What he saw there bewildered him. There in the clear water and still bright enough moonlight, he saw a large fish being eaten by three eels. By their size and distinctive colorings, he recognized them as eels he had caught. The largest one was blue speckled and the other two, yellow speckled. Had they followed the coral cave Wottok claimed trailed beneath the reef from the islet Darong across the canal? The fish was too large for any one of the eels to consume whole. They appeared to be fighting, writhing upon one another, each clutching tenaciously to the fish. It looked like the same one he had lowered into the well of Nahn Samohl earlier that morning. He watched as each eel tore its part away from the others then retreated out of his sight into the caverns beneath the pool's ledge. He ambled over to the well and pulled on the line tied to the hanging-spar, to which he had tied the fish, realizing immediately that the fish was gone. Had one or other of these three dared to enter the cave of Nahn Samohl and steal the fish from her? That was when he noticed an odor rising from the well. Had he noticed that before? He wasn't sure.

Ļainjin dove into the canal and swam over to Darong. The pool there was nearly four times as large and dotted with the giant clams the Saudeleur was breeding. Unlike at Idedh across the way, though, there was no ledge beneath the water's perimeter except at the pool's northwest corner, which was closest to Idedh, and that's where the eels liked to reside. Sure enough, once there, he saw what appeared to be the same speckled eels he had just seen disappear from the pool across the canal at Idedh. So, the under-the-reef passageway between the pools that Wottok had told him about must be true. Then how had the three eels managed to wrestle the fish away from the giant one, Nahn Samohl, or had they?

Returning to Idedh, Ḷainjin walked the perimeter walls and watched the half-moon set behind the mountains. Would he take wealth or title? Talupe had heard of his wealth yet left him rejected. What title had her man with the broken hand? None, according to Ewalt. Then Ḷainjin would choose title and make her wish she had shunned him not! With that bone caught in his craw, he took advantage of the last of the high tide and paddled back to Kelepwei to anchor his craft and sleep.

The next morning brought an eastern sky of bright red. The ocean had turned smooth as it lapped, like a sleeper's breath, on the surrounding reefs at low tide. Every canoe had long since crossed the reefs and plied its way to the kājokwā to assist in hauling it ashore. The day turned hot and sticky without even a whisper of air from the surrounding sea. The sun glared from a cloudless sky, yet the cooking smoke hung low to the ground and failed to dissipate. Men sought shade wherever they could and fanned themselves like fires with the warm, thick air wafting their sweaty faces. The noon tide brought boat after boat of breadfruit and coconuts, and then the Saudeleur ordered the sakau stones to ring out in the early afternoon to announce the feast for those who labored at sea. The rijeḷā, perhaps sensing a storm brewing, ordered their proas to be carried through the entrance of Kelepwei and left there. His craft safe behind the walls, Ḷainjin waded in chest-high water with the others to Pahn Kadira, where they knew Raipuinlañ's attendants would give them fresh, dry kilts to wear at the upcoming wealth-or-title ceremony.

The first round of sakau passed with word that seamen had successfully anchored the kājokwā behind the walls at Kariahn. As they arrived, the Saudeleur met them at the entrance and invited those who had asked permission to beach their canoes within the courtyard. Finally, the festivities began with singing, chanting, and the sound of the thwacking of their short hardwood spears. As the afternoon wore on, Ḷainjin noticed the smoke from the fires begin to swirl as a light breeze began to churn the dead air among them. There came a shift of expectation with the natural cooling of the evening preceding the setting of the afternoon sun. Amid the festivities, Ḷainjin rose and walked to the entrance of Pahn Kadira just as the Saudeleur put the wealth-or-title question to his friends.

"Did the Saudeleur also know that the great spirit was coming?" thought Ḷainjin as he looked out and saw what they had been expecting. Although the light, friendly breeze was refreshing and immediately began to dry the sweat that poured from his body, it was causing the many boats anchored in the retreating tide in the canal outside the compound to begin bumping gently against each other. A few of the wiser seamen had turned their heads to view the dark gray chimera creeping across the horizon.

Ḷōbwedi, who had arrived late and sat among the Saudeleur's contingent, was the first called. Although he appeared to speak fluent Pohnpeian, he had Ewalt there to assist with the prolonged explanation of the title he accepted, and the land associated with it. The Saudeleur called Ḷōbwilñawa next. As expected, he chose the same, even as it became gradually obvious to all that the gray had quickly overcome the clear blue of the eastern horizon and some sort of shadow was nearly upon them. The Saudeleur next called Lañinpo and his absent sister. He chose title for himself and, per her previous inclination, wealth for his sister.

Finally, as though he were master of the imminent specter about to descend among them, the Saudeleur hushed the sakau stones and called Ḷainjin. Like the others, he kneeled before the Saudeleur.

"Title?" he asked. Ḷainjin nodded his assent.

Then the Saudeleur held his arms wide. The sound of the first gusts rushed though the rustling palms, and their crowns nodded as though to his command. Cold, horizontal raindrops began to prick at their backs. With rain in face and wind in hair, the Saudeleur next announced to all who could hear that the newcomer had accepted the title Jau Areu. That he would be the new custodian of Idedh. And then, to the surprise of all, that he was the son of the famed Tarmālu and would enjoy his protection from the highest mountains of Pohnpei to its most distant shores. Ewalt's father, Wottok, flinching not from the rain, appeared from the crowd behind the Saudeleur and presented to him a large *wapepe* he had lashed together, by tradition, from the roots of the pandanus tree. The Saudeleur held his symbol high, defying the storm even as most of his followers had begun to head for the cover of the easternmost wall or, depending on their status, into one or the other of the thatch shelters.

Ḷainjin, who'd quickly lost track of Ḷōbwilñawa and Lañinpo in the tumult, had begun a search for Lipanmai when a strong hand gripped him firmly from behind. It was Ḷōbwedi. He bore the same serious yet light-throated expression he'd had when they last spoke. He beckoned Ḷainjin to follow and led him through the pummeling rain into the dimly lit house of the Saudeleur. The air had cooled, and although attendants were moving about and stoking his fire, the paramount chief was not there. Ḷōbwedi offered Ḷainjin a place to sit and dry himself before the fire.

"The title you accepted offers certain privileges. You may now enter his abode as you wish."

With that — and much to Ḷainjin's surprise — Ḷōbwedi took the liberty to walk over to one of many shelves of the Saudeleur's possessions and returned carrying a large cup, perhaps one of those pwentang Ḷōbwilñawa had mentioned in his stories.

"You should have told me you were the baby we left behind. I would have tried to cradle you with kisses on behalf of your mother — right there at that kājokwā. Do you not know you were the topic of her every conversation? She had a pastime game she would play. 'What is he doing now,' she would ask, and whoever she was speaking to had to play along and imagine an answer."

"Perhaps I neglected to realize my name was of importance to you."

"We loved your mother and followed her over horizon after horizon," Ḷōbwedi said, "and you wonder if her son would be important to us? You are the *ak* who flies low on the beach to warn us of what is to come. You are the feathers we tie to our sails to tell us *ṇatọọn*[136] or no!"

"To speak the truth, I have found it beneficial not to reveal who I am in order to get to the truth of what happened to her."

"Truth? You are the *wapepe* we cherish that guides our way home! Why would we steal one item of truth from your ears?"

[136] Sheet in or trim the sail.

"You are the—"

"Jau Areu," said Raipuinlañ, entering from his sleeping quarters behind the shelves where Ḷōbwedi had taken the pwentang. Unlike Ḷainjin and Ḷōbwedi, the Saudeleur had dried and changed his kilt. Outside, the squall was raging, and people had mostly taken cover. Here or there, a squeal or a shout echoed off the walls though the sound of thick rain pouring down the thatch onto the stones of the courtyard muffled all else.

"Is that the one?" asked the Saudeleur in Pohnpeian, reaching to take the pwentang from Ḷōbwedi.

"That's the one the wife of my Bar Nor trade brother gave me the morning we departed the Murik lagoon for the last time." Ḷōbwedi responded first in Pohnpeian and then in Kajin Rālik, but Ḷainjin's knowledge of Pohnpeian was now such that he understood well enough and shook his head to allow Bwedi[137] to continue in Pohnpeian.

Bwedi said something about his trade brother's wife handing the pwentang to him along with a small pandanus mat and telling him to wrap it up so as not to let it break against the hull. Then he made a joke, saying he always did exactly what she wanted him to do and that she was always so loud in her gratefulness he'd always expected her husband to object! At which point both men laughed as though this was the part of the story the Saudeleur relished most. It was obviously a story told many times and, having the benefit of hearing comparable stories of the Murik women's "generosity" from Ḷōbwilñawa and Lañinpo, Ḷainjin understood why they were laughing.

Then the Saudeleur reminded him of their last meeting, when Ḷainjin had asked about his mother and he had told him to wait and ask the Seekers. Now the Saudeleur seemed to be apologizing for something, offering a Pohnpeian saying — "half a story is a dangerous thing" — in his defense.

Ḷōbwedi turned to Ḷainjin and spoke in Kajin Rālik. "You see, only the women made pwentang, and that was the sort of thing your mother learned about," he said sadly, with empathy for his lost friend. "The twins' mother and your mother spent a lot of time with the women of Sigaba, learning their language, customs, and all their skills. I know they made a few pwentang

[137] Aka Ḷōbwedi; a Seeker.

because I went with the Kunai men and dug up mud for them, but I don't believe they ever made enough good ones to trade. They may not have even fired any, or if they did, they gave them away to their women friends as mementos. That's what women do! Right?"

"I don't understand what you're getting at," said Ḷainjin.

"When we left Murik for the last time," Ḷōbwedi continued, "we stopped at several islands along the way and gave away and received many gifts. Wrapped up as it was, I forgot about this pwentang most of the time." He went on to explain that when they had first arrived in Pohnpei, they cleaned many gifts from their proas and gave them to the Saudeleur. This pwentang among them.

"I was afraid to use this pwentang," the Saudeleur said. "I was afraid my attendants would break it. I knew the *wapepe* symbol and its meaning from Ḷōbwedi, but I did not understand the meaning of X." He handed the pwentang back to Ḷōbwedi.

Ḷainjin sat there with a look, he supposed, of confusion on his face. He had no idea what they were getting at.

"Then one day a few seasons ago" Ḷōbwedi explained, "we were sitting here, and Raipuinlañ handed the pwentang to me and asked what the Xs meant. So, I turned it over for the first time and instantly I knew it was your mother who'd made it." He handed the pwentang to Ḷainjin. "Here, look for yourself."

Ḷainjin accepted the pwentang. It was heavier than he imagined it would be. Fingers had clearly smoothed the inside, the lip, and base. Her fingers? Permanently fired to last forever and now passed on to him? What were the chances? Thoughts of his mother and his childhood without her swelled up in his throat. He was about to embarrass himself with tears when the Saudeleur pointed to the pwentang and rotated his finger in the air. Ḷainjin turned the pwentang over and there — etched and fired hard within the circular base — was the *wapepe* symbol!

"We have no knowledge of how or when it got to the Murik lagoon," Ḷōbwedi said. "The distance is considerable. But it is a trading center. Had we looked at the underside there, I'm sure we would have returned to Sigaba. We never would have left."

After studying the pwentang for some time and imagining what it would be like to try and piece it together if it ever broke, Ḷainjin's eyes focused on the same four X symbols that had been added to the original design. The center of the design is normally blank to represent the nonapparent searched-for island, but there in the center of the design was an X similar to the one he himself had sewn onto the design on his alele at Kariahn. Then, as if for good measure, there were Xs marking where the four quadrants crossed as the swells bent around the island. All these Xs had confused the Saudeleur and appeared out of place to him.

"Why the Xs?" Ḷainjin asked.

"That's why I knew one of them, probably your mother, made that thing!" blurted Ḷōbwedi. He crossed his arms to make an X. "She taught us to use that symbol as a sign to the other craft in our fleet if we needed help."

"You mean this was meant as a message that she's still alive and crying for help?"

"Believe me, I have asked myself that question season in and season out ever since the Saudeleur first pointed out the underside of that thing," admitted Ḷōbwedi.

"Half story very dangerous!" offered Raipuinlañ.

"If you think about it," added Ḷōbwedi, "all we really know is that at least one of them must have survived their capture and, for a season or two at least, made pwentang as part the bush-beach trade that somehow eluded our awareness at Sigaba."

When the Saudeleur reiterated the proverb of the half story for the third time, Ḷainjin realized that Ḷōbwedi — in connivance with Raipuinlañ or under his command — had probably not told the others. Obviously, it was in the best interest of Nahn Madol that the Seekers continue fetching the kājokwā needed to build the village. Ḷainjin could taste the blood as he bit the inside of his lip but spoke not another significant word. Better to think through all these conflicting emotions that welled up and consult with Ḷōbwedi at another time, and not in the chief's presence.

Later, Ḷōbwedi took Ḷainjin's hand as if he was keeping a child from straying away. He led him away from the fire toward the storm. The evening now covered in premature darkness, the children squealed as they played in the water draining off the eaves of the thatch roof of the Saudeleur's house, and three or four adults scurried from here to there under cover of an eave or pandanus matting. The combination of rain and wind pimpled Ḷainjin's skin, and he hesitated for an instant as they stepped out into the windstorm.

Ḷōbwedi squeezed his hand and shouted over the sound of the wind and pelting rain. "Never cringe in the face of an enemy, a storm, or a woman you want!"

Ḷainjin followed his example and sauntered slowly, as though unaffected by the tempest. They exited the side away from Kelepwei and stepped into an ankle-high mixture of chilly incoming tide, rainwater, and storm waves surging through the canals of the village. The light of the half-moon was completely undershadowed by the black clouds and horizontal rain assailing them. Ḷōbwedi led him down the canals to one of the many small islets at the northeast section of the village protected by the massive, double barrier walls that surrounded the superstructure of Nahn Dowas still under construction. They entered a small, raised hut with a fire pit that reminded him of Wottok and Kiton's modest home on the hill above. Ḷōbwedi's daughter fixed her gaze on the fire she tended. He introduced her as the only light in his world. She blushed and displayed a quick but beautiful smile as her father handed her the basket of food he had carried from the feast and told her to eat. Ḷōbwedi grabbed a fresh kilt from somewhere and handed it to him.

"And her mother?" Ḷainjin tied on the kilt and dropped the one beneath.

"Gone," he said, not specifying if she had died or run away. "We will sleep here tonight. I know you have many questions for me, and I owe it to your mother not to hold anything back."

As the tide rose and the storm waves began to surge violently through the village canals, they — cradled by the great walls about them — began a slow and pensive conversation. Ḷainjin's questions came quickly, like the tiny coals formed in a trough of soft wood after energetic abrasion by a hardwood spindle. Ḷōbwedi's answers came slowly, like the gentle aspiration needed to first smoke the tinder, then kindle the flame that began to burn within him.

"One question has gone unanswered my whole life," Ḷainjin said. "Who is my father?"

After a period of silence, Ḷōbwedi responded. "I will tell you the truth. You have made it clear that this is what you want. Your mother speared and bound the throats of men like so many fish on a stringer. Who says that Raipuinlañ himself was not one? She was slow to acknowledge your father. Undoubtedly part of her plan. Knowing her, she probably wanted all the *irooj* she had slept with at that time to wonder if you were theirs. She was very smart and thought through everything. Anyway, when we faced the storm, the mystery became clear to all her crew. The two argued up and down the shore as we all rushed to provision our vessels. They say she wanted him to stay behind with you. He insisted on accompanying her. His name was Kāmeto,[138] and he was a loyal member of her crew. He was her steersman. If she wanted to die, they would both die. That was his argument, and he was the only one to suggest that leaving the lagoon to protect the fleet might not be the best course of action. They could always repair the boats or remake them. All we heard her shout was what her fathers had taught her: "*Emejjia wa iḷometo.*"[139] Kāmeto kept his part of their bargain. They died together — or so we thought. After they took your mother, he was the one who led the others ashore. The Komba cut them down like pigs in the grass. So, who was right? Most of us survived the sea. Not so the shore!"

"That isn't the story I expected."

"None of this is likely to end up the way you expect."

"I must agree with that," Ḷainjin said. "Continue!"

Ḷōbwedi's daughter had retreated from the fire and begun tasting the food in the basket her father had brought her. The last of the flame had broken into mangrove coals, so she crawled forward with another stick and breadfruit-leaf stub to fan the fire back to light. On his part, Ḷōbwedi stepped to the door and walked out to test the strength of the storm. He returned just as the flame broke over the fresh firewood and dried himself in the flames.

"This is much better than heaving to and crawling into a rocking hull," he said, sitting down. "You are a strong man full of youthful energy. It's not going to be easy for you to understand an old man's reluctance to retrace his course and return to a nightmare he barely lived through in his past.

[138] Name: "Fly the ocean."

[139] "A boat dies slow in the open ocean."

Ḷōbwilñawa knows about the pwentang too. He hasn't seen it, but I told him as soon as the Saudeleur questioned me about it. Together, we decided not to tell the children until they grew up. Then when they grew up, our excuse was to give them more instruction to prepare them should they want to return. Disregard these excuses. If you want the truth… Okay, I'll admit it. We are cowards. Our life is comfortable. We brave a short season at sea each year and return as heroes with offers of wealth or title. Why would an old man risk all this to cast himself back into his past to see if just maybe, against all odds, he might perfect his story?

"Even if one or the other of them is still alive," Ḷōbwedi continued, "how would you overcome the longbows of the Komba? The Kunai told me they have never successfully attacked one of their villages on the hilltops. They see them coming!"

"I will attack them at night," Ḷainjin said.

"Attack which village? There are many, and the night brings its own problems. The kunai plain swarms with mosquitos that can literally drain a man of blood. That's why they crowd onto Sigaba, their tiny island off the coast."

"If you teach me where, I'll go. Once there, I'll think of something."

"Ḷainjin, trust me. You are unlikely to survive. Even your mother, I know, would say, 'Stay where you're safe.'"

"If that is so, why did she send that pwentang to me? Why is she calling for my help?"

"I grant that one or the other called for our help back then, back there," Ḷōbwedi said, "but look at you. You're a grown man. That was not under the last moon. That was how many seasons ago? Yes, I grant that we failed them back then, but they're probably dead by now. That place isn't healthy! There is much sickness and death to be encountered daily."

"If my destiny is to die searching for her, then that's the story your daughter will pass to her children and them theirs.'"

The young woman looked up at him briefly. Ḷōbwedi walked out once more into the storm, perhaps to gather his thoughts. Perhaps to garnish the strength for what he would say next. This time, he was gone for a long while. So long that Ḷainjin was about to fall asleep thinking about all he had heard.

When Ḷōbwedi returned, it was as though the gale had calmed him and swept away the last of his contention. He sat again before the hearth and picked at the coals with his daughter's fire stick. Then placed another stick of mangrove but refrained from fanning. His daughter had curled onto a mat in the corner, apparently sleeping. Finally, he looked humbly and deeply through the dim light into Ḷainjin's eyes and proceeded with a hint of hesitation in his voice.

"What did Ḷōbwilñawa have to say about those western men?"

"He told me you could trade with them, even the cannibals, and that they never steal."

"That's what I expected," Ḷōbwedi said. "He told you the truth but left out the one thing meant to kill you."

"I know they probably raped her! Rojak and I talked about that."

"That is the only thing they can steal — the life of a man but, more than that, the soul of the man. They can kill a man, boil his head in a pwentang, and hang it from the eave of their house, but they leave his spear where it lay to prove they had but one intention — to steal only his life. Taking the head is symbolic of capturing the soul. They can also take a man's woman or a boy's mother to disgrace him. The woman becomes the property of the men's house to serve their needs until no man wants her anymore. That's how they get around the stealing part. They've only captured her. Their purpose is to lure their enemies to their stronghold, where they hold all the advantages, where the avengers will be few against many."

"How can they be so—"

"Cruel?"

"That's it!" said Ḷainjin.

"Trust me, you have no idea what cruelty looks like, and it has two brothers. One called ignorance, the other revenge. Ignorance will frustrate you. It is unpredictable. Revenge will suck you in and cause you to defeat yourself."

"Strange, my grandfathers told me that too."

"At that place," Ḷōbwedi said, "on the strand above the high-water line of the beach where they captured your mother, there lies a carved log with an image of a man with a long nose that hangs down like a penis."

He looked back over his shoulder, as though to assure himself that his daughter hadn't stirred. "The Kunai tell what they insist is a true story of a man who came down from inland over the mountains. Not the hilltops where the Komba live, but beyond the mountains behind them. Mountains so high they appear impossible to climb. The man lived in one of the Komba villages for many seasons. Then one day, he appeared for the first time on the shore, that very shore where, many seasons later, they captured your mother. He had sent away the Komba who'd brought him there with several wild boars they had killed and his many goods to trade, and there he was, signaling to the Kunai from shore. The little Black man also brought tied domesticated pigs, and their grunting and squealing as he taunted them was very appealing to the Kunai.

"The Kunai are tall and brown like most of the other offshore islanders we dealt with, but Black and Brown alike, all western men go crazy for the taste of pig. They celebrate their dry season by setting fire to the kunai grass so they can chase the pigs down with dogs and spears. They too have bows, but they're much smaller than those of the Komba, and they use them only to fish. Anyway, the Kunai thought, 'This is only one man. He bears gifts. How much trouble can he bring?' You see, they normally don't invite the Komba onto Sigaba. They trade with them on the kunai, in designated places. Nevertheless, they sent enough canoes to bring all the man's goods, and they set him up in the men's house, but only then did they realize he had come to kill them."

"Kill them? How?" Ḷainjin asked.

Ḷōbwedi laughed. "That's only an expression they use when one group offers a feast to another that is so grand there's no way for them to properly reciprocate. They say, 'They killed us,' and from that time forward, they carry a lower status and have less say. He gave them all the pigs for a feast, traded all his goods in generous fashion, and took up residence in the men's house. The Black man stayed there for under a moon or two, making the acquaintance of most men on the island, and then quietly left without incident. True, they had not treated him as well as an offshore trader, but at least they treated him better than a Komba. The point is that everyone knew him, and from that point on, whenever a Kunai man met with a

Komba trade brother, they asked about him, and word of his feast and his prowess spread like a grass fire."

"Prowess at what? Trading?"

"He was developing renown as a trader, yes," Ḷōbwedi said. "In addition, he was becoming what they called a 'big man.'"

"You said he was a 'little man,'" said Ḷainjin.

"In western custom, a little man becomes big by generating feasts and feeding others, but it was the other things he did that they talked about most. He was exceptionally prolific. Within two seasons, he had provided bride gifts for four wives and had a child with each! That's the white magic–part. Then there is the black magic–part. Two local big men in hamlets adjacent to his both boasted they would kill him, and both died from the same cause. They stepped on fish bones. The Kunai loved him for his generosity, respected him for his white magic, and feared him for the black. They made him *akebu,*[140] and that is the only name he went by among the Komba, the Kunai, and other tribes up and down the hinterlands."

"What does akebu mean?"

"Forbidden man."

"Jeej."

Ḷōbwedi continued. "There's more. When they described the 'fish bones,' they sounded very much like the puffer fish–spines he had traded for in Sigaba!"

"I know puffer fish–spines are dangerous but—"

"They are the only bones that always leave at least one spine sticking up no matter how you scatter them. I realize they aren't naturally poisonous, so he must have put poison on the bones somehow, then planted them. Men dying of fish bones in the hinterlands… What are the chances?"

"Improbable," Ḷainjin said.

"Exactly. The Kunai were onto the akebu's story. Can you imagine the commotion when he returned at the beginning of rainy season, when there was little food, with even more pigs? They hadn't properly reciprocated for the last round. He had killed all the Sigaba big men once. Now he was after

---

[140] Komba word for a lineage leader who served as the priest or "forbidden man" of Lāpio cult worship and practiced the medicinal and magical arts.

their very manhood! They were all against bringing him ashore but had heard what happened to the Komba big men who had tried to compete with him. There he was, standing on the opposite shore, poking the pigs and making them squeal. Their women and sons all watching, all hungry. Every man feared he would ask for his sister. Yet every father secretly calculated the bride's wealth such a man could offer. They decided to invite him to the island one more time. They put him up in the men's house as before. They ate the pigs and were very much in his debt. Things went very much as before, except this time, as he sat in the men's house, he began to tell his story to one or two of them at a time.

"As the story goes, the akebu was a big man over the mountains," Ḷōbwedi said, "but a bad chief — who hated him for taking more wives and having more children than he had — banished him. The akebu bragged about all his children there without even mentioning those he had fostered among the Komba that all had heard about. Then, instead of asking for a bride as all expected, he began teaching about his religion. The concept there was simple and not very controversial. The Kunai, like the rest of us, believe our ancestors will help us in time of need. Because they had such limited land at Sigaba, they buried their dead on the kunai. A man would have to visit the grave of his dead father to ask his spirit for help. The akebu suggested they put a *lāpio*,[141] or image, where all the spirits of the ancestors could reside, right there in the men's house. That way, the *lāpio* could also overlook all the young men's initiations."

"Rojak told me to ask her brother about that."

"She is being naughty. She wants to know what her little brother let them do to him so she can tease him. As you probably already know, she hates the customs of the western men, but do not ask Lañinpo. He believes he isn't supposed to talk about it, and if you believe something bad will happen, it probably will. He already told me what he let them do. He said, 'made him do,' but I'm with his sister on this. He let them convince him he needed to let them do it. Youth is a competitive time for most boys. They're trying to test themselves to find out what they're like. You went through something like this when you had your tattoo ceremony. You experienced pain.

[141] Komba word for "effigy"; an image.

Carrying pain is what separates men and women from boys and girls. He let them erect his penis and insert a strip of fresh saw grass down into it and yank it out, causing him to bleed. The more times you let them do that the better. Boys of the same age group know how many times the others lasted. The point is to remove the 'black blood' that had probably accumulated from accidental exposure to the secretions of his mother or sisters. That's the reason why the uncle removes his nephew from his sister's house as soon as he can climb down the ladder and takes him to the men's house, to raise him there away from women."

"That is so ignorant..." Ļainjin furrowed his large brow.

"Well, when we go fishing with another," Ļōbwedi shot back, "if he's unlucky, do we not joke that he must have had sex the night before? Isn't that the same sort of thinking our ancestors brought from these dark places?"

"But that's just a joke," said Ļainjin, relaxing his brow again.

"But an ignorant one... Wait, we're just at the beginning," Ļōbwedi said. "Remember — instant death if you talk about any of this. They take what goes on in the men's house seriously. This little Black akebu kept bragging about how many children he fostered until one of the Kunai asked him what his secret was. He said it was because he had eaten so much semen as a boy. He was the most active of his age group. He went after the strongest of the bachelors in the men's house even until the morning of their marriages. By the time he was ready to take his first wife, he was bursting with semen that lasted him for life."

"He bragged about this?" Ļainjin was incredulous.

"He bragged about how much semen he had eaten and criticized their initiation ceremonies for not encouraging the older boys to feed semen to the younger ones. They would grow weaker as the seasons passed unless they improved the semen circulation on their island. That was his observation and his advice."

"I never heard... So, what happened?"

"The Brown men of Kunai, like those of most coastal areas, are originally from off-island," Ļōbwedi said. "True, they adopted some of the Black men's ways. They learned to hunt like them and plant like them, but they didn't mix with them. They didn't even steal their women even though the Black men stole theirs. The Kunai decided the akebu was a liar and never let him step foot on their little island again. When he returned two seasons later with the *lāpio* and the pigs for another feast, they refused to provide him passage. He left everything there to rot on the shore, including the *lāpio* he had carved and brought there with the help of his followers."

"So, you think this forbidden man was the cause of my mother's capture?" Ḷainjin asked.

"All I know is I have had this thought whirling around and around in my mind like the rock in a sling. Why did they attack us? The Kunai had traded with offshore islanders for hundreds of seasons, and whatever hostilities arose had never led to anything like what happened. I ask myself what had changed. This story of the forbidden man is the only thing I heard that comes to mind."

"Ḷōbwilñawa blames the blackstone," Ḷainjin said. "He says your group was trading for all the blackstone, and the Komba had a large crop of young men needing to take heads. They needed the blackstone for their circumcision ceremonies."

"The Kunai sent emissaries offering to trade blackstone for the return of those captured," commented Ḷōbwedi. "Nothing. No promises, nothing."

This time, Ḷainjin excused himself and walked out, but not into the storm. He stepped across the water-splashed stones along the edge of the house, pulled his manhood from between the strands of his kilt, and relieved himself into the streams of water falling off the eaves. The air was cool and filled with the sounds of water.

He looked down at his manhood as he held it. "Jeej!" He laughed to himself at the thought of Lañinpo giving it to a foreign man to harden and torment in that way. They must have bewitched him. How would he keep from laughing in his face when they next met?

Nahn Sapwe speaks

Ḷainjin reentered the house to find that Ḷōbwedi had placed a mat for him to sleep on. He lay back, listened for a time as the old man snored, and thought, "Truly, if a man has but one point of reference, he is libel to be made a fool by what he is told." He snickered to himself at his new friend Lañinpo's expense. Then he imagined his mother calling to him from a distant place. Out there was an island so big it would be impossible to miss, a long coastline and then an island situated like no other. He could find this place. He sat up as the vision of this destiny grew up before him, but what swayed his tree to its roots was the anguish of time lost. What he regretted most were seasons of otherwise unimportant endeavors that had sidetracked his story. He must answer this call to destiny. He must abandon this new title Jau Areu like a hermit crab that outgrows its old snail shell, abandons it for a larger, and discards that for a third. Yes, he had chosen title over the wealth that could have aided his journey. Truly, he had chosen poorly. Nevertheless, he must embark without hesitation, and he must inform Lipanmai!

He left the warmth of Ḷōbwedi's hearth behind and stepped out into the cold, nearly horizontal rain of the raging storm. The wave surge from the wind had combined with the incoming tide to fill the canal with more water than expected. Cringing not and motivated by impulsivity, he plunged into the windswept water and warmed himself beneath it as though curling up within the abandoned sleeping mat he had left behind. When the current threatened to sweep him off course, he angled his bearing accordingly. Without much effort, he retraced the path down the various canals back toward Pahn Kadira, from whence Ḷōbwedi had escorted him. There he found the great courtyard as abandoned as the canals and wondered if even the guards may have sought shelter. His craft and those of the others stood protected where they had set them within the walls. Shortly, still breathing heavily, he found himself tapping on Lipanmai's thatched and shuttered window. The shutter next to hers opened and beneath an extended bare arm, someone whispered, "Temple of Nahn Sapwe."

There, he found her alone, a single, unsheltered soul braced against the wind, struggling upward with a basket full of hardwood, climbing the slippery takai steps of the temple. Approaching her unnoticed and imagining she was shivering from the wind and cold rain, he yearned to shelter her in his arms but surprised her instead by taking the opposite side of the basket she was dragging. Overcome by the elements, she appeared not to notice who was helping her. The sound of the rain as it splattered the temple steps muffled even the thought of speech. They soon reached the topmost takai, which formed the flat, square temple mount. Beneath a low thatched roof but otherwise open to the elements was the now-roaring hearth of the never-to-extinguish fire of Nahn Sapwe that was her ward. The fire splashed them with light, and Lipanmai turned to see who had helped her. The surprise on her face flashed quickly into a broad, bold smile as they were overcome by the impulse to grasp onto the other's warm body. Dropping the heavy basket of hardwood, they embraced.

"Come," she urged, inviting Ḷainjin to enter beneath the open thatched shelter over Nahn Sapwe's hearth. She placed several more of the hand-sized mangrove logs into the hot flames before removing her skirt with a giggle and laying it out to steam before the fire. Taking a lime from a basket there and lying down before the flames, she peeled its green skin, exposing its tart segments. They lay like a fist into a cupped hand — she between him and the fire, eating a segment, offering one to him. He with his back turned to the water splashing down onto the cold, hard stone beneath him from the thatched eave above. He pressed one cheek against her curly, wet hair and wrapped an arm and a leg about her so they were both exposed to the heat of the blaze before them.

"Talk!" she commanded as he began to swish the water from her smooth, naked skin.

"I must go look for my mother."

"Where? Rālik?"

"No, west!"

"Truk?"

"No, farther!"

"That place we call Kataupaiti! Legend says nobody returns from there!"

"I make my own legend," Ḷainjin said. "I will return one day when I'm too old for you to want me."

"They will eat your soul. Their women will cut up your manhood and eat it for their morning meal. If you return, you won't be the same man who left."

"Then take me now while you can."

With this, Lipanmai rose and walked to the opposite side of the fire, where the thatch roof of the shelter was torn by the wind and had partially blown away. A length of thatch hung on a line and blew back and forth in the wind. She bit the line, jerking her head to free it, and returned, slowly enticing him with her nakedness as she bent the thatch around to cover her rear, coyly exposing her triangle of pleasure until she watched his manhood swell with desire. As the wind began to taper and the rain thickened and poured about them, drowning all thought of further talk, they coupled on the wet, bare stones her ancestors had mounted there. Her mouth tasted of lime. Later, they changed positions, and she covered her shoulders and back with the length of thatch as though she were a bird at nest covering her young. One upon the other, they rolled and ground themselves against the rough stone. He scuffed a knee here. She an elbow there. Finally, in their rage to unite, each managed to overcome the uncomfortable elements and satisfy the other deep in the loins simultaneous with the first flash of lightening, immediately followed by a surprisingly enormous clap of thunder from the spirit Nahn Sapwe.

After a few moments, she rose, attached her dried skirt about her waist, and beamed down at him, saying, "He blessed our being together." Then she curled up with him, and they slept there in each other's arms, one sheltering the other's very separate nighttime dream.

The morning, as one would expect, brought fair weather and light and variable winds, but there was no sign of the palu that day or the following several days. Then Ewalt arrived and brought news that Talupe had petitioned the Saudeleur over the palu's default. Ḷainjin and the others resolved to search for them the next day, light winds or no. Then, with the tide still high, as they relaxed under a sail canopy set up to shield themselves from the sun while telling tales of Manus[142] and Murik and Sigaba, the palu and Rojak finally appeared, paddling around the bend. Despite his immense size compared to the small craft he was paddling, Ḷainjin recognized him not until he saw Rojak paddling in the bow position of a second canoe — accompanied by another of his crew — and realized something must have happened to the palu's venerable proa.

No one spoke a word as the Satawan passed them, somber faced, with but a noble nod on his way toward Pahn Kadira. The moment Rojak drew near Ḷainjin, he asked her about the palu's proa.

She responded with a tearful shake of her head. "It's gone!"

"His crew?"

"Safe at Sokehs." Rojak looked Ḷainjin in the eyes, revealing her pain and then glancing ahead at the paddling palu. "Don't let him."

"*Eban*!"[143] cried Ḷainjin to himself, turning to the somewhat ridiculous-looking image of the palu — broad backed, sitting on the childishly small canoe — paddling toward the entrance of the Saudeleur's compound. Without further comment, Ḷainjin rose and dove into the tidewater after him. They arrived at the entrance simultaneously, and the palu told the attendants he was there to speak to the Saudeleur. Ḷainjin found himself sitting, sopping wet, nearly where he had been the night before.

The Saudeleur greeted them politely. The palu got right to the point. Speaking in Pohnpeian, he admitted he had lost the takai he'd intended to deliver and was in default on his agreement with Talupe. He respected the law and was ready to submit himself to Nahn Samohl's judgment. The Saudeleur turned to Ḷainjin, perhaps assuming he had something to add to the discussion.

Ḷainjin was quick to seize the opportunity to speak his broken Pohnpeian. "Jau Areu has measured well. This one too fat to reach bottom. Will jam on

[142] Part of Manus Province, and the biggest Admiralty Island, Manus lies in the Bismarck Sea north of Papua New Guinea.

[143] It will not; it cannot.

way down. He plans to shit in face of Nahn Samohl. She no can reach him. I petition you allow Jau Areu to speak Nahn Samohl. I'll take the palu's place. I think she not well. She my care now. You must know why she allows male eel to enter her home and steal her food."

"Not well?"

Ḷainjin raised his eyebrows and inhaled sharply with a wheeze in affirmation.

"Is she pregnant?" asked the Saudeleur hopefully.

"All I know, she does not eat!"

"What do you mean *speak*? What do you mean *not eat*? You don't speak with eels. They will tie your hands. They will take all knives. You won't be allowed to fight. No basket between you and her. Remember my words. She will eat your banana. When the sun rises, you will be pulled up dead."

"I am Jau Areu," Ḷainjin said. "I speak to eels. Does your title mean nothing? When can I speak to her? Earlier is better."

"Noon on the day of the next full moon."

That gave Ḷainjin nearly three quarters to prepare. "And if I arise from the well alive?" he asked.

"Then the debt is paid. That is the law," responded the Saudeleur.

"Then remember the words of Jau Areu: Nahn Samohl not eat. I find out why!"

As they exited Pahn Kadira, the palu kept insisting he wouldn't get stuck on the way down to the bottom of the eel well.

Later, with Lirojak[144] to interpret, Ḷainjin responded to his friend thus: "Wisim, you are a man of the sea with much sky inside. Your heart would burst, and you would suffocate in that hole. You know you would die down there even if the eel doesn't touch you. I saw it on your face as soon as you paddled around the corner. I know what I'm doing. Let me get you out of this. One day, you will owe me a woman with a big *puti* in recompense," he resolved, laughing. Then he asked, "What happened to your proa anyway?"

"It sunk!" replied the palu with a laugh. He said nothing more, and Ḷainjin needed to use the remaining light of day to reach Wottok on Temwen.

---

[144] Aka Rojak. Female Seeker; Lañinpo's sister.

"Impossible!" thought Ḷainjin a while later. He was attempting to hold wind in his sail as he drifted slowly toward the entranceway into the mangrove forest at Temwen's shore. At worst, a proa will swamp and need a good bailing.

"*Emejjia wa iḷọmeto,*" he chanted, giving up, lowering his sail, and beginning to paddle. He thought the palu must be joking, that he must have beached the proa somewhere in need of repair.

He wanted to speak to Wottok and get his advice regarding Nahn Samohl and the well at Idedh. It was that time in its cycle when the light of the three-quarter moon appears long after the orange sun retreats into a bed of glowing clouds on the horizon opposite. That time of the season when the air is saltless, and the sky is as clear as water in your hand. The tide recedes from the reefs more slowly as evening's darkness lingers, and its overseer rises late yet bright enough still to rule the night.

A few days later, he climbed the hill of this new world where his boundless, youthful energy and intuition had brought him. Wondering if this would be the last time he would smell this forest and view such sights from this height, he realized at that instant he would have to summon each moment of training and every word of confidence he had so far stored within to achieve the success he envisioned upon his descent. He knew what he had to do and why he had to do it. Now he was looking for the confidence and edge to get it done. Who better than Wottok to provide that to him?

When he arrived, his namesake the Jau Areu was sitting with Kiton, watching the moon as it slowly, almost imperceptibly, rose above the horizon.

As they met, they all repeated "*Kaselehlie*!" in turn, and Ḷainjin sensed they could see in his manner that much had changed since he last left.

"What did you learn from the Seekers?" Wottok asked.

"They related the story up to her capture off a small island called Sigaba, in an immense country far to the southwest called Papua. A group called the Komba took her up into the mountains that overlook the coastal plain. There are indications she has been involved in the pwentang trade."

"Pwentang?" Kiton hadn't heard the term before.

"Something better than that *jāpe* you use to heat your *nen*. Something made of mud that won't burn up in the fire. I'll bring one back for you."

"Oh, no!" she said. "Don't tell me you're planning to voyage there! Papua is a place of sickness and death. They ate her long ago, and if not, she doesn't want her only son to risk his happy life coming after her. Ḷōpako, look at me. Your mother would be my age. There is nothing left to save!"

Wottok laughed. "I would sail to Papua and beyond to save you!"

"You are a bigger fool than he is!"

"I will remember your words when things go poorly," Ḷainjin responded.

"What I fear is that no one will remember you!" Kiton said. "Ḷōpako, your glorious story of crossing the ocean to the stone village and grasping the title of Jau Areu. All this will be forgotten. Ewalt will tell the story to his children of a man from Rālik who left Pohnpei in search of his mother and died out there somewhere. Should things go poorly, I can be satisfied with that. After all, how many hundreds of stories of men who challenged themselves not?

"What about your mother's story?" she added. "Is it not on the lips of your people's neck-strings from north to south? Do your little girls not pretend they are she as they play among the boys with their toy canoes? Presently, the last they saw of her, she sailed up into the clouds. What greater end to her tale can you possibly bring back?"

"Kiton, a man must have bright thoughts when he begins such a journey," Wottok said. "Stop filling him with the dark worries of a woman!"

"I know, but somehow I can't help myself," she responded. "I feel his mother's spirit reaching out to me! Maybe I'm just an island bird satisfied by eating ripe breadfruit at the top of the tree, challenging not the sea!"

Getting to the matter he came to discuss, Ḷainjin posed his question to Wottok. "Do you know of a tunnel beneath the reef connecting the pools of Idedh and Darong?"

"Yes. Men have sworn they saw the same eel in both pools the same night. Then there is the fact that eels have often disappeared from the pool at Darong. If Nahn Samohl ate them, how did she get to them? Perhaps by clutching onto their mouths as they transited a narrow cave between one pool and the other."

"Is that how eels fight? One clutches onto the mouth of the other?"

"Remember, eels need to have their mouth open to breathe," Wottok said. "If one grasps the mouth of the other and clenches it closed, the other panics and quickly drowns."

"So, the biggest mouth wins?"

"I'm not sure if quickness or size wins. I have never seen them fight. We've never seen two in the same hole, right?"

"I saw three of the ones I caught in the pool at Idedh appear a little later at Darong," Ḷainjin said. "They were fighting over a fish I put in the well."

"Impossible! Normally, they would never enter the cave of Nahn Samohl! Was there one that appeared more dominant than the others?"

"Yes, the blue-speckled one. It was the largest and had a large chunk of the fish in its mouth. The others were sort of circling, looking for a way to take a bite."

"That is when an eel is at risk — when it eats," Wottok said. "It likes to withdraw into its cave and swallow slowly."

"Maybe something happened to Nahn Samohl. Is it supposed to smell down there?"

"No, nothing rots. They keep her hungry. She eats everything they put down there."

"Maybe they kept her too hungry," Ḷainjin said. "The whole island needs cleaning up. To me, that shows poor caretaking."

"Now you know why the Saudeleur has appointed you caretaker."

"Maybe too late. My bet is that Nahn Samohl is no more. My friend the palu is in trouble, and the Saudeleur has agreed to allow me to face the eel in his stead."

"No, Ḷōpako, don't do it," cried Kiton. "They will tie your hands and keep you down there from sunset until morning. That nasty woman will attack your appendages!"

"Not if she's dead!"

"Well, what about the others? You said yourself they enter the pool at Idedh from Darong, where they keep them," she continued. "You must feed them more fish, or they'll compete to tear you apart."

"No, that's not likely," Wottok said. "They'll smell him and stay away. They have already had him in their mouths, and they'll remember how that turned out! That was the most trying thing they ever experienced, and they're not likely to have forgotten who nearly suffocated them or what he smells like."

"Ḷōpako, even if Nahn Samohl is dead and even if the other eels don't attack, there is still the choking narrowness, the feeling of constriction and curtailment. I could not handle it. I would rather die first!" said Kiton.

"Better me than my fat friend," Ḷainjin said. "That's what I told the Saudeleur. And I warned him that his pet might be sick."

"You must convince him you did not kill her!" said Kiton.

Ḷainjin looked at Wottok. "Will the Saudeleur or his guards be watching me down in the well?"

"No, that part is forbidden. The law is clear that no one is to watch the trial. The point is that this is enforcement of the law and not a punishment. Not a killing at which others can gawk."

"How will I be tied?"

"The spar, as you know, is nearly as long as the well is wide, and they lower you down at the extreme of low tide. The line ties to a hole in the middle of the spar, which they place against your back but under your arms. Once they tie your wrists and suspend you, there's really no way to get loose. You can imagine that this is not a comfortable position. You can, of course, relieve the pressure by wedging your feet against the ridges of the takai walls of the well, but the guards will require you go to the bottom. If you refuse and wedge yourself above the water, you face the indignity that they poke you down with their poles. You can wedge yourself back up a bit as the tide comes in, but your appendages will hang exposed to the eel's grasp."

After that, the conversation turned back to Ḷainjin's mother and the stories of Papua that the Seekers had related. He asked Wottok where he could obtain enough *ekkwaḷ* to renew the lashings on his craft for his trip across the great current to the island of Papua. Despite Kiton's objection to the trip, Wottok presented several coils of *ekkwaḷ* to Ḷainjin as a gift, and he chose the thicknesses he required.

The next morning, they all ate breakfast before dawn and walked downhill to the water's edge together. Wottok offered his last advice. If Ḷainjin got himself untied, he should swim through Nahn Samohl's cave to the pool, where it would be safer to face the younger eels. Ḷainjin requested they inform Ewalt of everything that had passed. They gave the good-byes of friends who wonder if they will ever see each other again, and he paddled off into the high tide, through the mangrove forest and into the village.

He paddled to Idedh, beached his canoe high upon the entranceway, and began the laborious task of renewing each lashing. If he worked deliberately, it would take him several days to complete the whole project. He worked deliberately, paying little mind to those who paddled by other than to greet them with a respectful *kaselehlie.*

Then the tide became too low to navigate the channels, and he was all alone to explore the pool and prepare for his trial.

Those who had passed earlier must have spread the word that the newly titled Jau Areu who was to face Nahn Samohl the next day was so confident of his exoneration he spent his last day renewing the lashings of his proa. Over the next days, more and more canoes drifted by, and all they saw was his confidence. Truly, he would not leave to fate what he might accomplish by cunning and strength. Word of his whereabouts had apparently spread to the palu and Rojak because they appeared a few days later, she with a basket of food and coconuts, each paddling the canoes they had borrowed to round the island.

They found him wet of kilt, as he had been swimming in the pool. Ḷainjin was happy to see his friends because the day was running out and he could use their help with the lashings. But most of all, he was dying to hear what had happened to the palu's proa and tossed a coil of line to him. "Can you help me with a few of these? I'm expecting the Saudeleur to interrupt the preparations for my voyage with his silly trial."

"I can start on these." The palu indicated the square lashings of the many spars below the outrigger platform that run parallel to the hull and perpendicular to the outrigger booms.

Rojak grabbed Ḷainjin's ring and began cutting away one of the old lashings. "Why depart so soon? Where will you go? You manage this island now. You chose a title."

"Titles are for old men," he said. "Someday maybe, I'll return, take up my duties, and reclaim my title. Before then, I'll sail southwest across the kāleptak current." He wouldn't tell them why. He would leave that for another day.

"What will you do when the wind dies?" asked Rojak, cutting now at one of the great and all-important lashings where the outrigger booms tie to the kubaak.

"I will lower my sail, paddle at night toward the giant cross, and sleep by day," he said. "And wait for the forewinds of one of the many storms that circle that eastward-flowing current."

"What will you do when the storm hits you?" she asked.

"I'll take down my sail, fill my water-shells, and sleep below in the knowledge that my new lashings were tied by the most heroic woman on the entire ocean!"

"Ḷōpako, you have the knack for sweet mouth!"

"Then please, daughter of the ocean. Please tell me what I'm dying to hear. What story from the past days' storm?"

"It was entirely my fault," began Rojak. "I wasn't thinking and tied the line to the wrong place."

Ḷainjin looked to the palu for further explanation. Laughing, the big man slowly extended his hand horizontally and chopped it a bit as though sailing. Then he tilted it vertical, whistled, and lowered it quickly, as though the proa was sinking into the sea.

"What?"

It was Rojak's turn to elaborate. "He was already late on his delivery. He had planned to leave the morning we arrived with the kājokwā. So, I guess I was the cause of his delay. He knew the storm was coming and wanted to use its strength to move the takai around the island. It was a little stronger than we planned. We had two of them on the raft. Unfortunately, they had tied the two together better than they had tied them to the raft. We were in a hurry to take advantage of the coming storm. It hit us close to the passageway and sort of swept us out into the ocean."

"I know the place," Ḷainjin said. "That's where I got in trouble."

The palu nodded his head in assent. "That's how I got overconfident. The waves out there got really big really fast. We were all afraid the line to the raft would break, so I volunteered to swim back with a second line. The raftsman was busy at the tiller, and unfortunately, I tied it at the wrong place. I tied it to the lines that secured the stones together. A few moments later, a huge wave crashed down on the raft, pushing its nose down and breaking the towline. The stones now attached to the second line began to slip forward, and as the raft rose over the crest of the swell, the raft slipped out from beneath them. That second line must have caught at the very tip of the palu's stern because the heavy stones tipped it vertical before they dragged it, disappearing into the sea. We were all stunned, swimming in the dark, shouting for each other. The raftsman abandoned his raft, and luckily we all survived, but the sea took everything else."

"He swam to me very quickly," Rojak said, "and somehow, we all made it back to shore just as we heard Nahn Sapwe clap his thunder. I'll pay Talupe for the stones with my land and titles. I'll go to the Saudeleur, and he'll set the price."

"No," replied Ļainjin. "That won't be necessary. Do you want to give your lands and titles to Talupe? I don't think any of us feel she deserves to be paid." His eyes met theirs back and forth, and they provided no disagreement on this point.

He watched Rojak as she methodically and repeatedly tied her lashing tightly and with expert reiteration. She turned pensive. It was Wisim who asked the question they had come to explore. What was Ļainjin's plan, and how could they help?

"The best plan would be to feed the eels so much they would no longer be hungry," Ļainjin said, "and I would be safe down there. The Saudeleur must have expected I would do this. But look around. No one is posted to prevent me! Why? If there was any reason to worry, I would have fed them, but I have not."

Ļainjin told them he had no plan and there was no way they could help. He would rely on his experience with the eels, advice given, and his mental and physical abilities to come out of the well intact. He laughed. "With all appendages functional!" There was only one little thing he needed, and Rojak promised to bring it to him.

Ļainjin spent the cycle's remaining days there at Idedh, sleeping on his proa. Surely, wanting him to survive, the Saudeleur had expected he would feed the eel. Otherwise, he would have posted guards to protect the pond. Yet had he fished, the Saudeleur would likely have known this too, as his guards sit atop all the village walls and could report such comings and goings to him. No, the Saudeleur was playing a game of his own. Clearly, he didn't want to enforce the law against the palu, but then he had made that decision before learning the palu had lost his magnificent proa. What good was he now? The Saudeleur was encouraging Ḷainjin to cheat, yet if he did, would this not give the Saudeleur more power over him? Something inside him rebelled at the power of these chiefs over men. Better to skirt the power of the storm than to meet it head-on. Yet that tactic, as his mother had found out, was not without its own dangers. He was convinced he had chosen the right course by simply following the law in honesty — and by so doing, winning a true and lasting freedom for himself and his friend.

The eel well

On the appointed day, the guards arrived before dawn, each carrying a long hardwood staff. They took their positions as though they had been there for days. The Saudeleur's attendants arrived soon thereafter to prepare the feast he would sponsor in Ļainjin's honor. The plan, by tradition, was to lower him into the well at the noon low tide and feast until the incoming tide allowed those who did not care to suffer his screams to depart the island beforehand. The eel, according to legend, would play with her victim by day by writhing between his legs — boasting silently of her size — and scaring him nearly to death before retreating into her cave. Then at the second flooding after the moon had passed its crest, she would deliver her punishment. The Saudeleur and all but the guards would leave in the evening and return the next morning to await the uphauling of either the dead body or the badly mutilated and suffering body — whichever penance her verdict inflicted.

Ļainjin, on his part, didn't fear the eel he thought for sure was dead but the confinement of the well itself. Yes, he often crawled up into the extremely confined space of his hull on those nights he expected rain. However, he knew many men who would rather suffer the rain than such confinement, and he was a man known to have much open space inside. What if he panicked down there? This was his one dark thought. The other was, What was likely to happen if his plan to scare away his other slimy friends down there went awry? Nevertheless, he concentrated on the words of his grandfathers, who had taught him to hone his thoughts to the task of shaping his destiny rather than worrying about the possibility of failure. Meditating thus, he continued to putter around his vessel even as the crowd began to form. Talupe and her contingent, whom he tried his best to ignore, came first. But where was Rojak?

"It is *m̧ōm̧aan m̧aj*," Talupe teased, somehow knowledgeable of the Rālik expression. "Oh look, there she is!" she said in Pohnpeian, nodding toward Lipanmai, brought by the Saudeleur. "She probably already asked the Saudeleur to give her a Pohnpeian man once you're gone!"

Ļainjin, realizing the time of his trial was rapidly drawing near, tried his best not to let her words affect his concentration. Others arrived, then finally Ewalt and his friends from Rālik. Of immediate concern was Rojak. He had expected her to arrive before the others. Now she looked surprised by her late arrival. How would she inconspicuously deliver the most critical element of his plan? The Saudeleur was hovering over the canoe with Lipanmai next to him. Surprised by the new lashings, he repeatedly reiterated his warnings of the danger of the "half-told story." He was again trying to convince Ļainjin that his trip to the west was ill conceived and unlikely to bear fruit — belligerently oblivious, apparently, to the reality that none of the others surrounding them expected Ļainjin to live long enough to even consider such a trip. Most who came were traders interested in supporting the law they thrived by. Others perhaps to simply hear him die in the well.

Ļainjin was more convinced than ever that the Saudeleur's plan had been to allow him to satiate the eels beforehand and now fully expected he had. Ļainjin decided to introduce a moment of authenticity to him. "I did not feed them," he said softly.

The statement took the Saudeleur by surprise. As though his plans had been suddenly set aback. As though aroused from a dream. As though it had never occurred to him that Ļainjin would have so little interest in self-preservation that he would fail to see the obvious solution to prevail at his trial. There appeared a deep inner regret on the Saudeleur's face. Not an outer regret that Ļainjin would be sacrificed to Nahn Samohl, but perhaps an inner regret that he had failed to teach Ļainjin that the law was not there to restrain a Saudeleur's objectives but to promote them.

The next moment, Rojak arrived. However, the Saudeleur, angry like a little boy prematurely disturbed from his nap, motioned to his guards to begin. Ḷainjin rose and looked directly at Rojak as they tied his wrists behind his back, patted the waist of his kilt for possible weapons, and led him to the well. He stood there as the guards inserted the spar under his armpits behind him and pulled the line tight through the scaffold from which they would lower him.

Then, interrupting the Saudeleur from giving the signal to raise Ḷainjin over the well and surprising all with her disregard of decorum, Rojak rushed up to Ḷainjin, embraced him, and stuck her tongue deep into his mouth. She glared at the poor mortified Lipanmai as though taunting her staid behavior at the Saudeleur's side. Then Ḷainjin saw Rojak boldly scowl at the other Pohnpeian women among the group who had begun remarking to one another on her unacceptable demonstration of public affection. Finally, he saw her rejoin the crowd with her defiant, knowing smirk, and that was the last impression etched into his mind as the guards lowered him several arm's lengths.

As the spar beneath his arms was, by design, longer than the well was wide, he found he had to guide himself down diagonally with his feet to prevent it from jamming horizontally and prolonging the incredible claustrophobia that had suddenly afflicted him.

The water below the walls of the well was from the natural pool beneath and, of course, rose and fell with the tides. The builders must have simultaneously constructed the walls of the well as they backfilled the islet. The walls were made of takai, and the bottom few spanned the original crevice in the reef upon which they were stacked.

One of the guards, supported by his staff and silhouetted against the bright blue sky, peered down at him, probably making sure he was in the water and hadn't somehow braced himself along the ridges of the takai used to build the walls of the well. In an instant, the guard was gone, and all was quiet and pleasantly cool. Except Ḷainjin found himself unable to tear his eyes from that round view of light blue sky. It represented both life and freedom but, at the same time, would blind his sight and prevent him from freeing himself.

By tradition, the guards had not tied his feet, so he would be able to tread water in this smaller pool, which the sacred one's tunnel opened into.

Leaving the feet untied was a trap. The average fool, without the benefit of his arms to scull, would quickly exhaust himself and drown out of fright even before his appendages were clutched by the sharp, inward-pointing teeth of his unwanted lover.

Of course, Ḷainjin was no fool. He had inspected her tunnel the day before, entering it several times from the bottom of the larger pool at the other end and finding her absent. He had prepared his mind to relax, in order to lie back and float despite his tied hands and to take short, shallow breaths through his nose to keep his chest as inflated as possible. Thus, he had meditated in the cool, peaceful calm, oblivious to what might lie waiting at the pool's murky bottom.

It was now low tide, and the pool resembled those in which he and Wottok had previously fished for eel. Except this one was much more claustrophobic. The walls of the well ended above the pool. Floating on his back in the pool, he faced the first rows of crisscrossed takai directly above him that spanned it much like a ceiling and created the base of the well. Floating was not easy. To overcome the weight of the somewhat flat hardwood spar that spanned his back, he had to keep his lungs inflated to the maximum and then exhale and inhale again rapidly. Once the tide began to rise, the water in the pool at the bottom of the well would rise with it to the base of the well, forcing him vertical and preventing him from using this tactic.

He closed his eyes to prevent himself from focusing on the light above and kept his thoughts as far away as possible. He went back as far as he could remember, and there was Helkena, his surrogate mother, who had helped his grandfathers raise him. She was feeding him jekaro from the eye of a polished coconut shell. He loved that shell and now wondered what had happened to it. He loved the taste of the heated jekaro — so sweet. He also remembered the baked *bop*[145] and how he struggled to get it to fit in his mouth at first. She would then mash the sweet pulp from the core and feed it to him with her finger. But always she fed him from the core first, until his mouth got big enough and his teeth grew strong enough to bite down and suck the pulp on his own.

---

[145] Pandanus.

Later, as he grew up, she would also give him his pandanus raw in a variety of flavors and textures — some of which he would have to crunch down on to extract the raw pulp. This, he supposed, was why he had inherited the large mouth and strong jaws that he now used to his advantage. Yes, he loved his pandanus. It was the food of outer-island peoples. Those here on the high islands, to their detriment, couldn't be bothered with it. They would complain that the hairs got caught in their teeth, only to have them rot from their heads for lack of cleaning.

Jekaro and pandanus were his favorite foods, and always, when he consumed or even thought of them, he would remember the selfless Helkena, who would never let him call her "mother." She left Namorik with her husband and returned to Wotho when he was just a lad and had started his rijeḷā apprenticeship with his grandfathers. He never saw her again. But thinking of her now and remembering those faraway loved ones and comforting moments quieted his mind and sheltered him once again from the panic that might have otherwise consumed him.

Gradually, nearly imperceptibly, the seawater seeped through the stones that filled the island's base, and the water in the pool rose to the point where he was no longer able to float in it and needed to tread with his legs. However, before he became exhausted, the tidewater rose to the point in his trial where, were it not for the spar upon which he was suspended, he would be able to wedge himself within the walls of the well and rest there, feet braced against one side and back against the other. The well was about a third as wide as he was long, and its framework was square, made of pairs of takai crossed over the base of takai spanning the pool below. Between each successive tier of the seven or eight takai leading to the surface, they had fitted large stones. Because the spar was wider than the square of the well, they'd had to lower him down diagonally, with it passing at the corners. He was well aware that, unless they tightened the slack from above as the water rose, he could eventually rise high enough to turn the spar vertical and free himself from it. Of course, he could not count on them allowing this.

It was time to implement the first stage of his plan, before they took up the slack in the line caused by the rising tide. He lifted his leg over the slack so the line now ran from his back down between his legs before leading up.

The line, now taut, passed directly by his mouth. He repositioned the dried-pandanus-leaf packet that enveloped the blackstone Rojak had precociously shoved into his mouth with her tongue. Maneuvering the packet from the side of his cheek, he clenched down on it with his powerful teeth and jaws and began to grind doggedly through the pandanus until the stone eventually worked its way through one side. Holding the stone in his teeth, he then sawed, one by one, through the fibers of the line itself. It was a digit thick, but the stone was very sharp, and he eventually cut himself free.

With no tension on the line, he allowed the hardwood spar to sink and began working himself upward from the base of the well as the water rose, his back wedged on one side and his feet on the other. With his tongue and lips, he placed the thin pandanus packet, with stone still protruding, onto a ledge of the well. Then he wedged his way up slowly and deliberately, carefully focusing away from the light until he could see that the packet on the ledge was at the same height as the twine that tied his wrists together. After memorizing the features of the wall, he scooted rightward, the wall now behind him, carefully running his thumb over the area until it touched the packet and slowly grasping it between his thumb and index finger. The most critical part accomplished, he twisted his tied wrists until he could saw at one lashing, one fiber at a time. He had to rest his fingers often, but the blackstone eventually cut through, and his hands were free.

At that point, Ḷainjin wanted to retie the spar to the line, but alas, the hardwood was so dense it didn't float and had apparently sunk to the bottom of the pool. In case the guards pulled on the line or even looked down into the well, he wanted them to see what they expected. That was when he repeatedly dove down into the muck at the bottom of the cave. With a combination of light from above and from the pool at the other end of the tunnel, as well as finger fumbling, he found what he was looking for — and much more — after several dives.

When his face broke the water's surface just above the bottom of the well, he had the spar. He threaded the line through the hole drilled in the middle and knotted it as before. Then he found a pair of the stones that lined the well where he could wedge the spar to render it immovable. His hands and arms reeked of the smell of putrid fish. Confident now that he would survive, he rested as best he could by bracing himself in the well, bending at the knees, his feet on one side and his back against the other.

As the tide rose, Ḷainjin found himself having to keep as much of his body out of the cold water as possible. He had begun to shiver and remembered from the day before that the water near the surface of the pool had been much warmer than the water deep in the cave. He wondered if the sun-warmed water at the pool's surface would remain as the tidewater below seeped back through the stones of the island's base into the canals, and then to the very ocean that had brought him there. He would soon find out. When the light above him darkened into night, he decided he had waited in the well long enough to allow even the most eager to hear him scream to retire from the island. He decided to take the chance that no one would see him emerge from the adjacent pool.

He exhaled the air from his chest, sank down into Nahn Samohl's tunnel, and swam out its entrance and across the pool, careful not to break its surface until he was beneath the kōņņat tree that had grown at its edge. He was careful to emerge as quietly as possible despite his eagerness for a breath of air. Finding the water there to be comfortingly warmer, he felt like he had just sailed into the shelter of a calm lagoon after a rough voyage across the open ocean. Now that the pool was at full tide, he could crawl beneath the kōņņat's low-hanging branches, out of the water, and finally sleep.

When he awoke, the full moon was high in the cloudless sky. It reflected brightly in the pool. The air was still. Silent. His kilt had dried, and a ledge had formed around the edge of the tidal pond as the tide had long since retreated. Were he to drop back into the pool now, the splash might alert one of the guards he assumed the Saudeleur had posted. His back and shoulders aching from the hanging part of his trial, he curled up against the soft leaves of the kōņņat tree, searched for comfort among the sharp coral stones beneath him, and returned to his dreams.

Finally, the time for the next phase of his trial arrived. The level of the tidal pond had risen and wet his feet where he'd slept. The image of the moon had disappeared from the surface of the water. It had long since sunk behind those mountains he had not so long ago first viewed far at sea and wondered about their mystery. The night had turned darker, and he fully expected that the eels had entered the pool below. He could rush back through the cave, wedge himself up into the well, and keep himself out of the water until dawn, or he could try something else that Wottok had suggested, just to be safe. With the stones at the water's edge, Ḷainjin began rubbing his feet, which were hanging in the water, to extract as much of his scent into the pool as possible before entering. Wottok had promised him that the eels would not forget his scent and would be unlikely to approach him a second time. Then he entered the water and did the same to his wrists and forearms, scratching them with the stones nearly to the point of bleeding. It worked. The eels approached him not.

As dawn arrived, Ḷainjin dove back through the cave and up into the well. Even as he heard the first faint sounds of people congregating above, he lay back and floated at the base of the well as he had the afternoon before, except the cave was filled to its ceiling with water now. And this time, he reveled in the knowledge he had so far kept from those above. He had survived! The knowledge empowered him. He began to further plan his triumphant ascent, right down to whom he would leer at first. That moment came sooner and faster than expected. Soon the sounds grew louder and more numerous. He assumed that people were again gathering to see how fate had treated him. The line went slack for a moment and then quite taut again. Not unusual for the men above as the spar was wider than the well and wedged securely. He heard the guards shouting to one another and saw one peering into the well. That was when Ḷainjin dove down, grabbed onto what he needed, and surfaced. He dislodged the spar and hung onto the line as the men above quickly hauled him above the surface, into the blazing light and the collective gasps about him.

Somewhat blinded, he gazed into the astonished group of friends and onlookers who had gathered. Ḷainjin's eyes squinted at the crowd, searching for his target. There were Rojak and Ḷōbwedi, Lañinpo and Ḷōbwilñawa. There stood the Saudeleur and his contingent. Finally, his eyes met the bewildered gaze of Talupe and her man with the broken hand, and there he directed his triumphant grin. Quite surprisingly, no one rushed toward him as he hung precariously by one hand beneath the scaffold over the well, too high now to touch the ground. He feared that the surprised guards were about to let loose of the line and send him falling back down from where he had come. They had all cringed, covered their noses, and turned away. The Saudeleur appeared dumbfounded. There was Ewalt, and Lipanmai stood next to him. She bent over and began to puke. Finally, the guards lowered him a bit so his one foot could launch a swing to solid ground.

Then Ḷainjin looked down at the mammoth, stinking head and colorless, decomposing corpse of Nahn Samohl that he had dredged up from below and, with some effort, extracted from the well. By that time, the Saudeleur, Lipanmai, Talupe and her contingents, and all the onlookers — terrified and repulsed by the stench — began to flee the islet, almost in panic. Only his friends stayed to bear the insufferable malodor that clung to the air about them as Ḷainjin tied a line through Nahn Samohl's head and dragged her long body into the canal. He gave the line to Uerik, who on request, agreed to discard the carcass into the bay on his way home and return the next day, bringing Ḷainjin's bird from Jeilañ's house.

Ḷainjin asked Ewalt to bring his treasure from Kariahn and waded into the water. Sinking down, knees bent, he distractedly scrubbed the putrid oil of the decomposing eel from his body. He suddenly perceived the incredible beauty of his surroundings. Here, the sun-glaring, clear water of the canal, and there, a majestic, bright green coconut palm with its leaves lightly aflutter in the light breeze, above a couple of friendly white puffs cruising across a light blue expanse stretching farther than his eyes could see. These jagged, irregular walls with no two stones the same.

The history of this magnificent place was speaking softly to him. Perhaps the spirits of the men Nahn Samohl had killed were congratulating him, or perhaps those who had constructed these incredible walls some hundreds of seasons ago. Perhaps it was the spirit of Nahn Samohl herself, blessing him for having freed her from the dark hole in which she had been rotting. Or was it he himself who had opened his soul and was calling these spirits into union with him?

Ḷainjin felt his spirit grow as he looked at his friends in the entranceway, launching his canoe. They were strong of body. He saw much strength of spirit indeed, yet in each one, he saw unique weaknesses that might prevent them from successfully returning from the battle he envisioned, based on tales they themselves had told. They'd had their opportunity to save the mothers, but for whatever good reason, had turned away from it. Now it would seem like tempting fate for them to return there. He felt they would be fools rushing to their deaths, as had their companions on the kunai how many seasons prior.

"Ḷōpako, that's not going to work," offered Ḷōbwedi. "You need a proper bath. Let Lañinpo paddle you to my house, and I'll have my daughter grate coconut."

His friends finished launching his proa, and Lañinpo paddled it with Ḷainjin in tow. He turned on his back and floated behind from a short line, reabsorbing, filling himself again with the incredible expanse above. Lañinpo paddled with strong strokes through the retreating tide to Ḷōbwedi's islet, where the group apparently intended to meet, celebrate his trial, and discuss his departure. There, Ḷōbwedi brought immature coconut husks and helped him scrub the putrid eel's oil off his back. Then he sent Ḷainjin back into the canals and repeated the process, this time with coconut gratings, until the smell had sufficiently dissipated for him to sit with the group. By this time, Bwedi's daughter had produced much food, he had begun passing shells of jemañūñ, and an aura of festivity had settled upon the group. Ḷainjin was eager to eat but shunned the jemañūñ. He wanted only water and plenty of it.

"Ḷōpako, the Saudeleur asked us to speak with you one last time, to convince you this trip of yours is ill conceived," said Ḷōbwedi, turning to the others to solicit their comments.

"Ḷōpako, if I thought there was any chance my mother was still alive, I would take you there myself," added Lañinpo.

"Ḷōbwedi, did you tell them the story of the pwentang and the forbidden man?" asked Ḷainjin as he ate.

"I told them all everything."

"I assure you all, I don't expect any of you… I do not want any of you to accompany me. I will find the place that is too big to miss by myself. I'll take as many seasons as I need to learn as many tongues as it takes to find out for myself what happened to them. I'll trade my fortune. I'll learn their ways."

"Ḷōpako," responded Ḷōbwilñawa, "so many seasons have passed. I must warn you that it's not a healthy place where people live to a ripe age."

"Ḷōpako," pleaded Rojak, "that place is a nightmare. Should you ever return, it will haunt your nights for the rest of your life. I can't take a nap without waking with a shudder! It has been too many seasons. Our mothers are dead by now."

Interrupting himself several times to fill his mouth and swallow his food and drink, Ḷainjin delivered the following comments to his friends. "Ask yourselves this. We know that one of them survived the attack. The *wapepe* on the pwentang proves that. Whoever took them for whatever reason no doubt realized they were of great support for each other, and that made it more valuable to keep both of them alive and together. If all they wanted was women for their men's houses, why take these women from a group of newcomers? Why not take women from the Kunai or shame one of their longtime enemies? Did they need pwentang-making skills? Then why not take Kunai women, who had been making pwentang all their lives? No, it's clear they wanted our mothers because of their leadership skills. Who were these newcomer women who commanded men and learned languages and pwentang-making skills so quickly? If they decided to trade pwentang and needed someone to teach their women to make them and then monitor their production, these women would prove useful to them. Why kill them? Why not instead care for them? I am guessing that it's why they captured them and why they may still be alive, and I intend to determine if I'm correct and to succeed in finding out, no matter how long it takes. I leave as soon as my provisions are ready and my items of trade and my bird are delivered."

At that, he asked Ḷōbwedi for a sleeping mat and a place to lie. "There was no sleep down there and I'm exhausted."

He slept through the afternoon, and when he awoke, the tide was high, the sun had set, his friends were gone, and he was again hungry. Ḷōbwedi had had too much jemañūñ, and his daughter watched over him like a mother. The devoted, quiet girl brought Ḷainjin more food.

"We will cross the eastward-flowing current and sail together to the land of the islanders," said Ḷōbwedi. "I'll accompany you on your journey and lead you back to the place they took her."

Ḷainjin observed the worried look on his daughter's face. He lowered his eyebrows and grimaced to alleviate her fears that he would let her father accompany him.

"Thank you, Ḷōbwedi. A valiant offer, but my journey, if successful, is bound to end in a battle. I would rather face that alone. I'll use cunning and deliberation to defeat my enemies. I'll turn them one against the other. Better you two stay here, take care of each other, and await my return."

"No, Ḷōpako, your craft is too large for one man to paddle across the kāleptak current alone. You will never make it."

"Then don't call me Pako, because people have learned to call me that after I proved I can do whatever they say I can't. I'll sleep by day and paddle by night to conserve water and energy, and I'll cross this kāleptak like your blackstone that cut through the fibers of the line with which the Saudeleur had me tied. I'll surprise you as I surprised him and everybody else in my wake, and I will surprise this forbidden man of yours. Wait and see!"

Ḷōbwedi suddenly sobered such that Ḷainjin wondered if he had not been pretending a little. "Okay, then there's one more story I need to tell you before you paddle, just in case your stubborn rear ever drifts up at Sigaba."

"A solution to the mystery of the forbidden man, I hope!"

"No, but this just might save your headstrong hide from an untimely death by his hand."

"Then I'll listen carefully."

Ḷōbwedi continued. "While the forbidden man was on Sigaba, he took an apprentice named Setepana,[146] who accompanied him ashore, where he wandered through the kunai and, on occasion, involved himself with magic. On one occasion, he followed him to the river Kwama, where he collected blue bugs from overturned rotten logs and smashed them. These bugs were the food of an orange bird with a black face that the Kunai never eat because it is poisonous. Even touching this bird will turn your hands numb. He concentrated the bug juice by exposing it to the sun. During the process, the akebu stopped moving and had trouble breathing. That's when he told Setepana to catch him a puffer fish. That night, Setepana speared one on the reef by the light of burning *pāle*[147] and took it to the akebu the next morning. As you know, the liver of the puffer fish is deadly poisonous. Well, the forbidden man ate the liver of the fish and recovered after a deep sleep."

---

[146] The forbidden man's apprentice.

[147] Dried, braided coconut leaves used as torches for fishing; a coconut frond.

"And you think he used the poison from the blue bugs to kill the men in the hinterlands who opposed him," Ḷainjin said.

"Setepana thought so."

"So, one poison counteracts the other. The blue bugs are in the mountains, so he will be using that one on me. All I need to protect myself is the counterpoison from the liver of a puffer fish. Before I go after this forbidden man, I need to talk to a man called Setepana."

"If he's still alive!"

"Where can I get the provisions," Ḷainjin asked, "especially the jāānkun I'll need?"

"The Saudeleur is responsible for provisioning all debarking vessels. His water-shells are many, and he has them filled daily from mountain streams. He gets much jāānkun from the outer atolls."

"I wonder what he'll say. Probably something about the dangers—"

"Of a half-told story!" both men said simultaneously, laughing.

Ḷōbwedi asked Ḷainjin about his shark hunting. Ḷainjin related a few stories about it. Ḷōbwedi's daughter became more open and drew closer to listen carefully as they spoke. Finally, Ḷōbwedi got Ḷainjin to try a taste or two of his jemañūñ, and they talked until Ḷōbwedi got very drunk and fell asleep. His daughter's eyes peered thankfully at Ḷainjin as she curled up in her mat next to her father.

"Wealth has a negligible effect on people like her. She loves her aging father and is apprehensive I might take him away," he thought to himself, leaving them there and walking out into the night. The moon had risen into a cloudy sky. Black clouds hovered in the mountains, and a soft breeze brought a light mist and the smell of rain. Those clouds, they had told him, would hover and rain there day and night through the upcoming season until Tūṃur rose to blow them away. He covered the hatches of his canoe, reentered the little home, and was tempted again to sleep as the mangrove coals of their hearth faded and the dimmed moonlight found its way through its slatted walls even as the mist from the hovering clouds thickened and began to drip softly from the eaves. Tomorrow would be a momentous day. He needed to shake off the trauma of the eel well, rise refreshed, and set a determined course.

Kāleptak

He was awakened by the sound of Uerik softly calling his name from the entranceway. He had brought Ḷainjin's bird, and Ḷainjin found him there outside — tied to Uerik's beached canoe, pooping his goo and stretching his neck high. The Chief was waiting for someone to wave a fish before his beak and had a regal, yet confused expression on his face as he looked this way and that, no doubt wondering where all the children were.

"He hasn't eaten yet," explained Uerik.

"Good. He needs to catch his own food again and climb above the clouds before he turns into a taro plant."

"Jeilañ's children will miss him. They love to feed."

"Be sure to thank Jeilañ for me." As Ḷainjin was tying the Chief to his familiar perch on his craft, he saw Uerik turn to go. "Wait."

Ewalt had just appeared, coming around the bend from Kariahn. He had brought Ḷainjin's two alele full of his treasure. Ḷainjin opened them to Uerik and asked him to take whatever he wanted as a parting gift. Then he offered the same to Ewalt. They both went for the large shark teeth and, in turn, grabbed his bicep and drew him close. Each no doubt vowed within himself to remember him but probably thought they might never see him again. They launched themselves in different directions and paddled away.

Then Ḷōbwedi's daughter brought fresh coconuts from the day before, clutched at his elbow in the Pohnpeian way, and thanked him in the politest way possible in her language. "*Kalahngan en komwi*," she said and took her place at his stern to prevent it from scraping as he, too, launched into the canal.

Ḷainjin turned once or twice to find her still standing at the shore, watching him for a long time as he paddled through the cool mist still falling from the low, black clouds covering the horizon in darkness before the dawn. A faint, cold breeze was still blowing from the east, yet he suffered it with resignation, knowing what hot, listless, and sun-tortured days lie before him.

He paddled directly to Pahn Kadira to request provisions and found Lipanmai there among the other women, collecting water. They knew where to place the water-shells with their small funnels of pandanus leaves to catch the water dripping from the takai. This was one of her many attendant's duties she had told him about.

"Go away from me. You smell of Nahn Samohl's curse!" she said, leaving him to wonder whether she was joking or not.

"I need water for voyage!"

"You better have two lives for that voyage! The Saudeleur says no one returns from the cannibal islands." She removed a coconut-shell container from its place along the wall, sucked a little water into her mouth, then spit it out. "Too salty. You must ask the Saudeleur like the others."

Ḷainjin drew her close to him.

"Go away or I'll puke on your stinking face!" she teased.

"Then I lick that away before I go."

She left him there and headed for the house of the Saudeleur, returning shortly thereafter.

"Saudeleur no want talk. Come."

She led him to the Saudeleur's pantry hut, where she handed him a huge log of jāānkun.

"The Seekers already took most of it," she said, carrying two smaller logs of it to his canoe herself. Others brought him bundles of water-shells until his hull was full.

Her eyes shed tears as she waded into the canal to push his stern away. "I go with you. You stay with me," she promised in his language.

He turned back, water welling up in his as he repeated her words. "You come with me. I stay with you." He didn't know what that meant, but it sounded good and would prove prophetic.

She placed an open hand to her throat, raised her eyebrows, and inhaled sharply.

Suddenly, Ḷainjin noticed his friends were preparing to embark, and Lipanmai's words about their taking all the jāānkun came into focus.

"I will eat your little cannibal with mountain taro and spit his bones for dogs to chew!" the palu boasted in Ḷainjin's language, as though hastily memorized with Rojak's coaching. There he sat, laughing atop a makeshift leeward platform he had apparently lashed onto her proa during the night. Ḷōbwilñawa, who must have beached his proa somewhere, backed Lañinpo's proa into the canal while he climbed to his mast to raise sail in the light breeze. Ḷainjin and the palu followed suit, and the three boats slowly made their way out through the barrier walls of the village, over the fringing reef, and through the swells lapping its edge into the gray, cloud-covered ocean beyond.

They headed south in the light breeze and drizzling rain that morning, following the coast and catching their meals as they sailed.

"What had changed their minds?" Ḷainjin thought. "Was it the little speech I gave the day before?"

He later found out it had been Rojak, outraged that Ḷōbwilñawa had known of the design on the bottom of the pwentang but had told them not. She had been the one insisting they return even though she hated the men-centric culture of that part of the ocean the most.

He found himself spilling air, not wanting to pass Lañinpo's vessel out of respect for Ḷōbwilñawa's position as the rijeḷā, heroically accepting his responsibility to lead them. Ḷōbwilñawa began to bellow a rundown of their trip as he saw it.

Ḷainjin was to keep his vessel between his and that of Rojak. Watch would be the duration of one outgoing or one incoming tide. The rijeḷā would keep track of these as best he could. Rojak and Lañinpo were to relieve Ḷainjin for one tide each. When the rijeḷā slept, the palu would take watch command, and they would sleep in opposite shifts of one tide each. They would heave to only in a storm and tie up in the same order with kubaak to wind, lines tied through and lashed to the yoke of each boat. They must tie the yard and boom of each sail securely yet opened one hand more on the two craft progressively downwind to prevent the upwind boat from washing down upon them. They would utilize the tailwind of each storm to make way south or southwest when possible, but once they reached the middle of the kāleptak current, they would paddle due south to cross as quickly as they could. Until the rain stopped, they were to collect and drink the rainwater off their sails and outrigger decks and not touch the water in their provisions. Eventually, they would need every single drop!

Ḷainjin was glad to have someone else in charge. It took him back to his youth, sailing with one grandfather or the other. It was so comforting and carefree — so simple to follow the orders of someone more experienced. By late afternoon, he was able to look back and see the island shrouded in gray, white puffs nestled within the valleys among the green mountains.

Ḷōbwilñawa was right. The edge of the kāleptak current had swung northward early. Looking backward at the mountains as a reference point made it evident they were drifting slightly eastward on their heading to the southwest because otherwise, their stern would be pointing toward the island now. And clearly it was not. So, they were traveling south faster than west. A navigator must know such things. Ḷainjin reached over and untied his ever-alert companion. The Chief immediately spread his wings and rose, kite-like yet free, over his proa. Then he likewise drifted above the others, and when no one offered him a meal, soared off to search for himself over the smooth, slowly rising and falling swells. All of a sudden, he swooped down and scooped something into his narrow, elongated beak. "Probably a squid by the looks," Ḷainjin thought.

This new adventure of entering the backward portion of the sea excited him. He wondered how they would pass from one *añōneañ* season to another with no *añōnrak* to intervene. He had always thought of the seasons in temporal terms with no geographic component. Now he began to think of the kāleptak current as both a geographical and temporal suspension. Like a dream where one slips into sleep in the dark and wakes up in the light. What he didn't realize at that time, and could not have known about, was what lay ahead: the immense, islandless expanse; the deceptive lull of the eastward-flowing kāleptak current; and the sudden and violent storms that roamed its streaming expanse like nightmare spirits to threaten not only their sails and rigging but their very lives.

The rijeḷā must have been wondering how the other three would survive under the conditions ahead, knowing that only he and the palu had sufficiently hardened, like the pwentang they sought, as they headed into the midst of that merciless, fiery beyond.

The days and nights rolled forward like the irrepressible buñtokrear swells that raised and lowered their craft regardless of the wind's path. The nights brought relief from the sun but seemed too short. The days passed one long stretch at a time. The breeze began to swirl from one moment to the next, causing them to change their point of sail so many times they ended up striking. Then the days rolled forward even more slowly as they paddled. Even as the wind died altogether, and the surface of the water showed barely a ripple. Yet the perpetual rising and falling of the incessant swells undulating from the east never stopped, and the unseen counterflowing current beneath swept them eastward, contrary to their ostensibly westward progression. Day turned to night and night into day without event, save for the burning heat of the sun reflecting relentlessly into their eyes from every point of the flat, nearly motionless expanse drifting before and beneath them.

Ḷainjin paddled with eyes nearly closed as he peeped out through the burning sweat trapped beneath his brow, ceaselessly wondering when the stifling stillness would end. One by one, they drained the water from their netted coconut-shell containers. Their faces blackened beneath their funnel-shaped pandanus hats. Their lips cracked. Then he began to wonder if their destiny was to die of thirst there in the middle of who knew where. Yet Ḷōbwilñawa, he was sure, was ever aware of where they were. Had he not crossed kāleptak twice before and led them on annual kājokwā excursions along the northern edge of its flow many times? His aim, he had explained, was to keep them on the same tiring southwest course that he calculated — considering their eastward drift — would cut them directly south toward the cross of stars that he kept by night between kubaak and bow. That group of stars that appeared imperceptibly higher on the horizon from night to night as it spun ever so slowly upon the southern horizon like the apex of a gigantic celestial whirlpool, drawing them farther and farther into its duplicitous, contrary domain.

The moon had long since waned and come again. She was the single companion to comfort their nights, provide consistency in their world of motion, and promise reprieve from the terrible daytime glare. "Could I have made it this far alone?" Ḷainjin thought as Lirojak dove from her proa, pierced the rolling, calm surface amid the glistening fluidity, and swam to relieve him. He saw her hands clasp hold on either side of his bow and felt her drag immediately as he continued to paddle, now more aggressively. Then he heard the fibers of her skirt as she slapped it upon the deck of his bow.

"Keep paddling. I'm going to poop," she whispered.

"Why not poop off your palu's bow?" he joked.

"I would have to suffer his lecture on why this is no pursuit for a woman. How I should have stayed safe at Kelepwei, and his favorite, 'that eventually, a shark is sure to bite off my butt!'"

"How could it resist! What are you using to wipe?"

"My fingers," she joked.

"Are you trying to profane my boat?"

"Oh, that's right. Women besmirch while men only season. If it was not for women, you men would never have been born. Has any man ever thought about that?" Still hanging from his bow, she was forcing him to paddle all the harder to keep up with the boats on his right and his left.

"I'm using a piece of the husks I thought to save from the coconuts we started with if you must know. Do you want to inspect it? By the way, what have you been using as you leaned over the side thinking no one was looking?" She laughed. "The fibers of your kilt?"

"I have plenty of fresh coconut husk down here as well."

"Then we'll have a contest. I'll smell your butt and you smell mine," she teased.

"I'm afraid I'll come up with black on my nose," he laughed.

Suddenly she rose. "With typical immodesty," he thought. Her lean, glistening body was stark naked, hairy between long, slender thighs quickly sinking down into his hull, where she rubbed the water from her arms back into the sea and fastened a dry skirt she had left there, as was her wont. He remembered the first day by the kājokwā. She had done that, and he had immediately wanted her, but that was before he knew and came to respect the desire she and the palu shared for each other.

She motioned for Ḷainjin to switch places. He left his enormous paddle propped vertically in the stern hatch and moved forward across the deck on the outrigger side of the mast. She rounded the side of the lowered sail using the forward-pointing mast as support, carefully stepping over the sheet and second paddle he used as a spar to keep the furled sail hanging taut and out of the way.

"Do you want to know his secret?" she whispered.

"Only if I was a woman!" he laughed.

"He kisses me down here." Smiling from ear to ear, she nodded and glanced between her spread legs as she maneuvered the large paddle into the sea.

"Talk about unluck!" Ḷainjin joked. A common belief among Rālik men was that intercourse before fishing ruined a man's luck.

"That's how he got me back!"

"Who came up with that big idea, you or him?"

"Ḷainjin, you are but a baitfish. Once you grow into a big tuna and explore the depths of the ocean, you will know what makes a woman's body giggle."

"The big tuna!" Ḷainjin blurted this out so loud that the men in the other craft turned from their paddling to watch him writhe on his bow deck with laughter.

"What?" cried the palu in Pohnpeian.

"Nothing," Rojak called back in her language. "He's sea crazy. Too much sky inside."

Ḷainjin couldn't stop laughing, couldn't remove the image of the palu as a big tuna. He tried his best to distract himself by looking up at the stars, but the light of the setting half-moon was too bright.

"I must find the image of the big tuna among the stars." He pointed. "There, look. Do you see it?"

"No!"

"Well, I do. I'm going to teach the legend of the big tuna to my son," he promised.

"Ḷōpako, you make light of this, but it's a serious thing. A father teaches his son many good things, but he passes on much ignorance as well. We women aren't the cause of your bad luck. Our menstrual secretions are not the cause of any sickness. That's a myth western man created to keep us women subservient. I don't know how it originated, but there never was any truth to it. There is nothing unclean about a woman's body. Nothing to be afraid of down there."

Finally, to change the subject more than anything, he asked if she thought the stars were all the same distance away or whether some were farther than others.

"I think the big ones that shine under the moon are closer."

"Like that one?" Ḷainjin pointed to the evening star.

"Maalal.[148] Yes, that looks closer to me. The bigger the stars, the closer. Just like the island grows on the horizon as you sail toward it."

"Maalal — the ancestors called that one the tooth of the big tuna!" he joked, and they laughed again together.

"Ḷōpako, stop! He will hear you!"

Ḷainjin couldn't stop himself from bursting periodically into laughter again as he lay back on the deck and scanned the awe-inspiring immensity of the sky around them. Finally, his inactivity — combined with the coolness silently creeping from the depths below — chilled him to the point where he began to covet the warmth of his sleeping mat, so he crawled into his hull, covered himself, and fell asleep.

In what seemed but a few moments later and far sooner than he would have liked, her foot shook his. He knew it was time to take another turn at the paddle and relieve Rojak, who by now would need rest before relieving her companion. Sleepy and muscles aching, he rolled a log of jāānkun onto the outrigger deck.

Did she want to eat first? He cut a slice of jāānkun from the end of the log and placed on it a slice of yellowfin he had caught and dried before the wind died. He replaced her at the stern hatch, and they ate together amid the chilly, starcast night. The ocean-salted tuna and the tart-sweet dried pandanus mash made for heavy chewing silence, interrupted solely

[148] Evening star; Venus (evenings only).

by the intermittent sucking of water from the eye of the netted coconut shell they shared.

Rojak stuffed two large pieces of tuna between her large, gleaming teeth. Stepping one foot on his gunwale, she dove back into the ocean toward her proa.

Ḷainjin could see the silhouette of the palu turn toward him and raise his hand as she swam quickly, like a turtle with her head above the black, gleaming sea between them.

He raised his in response and then had to settle into an earnest rhythm to keep up with Ḷōbwilñawa, who had just relieved Lañinpo and always set a challenging pace. Rojak could sleep now, as it was the big tuna's turn to do a double shift. She had accomplished, no doubt, her intention to charm and tease them both and then wrap herself in the warmth of her sleeping mat, knowing she would capture their thoughts as she slipped away amid her separate dreams as they paddled onward, their common destiny continuing to unfold.

The colors of the day that dawned confirmed what Ḷainjin had expected from the evening sky. Later, Lañinpo took his turn to relieve him, and he retreated again into the warmth below, which on previous days had gradually turned into a pleasantly shaded yet somewhat stifling oven. The sun beat down upon the glaring, reflecting sea, sucking water from its surface even as it shriveled their fish dry, burned their skin, and parched their throats hoarse. He lay there amid the tens of empty netted shells, knowing the sea would sooner or later draw this water back from the sky. "The sea," he thought, "is patient, knowing it will eventually capture all. It will wait silently and patiently for the water stolen by the sun to fall again into its realm as rain. Somewhere close, a storm will form to prevent us from shriveling up like dead insects in this heat." That was the way of kāleptak — survived only with wisdom, patience, and the conservation of water. But the most important secret to escaping its entrapment was the infallible sense of direction possessed by the rijeḷā or the palu or true navigator, however called. Their consistent bearing was to the southwest and their heading, minus their eastward drift, south.

Ḷōbwilñawa's strategy was to utilize the first whiff of the storm's breath to raise sail and maintain their southward course. His goal was to utilize as much of the storm's energy as possible. He wanted to cover the equivalent of a day's paddle — even as the storm grew closer and the wind more violent — until the last instant of approaching danger, when he would order them to strike and drift, and collect water by funneling as much as they could from their sails into their netted shells. The tricky part for the rijeḷā would be to pick up the proper course again as the storm passed and its tailwind offered an even better opportunity to progress toward their destination. That would be the hardest part. With perhaps no sun or stars visible, with the surface waves tossed in multiple directions as the storm swirled around them, how was the rijeḷā to set course? Amid this chaos, he must somehow detect the eastward-flowing current itself as well as the countervailing westward-rolling swells of the ever-diminishing yet stubbornly consistent buñtokrear. This ability to escape kāleptak's clutch separated a rijeḷā, or one who knows, from those who found themselves entrapped in its eastward current amid its swirling, violent, and continuously emerging storms. They would die of hunger or thirst if not sheer exposure to the elements, leaving their craft to drift and swirl amid the kājokwā caught in its stream.

The tricky part for Ḷainjin would be to secure the boats together just as they struck their sails. This was necessary to prevent them from separating in the storm. He must use all his dexterity to receive the *anidep*-like, covered stone at the end of a leader line tossed to him by Lañinpo from the rijeḷā's upwind craft while tossing his own, coiled and ready, to Rojak's downwind craft. He must then tie his leader line to the thicker line drawn by Rojak and, at the same time, draw on the leader line thrown to him — and then tie off the ends of both at his yoke, setting the three craft in tow with each other.

True, they had practiced this several times. But doing it all in the teeth of the storm would prove to be much more challenging. The procedure's main objective, of course, was to keep the craft from drifting apart in the storm. Over time, the downwind boat, by plan exposing slightly more of its furled and secured sail, should eventually end up first in line. The stronger the wind, the more the downwind boat should point into it. The towlines would then line up to windward of the sails' yards and masts, preventing the rigging of the boats in tow from falling backward. This configuration would need only a single watch on the lead craft to stand post and to — by tiller — prevent them all from backwinding. The palu, too big to crawl into any hull, was the natural choice to hold this position.

The first storm hit that afternoon, but things did not go as planned. In Ḷainjin's mind, the rijeḷā waited a moment too long to order their strike. By the time his conch sounded, the wind's gust prevented Ḷainjin from quickly tying off his sail. He caught the *anidep* tossed to him by Lañinpo and tied it off, but by the time Ḷainjin was ready to throw his, the palu had drifted too far to receive it. Then, when Ḷainjin tried to retrieve the tie line he was supposed to tie up with, he had drifted too far from the rijeḷā's craft as well. And when Ḷainjin tried to haul his craft closer, the leader line broke. Therefore, to a person, they suffered the storm paddling through the waves to stay as close to each other as possible — and worse, had little time to funnel water into their containers.

Sometime in the middle of that night, the gusts passed. The rijeḷā sounded for them to hoist sail. Exhausted and chilled to the bone, Ḷainjin steered a course between the two others as best he could until daylight broke, the wind began to taper, and he felt comfortable feeling around in his hull for something to eat. By noon, the wind had died. They were able to tie up together, and they drifted and slept, too debilitated to talk for the rest of that day and that night.

The next morning, the rijeḷā announced they would change strategy. In the face of the next storm, they would continue sailing or luffing as necessary to secure the boats one to another first before sounding for them to strike sails. The problem with this plan, as Ḷainjin saw it, was that leaving their sails exposed to the wind for too long a period might result in a ripped sail or a broken mast. Either of which would handicap the remainder of their voyage. But they didn't carry through on the rijeḷā's new plan because it was eight days before the next storm hit. By that time, they had nearly depleted their remaining stores of water and, for two days, had ceased paddling from midmorning to midafternoon to conserve water. They didn't even raise their sails before the storm but tied up long before it hit and concentrated on collecting the rain.

Ḷainjin adjusted his furled sail to collect the rain and lay face down at the tip of his bow to fill one shell at a time as the fresh water poured into its tack and ran over his hand where the two *rojak* were lashed together. He filled them all in no time, drank his fill, and was ready and even eager to untie from the others and hoist sail into the tailwind as it passed.

But after three more storms and over one cycle of the moon, they were still in kāleptak's enduring grip. They had been out of water for days. That night, there was a circle about the circumference of the moon, which reminded him of his grandfathers' stories. There were places in the ocean where fresh water rose from fresh springs at the ocean's bottom. Supposedly, the sharks that circled these places enabled you to detect them. In his thirst-induced delirium, he imagined sharks circling and reached down to scoop up delicious-looking water from the sea. Alas, it proved too salty to drink.

The next day brought one final storm, this one weaker than the others, but they were able to fill most of their shells one final time. The next day, they began to feel a faint breath of air on the left side of their sweating bodies as they paddled ever southward. They could hold their sails with light paddle the next day, and by the third, their sails began to snap like kites as breath grew to breeze and its direction firmed from the southeast. The heretofore smooth, rolling swells began to ripple with small surface waves from a second direction that splashed once again upon their decks as their bows nodded in happy acknowledgment. They had entered the backward sea. Now they faced their ultimate challenge, to cross this sea in the face of its dry season and ration their water over the unknown distance yet to travel. Their success might depend on how far eastward kāleptak had diverted them and how far they could stretch their water. There would be no rain, so they would have to sail nonstop into an islandless expanse. Ḷainjin would learn what a terrible thing is thirst.

The rijeḷā ordered them to limit themselves to three containers a day, from which they were to sip and from which they were to remain in a state of constant thirst. Because of his enormous size, Lirojak allowed the palu to drink most of her daily ration. Therefore, Ḷainjin shared his with her. He also offered water to her brother when he took his helm and allowed him to rest. He never allowed them to dive from his boat without drinking first.

Soon Ḷainjin developed pain deep within his head. He slept at a moment's notice and began to drop his steering paddle into the sea. Were it not tied down, he would have lost it the first few days into the remainder of their voyage. His rigging backwinded twice. He found nothing to talk about when he was relieved, and he slept immediately and soundly once his aching head rested below. He counted eight days, then began to dream while still awake. He stopped watching his bird. When he heard the commotion when they sighted the smoke from the fire islands, he didn't bother a look-see. By the time they did arrive at Manus, he had not counted for several days — could not count, period.

They offered him fresh water, but he could hardly lift himself to sip it. He spent another day in the hull he had not risen from in how many days. He remembered strangers carrying him with much difficulty up a ladder high into a dark house. There, a woman speaking a foreign tongue laid him, without a mat, on a slatted floor. She woke him up periodically by pouring cold saltwater from enormous containers over him, then giving him fresh water to sip.

The Kingfisher

Ļainjin came to his senses gradually over several more days. Was he alive, or — like Jibke[149] — had he landed on the shores of the afterlife? Then he remembered with certainty that Lañinpo had, just the day before, asked permission to borrow his craft, but for what he couldn't remember. He pinched himself to make sure he was alive and not dreaming. Had Lañinpo returned? Was his boat safe?

She was the woman of the house, and she was the one responsible for torturing him with the cold seawater. What light entered the house came indirectly from below or from a space under the upper eaves, left open for the smoke to escape. He had realized the slats of the floor were over water long ago, when he kept hearing the sounds that her children made urinating through them. The water beneath him rose and fell with the tides, so he knew they were somehow over or close to the ocean. Canoes were tied to the house pilings and bumped irritatingly against each other. This was something an easterner who hated to beach his canoe without palm-frond skids would never allow, so right away, he lost respect for the men of the house. Especially so after he saw how they treated her. They had tattooed her face and shaved her head. They always spoke to her harshly and treated her like a captive attendant. Even her children, who always left with their father or played in tiny canoes on the reefs, seemed to treat her with disdain.

---

[149] Figure from the oral literature of the Marshall Islands who is given the impossible task of finding the source of the wind and lands in the mythical land of Eb.

Ḷainjin had never seen a woman without hair on her head, but if she felt embarrassed, ashamed, or guilty, it didn't show in her eyes. She held her head high and wouldn't tell him her name, so he called her Lipanmai in his thoughts and thought of her often. He followed her soft footsteps about the house, from one cooking hearth to another. He learned to turn to her as she approached, as she no longer forced him to awaken. She was the one, he remembered, who had sternly demanded pwentang after pwentang of cold ocean water carried up from below. Yet she was the one who had brought him the mat to sleep on and awakened him night and day to sip water or soup from a small pwentang. She alone attended to his many fears. She sat with him and patiently, smilingly mimed repeatedly over the several days it took him to understand that his proa was safe with his friends, who were well but had left to visit other villages and would surely come back for him soon. Her skin tone was lighter than his had been even before the sun scalding he had apparently endured. Her face was perfectly formed. High cheekbones dominated it, complementing her innocent smile. Bushy, wise eyebrows curved dark against her unblemished skin. Her ears appeared angled, alert.

She was Lipanmai in his mind, and he had dreamed of her during the days and nights of his delirium. Her determinedly spoken words "I go with you" had swirled in his thoughts since the moment he set to sea, and he was glad not to be alone now that his friends had left him. He contentedly lay there thinking of her in the darkness. The smoke from the fire stung his eyes such that he found himself breathing through the floor slats to suck in the breeze blowing beneath him. It felt good to be inside. At least here, the home's thick thatch protected him from the heat of the treacherous, overbearing sun that had crippled him. He enjoyed resting his aching body on the slatted floor, which gave as he turned from side to side, peering down into the shaded lagoon water beneath this dream-like abode. She was the one who had taken it upon herself to save him while what visitors she had seemed to carry on indifferently, absorbed in whatever preoccupations their village on the sea required.

She had even taken in the Chief, tying his leg to the rail on the landing below. It was the children, with all their comings and goings, who brought little fish to feed his bird that convinced him this house was part of a group huddled together on pilings above a common lagoon. They came and they went. The children, punting their tiny canoes back and forth with poles three times their size, pretended to be involved in important matters like their fathers. However, Ḷainjin observed that they simply added yet another level of unappreciated duties the woman of the house seemed obligated to fill. Rather than climbing up to her when hungry or thirsty, the children called out to her instead. So, she would leave her housekeeping chores and descend the rickety ladder to the canoe landing below to feed them.

She had no ground oven to bake, so she boiled their food in one or other of many pwentang that neatly adorned the shelves above each of two hearths on opposite sides of the room. She set her cooking pwentang upon three large, equal-sized stones over the coals of her fires. She stored her water in several much-larger pwentang that she had lined up along the walls in orderly fashion. He had never imagined a cooking fire built upon a wooden floor so lying on his side one day, mimed his question. She beckoned him to watch her and quickly stooped before her fire, allowing the bark strands of her skirt to slip free of her thighs. He watched her unblemished bare legs and dainty feet in the dim light of the hearth as she poked the edge of it with her firestick to break something loose. Then her beautiful legs returned and kneeled before his face. She had brought back a handful of a hardened mixture of wood ash and sand that she had apparently used to separate the fire from the thick mat below. She had answered his question, but like a fool, he could think of nothing else to ask her and that was that. After a moment, the legs retreated, and he turned on his stomach and wished he had thought of something else to ask.

Ḷainjin always thought of her husband as the Kingfisher,[150] a bird that haunted the mangrove forests of Pohnpei. Its bob of feathers and large beak made its head appear outsized to the rest of its body. While this woman of his remained unadorned, he always wore an elaborate turtle shell–comb in the unruly kinky bird's nest that encompassed his head. He wore rings of coconut shell in his stretched earlobes and adorned the pierced septum of his nose with a sliver of shiny pearl shell shaped like a new moon. Other

[150] Aka Malean.

things often hung about his neck. He often wrapped a pandanus band about one wrist or the other, if not an ankle. Only once did he speak of his lovely wife, and that was to brag how much his father, whose jawbone hung on one of his necklaces over his back, had paid for her. From Ḷōbwilñawa, he later heard of a woman who spoke of her sons as food for the Kingfisher. Like many other westerners, the Mwanus, he would learn, were head cutters who sometimes boiled, sometimes simply spiked, the heads of their enemies on posts about the village to be eaten by maggots, upon which the local kingfisher in turn would feast.

Though he showed no love for his woman, he had charmed her children such that their happiness hung on his every action. He would call to them from the landing below, "*Papu*!" or "*Ina*!"[151] The one called would jump down, without hesitation, from the house entrance into his outstretched arms. If his father agreed to take him fishing, the little boy would break, much to the Kingfisher's admiration, into a penis dance. According to what Ḷōbwilñawa would tell him, later in this same lad's life, he would use this same dance to taunt the recipients of his gifts to reciprocate in kind. His purpose in strutting and wagging his naked little manhood back and forth and up and down before his sister was to demonstrate, much to her envy, that he was the heir apparent to his grandfather's legacy. The boy's guardian spirit, the remains of his grandfather's skull and fingers, rested in a wooden bowl hung above the doorway under which he danced. Should the father's overconfident protégé awake and find his father had gone fishing without him, he would cry inconsolably regardless of his mother's supplications until a crowd of other children punted over to see what his commotion was about, and she would have to feed these as well. From such antics and others, he grew to understand why Lirojak hated this place and its seriously male-centric culture.

Nevertheless, Ḷainjin wasn't without respect for Malean,[152] which was the Kingfisher's name. At first, he thought of him as lazy as well as silly. Later, he would realize he was just all *kawas*[153] all the time. To be sure, he pointed this out to Ḷainjin daily. His way was to wake him immediately when he

---

[151] Generic terms for "little boy" or "little girl" among the Mwanus.
[152] Aka the Kingfisher.
[153] Titan word for "exchange."

entered the house. Sit and chew, and offer betel nut — which Ḷainjin always refused — and show him whatever he had received in trade that day with the Usiai.[154] He traded the fish, turtles, and other items of the sea collected by his nephews to the Usiai for coconuts, oil, sago, yams, taro, and the all-important betel nut and pepper leaves. In short, he was the hub of trading between many families. In his eyes, and perhaps in the eyes of his fellow villagers, this made him seem central to everyone's well-being. It was clear he was a good provider.

"Sisters — you?" The Kingfisher would ask this in his language every day.

Ḷainjin got tired of watching his feigned sympathy at his answer and learned to simply stare at his blood-red smile, stained with buai, as the Kingfisher invariably bragged, "Me — four!" Unsaid but understood was the result that he had a band of matrilineal nephews to command and rely upon at will.

He also traded shells drilled and strung by his wife and sisters to the Matankor[155] off-islanders for carved bowls, gourds, spears, and tools of blackstone. On these later trips, he would disappear for four or five days, but he didn't leave his wife and children alone, as his two younger brothers and their wives lived in rooms walled off in the back of the house with their children. These men, who only appeared to eat or start a fire with their fire ploughs and who apparently took turns beating their own wives, treated the Kingfisher's wife with the deference she deserved as she prepared the *kai*[156] for the lot of them. She, Ḷainjin was certain, would remain joyful no matter what, and for what reason he could never determine. He found himself wishing the Kingfisher would drown in a storm so he could free this captive woman and spend the rest of his days in her well-kept house, under the care of the beautiful woman preserved inside. But alas, he had his mission and she had her life.

As he grew stronger, Ḷainjin began to climb down onto the boat landing that opened to the dreadfully bright sea from which he came. He

---

[154] Bush people of Manus Island.

[155] People who live in inland housing on the smaller Admiralty Islands and on Manus's north coast.

[156] Titan word for "food."

preferred this spot of an evening, once the glare and heat of the day had passed. From here, he could sit with his bird and view the village. It reminded him of Nahn Madol with its surrounding bay of multicolored shades of blue upon which the village seemed to float and with the verdant green shoreline that trailed off into the westward horizon. But he longed for stones and walls upon which to climb and view into the distance from the vantage of height.

On occasion, when one paddling canoe approached another, a female passenger would suddenly cover herself with a pandanus mat and disappear into the hull until the other had passed. He wished to ask the woman of the house, but alas, had no way of questioning her as she had not seen the incident and he was at a loss to mime what had happened. Later, Ļōbwilñawa explained to him that women yet to be married had to hide themselves from certain of their betrothed's male relatives. Marriages arranged from youth were a serious and all-important part of their culture and were consolidated by periodic, reciprocal gift giving.

Then one evening, he was sitting on the landing and absently watching the children punting back and forth in the village — yet listening to the water splashing down between the slated floors above as she bathed. He was busy imagining her naked body and pretending she had asked him to enter that room and rub her skin with the coconut she had earlier grated when he observed distinctive sails approaching. His throat began to pang at the idea of leaving her behind, and he thought of crawling back into his mat and pretending to be unrecovered. He sank into ridiculous thoughts of how he might feign some reason to stay. Finally, after days of worry, there was Lañinpo, tending his craft and anchoring it a short distance from that of his sister. He should be relieved, he thought, but was not! His throat sank into his chest as the rijeļā began paddling toward them, then tied up to the landing beneath the overhanging veranda where he rested. Everything was occurring as though from a nightmare.

"Look at him! He sits like the village chief!"

Ļainjin glanced at the Chief. At first, he'd thought the rijeļā meant the bird. Having forgotten his manners, Ļainjin awoke into the present, rose, and helped Ļōbwilñawa tie off his proa.

"How is your life?" Ḷōbwilñawa asked.

"I feel like spent coconut gratings. Like somebody squeezed all the best out of me."

"Then you're still good enough for pigs and chickens to eat! Malean told us you were doing better, so we came to see for ourselves."

"He said he was going to a place called Mbuke."[157] Ḷainjin responded without thinking, as though watching himself speak.

"Yes, we saw him there. He never stops trading. His reputation grows and grows. He was but a boy and his bride but a child when I saw him last."

"Where does he keep it all?"

"All what?"

"His treasure," Ḷainjin said. "He comes and goes with all these items of trade. Where does he store them?"

At this, Ḷōbwilñawa broke out into such laughter that Ḷainjin began to feel foolish.

"He doesn't. Nobody amasses treasure here. They circulate their wealth to support the feasts their marriage customs require. He shows you those things because he wants you to be his *kawas* brother. He is still paying for Ngalen! Where is she?"

Ḷainjin just sat there dumbfounded. "Her husband led me to believe his father had paid for her."

Ḷōbwilñawa explained. "His father borrowed the wealth for her betrothal from his brothers. Now Malean trades to pay it back to them, and his father's bones watch from above that doorway to see that he meets his obligations." He pointed to the wooden bowl extending over a shelf above the gable.

"Ksomu! Stop hiding from your uncle! Where are you?"

Then he repeated something in her language he would later interpret as "a little sago to the mouth!"

Ngalen appeared immediately, as though she had been listening but from a polite distance. She had a fresh coconut for them in each hand and a smile as bewitching as the sunset on her face. Ḷōbwilñawa said something to her

---

[157] Consists of a small number of islands off the south end of mainland Manus. Manus Province, also known as the Admiralty Islands, is the smallest and least populated of PNG's twenty provinces.

in her language that made her laugh, and she turned her back temporarily to step down the ladder.

Ḷainjin could not keep his eyes off her coconut-oiled legs as she descended, and the aroma off her bathed skin captivated him. Then he glanced at Ḷōbwilñawa, who had been watching him. An embarrassing "he knows" pierced Ḷainjin's throat. She took Ḷōbwilñawa's hand and sat next to him as though they were cross cousins, and a second pang of jealousy pierced him. He was no longer himself.

"Is her name Ngalen or Ksomu?" Ḷainjin asked.

When Ḷōbwilñawa laughed and said something in her language, she removed her hand from his and cutely pounded him on the shoulder in feigned anger. Pretending to turn away from him, she smiled at Ḷainjin to include him in a joke he didn't understand.

"Ngalen is her name," Ḷōbwilñawa said. "And as you can see, she has never been bitten by a mosquito. She grew up here among these villages offshore and spends her days protecting her skin in the shade of her husband's house."

"What was that other name?"

"Ksomu?" As he responded, Ngalen pounded his shoulder again.

"Yes, that one," Ḷainjin said.

"That's a name I use to tease her. It's from a story about an infidel woman who pretends to be sick when her husband asks for food. He asks for 'a little sago for the mouth,' but she goes to the mangrove swamp instead and has sex with a bird called Karipo. That bird has a long neck because her husband, Ndrame, made it so when he found them together. He killed Ksomu there in the swamp, and to this day, there are many clams there at that place to prove the story true."

Ḷainjin objected. "That doesn't sound like a good name for Ngalen, that of a character who has sex with a bird!"

"Well," Ḷōbwilñawa said, "that's not the way the women here think of the story. Ksomu is a heroine who has the courage to shame her husband by having sex with a bird. Her husband was rude to her by coming home and demanding food. Better to have sex with a bird than with a man who does not treat her with respect. What is Ndrame to do now that everyone knows his wife ran off with a bird? He no longer has anyone to cook his sago, nor does he have anyone to have sex with. What woman will have a man who killed his wife?"

"None, I suppose," Ḷainjin agreed.

"So, that's the moral of the story. Every story has its own meaning based on its social context. Parents confirm marriages during their children's infancy. Kalowin told that story to me for the first time right here under this veranda. That was Malean's father. He paid an enormous sum of twelve hundred dog teeth for a girl he never looked upon one time."

"You mean he died before seeing her?"

"No, I mean in their custom, a father-in-law never looks upon a daughter-in-law's face. He didn't have to. Her loveliness was such that she was on the lips of the whole village from the day she was born. The sum he offered for her was legendary, so he referred to her jokingly as Ksomu to teach his son a lesson to treat her with respect. Now he looks upon her all he wants." Ḷōbwilñawa pointed up at the bowl. "He constantly presides over their wealth and insists they use it wisely."

"Well, please thank her," Ḷainjin said. "I would have died without her care."

After a bit of conversation between the two, Ḷōbwilñawa told him she said she had watched her grandmother cure many men of sun sickness. "She says it will attack him more quickly next time. Better he sails at night as much as possible and stays shaded during the day."

He continued. "Anyway, we met Malean at Mbuke. It's the only place other than the Papua coast where they make pwentang. There was one thing we needed to be sure of that we forgot to think about. What if there were other survivors of our fleet that we never knew about that got involved in making pwentang? So Malean asked the islanders about that, but the answer was no. None of our people washed up there. Our next stop will be Murik. We need to try to find out if they have other pwentang with the *wapepe* symbol to try to find out where they're coming from. Malean is trading for provisions for our trip and gathering many items that he wants us to trade for him."

"Why can't he trade them himself?" Ḷainjin asked.

"He intends to. He'll accompany us as far as the Murik lagoon and wait there for his uncle, who is still repairing his proa before making a trip of that distance."

"How far to Murik?" Ḷainjin asked,

"Two nights and two days."

"How far from Murik to Sigaba?"

"Another day or so, but we may decide to stop at one of the fire islands."

"I would like that!" Now excited about the trip, Ḷainjin quickly dropped his dream-like fantasy of perching like his bird in Ngalen's comfortable, dimly lit haven.

Ḷōbwilñawa spoke to Ngalen, who insisted they try her dugong soup before leaving. Ḷainjin said he'd been eating it for days but had thought it was fish soup with chunks of pig.

"Pigs are for feasting," explained Ḷōbwilñawa as each broke the shell of his coconut to use as a spoon to eat.

"What is 'dugong'?"

"It's like a pig that swims in the sea, but not fast like a porpoise. If the palu were a fish, he would be a dugong! Think of it that way."

As they laughed, Ḷainjin remembered the evening Lirojak had made the palu cry and reminded him of the rare sea dog he had seen at Bikar, the northernmost atoll in the Ratak string.

"I advise you to leave that bird here with Ngalen," Ḷōbwilñawa said.

"Why?"

"Because where we are going, they have bigger birds called 'sea eagles' that fly faster and would make quick work of it. And because you'll want to stop here again if we're successful. There are no other options."

When they left, Ngalen sent them with coconuts for the trip and insisted Ḷainjin take the sleeping mat. She wrapped a long string of shell disks she had drilled and strung it around his neck, softly touching his shoulder with her hand afterward. There was much discussion and laughter between her and Ḷōbwilñawa as she untied his painter, and Ḷainjin steadied the stern until she returned to midcraft on the landing. At the last instant, he instinctively reached out to her, and they intertwined fingers briefly as he thanked her in her language.

Ļainjin glanced briefly at the Chief, wondering whether he would see his friend again. He felt content to leave him in Ngalen's care. Then Ļōbwilñawa backed his proa away from the house, and Ļainjin saw, for the first time, the height of the immense green island behind them and the pure white of the slight and surprisingly shady sand spits that dotted the bay between.

"She said to use the shells to buy a long night for yourself at the men's house at Mbuke," said Ļōbwilñawa.

"Why would I pay to stay there?" Ļainjin turned back to see her, hands on hips, calling to her children, who were in a canoe between the pilings of the house next to hers, perhaps telling them to go and gather small fish from the reefs.

"Because that's one place where Manus men go to trade with the captive Matankor prostitutes from the dugong wars on the north shore." Ļōbwilñawa laughed. "She joked that your manhood is restless. It kept peeping out at her from between the fibers of your kilt as you slept."

Ļainjin, speechless, turned red with embarrassment.

"Ļainjin, don't worry about it. She's flattered. You will learn that women of whatever island don't need to hear a man say what they want. They're born with a sense for such things."

Suddenly, he felt exhausted again. What little exertion he had expended to embark had tired him. Ļōbwilñawa paddled hard, and they soon arrived at Lirojak's craft, where they found her dugong asleep like a baby in its crib. Ļainjin barely had the energy to greet his friends. Leaving the sailing to Lañinpo, he lay down in his hull, thought of Ngalen, and slept like a child gently rocking in her arms. The three craft departed for Mbuke to meet up with Malean.

They arrived at Mbuke sometime that night. He peered through the darkness at the Mwanus villages, which were like those off Manus, the big island, likewise built on pilings offshore of the Matankor, with whom they traded. The Matankor villages of Mbuke hid in the dense jungle of this second, much smaller high island. Ļainjin had learned from Ļōbwilñawa that the Usiai populated the big island of Manus. The Matankor populated all these surrounding offshore islands, and the Mwanus populated the surrounding coral lagoons of both Manus and Mbuke like a circle of colorful coral-eating fish endlessly swimming about their favorite coral head.

They would anchor offshore until dawn. Ḷainjin gave Ngalen's shell beads to Lañinpo and wished him good luck in front of the rolling eyes of his sister and as the palu remained immobile under her threatening stare. So, only Lañinpo accompanied Ḷōbwilñawa ashore. On his part, Ḷainjin would return to his new favorite activity — sleep.

However triumphant the nocturnal escapades of Lañinpo and Ḷōbwilñawa, they were prepared to sail at dawn. Ḷainjin awoke to the sound of Malean and Lañinpo loading tens of pwentang onto the outrigger platforms of his canoe, bundling them tightly with fishnet and dried coconut husk such that they couldn't jar each other in the waves. They sailed for Murik.

Ḷainjin took the helm for the first time that morning. It was a downwind run, and the wind was strong and steady from the southeast. But instead of feeling exhilarated, he quickly found the sun that rose over his shoulder overbearing, and by noon, he realized that something inside had broken again. He was sick and needed more sleep, and for the first time, he began to worry that maybe his strength *was* gone for good. For the remainder of the trip, Lañinpo served twice as much time as Ḷainjin at the helm. He did better at night. The sun had become repulsive to him. Yes, the island that loomed before him was compelling, but the sun's relentless glare diminished the excitement and sense of adventure. Had his struggle in the kāleptak current changed him for good?

The Bar Nor

Come afternoon of the third day, their three craft sailed by the mouth of the great river the others had told Ḷainjin about, but the giant lizards didn't appear. The dirty white water belched out from the mouth of a peninsula like sakau compressed into the sea. "It must have started as rainwater over the incredible mountains in the distance," Ḷainjin thought. And dirtied as it wound its way through the hinterlands and over the flat, jungle-covered plains that spread to the sea. The brown water followed the coastline in a westward-flowing current that swept below them but cleared as they passed a long stretch of coast covered with bleak gray beach sand capped here and there with shrubbery, vines, coconut palms, and stands of leafless green trees. Finally, they came to a coastal passageway into a verdant mangrove-infested lagoon, entered it, and hardened up to a Bar Nor village just west of the passage.

With its back to the sea, this coastal village reminded Ḷainjin of many similar villages back home except that it didn't face a clear, sparkling, blue-water lagoon but a dark-water maze of mangrove-covered islets, irregular saltwater lakes, and erratically shaped watercourses. These people called themselves the Bar Nor, or "mangrove men." As expected, the houses of this village were set upon pilings with their small, often outriggerless canoes huddled beneath. Each thatched pole house sprouted a rickety, pole-lashed walkway, sometimes leading inland and sometimes to the next house. If there was land betwixt this village that fronted the lagoon and the sea behind, it looked too narrow to support freshwater wells. "They must drink only by collecting rainwater," he thought. This would explain the pwentang that Malean had collected and piled high on his outrigger platform.

Like the kingfisher he was named for, Malean fluttered along the jumble of untidy stringer walkways made of pilings and poles lashed this way and that. Their arrival disrupted village life and a sort of festival atmosphere emerged. Naked, curious, and undisciplined children gawked. Women boldly stared past their buai nut–distracted men. Drums sounded as Malean searched, according to Ļōbwilñawa, for their trade partner. Meanwhile, the crew floated before the village like so many freshly cut coconuts awaiting collection by the thirsty crowd. Finally, Malean emerged and hailed them to where his partner had decided they were to tie up. No sooner had the proas been secured than a chirping, clicking sound began to emanate from within the adjacent houses and along the rickety walkways, and women began to unbundle and remove the pwentang. They had apparently received direction from Malean, who was himself distracted by still other women attempting to coax him away from his task at hand. Lirojak, who was apparently aware of the welcoming customs that temporarily liberated these otherwise chaste women, stood at her mast above her palu, who was still lounging at his lee platform position under the shadow of her paddle, amusedly watching the frizzy-headed beauties unload her craft's valuable cargo.

Lañinpo zestfully launched himself onto the landing, where a circle of women immediately set upon him, each trying to draw blood by pinching him with the pair of small clamshells each either held in hand or clicked together to produce the sound that seemed to energize them. Ļainjin, ill and tired out from the trip, dodged below and covered himself with the sleeping mat Ngalen had given him, hoping to avoid altogether the newcomer welcome he had heard so much about. Nevertheless, it wasn't long before he sensed his boat drifting. Somewhat alarmed, he rose and saw a diminutive woman sitting at the bow, paddling them furiously away against the wind, bent perhaps on crossing the lake into the maze of mangrove forest on the other side. She turned not back to the crowd that cheered from the landing behind but stroked deliberately on one side then the other, aback slightly from the bow that she straddled. Her bag of buai nut hung awkwardly about her neck. She was so short her feet didn't touch the water, and he could easily have overpowered the naked-backed little woman. Yet he felt trapped by events. Why embarrass them both before the others? It was better to play along at least until they were alone, which might be but moments away. He was both physically and mentally unprepared for sex with her. He wanted to lie back down in his hull but feared she would take that as an invitation.

Having crossed the narrow lake, now out of the wind, she hurriedly paddled them through a narrow, mangrove-covered waterway. His mast caught there under the overgrowth. They had reached a large, black, knee-like trunk upon which she scampered and tied off his proa. The water there was clearer and shallower with a bottom of brown, undisturbed mud. He felt like he was back in one of the eel pools of Pohnpei waiting for her to attack. She suddenly reappeared, facing him, and Ḷainjin couldn't help but smile at her. She was a woman much older than he, with a scrunched-up face and the largest buai nut–blackened smile he had ever seen. Her unarranged, frizzled hair appeared as wild as her eyes. She immediately bit into one of the nuts she had taken from her bag, parting it in two, then sprinkled white lime powder between the halves. Pinching them together again, she wrapped the nut up in a pepper leaf and impolitely popped the first into her mouth while she fixed a second for him. A warm glow of pleasure crossed her face as she crunched down on the concoction, balled it in one cheek, and scrambled onto the yoke of his proa. There, she sat uncomfortably close before him and offered the other nut with a grin.

He took it as a stalling tactic though he didn't care for or see the purpose of all this buai-nut compulsion. Ngalen had offered him the same under more chaste circumstances, and he did his best to make a show of chewing it before spitting it between the floor slats. He viewed it as a crude, addictive habit that threatened his plans and was likely to leave him tied to an unhappy life far away from home. Nevertheless, he nodded his thanks and began to chew.

She apparently took this as his assent to begin sex. She spread her knees and pointed her toes beneath the fibers of his kilt until they touched his manhood, at which point her wild eyes literally bugged out of her face and she giggled maniacally. For some crazy reason, all this stimulated his manhood to pop out at her from between the fibers of his kilt. Excited at this sight, she immediately dropped her skirt, bent over the yoke on her tiptoes, turned her bare butt to him, and held onto the mast, expecting a thrust from behind. At which point Ḷainjin decided to quit while ahead. Now that he had proved to her that she aroused him, he gently turned the stark-naked woman, hugged her compassionately, and tried to mime to her that he was too sick to have sex at that time and needed to lie down and sleep. To this proposal, she reluctantly agreed but insisted on drawing blood with her clamshell pincers from his calf. He discarded the buai nut into the water as inconspicuously as possible and crawled below, half-worried she might try to join him, but she had her pride and allowed him to rest as she apparently crunched on until her stash was exhausted. At which time she maneuvered the proa back out into the lake and victoriously returned them to the village.

They were just in time to reload Ḷainjin's boat with his share of the pwentang that Malean and their trade partner Kanari[158] had judiciously split off as his share in recompense for their transport. Kanari, Ḷōbwilñawa would later explain, was the son of their previous trade brother who had died. He would be the host for their stay. No sooner had they approached his house than the chirping began again along the walkways though Ḷainjin was able to escape his pursuers by pointing to the blood crusted on his calf. Ḷōbwilñawa assured him that, once inside, he would be free of the clamshells. The palu and Rojak were to stay at Kanari's house. He and Lañinpo were to sleep at Kanari's sister's next door.

The pole houses — or *iran*, as they referred to them — were like those of the Mwanus except the rectangular space inside was an undivided sleeping area. Ḷainjin found the inside strewn with mats and friendly people — a patriarch who was probably Kanari's father, two adolescent females, children from the house next door, a crying toddler, and his mother, busy preparing food. The rear wall facing the shore served as the storage area for cooking tools: small, flat, and other oddly shaped pwentang as well as huge ones. Some were for water and some for storing sago flour. Baskets of smoked fish hung from the ceiling on wooden hooks to keep them from rats. Other identical arm baskets, perhaps for trade, hung from rafters above the landing. This area facing the lagoon, Ḷainjin would learn, was the least

---

[158] A Bar Nor man who accompanies Ḷainjin to Sigaba.

smoky. He found the rafters directly above him crisscrossed with spears of various lengths. Again, there were no separate cookhouses. Their cooking hearths were also inside, as in Manus. He would later realize the smoke was for protection against mosquitos, which didn't grow in the saltwater swamps yet crept out from the mainland.

Exhausted and in no mood to mime, Ļainjin asked Ļōbwilñawa to tell his hosts to excuse him, as he would be lying down to sleep. Yes, it would be fun to gallivant around the village with Lañinpo, but he must concentrate on his recuperation if he was to prove good in battle. He placed his mat where directed, lay back, and fell into a dream-like state whereby he drifted in and out of sleep while remaining conscious of his surroundings and the movements and voices of the people around him. Other children giggled, screamed, and ran in and out. The adolescent girls chatted constantly, passed the boy who insisted they carry him between them, and took orders from their mother, who puttered endlessly from one fire to another as the pleasant smell of one food and then another filled the smoky, pleasantly dim environment. The mother disturbed him twice, once with two fresh coconuts shortly after he had lain down and later, during supper, to bring him a pwentang of sweet sago pudding. Lañinpo entered the house at supper time and placed his sleeping mat in the lagoon corner away from the landing. Later, he brought a woman he intended to sleep with, and though they politely kept their noise down to a minimum, it was obvious when they had finished the first time and then again before dawn, after which she left and Lañinpo fell back to sleep with a light snore.

The next morning, Ļōbwilñawa announced he and Kanari were sailing for Blup Blup Island to bring back pigs for the ladder ceremony he wanted to sponsor for his nephew. The plan was to be there by nightfall and return the next day. The palu wanted to accompany them, but Rojak had to stay to trade their share of the pwentang with the bush women for sago and would not hear of him getting "within chirping distance" of any of the offshore islands without her to fight off the women she knew "itched for new trade partners." Ļōbwilñawa instructed Ļainjin to stay put inside the *iran*, which suited his inclination exactly. Then Lañinpo, who seemed a new man, came excited to tell him about the woman he'd been with the night before. He had known her in his youth and remembered her name — Sarakena[159] — all these seasons. Did Ḷainjin not think it was a beautiful-sounding name?

Ḷainjin laughed. "Well yes, as long as it doesn't mean 'rat' or 'mosquito' or 'one who defecates in the house'! Take your name, Lañinpo. It sounds nice, but knowing you're a force before which men must strike their sails… That is a name!"

"I never asked what her name means."

"Should have spent more time talking and less time sliding in and out." Ḷainjin felt temporarily insightful, remembering the several attempts at conversation he'd had with Lipanmai.

"We spent a lot of time talking — just not in the house! She told me her history these past years, and I told her all about Pohnpei. She has not been able to marry because her brother demands too high a price for her. We talked a lot about how hard he is on her. I told her I will fix everything. How much can he be asking?"

"Not much, I would guess, in terms of what you accumulated back on Pohnpei. Waow, wait! You chose title over wealth." Ḷainjin laughed. "Maybe he'll accept a Pohnpeian title," he said sarcastically.

"I should be able to accumulate what he asks here within a season or two."

Shortly thereafter, he left. Toward evening, Rojak came by to wake Ḷainjin again and ask when Lañinpo had left and where he had gone.

"He left around noon and said he was in love with a girl called Sarakena." When Rojak appeared distraught at his response, he asked, "What's wrong with that?"

"Around here, it's one thing for a woman to give herself to a mariner. She's not supposed to allow him to parade her around the village before and afterward. They think they're fourteen seasons old again! I went with the village women to trade for sago with the Bush Murik. They all referred to Lañinpo as *naboag goan* — a flying fox."

"Like the ones in Pohnpei?"

"Yes," Rojak said. "They hold the fruit bat in low regard because it steals from other people's gardens. All the women talked about was Sarakena's

[159] A name: "all these seasons"; the woman Lañinpo meets again in a Bar Nor village.

brother and how upset 'the big balls below his little finger' were getting over the whole thing. I think they were warning me about all this. You know, they practice sister exchange here. If her brother expects me to sit around his smoky house sweetening his sago pudding, he's going to get quickly disappointed!"

"Do you think he would do something to Lañinpo?'

"Never! They treat us as honored guests who can do no wrong. I am worried about her. They say he beats her all the time."

"Why would he do that?"

"He wants her to stay virtuous so he can get a better price for her," Rojak said. "He thinks he owns her."

"I'm sure Ḷōbwilñawa and his Kanari will straighten it all out when they return."

"Perhaps."

"What about Malean?" Ḷainjin was curious now that she had wakened him.

"He's going from house to house, something he would never do back in the Mwanus villages. Their women are chaste as these women are, but they enjoy no holidays with offshore men like they get here. Men there can only have sex with captive women they pay to please them. Malean is eating bowl after bowl of sweet sago pudding and poking his banana into any woman who beckons while his trading partner goes house to house collecting these famous Bar Nor baskets to exchange for his share of the pwentang." Rojak peered up at tens of baskets hanging above. "Malean is popular around here, as was his father, whose trade partners Malean inherited. He's going to want you to trade his baskets to the Kunai for blackstone."

Ḷainjin hesitated. "But—"

"But we must return through Manus anyway, and neither the light baskets nor the blackstone will slow you down. It isn't like transporting pigs! Ḷōbwilñawa hates to transport pigs. I know his eyes widened and his throat coughed when Kanari asked him to sail to Blup Blup for pigs. However, he knows men here must fulfill certain roles with their trade partners and especially honor their bones by maintaining those relationships with their sons. The women say that Kanari's ability to lead his trade partner Lōbwilñawa out to Blup Blup provides him enormous prestige."

"Well, what does Malean want the blackstone for?"

"Not just any blackstone," Rojak said. "He wants large pieces to tip the harpoons they use on dugong. It's important for them to kill those things once they attack them. Wars have been fought over wounded dugong drifting up on an enemy's shore."

Having heard his uncle's name, the toddler uncharacteristically came up to Rojak on his own. She immediately embraced the boy. "So, this is the little chief." She said this facetiously, as the Bar Nor conspicuously had no chieftain. Fastidiously coddled, apparently since birth, he was the firstborn son who, per custom, was about to be taught by his uncle Kanari to climb the ladder at the house entrance for the first time as soon as he returned from Blup Blup. The child had developed an aura of entitlement equal to the village-wide ceremony about to take place and tugged at Rojak's simple necklace of small, white cowry shells until it broke. Then he cried when one of his sisters immediately swept him up, took the shell he was clutching, and returned it. In their language, Rojak immediately said he could keep it and offered it back to him. That was followed by his mother rushing up and slapping the boy's hand viciously before returning to her pwentang and leaving him with his sister, who attempted to shush him up by pacing him back and forth. It was clear that — even though he would forever remain the privileged person she, the rest of the household, soon the village, and even Ḷōbwilñawa believed him to be — she would mercilessly teach him to respect the property of others.

One by one, Lirojak picked up the shells of her broken necklace and politely retreated down the ladder to the landing below. Ḷainjin rolled onto his stomach, placed his cheek on the backs of his crossed palms, and tried to rest, as the sisters, one by one, took turns quieting the rambunctious little tyrant. He wondered how many more days it would be till his strength returned. Would it be gradual, or would he one day awake and be his old self again? Was he jealous of the constant care and attention the boy received from his mother and older sisters, considering he, as a boy, had rarely felt a woman's touch? He was certainly sick of the Kingfisher always asking him how many sisters he had.

The older of the two sisters seemingly inadvertently brushed his upturned foot, which extended past the end of his sleeping mat now and again as she sang and marched back and forth, trying to quiet the boy. Then she stopped and surprisingly interlocked her toes with his as she stood over him for a moment, giggling as she sang her charge away. Ḷainjin took that as an unmistakably bold invitation too fraught with unease to pursue. What were the unspoken rules of this trade-brother relationship? Intrigued yet wary, he slowly crawled forward upon his sleeping mat until both feet were within its lower border and rocked himself to sleep.

Thus, he rested through the next day and the next. Ḷōbwilñawa didn't return as promised, nor had Ḷainjin's strength begun to resurge. He kept himself squarely within the boundaries of the sleeping mat Ngalen had given him. That afternoon, Lirojak climbed the ladder, popped her head into the house, and announced excitedly that the palu needed to talk to him at the landing below. Ḷainjin lowered his uncharacteristically fragile body down the ladder and sat next to her proa, moored against the pilings. His view seemed to be swirling about him as though he had drunk jemañūñ, but it was good to be out of the smoky house. The palu, as always, sat in his spot on the leeward platform. It was clear from the beginning that they couldn't wait to announce something of importance.

"Has the rijeḷā returned?" he asked them.

"No, not yet."

"News of the rijeḷā was not why they came to talk," thought Ḷainjin.

"Okay," continued Lirojak. "It started with Wisim complaining about how much sago I was getting from the Bush Murik trading the large pwentang. He had come to realize that the large pwentang, used mostly as water containers, were therefore more valuable to the Bar Nor because they had no access to wells and had to collect all their water from rain. This is dry season, so he started trading the large ones to our neighbors for smaller ones and had me trade these smaller ones to the Bush Murik. And sure enough, the sago they offered was more that way."

"Well," Ḷainjin responded, "I guess it was worth floating the notorious Satawan trader all that way from Pohnpei! Now we'll have more sago to show up with at Sigaba, and unless I'm mistaken, their hungry season is coming up. They're just starting to plant their yams. Correct?"

"Yes. But wait! Wisim, show him!"

At this, the palu — with much obvious self-satisfaction — held up two small, new-looking pwentang, bottoms forward. Both had the *wapepe* symbol and Xs etched similarly inside each circular base. "Someone from Rālik is still making these!"

"Where did the Bush Murik get them?"

"Remember that fire island we saw to the south? The closest one, Manam."

"That's only a day away," Ḷainjin said. "Do they know if these were made there?"

"No, but—"

Rojak finished the palu's statement. "They don't make pots on Manam!"

Ḷainjin traced the *wapepe* design with his index finger. Had the palu just delivered a message that his mother had etched for him?

Suddenly, they heard slat drums beating about the village. On the incoming tide, he watched Ḷōbwilñawa's proa glide like the Chief through the passageway into the wind-rippled lagoon. Several black pigs were lashed prone upon the outrigger platform. At midproa, Kanari stood above the makings of the upcoming feast, braced upon the mast of the bulged-out sail, commanding the action. He had adorned his wrists and ankles with wicker bands as if he were the legendary hero Andena, arriving to bestow his gifts. Ḷainjin sensed that all eyes in the village had now turned to their trade partner, and he understood why they referred to their outrigger canoes as "sea eagles." They saw them as the thing of mystery and magnificent beauty they were.

They watched Kanari reach the end of the village, then call for *diak*, raise the *rojak m̧aan* from its place at the bow, flip the luffing sail forward to Ḷōbwilñawa, and victoriously, take his place at the helm. Now in full view of the gathering villagers starting to dance about, he sheeted to wind and steered them out of his sight, probably toward the point on shore where he intended to beach.

"Like us ri-Rālik, they say the man is the proa's hull, the woman the outrigger. That crap must have come from these male-centric westerners," said Lirojak, resting her foot on the palu's shoulder. "To me, the opposite holds true. Speaking as a woman, if I don't like my man," she vibrated his shoulder with her foot, "I cut him loose and look for another kubaak to tie up to!"

"Our Kanari pretends to be the sea eagle himself," commented Ḷainjin.

"The women tell me that just as those bags they make for their men to trade have four corners — or what they call *poang* at the base — so there are four traits of a big man. The first is to have many trade brothers, the second is to trade offshore, the third is to be generous in sponsoring many feasts," expounded Lirojak. She pointed to the many pig mandibles dangling from the porch beams of Kanari's house next door.

"The fourth?" asked Ḷainjin.

"The fourth is the one the women like best, but it's their secret! The temperament to turn his head and allow his wife or even his sister to seduce an overseas trader. They accomplish this by thinking of you traders as infants they pass onto their wives' and sisters' care. That's the reason for all the baby food, like sago pudding. The women absolutely love the freedom these periodic events provide them. But they're careful not to describe it that way. Publicly, they say the fourth *poang* is to be a strong warrior. However, to prove his strength, as part of the final manly initiation process, he gives his wife for one night to his sponsor. Guess who that usually is?"

"I'm guessing the maternal uncle."

"Correct," she responded. "So Kanari there will sponsor his spoiled little nephew at tomorrow's ladder feast. The very first thing he'll do is what he always does when he sees him — pull on his little manhood to reinforce this penis-centric bond they will develop and parade him about the village to the men's house to eat a pwentang of muddy sago they call *aragen*,[160] which the men make and only *they* can eat. Of course, I'm jealous because I would really love to taste that pig slop! When he is old enough to begin initiation into the men's cult, he'll play with his nephew's penis to harden it and then make it bleed. Ask my brother about that! I'm not supposed to know. Some nonsense about draining black blood — *yaron nungungu,* they call it. This supposedly harmful stuff needs bleeding out. They claim it's poisoning the boy has absorbed from his mother's and his sisters' menstrual secretions. The boy needs to get this bad blood pricked out, and of course, his uncle is just the one to do it.

---

[160] Murik word for pudding made of cane sweetened sago that only men can make and eat.

"Believe me, the women have many secrets too. They know what they're not supposed to find out. When Kanari decides to finalize his nephew's initiation into manhood, he gets to spear his nephew's wife in some men's cult ceremonial escapade. Men brag about how many sisters they have, but if you ask me, they're really bragging about all the nephews they get to molest and all the nephews' wives they get to lecherously poke. My little brother, big man he thinks he wants to become, looks at all these customs as so much sago pudding rather than what they all lead up to — cultural domination of men over women. Look at that hardwood mask hanging from the corner post. Look at that nose! It looks like a penis! That epitomizes their culture and expresses exactly what they worship around here."

Just then, the palu announced that Ḷōbwilñawa was paddling toward them. His initial intention had been to tie up next to Kanari's proa, but at the palu's insistence, after some maneuvering, several lines were thrown and secured, and they moored Ḷōbwilñawa up perpendicular to Rojak's proa and parallel to the high tide landing. He sat at his stern, outrigger to lagoon, bobbing slightly from the waves rippling shoreward from the southeast. His forearms dotted with clam bites. Lirojak closed her eyes and winced as the men looked at each other and grinned ear to ear. Just then, one of the pigs squealed out in terror in the distance.

At the palu's insistence, Ḷainjin handed a pwentang to Ḷōbwilñawa, who immediately turned it over to see the *wapepe* etched into its base.

"Yes." Ḷōbwilñawa was unsurprised. "Kanari says these are trade items coming through the upwind islands—"

"Manam?" asked the palu.

"Right. Kanari has promised to help us find out where these are being made. He wants to come along. It's a bit of a beat down the coast to Sigaba, so an extra hand will round out our crews. Is that all right with you, Ḷainjin?"

"Does he understand the danger? We all know this story could end ugly!"

"He is aware of all we know about what happened in Sigaba. I went over everything a second time with him. Don't forget his father knew your mother well, and we spent a season here after the Komba captured her. First, he feels a responsibility to his father's bones to help us. Second, Sigaba is a legendary place to trade. These western men are like ambitious spiders building a web. He no doubt looks at the prospect of finding a trade brother in Sigaba and strengthening his relationships along the way as buttressing and widening his trade web. Though he doesn't speak their languages outright, they use a sort of trade speak that may prove helpful to us."

"Tell what we want to hear!" bantered the palu in emphatic, broken Kajin Rālik. Then after an awkward pause, he roared with laughter. "How many bowls of sago at Blup Blup?"

The group, even Rojak, broke into laughter as the rijeḷā soberly folded his arms over his chest. If this was his attempt to emphasize a desire to remain silent, it proved counterproductive and appeared instead as an unsuccessful attempt to hide some of the still-red marks that the palu pointed to, forcing Ḷōbwilñawa to look down at them as though pretending to see them for the first time. This made the group laugh even harder and made his response appear all the sillier until he threw his palms at them in surrender.

"All this old man is going to say — too many!"

"Fat spider need web too! Why you no ask fat spider sail too!" asked the palu as everyone continued to laugh. Lirojak stabbed his lardaceous side harshly with the blade of her paddle.

"No, no," instructed the palu. He drew more attention from the embarrassed rijeḷā as he held up his hand, pretending to hold a small clamshell between his thumb and index finger. "Pinch like a woman!"

"You mean one of these western women! We women of Rālik are not like them. We do not chase after our men to pinch them with little clamshells. We are like the giant clam-shell that surrounds our man and makes him a part of us."

"No! I am fat spider. I like fly and land who knows where."

"No!" Lirojak argued. "Have you ever heard of a giant clam walking out of its shell? I have you trapped inside my protection whether you know it or not! You reside permanently attached to my shell by that strong mussel there between those fat legs of yours, and you have no tool to cut yourself loose. Dream if you will! You will never escape my clutches! A shark will surely eat you as soon as you leave my protection. Your story is intertwined with mine as sure as the tide turns to the cycle of its mistress."

"Yes! Yes! I know! But make me little bites also. Tomorrow I must feel some respect at village feast."

She maneuvered back onto the proa, kneeled over him, and began pinching his belly and sides, at which he laughed hysterically like a tickled little boy.

That evening at dusk, as promised to Ḷōbwilñawa, Kanari brought one of the village's most experienced mediums to seek answers to their questions about their two mothers. They sat in the big undivided room next to the smoky hearth closest to the corner where Ḷainjin slept. Lañinpo was still absent, but Rojak and Ḷōbwilñawa were there. Uncharacteristic of the Bar Nor, Kanari's sister served no food nor drink. This was all seriousness. The medium's eldest son had died a few seasons back, and though he had often spat at her when alive, he had become a better boy, meek and at her disposal now that he had entered the world of the spirits. Kanari told her story to Ḷōbwilñawa, who interpreted for Ḷainjin and Lirojak. The palu, as was his wont, remained on their craft. The medium was a dark-skinned woman with disheveled, uncut hair. She smiled not but turned back her lips as she spoke to reveal her black, buai-nut mouth. She spoke only to Kanari and acknowledged the rest of them not, as though they did not exist.

The séance began with her calling after her son, who appeared to her immediately. He was told to fly to the Kunai and inquire with the spirits there about the women who had made the pwentang that sat on the mat before her and upon which her fingers rested as she traced the designs etched into the bottoms of each. She implored the boy to memorize the design, look for it wherever he flew, and report back quickly. Then she sat, proud and confident, apparently awaiting his return. Except he didn't return, and she sat and sat and whistled softly as though mimicking the sound of the southeast wind blowing through the thatch hanging from the lagoonward-facing eave above. Thus, she sat tirelessly through the night as Kanari's sister's family, and the rest of the group eventually rolled themselves within their mats and went to sleep. Ḷainjin himself finally surrendered, after a long, pensive wait, into a fitful, restless doze. Then deep into the night, he was awakened by a serious jabbering, as though her son had returned from his trip and the medium was interrogating him about what he had observed.

Unfortunately, there was no interpretation of what she had said, as Kanari and the others were only gradually coming to their senses.

After much discussion between her and Kanari, she curled in front of the fire and went to sleep. Only then did he provide his synopsis of the story her son had supposedly brought back from the spirit world. He had found both mothers huddled by a fire high in a tree. Surrounded by many of the pwentang with *wapepe* insignias, both were alive, though cripplingly wounded and not well. The spirits of their followers circled and continued to fight the men who had murdered them. They flew among swarms of insects to attack them and their children. Others lurked and molested the bodies of their daughters, coaxing them to die so they could ravage them truly. The Manam Island fire cone attracted them all. There they lusted after the dead daughters and sisters of their enemies who haunted that place. They longed to return to the islets of their childhood and search for the souls of the loved ones they had left behind. Yet all — to a man — remained committed to the two women they had died for and huddled about their fires amid the cold of the night, longing for their release.

The next day, they held the feast of the ladder. Kanari had decorated it with trinkets and netted bags of delicious nuts he'd obtained on Blup Blup. The practiced nephew scampered down, then back up the ladder like a little gecko. His uncle paraded him through the village like a hero with a much-valued heraldic necklace strung around his neck. His uncle allowed him, from time to time, to clutch a family basket in which his other uncles placed a boar's tusk or such. Ḷainjin, feeling a little stronger, accompanied Ḷōbwilñawa, Kanari, and the boy to the men's house, which was longer than the houses and had elongated gables that stuck out like noses at each end. They had to separate bark strands that hung across the entrance to enter. That, according to Ḷōbwilñawa, represented crawling beneath their mother's skirts. They were now in the presence of men only. Inside, there was much ceremony — pretty much about nothing as far as Ḷainjin could tell. Then again, he understood not the special words and short chants spit out as the men greeted the little charlatan.

The elders, concentrated on their eating, sat pompously at the far end before the light of a fire. Younger men carried food back and forth. Mothers' brothers raucously joked with sisters' sons, groping each other and spilling bowls of food in good humor. They all made much fuss over the belatedly firstborn son, who continued to collect trinkets in the man-sized heraldic purse. Because he was in the men's house for the first time, they initiated him with a bowl of *aragen*. They served the same bowl of cane-sweetened sago pudding to Ḷainjin, except his had a generous slice of pig liver plopped on top. The *aragen* had no secret ingredient and, as far as he could tell, tasted exactly like the stuff he'd been eating all week. He quickly grew tired of the ceremonies, which were hard to understand, and returned alone to the house of Kanari's sister. No doubt due to the absence of the little tyrant, he slept uninterrupted for the first time in many days.

By evening, Lirojak had entered the house at the shore end and interrupted his sleep by bringing a sobbing young woman whose face, arms, and breasts appeared beaten. Ḷainjin recognized her as Sarakena, the woman Lañinpo had slept with the first night. She held her hands over her bruised and puffed face as if to hide the proof she had done something wrong. "Her brother beat her!" announced Rojak. "I need to find my brother before he does something stupid." She spoke earnestly to the woman in her language, repeating the name of her brother twice, and told Ḷainjin to try to keep her there.

He held his palms forward as if to ask, "How?"

Then Rojak left and caused quite a bit of commotion with the palu in their boat under the house next door.

Several awkward moments passed as Ḷainjin sat speechless before the crying victim. Then the woman of the house gratefully rescued him. She commanded her daughters to bring water and food for their guest and began a long discussion that stopped the crying and allowed her to vent her anxiety. At some point, Ḷainjin fell back to sleep. When he awoke, Sarakena was gone.

Finally, Lirojak returned with her brother. She was sweaty and disheveled, and peeved that he had let her go. He wished it were not so.

"But what was I to do?" Ḷainjin thought. "Tie her ankle like his bird and leave her to poop through the cracks in the floor?" But he kept his mouth shut, as she was in no mood for excuses.

Lañinpo, also angry, went to his corner to lie down. "Who gave you permission to fight on my behalf?" he asked his sister angrily. Yet those were his last words as he, too, perhaps realized she was so out of control that further words were pointless.

When Rojak angrily unfurled the sleeping mat she carried, two short and blunt Pohnpeian hardwood dance staffs rolled out on the floor. For some reason, she was planning to sleep there. "I seek permission from no man, and I fought on my own behalf! It wasn't you he was dying to spear!"

"What happened?" Ļainjin asked.

"I decided to sashay over to the men's house, carrying my sleeping mat, to call out the battered one's brother. As soon as he saw the sleeping mat, he considered me a dog in heat and invited me to his house, but I insisted we walk the shorter distance to the oceanside and do it there. As soon as we were alone, his dirty hands were all over me. He stunk of shit, but I played along and let him feel where he wanted for a while and then unfurled my sleeping mat and those cute little dance staffs rolled out in the moonlight. That surprised him, but then I dropped my skirt, and his penis stuck out at me straight as an arrow. I wiggled my tail at him and playfully tossed him one staff and tapped mine gently against his, as if I had some perverted game in mind. He stood there naked and fending off my gradually more aggressive blows until *wōt jeej*! I poked him a good one right in the chest. That cooled his erection like a splash of chilly water. After I bruised him a second time, on the arm, he realized I was out to hurt him, so he swung his staff at me like a club. The second time he tried that, I parried my staff along his, sliding it down to his hands so hard he dropped it. When he bent to pick it up, I slammed him in the mouth and broke his teeth. Then followed with a blow that I imagine crushed his cheekbone and put the poor boy to sleep. I used a piece of blackstone to carve an X on his good cheek and on the side of his butt, where it shows, to remind him to parry with a woman rather than attempt to club her. I'm sure he learned his lesson."

"Learned his lesson or no! He will never hit Sarakena again. I've asked her to come away with me," responded Lañinpo from the corner.

"Just like a man! Instead of coming up with a rational plan, he dreams. What makes you think she would be happy away from her friends and family? A woman here does not offer herself to a voyager because she expects him to take her away. She does it so he'll return with more items of trade. Make her rich. Give her blackstone and shell rings and a dogtooth necklace with which to remember you. Treat her the way they expect her to be treated."

"Her brother would just take her gifts for himself."

"Not likely!" thought Ḷainjin. "Unless he's looking for another tryst with your sister."

That ended the conversation. Lirojak plopped down on her mat and slept next to him. He hardly slept, listening to her heavy breathing. She must have had another fight with the palu — which would have started, undoubtedly, when she took her sleeping mat from her proa and marched off with it in hand. She began carelessly to expose her long, narrow thigh in her sleep. In her fight, she had skinned her knee somehow, and Ḷainjin wished he could wash it. He realized how much he wanted her. He had never met a woman who hardened a man upon her approach then withered him when she spoke. He realized he was starting to recover from the sun sickness but wasn't foolish enough to cross a mentor like the palu.

The morning next, he had but one thing on his mind. Lirojak and her brother had left early. Then, per their routine, the mother of the house and her younger daughter went for water, leaving the older to tend to the boy. As it turned out, all Ḷainjin had to do was offer her his hand, and she set the boy to cry on his own. Ḷainjin would never forget the look of horror on the little chief's face as his sister quickly grabbed something from the shelf above the smoking hearth and led the newcomer over to the corner. There, she bent over, flipped her skirt upon her back, and held tight to the mangrove corner poles of the thatched house-frame, inviting Ḷainjin to mount her. It seemed to him the whole house shook on its pilings as the boy continued to cry behind them and their hips desperately jerked in unison, and he felt it was about to be over when he realized what she had grabbed onto. Bracing herself and still clutching onto a cross pole with one hand, she pinched him hard on the wrist of the hand grasping her hipbone. It smarted such from her little shell that he temporarily lost his overpowering urge to release himself. Then she did it again to the back of his thigh. Then elsewhere, laughing at him or perhaps at her ever-screaming brother as together, they shook the house to its rafters until finally, she lifted her head toward the ceiling. Perhaps in satisfaction or perhaps from sheer exhaustion, she dropped the shell, clenched his butt cheeks with her nails, and coaxed him to finish what he had started to do more times than he had counted.

Later that day, he took Lirojak's advice and gave the girl shell armbands and a necklace of trochus shells, which he saw her wear proudly until the day he sailed away through the passageway and out to the sea from which he had come.

That afternoon brought the terrible news that Sarakena, the battered woman, had hung herself by a pool where her sister went to wash. Sarakena had left several gifts for her sister at the base of the tree, which she assumed were to offset the trouble she caused her. The sister had completed the burial before news of Sarakena's death spread through the village. Had she been male, the nephews would have performed elaborate ceremonies. Everyone attributed the death to the brother's beatings. Shamed by her death, he fled the village unseen. Some suggested he might have traveled with the Mountain Arapesh,[161] who had come to trade and left.

Quietly, the sister fashioned a small model outrigger canoe from dried coconut leaves and brought it to a very somber Lañinpo. Apparently, they took it to the shore of the passageway and set it to sail in the outgoing tide, releasing Sarakena's spirit to fly ahead of them to the cone of fire on Manam. That tragic experience led Ḷainjin to believe it was impossible to beach on a distant shore and, as newcomers, act a part other than expected and depart without leaving a debacle in their wake.

Early the next morning, they loaded down the three boats to their limits with pandanus-bundled sago and, with much misgiving, tacked away to wake. They faced a stiff southwest breeze that promised headwinds all the way to their destination.

[161] The Arapesh were a horticultural people living in the northeast lowlands of East Sepik Province. The Mountain Arapesh were a tribe of Arapesh living in the highlands above the Sepik who had migrated there for trading purposes.

Kakar

Ḷainjin was happy to accept his new crew member. Though neither spoke the other's language, the two men communicated silently, and Kanari was quick to learn the few additional words needed to follow Ḷōbwilñawa out to sea and then tack back toward shore. Their leader's intention was to hug the shoreline as much as possible all the way to the gray, smoking mountain ahead, which Ḷainjin, after all he had heard, imagined would rise from the surrounding sea like the decomposing breast of a floating corpse. Kanari flinched not, turned not, when facing the sea sprayed from their plunging bow but continued his seaman-like manner whether minding the sheet or taking his turn at the tiller. A hearty, handsome man with a confident yet self-deprecating laugh, he held his big-man status at bay and bragged less than Malean. Ḷainjin could see that for Kanari, sailing wasn't just a means to an end, as it was for Malean, but a joy unto itself. His pleasure to be at sea was refreshing, and Ḷainjin absorbed the inspiration he needed from his new friend. Their comradery grew as they continued their back-and-forth approach to the ugly, smoke-capped mountain. Mysteriously scraggly, it loomed incredibly higher and higher at each approaching tack.

Thus, they sailed. They ate as they tended the tiller and lines. They traded places as the day rolled on. They laughed at each other when an unanticipated, wind-sheared wave splashed one and then the other. As the hazy afternoon turned to evening, they realized they wouldn't reach their goal until deep into the night ahead. The moon rose slightly waned, and its comforting light, which shone bright beneath the haze from the smoke above, glistened upon the dark waves, now lessened in lee of the island to windward. Finally, Ḷainjin grew tired and mimed to tell his companion he needed to go below. He slept soundly until awakened later that night by the sound of boats bumping as his companion and Ḷōbwilñawa discussed the supposed strategy in the language of Bar Nor. They had entered a calm, mountain-sheltered bay before a village on Manam Island's northwest periphery, and Kanari was the first to identify as Siassi the proas that lay at anchor. They decided to join the anchored proas at a respectful distance and wait until dawn to go ashore. Ḷainjin slept again, and when he awoke late the next morning, found his companion gone.

The island's periphery was a verdant green ringed by black sand shining bright in the early morning sun, which shone beneath the white smoke belching from the fiery eye of the cone. This was where the spirits of the dead supposedly flew like a *wūnaak* hovering above their prey. The leafy green turned a rocky gray as the mountain rose skyward to the top. There, it belched the smoke that trailed into the wind back toward the direction of the travelers' downward approach. Ḷainjin wondered, "Was it possible to climb those rocky slopes and peer down into the fire they say never snuffed?" But alas, he sensed a change in fortune as Ḷōbwilñawa, standing upon his deck, clasped his hand onto Kanari's and leveraged him up from the sea.

Kanari had just swum from the Siassi proa, where he seemed to have gathered news they needed to proceed with their plans. A prolonged discussion among the four in the language of the Bar Nor ensued as excitement grew among them, and the palu and Ḷainjin glanced at each other hopefully. Finally, the rijeḷā announced that Kanari had gleaned from a Siassi youth left at anchor that the pwentang they were looking for were not, in fact, made on Manam. They were a trade item the Siassi regularly obtained at Gitua, a village along the coast southeast of Sigaba. The youth said the pwentang were indeed made by the Komba in the hinterlands, who transported them to Gitua by river and traded them on the day of each full moon of the trading season. These Siassi craft in the harbor had just come from there by way of Karkar Island. Ḷōbwilñawa saw no point in going ashore. They would head directly to Sigaba and make plans to intercept the Komba by the next full moon.

Kanari objected. After further discussion, it became clear to Ḷainjin that Kanari had won the debate. Ever the trade brother, he wanted to first offer gifts to the Siassi to seal their friendship, and he felt it prudent to go ashore and offer to trade with the Manam Islanders to maintain a sense of normalcy. He challenged the group not to act like fruit bats coming to steal in the night but to reveal their true mission. "You are children searching for mothers," Kanari argued. "Who among them could object to that? Your story is an honorable one. Generations will pass your story from father to son, and they will remember you as honorable men. So, if craft like yours appear among them again, they'll treat the wayfarers as such."

Therefore, they beached their canoes on the black sand and, as the tide retreated, presented gifts to the Siassi. Kanari held the symbol etched into the pwentang's base for all to see as the reason for their return after so many seasons, and truly, they departed as friends, with more from the Manam Islanders than they had given. Except Ḷōbwilñawa had to laugh because his craft was weighted down with the very thing he hated to transport. Each of their craft embarked with a squealing pig, lashed and defecating, upon each outrigger platform.

Again, they turned their faces to the wind and tacked toward the endless, ever-changing shore of the colossal island to starboard then back to sea and back again, all the while headed on their next bearing — Karkar. Much larger than Manam, its principal mountain appeared similar but held a verdant green all the way to the top, and the fire that had once perhaps bubbled up from the sea, spitting black rock to create its shores, smoldered still in its throat. The wind blew such that tacks to sea were short but those toward the island were long, so their progress was fast, but not fast enough to reach the offshore island by nightfall. As a result, they sailed on through the night within the narrow strait between Karkar and the coast. As mimed by Kanari, that was the safest course due to seemingly certain beheading on either shore.

By afternoon, they reached the next pendant of the offshore necklace of fire islands that adorned this selfsame southern sea his mother had traversed how many seasons before. This one, called Bagabag, was smokeless now, perhaps having had its fire snuffed long ago. They came upon a narrow but long sliver of reef a moderate paddle to lee of shore where Ḷōbwilñawa determined they should rest. They were now but one day's journey from Sigaba. There should be no more tacking, as their destination lay but two fingers east of south, and a close-hauled course would put them right on target. His plan was to fish during the night and clean, salt, and dry their fish on their way the next day. They would arrive the following morning with fish to gift along with Kanari's pigs and, of course, the sago to trade. This was apparently the very circuit they'd sailed seasons ago when his mother had led the group to trade for the blackstone she sought to amass for their trip home. The palu dropped anchor, and the other two boats were tied hull to hull to his stern, using coconut husks as a buffer between with sails hanging and pointing in opposite directions. They rested that way in peace, but what they didn't count on as they slept were the possessive islanders who watched from shore and viewed them as poachers on a reef they owned.

Ḷōbwilñawa woke the group at sunset, suggesting they had slept long enough and promising they could rest again once they caught their share of red fish. Kanari's desire to discuss their strategy for the upcoming battle against the forbidden man in the hinterlands above Sigaba kept breaking through their frenzied fishing. He spoke between chants of friendly competition. He probed the others with questions as he battered his large catch with his club, crushed the heads of his smaller catch with his teeth, and sliced bait to attract his next victim. The rijeḷā interpreted the gist of his words, absent the chants, to Ḷainjin and the palu, only occasionally commented upon by Lirojak, mostly in Kajin Rālik. The rijeḷā began by pointing out that Kanari's greatest concern was that the traders of Sigaba would object to the killing of any of their Komba trade brothers and would potentially warn them of their intentions. The group must not fear that their actions against the forbidden man would cause trade with the Komba to diminish. The opposite would be true because the group would have him, Kanari. He would promise to reestablish the old trade route between the Bar Nor and the Kunai. The group must vent their plans openly in the men's house so every Kunai would come to believe his Komba trade brother will be safe from revenge.

"The men's house. Where else?" Lirojak questioned Kanari in such a way that he noticed not her sarcasm. She addressed him yet spoke in her language, which he hardly understood. "I'll stay with the women and mime the Bar Nor recipe for sago pudding."

"The Kunai trade brothers should know it isn't their strategy to fight their way through to the women but to steal them away in the night," Kanari said.

"Like fruit bats?" she asked.

If he had caught her sarcasm, he didn't show it and continued. It was important to stress that they planned to attack at night, as most of these islanders fear night spirits and rarely venture from their home fires. Their group must explain their plan to the Kunai immediately. One word of warning passed by a trade brother to the forbidden one and their heads would hang from Komba house posts.

"Except for me!" Rojak interjected again. "I get to make pwentang for the rest of my life and probably get poked by one or more of their pathetic bananas until my tummy explodes with another of their vain little insects."

"I, too, will die before I allow that to happen!" added the palu.

"They'll giggle like excited children as the fat from your rump drips down to sizzle their fires," she responded. "What a catch you'll be! Better than a dugong!"

"I'm not going to shit for a week before this battle," the palu said. "I'll let loose as I die, and they can have the fun of their lives cleaning me for their feast."

"No one dies. Only the forbidden one," Kanari said. "That must be our plan from the day we arrive. No boasting about killing — only retrieving what the forbidden one stole from you. Look at me! They cannot kill me in battle! I do not boast! Yet I have *kakar*!"[162]

Confused, Ḷainjin turned to Lirojak.

"That means he forced his wife to have sex with his ugly, old uncle," she responded. Though Kanari's understanding of their language included only commands and sailing terms, she was careful to speak softly so even if he could have understood, he could not have clearly heard her words. On his

[162] Small ceremonial spears kept in the Bar Nor men's house that can be touched only by those men who have successfully been initiated into the kakar cult; bravery in battle.

part, Kanari held such a proud and boastful expression that Ḷainjin could hardly stop himself from laughing. Especially when she turned her head away from his, mimed "nine times," poked her finger in and out of the eye of her hand, and made a face of drudgery.

"What is *kakar*?" asked Ḷainjin of Ḷōbwilñawa.

"They're small, carved spears about that long," he said, showing a distance of about the length of his foot between his hands. "They have feathers tied to them."

Kanari confirmed the length with his hands as Ḷōbwilñawa spoke.

Ḷōbwilñawa continued, "I have never seen them, of course. They keep them on a shelf high in the men's house, but they told me that, as part of the final initiation process, they allow the warrior initiate to touch them. If he faithfully undergoes the initiation process, he will not die. Anyone else who touches them will die immediately—"

"Like a woman, for instance," interrupted Lirojak.

"Yes, definitely a woman."

Kanari affirmed this by making his eyes big and forcing a closed-lip smile before crunching into the head of his latest catch.

"A woman or any noninitiate or even an innocent child," continued Ḷōbwilñawa.

"Okay, so I definitely don't have *kakar*," blurted Lirojak, "and I'm sure I am likely to die if I don't follow directions. So, I promise you to strictly keep to myself how many of those kinky-haired dogs I intend to kill." She grabbed Kanari's shoulder and shook him. "No offense, *kakar*. I love your hair. I find it very manly. Jeej! I'm sorry! I think I used that hand to wipe my *jukkwe*[163] this morning!"

Everyone, including Kanari, laughed at his expense. It was a joke that only such a group at such a time could share without offense taken.

Their coconut-leaf baskets, once filled to their brims with drink, now received one energetic, prickle-spined red fish after another. The circular wind clouds marched white across the horizon. The oblong moon rose in the sky. Those clouds passing directly beneath its light turned gray as the multifaced personality of each was exposed in imaginary detail and as each

---

[163] Sand clam; bivalve word used to refer to one's vagina.

cloud, as it was slowly silhouetted against the black, star-dimmed sky, cast its shadow down upon them. There sprang much competitive, good-humored chanting from the group that night. How often had Ḷainjin seen fishers argue peevishly over where to fish, then break out in brotherly comradery once their basket began to fill? Now, especially so between Kanari and Lirojak, whom he characterized as just another night fish. She was easy to engage yet nettlesome once landed and troublesome to dislodge. She would learn to accept Kanari as but a branch on an otherwise useless tree that she could — if need be — bend to her will.

They fished through the better part of the night until they judged they had caught enough. All but one wanted to return to sleep before the next day's journey. Ḷainjin slept soundly until awakened by something astir — by what, he wasn't yet sure. He popped his head out of his hatch. Was there treachery afoot? Kanari had launched himself onto Ḷōbwilñawa's boat and done something that had audibly upset the rijeḷā.

Rojak and the palu began to unfasten the tie lines that bound their hanging, unfurled sails. Other lines began to fly, and commands barked in hush. Ḷainjin noticed their array of three boats turning slowly off wind and realized Kanari had cut them free of their anchorage! They were drifting, and all were making ready to sail. Why?

In the interim, Kanari had hopped back aboard and, by instinct, rose to stand at the yoke of his boat. Pressing his weight against the still-unfurled sail, he fought the force of the breeze that could otherwise have backwinded them and caused their rigging to collapse. Kanari ordered Ḷainjin to take the stern, where he managed to turn the boat to wind, and once broadside to it, they faced the source of all the commotion. There in the sea to landward was a line of perhaps ten equally spaced paddling canoes, silently but rapidly approaching. Kanari immediately raised sail although they were facing the line of aggressors and pointing in the opposite direction of their companions. No sooner had he tied off his halyard than the first spear pierced his rigging, and his impulse was to drop into the hull to diminish himself as a target.

Ḷainjin immediately eased their sheet to pick up speed and fill their sail into an off-wind run, avoiding most of the closest adversaries and heading toward their flank. Kanari pulled the barbless hardwood spear from the sail and held it high. Fearlessly exposing himself, he taunted the paddling men with it. Ḷainjin heard Kanari shout his name several times as well — and the words *kakar* and "Bar Nor" and the Bar Nor word for "trade brother." Then Kanari unfastened their pig and laughed as the wild thing scrambled into the sea to the uproar of their adversaries. Were those cheers or war cries? Had that been done to distract them or to offer recompense for the fish taken?

The wind swept them onward, and they approached the end of the line of canoes. They had been caught headed in the wrong direction, and it became clear that the last canoe had successfully flanked their retreat. The wind direction wouldn't allow Ḷainjin to get downwind of them without dangerously backwinding or tacking, so he decided ramming their canoe appeared the best option. Their two opponents now stood bravely at each end, spears in hand, ready to battle yet obstructed by the large, billowing sail rapidly closing upon them. Just as Ḷainjin and Kanari were about to crash into their opponents though, Kanari — still singing as though among friends — flopped to the deck, sheeted hard into the wind, and cut a course that just bumped their bow enough to toss them, off-balanced, into the sea. Then he jumped to the outrigger platform, spear in hand, to face the next attackers in line, deftly batting down a weakly thrown spear aimed at Ḷainjin. Finally, Kanari humorously taunted the man who had thrown it by raising his voice and singing all the louder.

With that, they were free of them. "And if that was *kakar*, it was a handy thing to have aboard," Ḷainjin thought. However, *kakar* was far from over that morning. As soon as they had sailed sufficiently inland of their enemies to safely *diak*, Kanari insisted they close-haul their way back to the group. And since they and their opponents had brought no bows to the battle, he taunted them all the more, dropping his kilt and performing his best impression of a Manus penis dance without the gourd! Though their enemies knew not the meaning of his taunts, the good humor of Kanari's antics even won a few to laughter.

Later, Ḷainjin and Kanari tacked back to sea and joined their companions, who were drifting in wait for them. They acknowledged that their Bar Nor companion had saved all their heads. Respect even seemed to emanate from

Lirojak, although she couldn't resist chiding Kanari that she thought he had claimed these islanders "feared the night spirits." To which he simply pointed to the dawn as if to explain that early mornings didn't count.

They set a course south of southwest, eating the smaller fish and salting and drying the larger ones as they sailed toward the mountainous mainland, missing the next fire island in the necklace. Called Arop, that island, according to Ḷōbwilñawa, had a freshwater lake cratered at its center. This was a beautiful part of the coastline. Now to leeward, it sheltered smooth seas that washed upon fringing reefs sporadically bordering tan sand beaches or gray craggy coasts. From these sprouted a narrow band of forest followed by grassy fields rising into hinterlands before the highest mountains Ḷainjin had ever imagined that fostered the only rain clouds upon the horizon. If this was truly whence the forbidden man came, that would by itself make him a formidable opponent. Every so often, they had sailed past the mouths of slow-moving rivers that carried fresh water from such heights. How far could they paddle upriver? he wondered.

They ended up rather across the strait from Arop at a seemingly isolated reef off the mainland where, like mother turtles, they saw no shore fires. The sea floor dropped precipitously to the ocean side of the reef, and they fished as if on the edge of a cliff, with no fear of snagging their lines on its sharp coral. There, they caught jacks before sunset, then grouper in the dark, and finally, big-eyed red fish once the moon rose and brought the reef to life. Just to be safe, they rotated their sleep to make sure there were no surprises like the night before.

The next day, they trimmed a close cut into the wind, and at Kanari's advice, sailed as near to shore as possible, confident they could outsail any assailants and wanting to remain as undisclosed as possible to the hinterlands. The kunai grasslands grew upon and between two adjacent peninsulas that stuck out from the mainland like the breasts of a woman. Long before they approached the first, the unmistakable scent of burning grass pervaded the hazy air, and the light gray smoke from tightly controlled Kunai brush fires swirled in columns across the gradually rising plains like sea spouts in a gale. All three commented on it from time to time, as one would the turning of a season. They appeared inspired at the first nostalgic scent of it. Charmed by the sight of it. Over and above their mission, it was clear they were returning to a land that held a singular place in their memories, and their eyes glossed over as though returning home from a long absence.

From the tip of the first plump, grass-covered peninsula flowed the waters of the river Kwama, where the domain of the Kunai begins. From the mouth of the Kwama to the tip of the adjacent peninsula where Sigaba lay, their approach would now be visible to the islanders there.

Ḷainjin viewed the small island in the distance skeptically. Sigaba had been much larger in his imagination. Based on stories told, he knew that hidden somewhere within that second peninsula was the small lagoon where they had captured his mother. The realization that he had successfully come so far to meet her calling welled up in his throat and suddenly reawakened the spirit that kāleptak had deadened. He had — without realizing until now — successfully overcome its test of endurance. From the low islands of his birth to the stone village to the thatched house upon the sea to the great mangrove swamp of the Bar Nor to the necklace of fire islands to the kunai now stretching before the hinterlands there above him, he realized suddenly that he had been searching for something more than his mother. He had been searching for the man he now, by trial, had become. His strength of spirit — the feeling that he could accomplish whatever he wanted — came back to him in that moment and whispered a promise to never again desert him.

Ḷainjin's left hand clutched the mast as he stood high and braced himself to see through the smoky haze of the Kunai fires that billowed and curled across the grassy peninsula. As explained by Ḷōbwilñawa, they were routing the feral pigs for food, yes, but also to rid their gardens of them. The planting season was at hand, and the pigs were wont to tear through the waist-high fences the people constructed in rectangles around their yams. Kanari continued to steer a course as close as possible to the shore. Here and there, Ḷainjin could see through a break in the trees that lined the coast to the hillsides beyond. There, he saw the broken outlines of the square, individual plots of land cleared of the tall grass and somehow fenced. The distance between the island — before which he could see fishing canoes — and the distant plots on the hills was great. "These busy people are walkers," he thought. Yet they were also fishers and, of course, traders. Their little island, he would soon learn, hosted two sheltered lagoons and was a perfect attraction for sailing vessels. An outer lagoon, between the island and shore, was enclosed by the same fringing reef that protected the island. It was wedged like a bubble between the island and the shore, which enclosed a second, much larger lagoon surrounded by land like the pincer arms of a crab, leaving only a relatively narrow mangrove-encroached passageway between the two.

As they approached the island of Sigaba, Ḷōbwilñawa judged the tide still high enough to cross over its same western reef, which would be their pathway to the mainland at low tide. Those ashore, he realized, must have left the island in the middle of the night and swum in the morning tide or paddled canoes through the passageway into the inner, mangrove-enclosed lagoon. With barely enough freeboard, the group crossed the reef to a cheering crowd of men and women who obviously remembered or had heard stories of their unusual craft. They then crossed the blue water of the outer lagoon and landed on the windward side of a long, sandy shoal that pointed toward shore. A few men, more women, children, boys with heads shaved and painted red… All stood without fear, ready to welcome them. It proved an obviously emotional experience for the three who had departed from there so many seasons ago, as though returning to their home island after a long and arduous absence.

On his part, Kanari — ever the warrior — kept warning that the spectacle would attract the notice of their nemesis, looking down from the hinterland. With the help of Ḷainjin and the palu, they immediately began to dismantle their conspicuous sail riggings. And with the help of Ḷōbwilñawa's language skills, they solicited a group of locals to carry the proas through the jumble of the untidy Sigaba village to several boat shelters, where they were invited to conceal their distinctive-looking craft. Then Kanari wanted to know if there were any Komba trade brothers ashore. No, there were none. Hearing this, he appeared relieved, willing to rest and wait for the others to return from their day on the kunai.

The Kunai

That very evening, once the other elders had returned from the kunai, the group sat in the men's house without, of course, Lirojak. They later learned that she was happy enough to sit with former playmates and laugh and relearn the language. As directed by Kanari, Ḷōbwilñawa passed the pwentang around the room and announced their plan to find and free the mothers of the group. He explained their intentions from beginning to end, to leave no room for misunderstanding or false conjecture among them.

Ḷōbwilñawa was surprised to learn that the elders already knew of the trade in pwentang with the Siassi, and he explained this to his group. But the Kunai seemed more upset with their distant cousins in Gitua who had facilitated this trade. It was causing them much hardship. The Komba were lazy and only produced a limited amount of mountain taro, and most of it was now going to Gitua. The Komba were now trading more than ever before to these distant and greedy dogs. They insisted Ḷōbwilñawa use that word when referring to them. The Kunai would have stopped that river trade long ago were they not afraid of the akebu and his infamous magic.

On hearing this, it became clear that the forbidden man had the Kunai so intimidated they only referred to him by title. However, if the Rālik mothers were the ones responsible for the pwentang and the outsiders planned to release them, so much the better, they concluded. Kanari insisted they count heads. After discussion back and forth, Ḷōbwilñawa finally agreed to ask on Kanari's behalf how many initiates among them were "headless." This could have been a brilliant question. His intention was to motivate them to fight beside them on the mothers' behalf, but they were so afraid of the akebu that they were embarrassed to answer. Kanari insisted on an honest count. He learned that the number, among several *nambwe*,[164] had increased over the past years as only the very bravest of their young men dared to kill a Komba and pass initiation. So now, most adult men were headless — or as Kanari referred to them, "noncountable." The numbers were now too great to keep track. It was easier to remember those who had taken heads. Most of the elders, but only a few of the younger men, raised their hands.

With Ḷōbwilñawa interpreting, Kanari insisted he could not talk to those among them who were headless and requested that only those who had achieved full manhood scoot forward. He encouraged these to lead the others into battle against the forbidden man, pointing out what they, of course, knew — that many of the akebu's followers were not trade brothers of the Kunai and were ripe for picking.

At one point, according to Ḷōbwilñawa, Kanari challenged them thus: "You ask, 'Who is this newcomer who stands before me and asks that I listen to his words?' I am *kakar* of Murik who has taken many heads and flinches not in battle or in trade!"

Unfortunately, his plea remained embarrassingly unanswered. Such was the breadth of fear the forbidden one had instilled among them. But the Kunai proved happy to trade their blackstone for Malean's Murik baskets and sago, and eager to establish trade relations. Though to a man, they henceforth referred to Kanari as Kakar, as though that was his true name or title, and none of the headless men would speak or even raise their eyes to the Bar Nor warrior. Ḷainjin wondered if Kanari's talk had not been counterproductive. At any rate, it was clear as water that the akebu and his Komba allies had intimidated these Kunai men. Their group must plan to fight alone — or as Kanari put it, "Better than counting on the noncountable."

The next day, the embarrassment and the tension of the meeting the night before seemed to dissipate when, at the invitation of the islanders, the group paddled ashore in Kunai canoes, tied them amid the mangrove surrounding the lagoon, and joined in their daily activities. They soon

[164] A group of initiates to manhood of approximately the same age.

realized the benefit to their mission this exercise provided them. All but Kanari had been at sea so long their legs were weak, and their performance at walk and work humiliated them. Lirojak and the palu stayed behind. She objected to their custom of not allowing women to touch the yams. Among them, only Kanari had the stamina to participate in any meaningful way.

Finally, after an exhausting march into the hinterland along well-worn pathways, amid scorched hillsides and stands of tall grass, they could look back and see the island far below. There, they came to the squared-off garden plots the Kunai tilled and weeded. First, though, they continued the process of digging up the last of the previous season's yams. Then they replanted others anew after softening the earth into individual mounds they referred to using the same word for the mountains on the fire islands in the distance. While Ḷainjin's people marked the passing of the seasons by keeping track of the rising of stars, the Kunai tracked their seasons by having a name for each moon. This was the time of *kasau nawoi*[165] under the moon they called *makisa*,[166] when food from the previous harvest is still abundant. But by *gi*,[167] the Kunai would have eaten or replanted these leftover yams from the previous season, and by *totori*,[168] they would be dependent on trade with the mountain people to sustain their village. By *sulu*, the rain would begin. The yams planted today would have just begun to grow, and the Kunai would be hungry without trade.

Others, who had lugged large, flat-tipped digging sticks they called *soka*, used them to dig up the stubborn roots of the tall grass where they had decided to till new plots. They crossed the tips of two *soka*, speared both into the roots, and pried one clump after another at such a feverish pitch that Ḷainjin grew tired just watching them. Still others repaired the fences necessary to ward off any yet-unkilled feral pigs. The Kunai made their fences by pounding two rows of vertical poles into the ground and piling cane horizontally between them. This, they told Ḷainjin, was more of a bother than an absolute deterrent for the rapacious pigs. Their hope was that

---

[165] Time to make yam hills in earnest; language of the Kunai.
[166] Kunai word for "May."
[167] Kunai word for "July."
[168] Kunai word for "August."

the pigs would move on to an easier plot that was already in the process of being rampaged. Meanwhile, the women hauled the food and water and were doing their part by lighting fires and preparing meals for their men. Everyone seemed in high spirits as apparently, during the next season, torrential rains would trap them indoors in their small village for an interminable number of days.

That evening, the group returned — feet sore, legs aching, and feeling vulnerable. How were they to strengthen themselves for the upcoming battle in the remaining days? They had already decided they needed to attack at night. It was general knowledge up and down the coast that the mainland islanders, fearing ghosts and black magic, *did* stay inside all night and ventured out into the dark only before dawn. Even if their legs were strong, even if they knew exactly where to find their mothers, such a nighttime trek might leave them too exhausted to fight. Fortunately, Kanari had already devised a plan for them. They would travel to Gitua before the full moon, capture the same canoes that had brought the Komba traders downriver, and paddle them upstream that evening, appearing to anyone watching from a distance to be the expected Komba. Later, they would disappear somewhere into the night, fresh and ready to attack.

They had their plan. Now they simply had to work to harden themselves to the point they could successfully carry it out. They learned to dig large clumps of kunai roots with the heavy *soka* tools, plan and execute large-scale grass fires, and run down and kill the wild boar the villagers loved to feast upon. In the interim, two separate and fortunate occurrences would serve to enhance Kanari's seemingly workable plan.

Rojak would learn that one of her best friends from her youth, upon the death of her father, had moved seasons before to Gitua with her mother, who was from there. They decided she and the palu would walk there along the coast to strengthen their legs and gather what knowledge they could. One morning, with the tide too high to walk, Lirojak and the palu waded and swam across the reef that spanned the narrow passageway into the inner lagoon and reached the eastern shore of the crab's claws. They looked odd as they proceeded down the sandy shore. She — tall, fair-skinned, and slim — walked ahead, turning encouragingly. He — of moderate height, dark, and heavy — followed somewhat reluctantly. The result of their sojourn would add details to Kanari's plan.

A second incident occurred one day while Ḷōbwilñawa was puttering with his beached proa. One of the accomplished initiates, Babwa Wangumu,[169] had approached him, wanting to speak with Kanari. Apparently, his speech had speared the young man's throat, and he'd told the elders he had information through his trade brother that should be helpful to them. Babwa was one of the few successfully initiated among his *nambwe* and had killed a Komba in fair combat. Babwa and the Komba had encountered each other by accident, up close and alone, on a pathway surrounded by tall grass high upon the kunai. The Komba immediately reached toward his quiver for one of his long arrows. However, before he could thread his long, unwieldly bow, Babwa struck him with his *soka*, then choked the life from him with two hands to his throat. He hid the dead man as best he could and, the next day, bravely returned to the body with a knife to cut away his prize and victoriously return it to the village for boiling. Later that same season, Babwa cleverly used his sister to attract a second Komba. He chased the man down and speared him from behind like a pig.

"This is a man we can surely trust!" insisted Kanari as Ḷōbwilñawa related his story. He went on to describe how he had used his newly attained status to develop trade-brother relations with the Komba, who now treated him with the seriousness he deserved. His Komba trade brother was an older, very experienced trader they called Ilisa.[170] He had mentioned to Babwa that all the elders in his hamlet were unhappy with the semen-eating culture introduced by the akebu but that those who spoke up were quick to die from his magic. Their bodies would suddenly become lifeless, their panicked eyes slowly sinking into their dying faces. Ilisa hated the way all their sons were staying up all night playing with each other in the men's house and sleeping instead of working during the day. Everything spoken by the akebu now was about semen, virility, proliferation, and filling the hillsides with his followers. Babwa was certain he could convince his trade brother Ilisa to solicit his hamlet to bond with their goal to kill the akebu

[169] An accomplished Kunai initiate who killed two Komba.
[170] An older, experienced trader; Babwa's Komba trade brother.

and not fight to protect him — and not prevent them from reuniting with the mothers and returning them to their home islands.

Ḷainjin and Lañinpo agreed the proposal was risky, but catching the whole hamlet unaware and attempting to fight them all was riskier. Again, they agreed to put their lives in the hands of the decisive Kanari and the budding trade brothers Babwa and now Ilisa. But how many others? These were the concerns that darkened Ḷainjin's throat over the next few days as he made his daily trek onto the kunai and lent his hand to the backbreaking work to regain the strength his legs were sure to require. Yet now and again, he would glance up at the puffy, white wind clouds, turn his ears to the direction of the strong breeze, look out over the blue expanse stretching to the smoke-belching fire islands, and remember how and from whence he had come. Then his confidence would flood back as sure as the tide. He would remember who he was and quietly put one foot in front of the other, single-mindedly proceeding toward his story's end.

Then came Lirojak, rushing back from Gitua and leaving the palu there with her friend Kou. She brought the tale of Kou, whom she had found pregnant in Gitua and under the care of her mother. Unbelievably, her husband was one of the Komba who transported the pwentang from the hinterlands to trade with the Siassi. Everything Kou told her confirmed what Kanari had gleaned from the off-island traders at Manam. She expected her husband back the day of the full moon. Sometimes, the Siassi would arrive in their large twin-sail canoes one or two days before because her husband only stayed for the afternoon and then left to paddle back the way they had come. It was his job, along with a companion, to paddle two outriggerless canoes filled with pwentang from the foot of the hinterlands down to Gitua. Sometimes, the Siassi trade brothers would arrive in their large twin-sail proas one or two days before the appointed day. Her husband would only stay for the afternoon and then leave to paddle upstream before dark.

"Kou has become very stupid," complained Rojak. "She describes her man as 'bursting with semen' and can hardly wait for his return. She told me once her child is born and she returns to the hinterland, instead of resuming relations with her... They must not cross paths for two dry seasons. In the interim, he'll live in the men's house again and take up his responsibilities to inseminate the boys or take another wife or both. It's that forbidden man and his Sambia[171] kin who have completely indoctrinated her into their ridiculous life of penis worship! Once among them, women can't even walk on the same path as men."

Rojak continued, and Ḷōbwilñawa seemed careful to interpret her every word to Kanari. When the Komba — unlike her "semen-bursting" husband, who was one of a few quick learners — were slow to adopt the akebu's instructions, he abandoned them to themselves and left their hamlet for a season. But he returned the next, bringing his Sambia kin from the highlands atop the mountains. No one knows how he climbed so high or how he returned so fast. There is no path. He allowed them to build a village close by but higher upon the hinterland. Higher because they were smarter than the Komba and understood the importance of proliferation to crowd out potential enemies. The younger Sambia boys he brought quickly taught the Komba boys the five steps of initiation. The first, called *moku* or something like that, occurs after a boy's seventh dry season. At that point, the boy leaves his mother for good and goes to sleep in the men's house. Kou could not remember the name or meaning of the second stage or the third, but at fourteen dry seasons, the boy gets his puberty rites and can no longer eat semen. He then has the responsibility to inseminate the younger *moku*. Therefore, according to Kou, a boy has only a limited amount of time to reach manhood, ingest the lifetime of semen necessary to impregnate his wives, and maintain his future responsibilities to the semen-collecting enterprise.

As Rojak spoke, Kanari became visibly agitated with her. He kept breaking in to question her about the men's house. He appeared uninterested in all the semen talk as though he already knew about that or that it wasn't relevant to the battle he was planning.

"I didn't ask her where exactly the men's house is, but everything Kou said led me to assume it's in the Komba hamlet. The Sambia go there to engage in their semen trade. I tried to appeal to her sense of reason. What

[171] The Sambia people lived in the Papua New Guinea Highlands. They practiced polygamy, sister exchange, strict separation of male and female duties, and semen exchange through ritualized obligatory homosexual practices.

about the men in Gitua? What about the men in Sigaba? What about my brother? How do they get their semen? She replied, 'The same way. The men down here just don't talk about it to their wives and sisters. Only the Sambia are smart enough to acknowledge its importance. After all, they come from the highest place on the mountains. They must be smarter than us all.'"

"Apparently these people associate height with intelligence," thought Ḷainjin.

Kanari released a storm of questions as though he had been holding his breath, just come up for air, and required another question before she had answered the previous one. Ĺañinpo interpreted one after the other. "Where do they keep their bows?"

"Who?" Rojak asked.

"These young men! When they enter the men's house! Where do they put their bows?"

"I don't know. I didn't ask."

"No more woman's talk!" Kanari continued. "She didn't ask any of the right questions. We need men's details to succeed! How wide is the river and how swift? How far up is the river navigable by your proa? Where is the sun when the traders arrive at the village?" Kanari then stopped and stared at her in disbelief, perturbed at her for wasting so much time with this valuable informant talking about the semen custom rather than what the group needed to know to stay alive up there. He spoke a few remarks to Ḷōbwilñawa in anger that, perhaps out of politeness, he did not interpret for the rest of them.

"If you wanted answers to those questions, you should have prepared me before we left! You probably didn't dream we would be so successful! After all," Rojak continued, "I'm only a woman on a separate path with stinking secretions that could sap your manhood to touch, so you probably don't want to listen to what I did find out about our mothers, the forbidden man, and where they all live."

There followed a moment of silence among the group as Ḷōbwilñawa interpreted at least part of what she had said to Kanari, who on his part, had perked with greater interest.

"Did Kou say they're alive? Are they the ones making the pwentang?" asked Ḷainjin.

"Yes, I know this for sure. Kou and her semen-bursting husband lived in the same hamlet with them."

Ḷainjin spoke to the group with honest and genuine gratification. "I knew it. I mean, I've felt it all these seasons."

"Well, listen to this," continued Rojak. "Do you remember how Kanari's medium told us she found them that night back in Murik?"

"Huddled by a fire in a tree!" answered Ḷainjin.

"Well, the forbidden man" — Rojak blurted this out with much elation — "keeps our mothers trapped in his tree house!"

Kanari had been listening intently to all this, but Rojak had avoided mixing in any of the Murik language she knew, so he had only heard his name and witnessed the reaction among the group. He turned pleadingly to Ḷōbwilñawa, whose eyes deferred to Lirojak for her permission to interpret. On her part, she just sat self-satisfied, staring at Kanari until he mumbled his apology. At which point she raised her eyebrows and inhaled sharply in assent.

Once Ḷōbwilñawa had interpreted, the tone of Kanari's next questions about the tree house were more instructive than chastising. They needed to know how people ascended into it. How high? How many ladders? Do they pull them up at night? They needed to know how close to the Komba hamlet. How far from the Sambia, and was it visible from their hamlet? Then Kanari helpfully summarized where they stood in their plan of attack. They must be ready by the next full moon. They must listen to him. He had *kakar* and knew of such things. It was clear they would get no help from the Kunai other than through Babwa and his communications through his trade brother Ilisa. The most they could hope for was that they still the bows of those Komba discontented with the akebu's leadership. If they could disable the bows of the young men and others in the men's house and avoid alerting the Sambia hamlet, they would have a chance to climb the tree house, kill the akebu, and free the mothers.

If the group was successful in freeing the mothers, and especially if they were not, they must have their proas ready to sail quickly past Gitua. The Gitua benefit from the Komba trade with the Siassi and may want to punish them for their interference. They must coax or otherwise capture this pregnant woman and take her upriver to lure her husband and the other

Komba ashore, where they could disable them, take their canoes, and return them upriver as expected. Lirojak must stay with her friend and the captured men and guard their proas until their return. In the interim, she must go back to Gitua and glean the necessary information slowly and casually as time passes so as not to alert suspicion. Lirojak agreed and returned to Gitua with Kanari's various questions in mind the next day.

As the moon continued its cycle toward the fateful day, they relentlessly continued their daily toil on the kunai. Gradually, the muscles in their legs regained their strength and became ready for battle. Lañinpo, on his part, visited his sister in Gitua to study the whereabouts of Kou's family's house and explore the river.

With Babwa's help, Kanari and Ḷōbwilñawa met with Ilisa and easily solicited his agreement not to interfere with their plan to kill the akebu. And contingent upon permission from his elders, he even agreed to participate. Through Babwa, they learned from Ilisa that the akebu traveled widely among neighboring Komba villages because he had wives in other hamlets. However, he always returned to sleep in his tree house, as he probably feared retribution for the lives he had taken with his magic. The akebu carried a toy fishing bow with tiny bamboo arrows in a pigskin pouch. Ilisa told a story he had heard, that one afternoon the pigskin quiver attracted the tongue of someone's pet. The dog had died much the same death as those of big men in these various hamlets who had opposed him.

Not that he wasn't respected for his generosity, continued Ilisa through Babwa. The akebu sponsored magnificent feasts to honor each of his family occasions in these hamlets where he had taken wives. These wives were young, and his children were many. They respected him but loved him not. They followed him without admiration. They mimicked his culture without belief because he was not one of them.

"He is a man apart with foreign ideas we do not accept," interpreted Babwa.

Ḷainjin, on his part, forgot not the advice of his friend Ḷōbwedi. With the help of Bwilñawa,[172] he sought out the fisher called Setepana, befriended him, and heard his story of the akebu and the source of his magic for himself.

---

[172] Aka Ḷōbwilñawa; the rijeḷā.

"There is an orange-and-black bird in the forests above the kunai that numbs the hand that catches it," Setepana said. "The akebu traced the poison to the bird's food source — a blue beetle. This ground-up beetle is the source of the akebu's magic."

Ḷainjin had heard the story of the counterpoison himself. Learning from Setepana where among the ocean reefs this fish lived, he speared one and experimented with its poison. Then he formulated his plan, which he kept to himself like the knife ring the Saudeleur had presented him. What Ḷainjin lacked in *kakar*, he would make up with cunning. By the time the fateful nights cycled forward, he was both strong and ready — and had his own pouch of salted and dried puffer fish–livers at the ready to counteract the poison arrows of this akebu. He had already sampled minute quantities and become familiar with its effects.

As he watched the round moon rise and the tide retreat at sunset, he communed with his white, puffy, and ever-in-flux friends. One after the other, they had accompanied him for so long and from so far away he imagined that each had their own spirit, each their own ever-changing view of the world rushing below. Each their own ever-changing story. Ḷainjin was happy to be who he was, where he was — and ready to do whatever he had to do. He was ready to change with the passing of time and move forward to face whatever fate would bring. He napped again and then again, as the moon rose higher, the tide lowered, and the reefs surrounding Sigaba became more apparent and hollow sounding with the waves now plunging beneath them. Once the moon had drifted westward on its trek beyond the mountains, as the tide turned and the reefs disappeared beneath the sea, it was time to begin their fateful journey.

Their proas at the ready, they launched all three, with Kanari accompanying Ḷōbwilñawa in the lead and Lañinpo sailing his sister's proa. Ḷainjin followed the other two. They hugged the coast into an oblong bay. Once the moon had disappeared and the sky had darkened, they were ready to attempt passing the village. Then, as silently as possible, they tacked into the mouth of the river, which was perhaps twenty-five arm's lengths wide. Although the river current was flowing against them, it was weaker than the incoming tide and swells from the sea. This slack allowed them to quickly proceed in quiet single file, past the sleeping village along the opposite bank of a river. The breeze now from behind them, they loosened their sheets, puffed their sails, and paddled now and again until they left the village behind. This breeze then tapered and died, in lee of the trees that lined the river's shores. They lowered their sails and paddled for all their worth against the current. The deep hulls of their canoes, which allowed them to make good against an oncoming wind, now caught in the current, causing them to want to drift backward in the stream.

The river wound back behind the village they had passed, which had previously been explored by Lañinpo. Entering the kunai, it turned sharply in the opposite direction before bending back again, forming a "thumb" of kunai grass bordered by river. This thumb seemed to Lañinpo like a good place to hide their canoes and ambush those coming down the river. Kanari agreed. It stuck out like a peninsula formed by the river's winding passage. The footpath leading from the village to the kunai penetrated it not, so villagers were likely to pass them by without noticing their presence. They beached their proas, and Lañinpo would now begin his mission to return to the village to fetch the palu, Rojak, and her friend Kou.

Now all that appeared left between them and the morning, when their plan would ripen, was the second foretelling of Kanari's medium. They must suffer the swirling spirits of the night in the form of swarms of mosquitos that blackened their now-sweaty bodies and drove them back into the hulls of their proas and beneath their matting. Sleep came not as they twisted and turned and longed for sunrise, the insects droning and sucking blood from every exposed surface. The misery was outside the realm of anything Ḷainjin had ever experienced or imagined. It was worse even than the calm, the treacherous sun, and the thirst of kāleptak. As he lay there curled within his sleeping mat, he came to realize why these western islanders thrived amid the thick smoke of smoldering coconut husks. The hearths they slept among protected them from the torture of these malicious insects that owned the night.

Only the sounds of Lirojak and her palu rejoining them brought comfort though he rose not to meet their charge — whom he could hear, he guessed, relentlessly questioning them regarding the safety of her husband. As planned, of course, they had solicited her participation by promising to leave him unharmed, but Ḷainjin could hear her requiring them to repeat their promises from time to time until light came and the insects retreated reluctantly. Their torment gradually ended, and he was able finally to sleep.

He awakened to the sound of Kou crying again. Had she ever stopped, or had he simply been able to ignore it in his sleep? This time, Ḷōbwilñawa was seriously interrogating her, with Rojak assisting with the interpretation between the two in a voice sympathetic to her young friend. Ḷainjin raised himself from his hull to drink from the mouth of a fresh coconut as he listened to the back and forth, which Rojak later clarified.

"Why are you crying?" Ḷōbwilñawa asked. "No one plans to hurt you, your child, or your husband. You must not look fearful when you beckon your husband and any others ashore. Whoever panics and tries to paddle away will be in danger. We won't allow them to escape and will do whatever necessary to prevent them. We plan to leave them unharmed. All we plan to do is borrow their canoes to paddle upriver."

"No! You plan to kill the akebu and free the mothers!"

"Yes, but these things are out of your control. You must concentrate on saving your husband by calling him ashore and encouraging him not to fight. We have no reason to harm him unless that becomes necessary. Do you understand this?"

More weeping. Ḷōbwilñawa and Rojak were obviously not getting through to Kou, and she appeared to be turning against Rojak. Then Lañinpo, charged with watching the path that edged the kunai and crossed the landward base of the thumb, quietly joined them with more bad news. A group of men with bows had just passed, headed upriver. Luckily, their old dogs hadn't smelled him.

"That was because of her mother!" Rojak said. "Kou warned us her mother wouldn't keep our dragging her off into the night to herself."

"Not to worry." Kanari spoke slowly, thoughtfully, through Ḷōbwilñawa. "Let them come. Our spears against their bows. In this grass, we are like poisonous snakes that can strike them before they react. If they come by river, we dive under the water, overturn their canoes, and bite them like sharks with our *rajraj*."

Then he turned to Kou. She didn't understand Ḷōbwilñawa's Kajin Rālik but appeared suspicious of what he had said. Kanari raised the *rajraj* Ḷōbwilñawa had given him, directed his gaze directly at her, and warned her in his own language. "Save your husband from this!"

Kou turned to Rojak and then Bwilñawa and, when no interpretation came, began crying again.

Kanari assigned Ḷainjin the task of peering out through the tall grass at the upstream edge of the thumb to view the river ahead and quietly notify them the moment the Komba canoes appeared. Lañinpo returned to his post toward the edge of the pathway to the kunai that edged the first downriver bend below the base of the thumb. If he entered the river from that point, he could potentially prevent a canoeist from escaping their ambush. Luckily, when the dugout river canoes appeared around midmorning, there were only two with a single oarsman in each. It was immediately clear why — because they had weighted down and filled the canoes with pwentang. Kou had gained her composure, and as her husband came rounding the nail of the thumb, she hailed the surprised man, who immediately debarked and held to his canoe at the riverbank. He assumed she wanted to come aboard until Kanari and Rojak appeared with the ropes they intended to use to restrain him.

Ḷainjin's concentration at this point was on the second man, who was drifting midstream and listening to Kou's entreaty that he come ashore as well. Instead, the man's eyes slowly studied the situation and he panicked. But before he could dig his paddle into the stream, Ḷainjin had dropped his kilt and dived after him. The man's first thought was to outpaddle his swimming, but once Ḷainjin reached his stern, his next tactic was to stand, turn, and attack him with his paddle. Ḷainjin warned him several times with his *rajraj*. Toyed with him just long enough for Lañinpo to surprise the man at his bow, at which point he surrendered with a nervous smile.

Though restrained at their feet with hands tied behind their backs, Kou and the two prisoners visibly calmed as the morning passed. The first thing Kanari did was to pile the pwentang amid their little circle fenced by the weeds away from the riverbank. Having the pwentang there next to the men may have relieved them of an additional worry, that they would be punished for their loss. They were still alive, and their heads were not hanging by their hair, which was apparently the result of most assaults on the kunai. Kanari — through Ḷōbwilñawa through Kou — divulged his plan to them. All they wanted was their mothers freed. They had been in captivity far too long to account for any offense committed against the Komba. Yes, the akebu may die in the process, but either way, the canoeists wouldn't be the ones blamed, as the pwentang would remain in their possession. They were going to take their canoes upriver pretending to be the canoeists, with one paddling and the other lying down as though cargo. They would then climb the akebu's tree house and free the mothers.

Rojak had already learned from Kou that they must leave their canoes at the fork of the second tributary. This was where the pwentang were fired with grass from the kunai and stored. From there, they could see the tree house of the akebu higher up on the hinterland. Kou and the two prisoners looked at each other in disbelief that Kanari's plan was likely to succeed.

"What about his magic?" asked Kou's husband sardonically — using Kou's language.

At this, Kanari's eyes sharpened as though he was about to go into one of his *kakar* tirades, but then they softened and appeared almost amused as he responded.

Ḷōbwilñawa seemed to agree and interpreted into Kou's language as best he could: "If we succumb to his magic, then by tomorrow morning, Rojak will set you free and flee for her life, and you two will have the pwentang and two of their proas to use, to either continue to follow the akebu or run from his magic. Either way, you're better off than you were paddling down the river this morning."

Much discussion between Kou and the other two ensued until the rationale of Kanari's statement was comprehended.

That proposal served to cast the canoeists into thought, and Ḷainjin decided to use the quiet to sink back into his hull and catch up on the sleep he had missed the night before. To prepare his thoughts for the battle ahead, he meditated over the three elements of battle, according to his grandfathers. These were patience, distraction, and surprise. Planning was important, of course, and Kanari's plan to naturalize the forbidden man's reluctant followers and disable the bows of the boys in the men's house was a good one. However, his grandfathers had also taught him that the course of a battle seldom goes according to plan. There are too many possibilities for everything to fall into place properly, and that is where patience becomes essential. Patience would reveal the proper moment to distract and surprise.

According to information Rojak had gotten from Kou, tree houses were not part of either the Komba or the Sambia way of life. There were no others in the village, so it would be easy to spot. Obviously, the forbidden man had built it not to hide himself amid a cluster of trees or branches but to stand out as part of his "higher is smarter" theology. He must have brought the knowledge to build it from his travels prior to Sigaba. Apparently, he knew to choose a tree with no branches, or stubs of them, on the trunk below. He knew to leave enough live branches at the top to prevent the tree from dying yet not so many to cause the house to creak as the tree swayed in the wind. He probably wanted to keep the house as quiet as possible, to hear anyone climbing from beneath them.

Kou was insistent that the akebu never allowed the mothers to climb down. No one had seen them up close for a long time. They lowered their excrement and raised water for bathing in the same heavy nets used to lower the pwentang ready for firing. The women of the village took turns emptying and burying. And on occasion, when the akebu was traveling, the captives would toss down small pieces of blackstone from the treasure he had received as the primary trade item he solicited from the Siassi in exchange for the pwentang. The tree house must be a storage facility for both and must have a spool of some sort overhanging from its eaves to allow those on the ground to pull the heavy clay up to the women and lower the dried pwentang for firing. As this spool turned, it would make a noise to alert the akebu that someone below was pulling something upward.

Men who solicit revenge know the night is their enemy. It was unlikely that the akebu would sleep through a sound like that. According to Kou, both ends of the rope hung down from the eave of the house. One end was staked to the ground, but he kept the other end tied to one of the large forks in the tree under the house. That end passed by a large window flap where, once opened and tied vertical beneath the eave, the net could swing into the house for filling. If someone tried to climb this rope from below, the spool would move. The akebu would hear the sound and could always cut the line. However, should they succeed in freeing and quickly lowering this net end to the hill below, a man could rapidly climb the tree if tied to it and propelled upward by two men pulling from below. If they kept the line moving, the akebu would not be able to sever it.

Then there was the ladder, made of three vines hung from the front of the tree house and staked to the ground. It had steps of sticks lashed horizontally across all three. Likewise, this was bound to cause the house to shake should someone begin to climb. Nevertheless, might these two less than quiet ties to the hill beneath provide the distraction necessary to surprise and overtake the akebu?

If the tree house stood alone and was at the height of ten or more men, as Kou had estimated, and if his weapon of choice was a small bow, he was unlikely to shoot his poison-tipped arrows upon first hearing someone climbing the ladder. Such a shot would prove unsuccessful if the one climbing wore a sun hat and light sunshields for protection. Nor was he likely to cut the ladder loose unless he saw a host of intruders attempting to climb. That was his exit in case of fire, and cutting it would be his last tactic rather than his first. Nevertheless, the plan was for the one climbing the ladder to tie himself to the end of the rope as a safety line secured by the men below. They all agreed the akebu was most likely to wait for his assailants to arrive close upon him before shooting. In addition, they hoped he would sound an alarm with his conch shell. This to leave those climbing vulnerable to arrow attack from those answering his alarm.

Kanari and Babwa's Komba contact Ilisa had worked out a plan for this contingency and had gotten it approved by the Komba elders. As immediately as the akebu's alarm sounded, Ilisa would set fire to a house in the Samba village. All would then think the alarm was due to the fire.

Kou had told of a lookout platform built upon other limbs overhanging the tree house. Ultimately, Ḷainjin's plan was to drop through the roof from this platform and maneuver himself in such a way that the akebu would be expecting a slap from the back of his hand. Instead, in his last moment alive, from the corner of his eye, he would see the white shark tooth and be surprised by his life's blood spurting from the side of his neck.

Such were their plans as repeatedly discussed, and such were the thoughts swirling in Ḷainjin's head that afternoon as he drifted into and out of light, sweaty sleep in the hot, stale air within the hull of his canoe. Then, when it must be late afternoon, he heard commotion as the palu, Lañinpo and the others moved the paddling canoes to the riverbank. "It must be time. If this is good-bye, then so be it," Ḷainjin thought, fingering the inner wall of his hull. Hewn many seasons ago by his boyhood friend, it would be a source of inspiration for the battle ahead.

He rose confident to face his destiny. He wanted to speak to Rojak, to ask her to promise to take his story to Namorik should things not go according to plan, and that was when the first of a series of critical and unexpected twists occurred. For some unexplained reason — Wisim perhaps too fat for the canoe — Rojak announced that they had decided to switch parts in their plan. The palu would be staying to guard her friend Kou and their proas. Rojak demanded to be one of the three children climbing the tree to retrieve the mothers. That change was to push Ḷōbwilñawa off his part as one of the three climbing, leaving him and Kanari to guard the hill below. It wasn't as though this had not occurred to Ḷainjin before. Should he fail, his story would be lost forever in the hinterlands of this strange and uninviting island, his spirit likely intertwined with that of his nemesis the forbidden man, destined to swirl in nightmare forever about the fires of Manam with no one to pass his story on. There would be no thoughts of him, no one calling him to those beloved Rālik coral necklaces floating there in all their beauty, endlessly awaiting his return. It was now time to cast his lot irretrievably and find which destiny would be his.

They launched the two dugout log canoes. Flat bottomed, they had identical up-tapered ends. Ḷōbwilñawa paddled the first with Kanari lying prone. Lañinpo was in the second, with his sister and Ḷainjin lying next to each other like so much cargo in the hull. He slightly higher, somewhat on his side. She lying flat. He offering his upper arm as a headrest. The sun soon crept below the high mountains ahead, leaving the sky still blue from the sea behind. The temporarily calm river beneath them ran cloudy through the red earth of its banks.

Never-resting damselflies darting in and out made Ḷainjin wish he could fly, but now, while he was still alive. Rojak's well-shaped, sweaty face turned to his. He wanted more than ever to embrace her, to roll himself into the cradle of her long and slender legs. She smiled, knowing perhaps that he would do anything necessary to protect her. Though he knew, in her courageous throat, she desired not the protection of any man. How lucky was her palu to have attracted her in her youth, to have lost and then lured her again into his snare? Alternatively, perhaps that necklace, made by his woman on Satawan, was now captivating her? Ḷainjin wanted to take it from her neck and toss it into the river to see.

Ḷōbwilñawa, as strategized, was to set a pace that would reassure the forbidden man — or anyone else spying from afar — that his men were returning to him as planned yet, ultimately, too slowly for them to arrive before dark. The men assigned to wait for their arrival would then return to their homes before dark, as was their custom. Ḷōbwilñawa paddled at a reasonable clip until reaching the first fork in the river, then much slower once the river narrowed and the current became swifter. Once they had passed a clearing upon the kunai between the otherwise tree-lined banks of the river, they saw the tree house unmistakably commanding the sharp rise to the hinterland, and he led Kanari and Lañinpo to a bush-covered spot where they tied up and waited.

Shortly thereafter, the enemy from which there was no escape attacked, and their misery began. Blood-sucking mosquitos, as if tiny blood-lapping bats, swarmed out of the kunai and tortured their warm bodies, leaving a wake of dead black insects mixed with live red blood smeared upon their faces, arms, breasts, and backs. This, Ḷainjin used to his advantage. He lay upon her to protect their breasts and laid his hands over her neck and face as she used her hands to rub his back and her feet to rub the backs of his exposed thighs. Lañinpo, on his part, turned his back to them and swatted himself violently with a branch torn from the bushes, as did the others. How long they continued, too self-occupied to observe the moon's progression above, was hard to tell. All were captivated in the throes of their own suffering.

Finally, Rojak's brother took up his oar and paddled them the short distance to their destination. She simply clasped Ḷainjin's hand for a short time when they rose from the riverbank and found the open thatch hut that served as a temporary storage for the pwentang before and after firing. Their thoughts henceforth fixated on literally keeping their heads. Their movements would be swift, and their eyes, their whole selves, concentrated upon the various tasks of their plan. They would follow the path that led directly from there to the tree house. Kanari and Ḷōbwilñawa would head directly into the village to silently find and remove the strings of each bow they found hanging from the laddered entrances to the stilted thatched homes, which would be smoke filled and closed windowed. They could see the tree in which the house sat, high upon its three-pronged fork, smoke pouring from beneath its eaves. Each fork rose above the peaked roof and subsequently supported a small lookout platform above its peaked, thatched roof before branching into the few live tufts left upon the tree.

Ḷainjin imagined the akebu sitting there atop his post earlier that evening, searching the river for signs of his canoes approaching. Then retiring inside, closing all windows, and firing the damp, smoldering husks that would protect them from the swirling spirits of the night. Would he imagine that the sounds he was about to hear were his traders returning with blackstone to add to his treasure? Could Ḷainjin reach that platform or the fork supporting it without detection? He could see Bwilñawa guarding the corner of the men's house. What was taking Kanari so long? Finally, they signaled. Ḷainjin squeezed Rojak's hand as he glanced into the courageous soul within the shiny white-and-black eyes glistening back at him in the moonlight one final time. Their moment had come, and then he was on his way toward the trunk of the tree.

It proved to be much broader than described — the bark smoother, the first fork much higher than expected — but this was Ḷainjin's part, and failure to reach it would surely doom any prospect of success. It was much fatter than any coconut tree trunk and branchless, unlike any breadfruit tree he had ever climbed, but he attacked it as a naive young dog might a wild boar, with no thought but rage and without care for its life. His legs ached to the groin as the sides of his feet clutched its smooth but thankfully dry sides. His hands gripped to the very nails as he reached, clasped, and raised himself once and then once again. Silently, never groaning, never stopping, never minding the hovering hordes biting about him, he reached — how, he would never know — the first fork and place of rest. All was still silent in the house above him. His heart pounding still, after his moment of rest, he attacked the tree again. This time, the trunk had narrowed, the trifork was closer, and he more easily reached his goal. He opened the little pandanus pouch he had tied to his kilt and placed one of the puffer fish-livers upon his tongue. In the past, this had been enough to cause his vision to spin and the strange peace of a dying man to seep down into his throat. Taking Setepana's advice, he squished it between his teeth but swallowed it not. He might need to spit it out should he not meet with the akebu's poison or be unable to find it. Swallowing a smidgen of saliva, he waited patiently, looking out over the expanse of the kunai below — all the way around the peninsula to the open, glistening sea, all the way across the strait to the islands of the Siassi. Finally, once he felt the disorienting effects and growing nausea from the poison fish take hold, he waved to his companions. They headed toward the base of the tree, and he untied and lowered the net end of the rope.

Ḷainjin could hear the spool squeak as he smoothly and silently climbed the forked branch that curved around the house and led to the platform above it, but he stopped just short of it, seeing that the platform rested on the roof peak and not wanting to alert the akebu of his presence there. A few moments later, he heard the spool strain as the line from the ground tightened. Then the whole house below him began to creak as Rojak began her ascent. His plan was to drop through the thatch of the roof the moment the akebu sounded his conch. He began feeling softly for the roof poles beneath the thatch with his foot, with the intention of falling between them. But instead of the alarm he had expected, he heard a frantic slapping by the window on the far side of the house. The akebu must be trying to create a flame to light the house. The light was good, and now Ḷainjin didn't have to worry about dropping down into the hearth. He quickly calculated that shelves of pwentang probably lined the thatch wall beneath him. So, he planned to drop through as close to the ridge pole as possible. His head began to spin out of his control, and his vision began to break up as though his eyes were four rather than two. Time seemed to stand still, moments to linger. He lost track of exactly where his climbing companions were. Should he jump or be patient?

Finally, he heard the akebu rushing beneath to the entrance — perhaps to view who was climbing from below. Then he heard the conch streaming out into the night and, without hesitation, jumped through the thatch roof. His weight was enough to snap the thatch lashings, and he broke his fall by reaching for a thatch pole that snapped in two. The floor beneath him gave but did not break. He saw the mothers there, coming out from under their mats in the corner close by the hearth. He heard the akebu speaking to someone, still directing his smoky little world about him with deliberation. He was small in stature. Smaller even than the Komba captives they had left tied below. His nose was quite broad, and he was very black. His face squished from forehead to chin.

Ḷainjin saw him drop the conch and thread his little bow with an arrow. The gray-haired mothers were speaking, probably warning him in the wrong tongue. "I am your son, Ḷainjin," he said in their language, turning to face his nemesis. The akebu appeared almost childlike as he drew his bow's string and pointed its arrow directly at him. A hopeless-sounding wail arose from one of the women, who rose and scrambled unsteadily to the corner. Nevertheless, Ḷainjin stepped forward, seeking the little man's poison, chewing and swallowing the last of the liver in his mouth. Happily, the little arrow barely pierced his right breast. He tore it out and stepped quickly toward the akebu as he attempted to thread his bow a second time, but Ḷainjin arrived in time to take it and toss it aside as would a father angrily disabling a son. Then the little man stabbed him in the other breast with a second arrow deftly drawn from his quiver. Ḷainjin wrenched the pigskin quiver from him, then threw it so hard against the thatched window flap that it tumbled down and away. The akebu, who must have been surprised his poison was taking so long to affect him, started to slowly, strategically retreat, all the time continuing to talk as though directing someone unseen.

For his part, Ḷainjin felt confident he had now eliminated any threat and relieved he was recovering from the urge to regurgitate the puffer fish–livers he had eaten. Then two things happened simultaneously. Lañinpo jumped through the roof, *rajraj* in hand, and Rojak reached the top of the ladder, raised the flap over the window, which served as the entrance, and began to climb inside.

The akebu shouted something that caused one of the mothers to lunge forward unsteadily. Her legs drummed across the slatted floor as she screamed in Kajin Rālik, "That's your sister!"

In that same moment, another diminutive figure lunged from somewhere to poke Rojak in the chest with a spear. Ḷainjin would carry the surprised, instantaneous defeat in her eyes with him. This, just as the mother reached for Rojak's hands, slipping away from the window posts, and footless, followed her out, falling with her into the night. Ḷainjin, of course, rushed to the window, opened the flap, and saw the two lying lifeless together on the hill below. "She was supposed to tie herself to the hoisting line anchored by one of the men below!" he thought. "In her haste, she must have forgotten." No longer able to control his nausea, he threw up into the clear outside air and then turned in delirium just as Lañinpo caught the akebu by the hair, cut his throat, and began sawing at it in a bloody rage as his little brother whimpered and watched from the corner. The last thing Ḷainjin remembered before slipping away was the face of his mother, tears flowing, crawling toward him in the firelight.

The promise

Ḷainjin awoke late the next morning and knew from the rock of his proa that they were safe and out at sea. Overcome by nausea, he rose quickly through the hatch above and belched the little water left in his stomach into the ocean.

There she was, slowly paddling out to sea. An attractive, spry-looking woman, calm and fully in command of the large craft and his oversized oar. She had been the objective of all his endeavors, and there she was — free at last. Her enthusiasm was liberating, like the wind in her unbundled gray hair. But at what terrible price? She broke the joyful moment by turning her gaze in a matter-of-fact way toward the body that lay between them.

"Her brother said you would want to say good-bye to her."

The badly bruised body of Rojak lay strapped over the outrigger platform. Her one leg dangled into the sea. Her long, wet hair sprawled about as if she had just swum to him and was about to rise and swirl it into a bun, as had been her habit. A shudder of horror as he recalled the night before passed through him. This wasn't how he had imagined their reunion.

"The little brother that murdered her?" he asked.

"He just followed his father's orders. Lañinpo didn't have the throat to kill him. For what purpose? They're brothers." She pointed with her eyes to the sails hugging the coastline on the horizon. "He accompanies his brother and Kanari to Murik to seek a new life there. I hope it's all right. I told them we are heading out to sea."

"Yes, that's okay. I have no love for that place."

"Can you raise sail then? We need to get her to sea before she starts to stink. We don't want her swelling up and washing ashore. Of course, I couldn't raise that sail by myself!" She steadied herself with her free hand, untucked her legs from beneath her, and beat the footless stumps upon the deck. Making light of her condition by launching a humorless joke in such a silly way left him curiously amused by the spirited old woman, who sent herself into a coughing fit as she laughed.

His thoughts immediately turned back to the night before and the drumming sound of Rojak's mother racing unsteadily across the slatted floor to grab onto her hands, following her haplessly through the thatch-shuttered window that opened to the floor. She'd also had no feet.

"Let's go! *Wūj uwaṇ in jān lōḷḷap in*!"[173]

"What a character, this mother," he thought. Despite all the anguish, he loosened the sheet, pulled the halyard, and watched her steer them out into the strait toward Arop.

"Then what about her man...? We call him the palu."

"It was a pity to see such a big, strong man stuck with so many little fishing arrows. It must have been the Gitua villagers. They set fire to that little thumb by the river from the downwind side and surrounded him like a wild boar. The slow-burning fire and small arrows shot from afar gave him enough time to drag both proas safely out of the fire's path to the riverbank before collapsing there upon the shore." She pointed again with a strong, red clay-dyed hand to the two sails on the horizon headed on a northwesterly course. "Lañinpo and Kanari will let him to sea."

"What about Ḷōbwilñawa?" asked Ḷainjin.

"Lañinpo says Kanari and Ḷōbwilñawa both rushed down the hill to distract the single Komba with a longbow who was about to shoot an arrow at that one there as she climbed." She pointed again with her nose to poor Rojak, sprawled prone, lifeless, and ashen across the outrigger platform, and reached forward to loosen the sheet. Ḷainjin adjusted it for her instead.

"The onlookers said Kanari ran faster," she said, "but our friend was closer at the time the Komba made his choice. Kanari didn't give him time to draw a second arrow. He takes the Komba's head back to Murik."

"And Ḷōbwilñawa?" Ḷainjin remembered the rijeḷā's reluctance to return to that place and his heroic acceptance of the mission. His eyes drifted back

[173] "Pull this gray hair from this old lady!"

to the hinterland they had left as if to say good-bye to the hero he had first met that day of the kājokwā.

"We had to leave him there," his mother said. "Two of your Komba allies appeared and helped me to the river. We had to get out of there. They said they would bury him."

"Poor Ḷōbwilñawa. He didn't want to return. He had built a good life in Pohnpei."

"Lucky for me, he changed his mind and escorted you here to set me free." She triumphantly sniffed the clean ocean air with a warm smile, showing a moment of gratitude, thanking them all for what they had accomplished.

"I'm surprised Lañinpo returns to Murik."

"Lañinpo takes the akebu's stinking head in a basket. He has passed his initiation. Kanari has him convinced he must now touch the *kakar* spears. You don't mind missing that, do you?"

"No," he said. "I, too, am anxious to get to sea." The truth being, he hated that place but thought fondly of the red-mouthed woman who had captured his proa and Kanari's niece, who had helped him shake the walls of his sister's pole house.

"I'm sorry. I know that you're in mourning for your brave friends. It's just… I promised myself, if I ever got free, I would never set foot on that island again." She broke into lighthearted laughter and beat her stumps a few more times to make sure he'd caught her self-deprecating joke. Her laughter was infectious, but…

"How did you lose—"

"It's an ugly story, and enough sad stories for one day. I'll tell you another."

There was so much to lament that Ḷainjin didn't know where to start, but she would have none of it. Putting voice to her newfound freedom, she soon began to sing her triumphant chant, a chant, he later learned, that she and her dearest friend had contrived over the seasons as they daily fashioned the akebu's pwentang. They sailed that way out into the strait, both enjoying the seasonally fair weather, the fresh breeze, and the salty air. Free at last of the insect-infested, smoke-laden villages ashore.

Soon, though, it was time to say good-bye to his beloved friend Rojak. One part of him wished they had joined themselves in passion; another was happy not to have known her that way. She was one who had desired not a man's conquest, only his acceptance, and alas, the very nature of men's upbringing prevented that. He embraced her at last, hugged her limp, cold body tightly beneath her lifeless arms, and kissed her on a curiously unbruised spot on her shoulder. Refusing to look again at her torn, pale face, he allowed her to slip again from the grip of life, into the infinite, transparent blue of her untimely place of rest.

His tearful eyes met those of his mother, who felt his pain and opened her arms. He bent forward into her lap. Put his arms around her and wept there as a child. He didn't want it this way, hadn't realized he would have to sacrifice his friends for her freedom. Many years of loneliness crept out of him as he sat there, bent over awkwardly as she patted his back and tried to console him as the grief poured out.

By what chance had their stories endured to come together as one? How many had helped them? How many souls had offered their friendship, given their very lives for these moments to occur? He enumerated without counting. "Why not make the most of their sacrifice?" he concluded finally, without contriving to wish otherwise.

Old woman that she was now, she did not smell as he had remembered from childhood, but he had longed for her embrace for such a time that, even in this awkward position, it felt satisfying. He wished she could hold him in her arms and squeeze him as a child, but alas, he was too big now. They were on a boat, and the ocean was calling.

His mother allowed him to hunch himself into her lap, lost in his memories, for quite a while. Then she politely requested that he hoist their sail again and point them off to he knew not where. Gradually, her zest to put distance between them and the mainland they were leaving, her triumph at fulfilling her so-long-awaited plan to be free, and her joy to have awakened from season upon season of nightmare began to affect him as well.

"How does that *ikir*[174] go again?" he asked. True, she reserved her expressions of love for him due to circumstance. She had left him shortly

---

[174] A navigational poem.

after birth. How could she make up in a day for all the loneliness she had committed him to? Yet he had traced her path across an ocean to set her free. So it was that she began with enduring passion to teach him their poem that recounted their travels from Epoon in the south to Mili in the east to Bikar in the north to Pohnpei in the west. It related all the seamarks that tied together all the stories they had grown up hearing. It told of freshwater springs circled by sharks and birds and turtles and all manner of ocean life. It was a song of courage and optimism. It strengthened the spirit and granted confidence to moments of weariness. Through this *ikir*, she intended to instill the confidence he would need to succeed in his journey home.

Ḷainjin absorbed it with passion even as the strength of her singing seemed to wane as the days passed. Slowly, it became obvious to him she wasn't as strong as she pretended. She periodically broke into fits of fever and coughed disconcertedly. Eventually, her much-beloved sun and fresh air seemed to turn against her.

He was happy when, not a day too soon, the green mountains of Manus rose upon the horizon. He began to imagine the taste of Ngalen's dugong soup and longed to see her face and, yes, the indifferent gaze of his conceited bird! He understood now that the rijeḷā had done him a great service by planning this last stop on his way home. They would need serious provisions for their journey back across the great kāleptak. He remembered the palu's instructions to Satawan — to keep his face north as its countercurrent swept them east until they could see little Liṃanṃan nightly, just above the cloud line, to guide him there. The palu had warned that there would be no islands in between! That must be their first destination. Ḷainjin must tell the palu's woman and family the whole story of his valiant end no matter the pain or the anguish it might cause. At minimum, he owed them that. Thereafter, they must traverse the sea on short legs, as it had become clear his mother's body was less strong than her spirit demanded of it.

Slit drums resounded upon their arrival, and the village of stilt houses built upon the reef was exactly as Ḷainjin had left it. The Chief cold-glanced at him briefly before raising his beak skyward and downing his lunch from the quick fingers of Ngalen's son, who seemed proud to demonstrate how well he had kept the bird. Malean was ecstatic with the number, shape, and size of the blackstones traded for his Murik baskets. Ngalen was as beautiful and her house as immaculate as ever. She was a gracious host to them, and Malean was quick to provide them the needed provisions. He even took Ļainjin spearfishing in the shallows by torch light on a black night and invited him to the shady men's islet, where canoes were in various stages of construction.

His mother enjoyed toying with a tongue she had long since forgotten. On his part, Ļainjin managed to mime the gist of the unfortunate death of the rijeļā yet alight the hope of a new trade route for Malean through Kanari and Lañinpo. He would have liked to stay longer to give his mother more time to recuperate from the first tack of their journey, but rainy season was coming to these backward seas, and she was eager to begin the second leg. They left on a gray day amid light winds from the southeast. He decided to leave the Chief tied to his perch on the outrigger booms, lest he fly back to Ngalen. His mother resumed her chant as they rounded the island's east end and headed due north, leaving behind the smoking fire islands to the south as an ever-present daytime quadrant marker upon their stern.

Although his mother had peppered his chanting lessons with legends Ļainjin had heard many times before, he now treasured the character of each word as if it were a valuable piece of blackstone. She teased him about his love for Ngalen, which she said had emerged like sweat from his face every time he looked at her.

"One day soon," she prophesied, he would find the one who would "fulfill his destiny."

"Out here in the middle of nowhere?" he joked.

"All the easier for a thing of beauty to stand out. Like an island on the horizon or a turtle on an otherwise empty shore. There is no such place as nowhere. There is only the here, and the only question is, are you able to seize the moment?"

"That is very confusing!"

"Good! Then let that be a riddle you must solve!" she said.

"You must give me more clues!"

"Like looking through a window with the shutter open from a distance. You may see her, but she may not notice you. A man must cultivate a timeless presence about himself. First, not to gaze but to look directly at her.

Second, not to just look but to see and evaluate. Finally — and most important of all — to acknowledge the spirit within her crying out to be noticed. Never ignore a woman for more than a moment, or she will take flight like a bird and may be gone forever. She seeks consistent acknowledgment. You see a man fishing. You acknowledge his presence out of respect. A woman deserves no less."

They sailed on for days like that. She probed him between shifts, politely invading his very sense of himself as she attempted, perhaps, to carefully make up for the childhood they had never shared. She made him relate, one by one, each season of his life from the time she had left him there before the storm. She encouraged him to recall much that he had forgotten. He refrained from asking about her captivity. That was what it was, and she wasn't eager to speak about it. Instead, he delved into the meaning of each line of the *ikir*, and she never tired of explaining. On her part, she learned what they had taught him and sought to plug what holes in his knowledge she found. He tried his best to understand and to remember as it became increasingly clear, from her periodic shivering and sweating, she was ill. They guessed her failing health would limit their time together, and this gave a certain urgency to their talk.

Then one day, out of her own volition, she began speaking about her captors.

"You know they don't have *irooj*. There's not an *irooj* on the island. So, they lack a unifying principal. That's probably why they have so many languages and ways of life. No one to consolidate power. Hundreds of different tribes, different languages even. A member of one tribe kills a member of another all the time, but they do so selectively. It's part of becoming a man. 'Head-hunting,' they call it. Taking a head from a neighboring tribe and perhaps adorning their men's house with it.

"The forbidden man was not Komba. He was Sambia. He came from an entirely different language and way of life. Think about it. He had nothing when he came down from that mountain. It took a lot of courage to just show up the way he did. He didn't share their religion or beliefs of why this or why that. But no matter, he worked the gardens hard and they respected that. The higher up a man comes from, the smarter, and he learned their language quickly enough. With those people, generosity is everything and he was very generous. He fed them pig, and that was what they wanted to eat. That probably sounds funny — headhunters and generosity. They're easy to get along with, really. The secret is to become a trade brother. That was one custom they shared. The akebu figured that out right away.

"Another was respect for dead ancestors. His ancestors resided over the mountains where they had buried them. The Komba travel in groups for protection except to visit their ancestors. So, he fashioned what he called a *lāpio*, a statue that the dead spirits could haunt. He placed it in the men's house and prayed to this regularly. The Komba adopted his custom. Why travel out alone and risk a beheading when you can talk to your ancestors right there in the men's house? That's an example of one of his practical contributions to the Komba way of life."

"You sound like you, too, respected him," Ḷainjin said. "They told stories in Sigaba that he'd poisoned the other big men, and that's how his stature grew so fast."

"That's probably true. He could be very generous, but he also had a cruel side. For instance, in typical big-man style, he would trade the blackstone he got for our pwentang for wild pig and throw a feast for his followers, or he would pay bride-wealth on behalf of a young man seeking wives. He traded for fish too. He knew we liked fish, so he would reward us with it. We'd wait up for his traders to return upriver and cook them. The fish already cleaned for the long trip upriver were still fresh. We'd build a fire right there in the house and eat as much as we wanted. Just like in days past, out among our atolls.

"He had many wives himself in the surrounding villages. The gardens of these women were productive. He used it all to his advantage when he'd throw a feast and feed people. The trader in me respected that. He distributed everything, and the people saw this. He wasn't amassing wealth for himself or even his Sambia relatives. They respected that.

"He would not acknowledge us captives publicly. We didn't share the respect his wives shared, but privately, he would give us choice portions of meat and vegetables. Obviously, he didn't have to do that. He could have treated us like Matankor treat their captive prostitutes. We were his property. He could have fed us anything, but he fed us well. He even partitioned off a little place in the house with a fiber curtain for us to make ready. Even when we tried to escape. He warned us plenty of times about what he would do—"

"What?"

"Now we're talking his cruel side. He warned us. Told us exactly what he would do if we tried to escape again. But he would be away for days visiting his wives and their families. We tried to run away several times despite his warnings, but each time the Komba caught us. And he would reward them very generously. They waited for us to attempt to escape again and tricked us into trying, and we could be sure they would report it as soon as he returned.

"Finally, he kept his promise.

"I woke up one day after he poisoned me, and one foot was gone. Can you imagine the horror? There was my stump all bound up in medicine leaves, and there he was eating my foot by the light of his hearth. Enjoying his prank like a cruel little boy who bullies his friends to get his way. Lañinpo's mother thought if she gave herself to him willingly, he would spare her. He'd mount her from behind from time to time like she was a dog. She softened him not. He roasted her foot just as he did mine. One by one, he ate our feet. He ate the second foot after the first one healed. 'Why waste such a delicacy?' he would say. He could poison us at will, and he knew how to mix his poison to induce sleep and not death. It was a lesson we would not forget again. She offered herself not after that.

"When someone takes your feet, they basically take your life — your mobility. From that point on, escape was hopeless, and we accepted our life there as all we would have. She raised his son. He grew up listening to his father, and that was all right because he treated us well. He was an ambitious boy and oversaw lowering and firing the pwentang. He was the one to coordinate with the men below, reach outside, and lower the net through the window. He studied with his father and occasionally accompanied him on his visits to the villages.

"When you dropped through the roof and told us who you were, we were surprised, but in our long-buried dreams, we expected someone to rescue us. Rojak's mother knew the moment Rojak opened the window who she was. She also knew her son would do exactly what the akebu told him to. Pitiful thing… Without feet she had no leverage, but she held on to her daughter until the fall broke her neck. We left her there along with Ḷōbwilñawa. What could we do? Rojak was still breathing, so her brother carried her along with the little man's head. That head!

"He didn't deserve that desecration. 'Stop already!' I shouted at Lañinpo. But he was set on sailing away with that head. Kanari carried you after they lowered us in the net. Do you remember that? A few Komba appeared and — surprisingly — helped me. Kanari and Lañinpo wanted us to accompany them back to Murik. I refused. I told them I had experience with the poison from the arrows and you just needed to sleep and we would bury Rojak at sea.

"You know, they say if they eat you, or take your head, your soul will have no shape in which to reside in the spirit world. I guess I'll have no feet," she joked, "so I plan to hitch a ride on a porpoise — or if I fail to catch one, a mother turtle!"

As gradually as one season turns into the next, the first currents of the great, silent kāleptak stream began to sweep them eastward even as they continued their northward bearing. Moderately, the winds began to swirl and die, and Ḷainjin and his mother had to drop sail and paddle. This was the part of the journey he feared most. That was when she taught him the secret to crossing kāleptak, which was to avoid paddling during the noon hours with buñtokrear as the only point of bearing. Whereas the east sun in the morning and the west sun in the evening and the stars at night allowed for a more accurate bearing, less spent energy, and a more efficient use of water.

When the terrible storms swept over them, she refused to let him try to take advantage of the winds, explaining that their direction changed too quickly to hold a proper bearing. It was more efficient to concentrate instead on refilling their containers with rainwater. They must hold an exact northward bearing with each stroke exerted. They must not waste a single stroke off bearing. And so the days rolled forward under the cycle of the sun's morning and late-afternoon glare and the gentler glow of their mistress moon as she waned and grew and steadied their way.

The last thing his mother explained to him was this. She wanted him to retain her story deep in his throat. Never to repeat it to a single soul. She explained her reasoning this way. There are moments in a woman's life where, provided she is truly present, her future will reach back to guide her to her destiny. Ḷainjin was one of few men ever to have learned to visualize his life in this way. It meant holding true to life's bearing. It took tremendous commitment and concentration for a man. It comes more naturally to a woman, who knows she must bear her child. In that moment and thereafter, she feels the guiding hand of her future upon her. Although his mother could have died many times during unspeakable trials, she lived on by this guiding hand, as she believed against all odds they would be together again. But her true story was too cautionary for any woman to hear.

"Let the young women bloom like flowers along your path. Better to let them hear my story as they have heard it before — leading my fleet out to sea in the face of certain storm. Pass on my *ikir* to all who would learn, but never repeat this part — dying footless, wishing for the life that could have been. Let some woman somewhere, someday hear of my courage and reach forward unafraid to achieve her destiny, my misguided end unknown to her. Let your daughters do the same. Promise me you will discourage them not with your fear of the struggles they may face. To what end should you cause the color of petals to fade before their time? Let her fear not the sea, for we have entered that place before her, and our spirits are there to buoy her up. Stop not at Pohnpei but return rather to the islands of your birth. Let your destiny unfold there amid the language and life of your forefathers."

Ḷainjin paddled hard across the smooth water that night. She paddled as well as she could from the bow. Before the dawn, he lay to rest for a moment and quickly fell into an exhausted sleep. When he awoke, he felt the first mild breeze from the northeast, and he sensed the great kāleptak was finally behind them now. Then he found her slumped over lifeless on his forward deck. Their time together had been too short. Too much left unsaid. She had completed her part to get them into the wind that would carry him onward. For a second time, a loved one would pass from his arms into those of the sea. Hovering about him as he released her were the memories of all who had helped him get to this point on the ocean that was his life. There was

Ļōbwilñawa, of course, and the palu, but now Rojak as well as the spirits of all those others who had helped him. They surrounded him now as he lowered her into the transparent blue, promised to keep her secret, and watched her body sink until it was no more. He could imagine her spirit rising again from the depths to mingle with the others about him. They strengthened his aloneness.

You need not hear the story of his sail north to Satawan. The season he waited there among the palu's family for the westerlies. How, keeping his mother's direction, he passed his chance to land again on Pohnpei but traveled instead to offshore Namorik. You now know why he turned away from friends and family there. Why he dropped his true name. You have seen his days turn as his mother predicted, joining those of Liṃanṃan amid the sun-drenched quietude of Lae. You now know why Ļainjin promised her never to speak of her story and why, untold, it had to pass with her body back into the sea from which it had emerged.

The legend now turns to Ļainjin's hero child Ijokelekel — born to Lipanmai — who unwittingly searches for the father he never knew.

Glossary

ak — The frigate bird: *Fregata magnificens.*

akebu — Komba word for a lineage leader who served as the priest or "forbidden man" of Lāpio cult worship and practiced the medicinal and magical arts.

alele — A flat purse- or pouch-like basket plaited with processed pandanus leaves and used for valuables.

Andena — The elder brother in "The Two Brothers," a folktale told by the Sepik area peoples.

anidep — A game in which a foot-sized cube of woven pandanus leaves is kicked back and forth within a circle by clapping participants.

añōneañ — "Call of the north"; the southern solstice, which annually coincides with winter in the northern hemisphere.

añōnrak — "Call of the south"; the northern solstice, which annually coincides with summer in the northern hemisphere.

Ant — A coral atoll seven miles east of what is now called Pohnpei.

Antares — Aka Tūṃur.

aragen — Murik word for pudding made of cane-sweetened sago that only men can make and eat.

Arena — The younger brother in "The Two Brothers," a folktale told by the Sepik area peoples.

Babwa Wangumu — An accomplished Kunai initiate who killed two Komba.

bal — The foot beneath the clew of the lateen sail where its vertical gaff and horizontal yard join.

Bar Nor — Melanesian peoples inhabiting the Murik Lakes region of what is now Papua New Guinea; a coastal, intertidal area characterized by connected inland lagoons seasonally flooded with overflow from the Sepik River.

blackstone — Obsidian; volcanic glass.

bop — Pandanus.

buai — Areca nut, often chewed wrapped in betel leaf (*Piper betel*) with a sprinkle of slaked lime: calcium hydroxide, $Ca(OH)_2$.

buñtokrear — Swell that "falls from the east."

Bwedi — Aka Ḷōbwedi; a Seeker.

Bwilñawa — Aka Ḷōbwilñawa; the rijeḷā.

Chief — Ḷainjin's pet frigate bird.

dāp — Moray eel; marine eels of the Muraenidae family.

diak — To tack or, more specifically, shunt. The tack of the sail is transported from one end of the canoe to the other, keeping the outrigger to windward.

Eban — It will not; it cannot.

Ebar ṃṃan wa ne wam — "It is also good, that boat beneath you."

Ejelok eṃṃan in wane — Literally, "there is nothing good about that boat!" An idiomatic way to highly praise the obvious.

ekkwaḷ — Sennit; coir fiber line made from processed coconut husk fibers.

Ekūtañtañin eṃṃaan — "A man is an inchworm at sea."

Emejjia wa iloṃeto. — "A boat dies slow in the open ocean."

Epoon — A neighboring atoll seventy-three miles south-southwest of Namorik.

Ewalt — Ḷainjin's interpreter.

gi — Kunai word for "July."

Idedh — One of many man-made islets on the reef off the coast of eastern Pohnpei.

iedik — Literally, "small time"; neap tide.

iielap̧ — Literally, "big time"; spring or extreme tides during full and new moons.

ikabwe — Mackerel.

ikir — A navigational poem

Ilisa — An older, experienced trader; Babwa's Komba trade brother.

interpret — To provide an oral translation.

irooj — Chief.

jāānkun — Sun-dried sheets of pandanus pulp rolled into a log and wrapped in a sheath of pandanus leaves.

jāpe — A wooden, trapezoid-shaped vessel carved from breadfruit wood and used to knead breadfruit; the constellation Delphinus, the dolphin.

Jau Areu — Pohnpeian title: master fisherman.

Jebro̧ — Aka Pleiades; constellation.

jebwa — A battle dance; a fierce reenactment of a classic fighting style passed along from previous generations.

Jeej — An idiom used to express surprise. Translates roughly as "heck" or "darn it." A short form of "wōjjej."

Jeilañ — The Pohnpeian who looks after the Chief.

jekaro — Also called "tuba," "toddy," and various other names; the sap of the coconut palm tapped from the flower bud as it grows and continues to protrude between its mature frond leaf and the less-mature inner fronds of the palm's inner crown. The skill of making jekaro is practiced worldwide wherever palms grow.

jemañūñ — Fermented jekaro; tuba.

Jibke — Figure from the oral literature of the Marshall Islands who is given the impossible task of finding the source of the wind and lands in the mythical land of Eb.

jowi — Clan or tribe.

jukkwe — Sand clam; bivalve word used to refer to one's vagina.

kai — Titan word for food.

Kajin Rālik — Language of the Rālik Islands, now the western chain of the Republic of the Marshall Islands.

kājokwā — A tree trunk adrift in the open ocean or washed up on the shore.

kakar — Small ceremonial spears kept in the Bar Nor men's house that can be touched only by those men who have successfully been initiated into the kakar cult; bravery in battle.

Kalahngan en komwi — Pohnpeian for "thank you."

Kalbōk — L̗ainjin's fishing, shark-fighting friend for life.

kāleptak — Swell that "slaps from the west"; the countercurrent of the Intertropical Convergence Zone, which periodically streams through the islands just north and south of the equator.

kallep — Trap-jaw ant: *Odontomachus simillimus.*

Kāmeto — Name: "Fly the ocean."

kaṃōḷo — A newcomer celebration.

kanakan — Pohnpeian for "good."

Kanari — A Bar Nor man who accompanies Ḷainjin to Sigaba.

kapilak — A gale sometimes associated with the first morning's sighting of the constellation Aries.

Kariahn — A Pohnpeian islet where trading takes place.

kasap — Pohnpeian for "frigate bird."

kasau nawoi — Time to make yam hills in earnest; language of the Kunai.

kaselehlie — Pohnpeian for "hello."

Kataupaiti — Legendary origin of the first voyagers to settle in Pohnpei.

kawas — Titan word for "exchange."

Kelepwei — A man-made islet across from Pahn Kadira used to house visitors.

Kiberikrik kōjatdikdrik — "Steer into wind and hope to win"; a sailing axiom when racing an outrigger canoe. The lateen sail takes a remarkable cut into the wind, rarely gets caught in irons, and in a smooth-water lagoon environment, does not always require a "belly" to perform competitively.

kihr en eiwel — Pohnpeian for "red snapper."

the Kingfisher — Aka Malean; Ngalen's husband.

kino — A fragrant, broadly lobed fern (*Phymatosorus grossus*) often used to spice earth ovens; grows at the base of trees.

Kiton — Ewalt's mother.

Komba — The mountain or hinterland villagers inland of Sio (Sigaba). They live on the Huon Peninsula of New Guinea and were both enemies and trading partners of the Kunai.

kōṇṇat — A short, sprawling tree that grows next to the shore; beach cabbage: *Scaevola taccada*; "naupaka" in Hawaiian.

Kosrae — An island about 300 miles southeast of Pohnpei that is now one of the Federated States of Micronesia.

kubaak — Outrigger float.

kubaak en kapako — An outrigger float for shark hunting.

Kunai — "Grass men"; also, the New Guinea pidgin English term for "grass," or *imperata cylindrica.* The edges of this grass are narrow, serrated, and very sharp. It catches fire easily and is between two and ten feet high.

Ļainjin — Tarmālu's son.

ļañ eļap — "Big wind"; typhoon.

Lañinpo — A name: "heavy weather requiring the striking of sails." A Seeker; Rojak's brother.

lāpio — Komba word for "effigy"; an image.

Lenkar — The stories of Lenkar and Jebro are told in *Man Shark*, the first volume of this series.

Li — Female prefix used to emphasize respect.

liet — Pohnpeian for "cannibal" or "cannibal peoples."

Liṃanṃan — Irooj's daughter; Ļainjin's chosen one. A name: "woman beautiful." "Li": the female prefix; "ṃanṃan": "very beautiful." The north star, Polaris.

Lipanmai — A Pohnpeian name meaning "woman under the breadfruit tree."

Lirojak — Aka Rojak. Female Seeker; Lañinpo's sister.

Lō — Male prefix used to emphasize respect.

Ļōbwedi — A Seeker; aka Bwedi.

Ļōbwilñawa — A Seeker; aka Bwilñawa; the rijeļā. "Ļō": the male prefix, used to emphasize respect.

lōjkaan — Marlin.

Lōktañūr — Tūṃur's mother. The story of Lōktañūr and her twelve sons, who became stars, is the cornerstone of Marshall Islanders' knowledge of seasonal weather.

Ļōpako — Aka Pako; Ļainjin's nickname. Literally, "man shark." "Ļō": the male prefix; "pako": "shark."

Maalal — Evening star; Venus (evenings only).

Mailap — Mailap and the Trukese pronunciation Mājlep are both names for the star Altair.

ṃaj — Approximately April.

Mājlep — The star Altair. See Mailap.

makisa — Kunai word for "May."

Malean — Aka the Kingfisher; Ngalen's husband.

Manam — Known locally as Manam Motu, Manam is an island located in the Bismarck on the northeast coast of mainland Papua New Guinea. The island was created by the activity of the Manam volcano, one of the country's most active.

Mānnijepļā — A mythic bird that flew passengers from one island to another.

Manus — Part of Manus Province, and the biggest Admiralty Island, Manus lies in the Bismarck Sea north of Papua New Guinea.

m̧arm̧ar — Flower leis.

Matankor — People who live in inland housing on the smaller Admiralty Islands and on Manus's north coast.

Mbuke — Consists of a small number of islands off the south end of mainland Manus. Manus Province, also known as the Admiralty Islands, is the smallest and least populated of Papua New Guinea's twenty provinces.

m̧ōm̧aan m̧aj — Literally, "a man is an eel," which means that he always develops a relationship with a hole. *Mōm̧aan* means "man"; *m̧aj* means "eel."

Mountain Arapesh — The Arapesh were a horticultural people living in the northeast lowlands of East Sepik Province. The Mountain Arapesh were a tribe of Arapesh living in the highlands above the Sepik who had migrated there for trading purposes.

mpwein tenek — Pohnpeian for the sweet, spongy endosperm of the newly sprouted coconut. It can be eaten raw or cooked into a dessert-like dish with arrowroot and coconut milk.

Murik — The Murik Lakes lie just north of the mouth of the Sepik River. The Bar Nor live in five or so villages along the banks of its mangrove swamp. It was a precontact maritime trading center similar to Sigaba.

Mwanus — The people living in villages who build on the reefs of Manus and the other islands of what is now called the Admiralty group.

mwenge — Food; to eat. Similar to "m̧ōn̄ā" in Kajin Rālik.

Nahn Madol — A Pohnpeian village on the reef.

Nahn Samohl — An eel.

nahnsapw — Pohnpeian for "coastal or cultivated land."

Nahn Sapwe — Pohnpeian spirit of thunder.

nambwe — A group of initiates to manhood of approximately the same age.

Namorik — Literally, "small lagoon"; an atoll in the southern Rālik Chain of what is now the Republic of the Marshall Islands. Where Lainjin is from.

nanwel — Pohnpeian for "the mountains," or the area outside human authority.

ṇatọọn — Sheet in or trim the sail.

nen — Fruit from *Morinda citrifolia*, a small tree prized throughout the islands for its medicinal properties; a tonic thought to promote health. Also called "noni."

ñeñe — The length across the breast from fingertips to fingertips; one fathom.

ñiitwa — Crooked-tooth barracuda; genus Sphyraena.

Oljipa and Oljopa — According to *The Book of Luelen*, these men came to Pohnpei on the seventh voyage of settlement. They came from a place referred to as Kataupaiti and were instrumental in the construction of Nahn Madol.

Pako — Shark. Ḷainjin's nickname: "man shark."

pāle — Dried, braided coconut leaves used as torches for fishing; a coconut frond.

pali — Alternative spelling for "palu." "Traditional navigator" in the languages of what are now the Western Caroline Islands of the Federated States of Micronesia. Wisim is "the palu."

papu; ina — Generic terms for "little boy" or "little girl" among the Mwanus.

Pohnpei — Currently one of the principal island groups that make up the Federated States of Micronesia, located in the Eastern Caroline Islands.

proa — An outrigger canoe rigged with a sail.

pwentang — Titan word for "cooking pot."

Raipuinlañ — The wealthiest chieftain; the Pohnpeian Saudeleur.

rajraj — A knife or sword-like weapon uniformly edged with shark teeth.

Rālik — The western chain of atolls of what is now known as the Republic of the Marshall Islands.

Ratak — The eastern chain of atolls of what is now known as the Republic of the Marshall Islands.

ribwinbwin — Literally, “person who counts.”

riia — “Bones from where?”

rijeḷā — Literally, “bones that know”; navigator; captain; pali; palu.

ri-kwōjkōj — Literally, “bones that cast fortune”; fortune teller.

ri-Rālik — Bones of Rālik, the western chain of what is now the Republic of the Marshall Islands.

rojak — The individual booms of the lateen sail. Vertical boom: rojak ṃaan; lateral boom: rojak kōrā.

Rojak — The female Seeker; Lañinpo’s sister; aka Lirojak.

rojak ṃaan — Literally, “spar man” or “spar in front”; the vertical boom or yard of the triangular lateen sail.

sakau — Kava; a drink with anesthetic properties made from the mashed roots of the propagated *Piper methysticum*, or pepper plant.

Sambia — The Sambia people lived in the Papua New Guinea Highlands. They practiced polygamy, sister exchange, strict separation of male and female duties, and semen exchange through ritualized obligatory homosexual practices.

Sarakena — A name: “all these seasons”; the woman Lañinpo meets again in a Bar Nor village.

Sareid en Sahpw — The father of Raipuinlañ.

Satawan — One of the outer atolls of the Truk group.

Setepana — The forbidden man’s apprentice.

Siassi — A volcanic island (Umboi) between the mainland of Papua New Guinea and the island of New Britain. It was a third center of precontact trade concentric with Sigaba.

Sigaba — Later called Sio Island, a “place of mixing.” A precontact trading center located off the Kunai coast of the Huon Peninsula of southeastern New Guinea.

Sokehs — An island with a mountain cliff on the north side of Pohnpei.

sulu — Kunai word for October.

takai — Pohnpeian for “stones”; essentially the same word as in Kajin Rālik: “dekā.” Takai are hexagonal basaltic crystals that date back to the volcanic origin of the island.

Talupe — The ambitious Pohnpeian woman who captures Ḷainjin's attention.

Tarmālu — Ḷainjin's mother.

Temwen Island — The island inland of Nahn Madol whose surrounding reef supports the city.

Titan — The language of the Mwanus.

totori — Kunai word for "August."

Truk — The next island and language group west of Pohnpei.

tuba — Carolinian for "jekaro."

Tūṃur — Aka Antares, the brightest star in the constellation Scorpius, including Tau, Alpha, and Sigma.

Uerik — Ḷainjin's Pohnpeian friend who estimates that "six men could paddle a takai down the mountain."

Usiai — Bush people of Manus Island.

Wa jab depet āne — Literally, "boat does not pierce islet." This proverb means that a canoe's hull does not pierce the sand of an islet without bearing gifts.

wapepe — Literally, "boat floating." The symbol represents the four swells, one from each quadrant, converging upon an island in mid-ocean.

Wa tutu! Wan eman — Boat spray; the bath of a man.

Wisim — Aka "the palu."

wōjjej — An idiom used to express surprise.

Wōt jeej — The same as "jeej." An idiom used to express surprise that translates as "heck" or "darn it." Demonstrates more deliberation than "wōjjej."

Wottok — Pohnpeian elder; Ewalt's father.

Wūj uwaṇ in jān lōḷḷap in! — "Pull this gray hair from this old lady!"

wūnaak — Flock of seabirds diving for baitfish driven to the surface by tuna.

Bibliography

Athens, John Stephen. "The Discovery and Archaeological Investigation of Nan Madol." *Micronesian Archaeological Survey reports.* Saipan: Historic Preservation Office, 1981

Bernart, Luelen. *The Book of Luelen.* John L. Fischer, Saul H. Riesenberg, Marjorie G. Whiting, Eds. Canberra: Australian National University Press, 1977

Chamisso, Adelbert von. *A Voyage around the World with the Romanzov Exploring Expedition in the Years 1815–1818 in the Brig* Rurik, *Captain Otto Von Kotzebue.* Henry Kratz, Ed. Trans. Honolulu: University of Hawaiʻi Press, 1968

Gladwin, Thomas. *East Is a Big Bird.* Cambridge: Harvard University Press, 1970

Groves, William C. "The Natives of Sio Island, South-Eastern New Guinea." *Oceania Publications.* University of Sydney, 1934

Harding, Thomas G. *Kunai Men.* London: University of California Press, 1985

Harding, Thomas G. "Money, Kinship, and Change in a New Guinea Economy." *Southwestern Journal of Anthropology.* University of Chicago Press, 1967

Harding, Thomas G. "Precolonial New Guinea Trade." *Ethnology.* University of Pittsburgh, 1994

Herdt, Gilbert H., Ed. *Ritualized Homosexuality in Melanesia.* Berkeley: University of California Press, 1984

Herdt, Gilbert H. "Semen Transactions in Sambia Culture." *Ritualized Homosexuality in Melanesia.* Gilbert H. Herdt, Ed. Berkeley: University of California Press, 1984

Key, C.A. "The Identification of New Guinea Obsidians." *Oceania Publications*. University of Sydney, 1969

Lee, Vincent R., Nancy G. Lee. *The Sisyphus Project*. Wilson, Wyoming: Vincent R. Lee, 1998

Lewis, David. *We, the Navigators*. Honolulu: University of Hawaii Press, 1972

Lilley, Ian. "Prehistoric Exchange Across the Vitiaz Strait, Papua New Guinea." *Current Anthropology*. University of Chicago Press, 1988

Lipset, David. *Mangrove Man*. Cambridge University Press, 1997

McElhanon, Kenneth A. "Komba Kinship Terminology." Ethnology. University of Pittsburgh, 1969

Mead, Margaret. *Growing Up in New Guinea*. New York: HarperCollins, 2001

Petersen, Glenn. "Lost in the Weeds: Theme and Variation in Pohnpei Political Mythology." *Occasional Paper Series 35*. Honolulu: Center for Pacific Islands Studies, University of Hawai'i at Mānoa, 1990

Ploeg, Anton. "Dependency among the Kovai, Siassi, Morobe Province, Papua New Guinea." *Oceania Publications*. University of Sydney, 1985

Riesenberg, Saul H. "The Organisation of Navigational Knowledge on Puluwat." *The Journal of the Polynesian Society*. The Polynesian Society, 1972

Sahlins, Marshall D. "Poor Man, Rich Man, Big-Man, Chief: Political Types in Melanesia and Polynesia." *Comparative Studies in Society and History*. Cambridge University Press, 1963

Specht, Jim, Ian Lilley, William R. Dickinson. "Type X Pottery, Morobe Province, Papua New Guinea: Petrography and Possible Micronesian Relationships." *Asian Perspectives*. Honolulu: University of Hawai'i Press, 2006

Stasch, Rupert. "The Camera and the House: The Semiotics of New Guinea 'Treehouses' in Global Visual Culture." *Comparative Studies in Society and History*. Cambridge University Press, 2011

Terrell, John. *Prehistory in the Pacific Islands*. Cambridge University Press, 1988

Terrell, John E., Robert L. Welsch. "Lapita and the Temporal Geography of Prehistory." *Antiquity*. Cambridge University Press, 1997

Thomas, Stephen D. *The Last Navigator*. New York: Henry Holt and Company, 1987

Younger, Stephen M. "Violence and Warfare in Precontact Melanesia." *Journal of Anthropology*. London: Hindawi Limited, 2014

www.ingramcontent.com/pod-product-compliance
Lightning Source LLC
Chambersburg PA
CBHW020838020726
47497CB00005B/1162